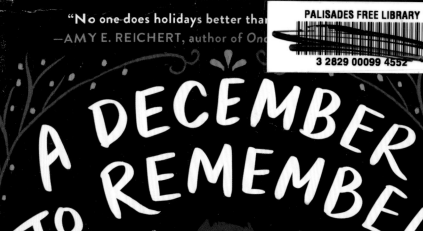

"No one does holidays better than
—AMY E. REICHERT, author of *On*

A DECEMBER TO REMEMBER

a novel

JENNY BAYLISS

Author of *The Twelve Dates of Christmas* and
Meet Me Under the Mistletoe

2. 11/23

Praise for

THE TWELVE DATES OF CHRISTMAS

"With its cozy, small-town setting and adorable premise, *The Twelve Dates of Christmas* is the perfect book for anyone looking for a charming holiday romance." —*PopSugar*

"We can't get enough of this twist on the '12 Days of Christmas'!" —*Country Living*

"Bayliss delivers delightful holiday atmosphere and believable romantic tension in her cute and cozy debut . . . By turns tender and hilarious, this adorable rom-com is sure to satisfy." —*Publishers Weekly*

"Charming . . . This slow-burn rom-com set in a small British village at Christmas will be the perfect cup of tea for fans of Marian Keyes or Helen Fielding." —*Library Journal*

"Fans of the best-friends-to-lovers and second chance tropes will savor this." —*Booklist*

"[A] nice cozy rom-com novel, one with a bit of an edge, a larger meaning, and a satisfying ending." —Minneapolis *Star Tribune*

"Fans of *The Holiday* will adore this quaint English countryside set romance. . . . Feels like getting a hug while sitting under a thick blanket with a cup of tea on a wintry afternoon." —*Refinery29*

A
DECEMBER
TO
REMEMBER

ALSO BY JENNY BAYLISS

Meet Me Under the Mistletoe
A Season for Second Chances
The Twelve Dates of Christmas

A
DECEMBER
TO
REMEMBER

A NOVEL

JENNY BAYLISS

G. P. PUTNAM'S SONS
NEW YORK

PUTNAM
— EST. 1838 —

G. P. PUTNAM'S SONS
Publishers Since 1838
An imprint of Penguin Random House LLC
penguinrandomhouse.com

Library of Congress Cataloging-in-Publication Data

Names: Bayliss, Jenny, author.
Title: A December to remember / Jenny Bayliss.
Description: New York : G. P. Putnam's Sons, 2023. |
Identifiers: LCCN 2023028534 (print) | LCCN 2023028535 (ebook) |
ISBN 9780593422243 (trade paperback) | ISBN 9780593422250 (ebook)
Subjects: LCSH: Sisters—Fiction. | Fathers—Death—Fiction. |
Estranged families—Fiction. | Inheritance and succession—Fiction. |
LCGFT: Domestic fiction. | Novels.
Classification: LCC PR6102.A975 D43 2023 (print) |
LCC PR6102.A975 (ebook) | DDC 823/.92—dc23/eng/20230626
LC record available at https://lccn.loc.gov/2023028534
LC ebook record available at https://lccn.loc.gov/2023028535
p. cm.

Printed in the United States of America
1st Printing

Interior art: Holiday ornaments © GoodStudio / Shutterstock
Book design by Alison Cnockaert

For my siblings, Lindsay and Simon,
without whom I would be lost. Love you xx

A
DECEMBER
TO
REMEMBER

PROLOGUE

FIVE YEARS AGO

AUGUSTUS BALTHAZAR NORTH chuckled to himself as he plucked the tiny, feathered cuckoo from the mechanism in the old clock and, using sticky tack, stuck a small wooden Monopoly house in its place. He closed the clock and stood back, satisfied.

"And that's the last one hidden," he said to his curiosity shop. "It's down to you now to keep them safe."

As though in answer, all forty clocks on the wall began to chime. Three sonorous tolls marked the lateness of the hour, and the moon peered in through the window for good measure. Artemis rubbed herself against the old man's ankles, her long bouffant tail curling around one leg, then the other. Augustus smiled and looked down at her.

"That goes for you too, my faithful friend. And take good care of yourself while you're at it, though I know you will."

Artemis mewed and favored him with a long slow blink in response. She was a puffball of black fur with a circle of white around each eye as though she were wearing spectacles. She moved with the unhurried elegance and quiet intelligence of a feline librarian. Artemis belonged only to the curiosity shop, though she was fed and pampered by everyone in Rowan Thorp.

North Novelties & Curios had been passed down through the North family ever since Patience North had had the land put in trust for her by her father ahead of a promise of marriage, which never came to pass. Exasperated by her unwillingness to take a husband and her unfathomable yearning for independence—and secretly impressed by her tenacity—her father allowed her to open the shop in 1740. It was indeed a curious shop, packed to the rafters with miscellanea, trinkets, and bric-a-brac that time had rendered antique.

The shop smelled like old books, leather, woodsmoke, and the heady scent of incense sticks, which had seeped into the very fabric of the building.

Every inch of wall that wasn't covered in display cabinets was hung with oil paintings or clocks: ornately carved Viennese pendulum clocks, old railway station clocks from India and Baltimore, and dainty hand-painted French enamelware clocks on long decorative chains. The paintings were an eclectic mix of Turner-like landscapes, flouncing Renaissance figures, and austere still lifes in the style of the Old Masters, which for all anyone knew may have been the real McCoy.

The shelves that housed the shop's treasures were practically their own ecosystem. The curious flora and fauna of antiquities seemed to have grown organically down the centuries; it was hard to decipher, for example, where the black pearls began and the Georgian sugar tongs ended. The shop gave the impression of a place that had been carefully and haphazardly curated by a mischievous poltergeist, and who was to say that it hadn't been?

The shop was lit by wall sconces and lamps dotted about, which bathed everything in a warm golden glow.

"Ah, how I love you," Augustus cooed to his shop. "And I'll

miss you. But I have kept my other mistress waiting far too long!" He winked, and the shop seemed to sigh in response.

The clocks struck the quarter hour; time he was off. The open road was calling him to it as it so often did, and as always, he was powerless to resist. He took one last look around at his beloved curiosities. "Look after my girls." He waggled a warning finger. "They will need you, mark my words."

The old man pulled the door closed on the shop and locked it. Then he made his way slowly up the dark street to the solicitors' office of Steele & Brannigan. An owl hooted. It was a clear night, the first hint of winter just discernible by the peppermint freshness in the air.

"Just in the nick of time."

Augustus checked the seal on the thick brown envelope and posted his final instructions through the letterbox. "There," he said. "That's everything."

As he strolled back the way he had come, he made sure to soak in the little high street, the home of his forebears, and commit it to memory. He glanced up at the darkened windows above the greengrocer's and acknowledged his wistfulness tinged with regret, or it may have merely been the steak and kidney pudding he'd had for supper repeating on him. He was what he was, and he was too old to fight against it now.

He climbed into his trusty, crusty camper van, which had seen almost as many years as he had, and pulled slowly out of the village, following once more the siren call of fresh fields and far-off mountain roads waiting for him.

1

PRESENT DAY

MAGGIE, SIMONE, AND Star's father had died as he'd always wanted to: quietly and without ceremony, in his beaten-up van in the middle of a forest in the Italian Alps. His age, like the rest of him, had always been an enigma, though it surprised nobody to learn that he had died just shy of his ninety-sixth birthday; Augustus was one of those curious beings who seemed always to have been old and yet equally never to have aged.

In a handwritten note found tucked into his breast pocket, Augustus had bid farewell to his three estranged daughters and assured them that he had enjoyed a long and happy life, the memories of which he would carry with him into the next world.

The very existence of the note had broken Star's heart. Maggie, the eldest of the three, had called her discordant sisters as soon as she'd received the news of their father's passing.

"But that means he knew he was going to die," Star, the youngest, had sobbed over the phone.

Maggie, who as firstborn was unwillingly cast in the role of materfamilias, tried her hardest to push conviction into her voice. "Not necessarily. He might have carried it around in his pocket for years, just in case," she soothed.

"Dad never planned a thing in his life." Star sniffed loudly. "He was a free spirit. No, he knew he was going to die, I know it. It's too sad. I can't think about it."

Simone, the middle of the North sisters, had been less demonstrative in her grief upon receiving Maggie's phone call, but Maggie could hear the shake in her voice.

"Was he—was he alone? When it happened?" Simone had asked.

"I believe so, yes. But the doctor I spoke to assured me that he died peacefully in his sleep. That's something to be thankful for, isn't it?" It was hard to put a positive spin on the death of a parent, even one who had been absent for most of their lives, but she was giving it her best shot.

"I suppose so," Simone had said. "I mean, I know we weren't close for the last twenty-odd years, but even someone as careless with people as he was ought not to die alone . . ."

"He wanted it that way. No fuss. Just him and the mountains."

Though it was the truth, saying the words didn't bring Maggie peace.

THE FUNERAL TOOK place on a bleak Tuesday in November; the fat rain and black pregnant clouds felt fitting for the occasion. Despite the weather, the whole of Rowan Thorp village had turned out to honor the man known affectionately by the locals as "The Wizard of Rowan Tree Woods." Augustus had been roguish and charming and quite frankly a randy old bugger who was adored as much for his sparkling manner as the trouble he caused.

At the front of the church a large picture of the man in question rested on an easel: long white hair pulled back into a plaited rope, a beard to match, a devilish grin, and bright green eyes that twinkled with mischief. His collection of jaunty waistcoats, which he always wore beneath an old tweed jacket, only added to his disheveled country squire image and made him irresistible to any who crossed his path.

Word of his passing had brought a flood of mourners from across the globe, wanting to pay their respects to the man who had been so loved by all and yet known by none—not least his three daughters.

"I thought only royalty got this many flowers when they died," said Joe as he helped Maggie lay out the hundreds of bouquets and wreaths that had been delivered to the church ahead of the service. "I've seen postmarks from as far as Alaska. One of them says it's been sent from a rainforest!"

"My dad was a well-liked man," Maggie replied, standing and stretching out her back.

"Some of these note cards are borderline soft porn."

She smiled. "Like I said, well-liked."

"What did he actually *do* when he was off on his travels?"

"Played his lute, read tarot cards, seduced women. He used to take some of the rowan wood from his woods out back and whittle it into love spoons and forest animals."

"To sell?"

"Sometimes. Sometimes he gifted them. Really, he did it for the love of it. It was a way of meeting people; who could resist coming to talk to a man playing a lute and whittling in a purple nag champa–scented van?"

"No wonder they called him a wizard."

"I think you two would have got on well. He had a twinkle about him," she said fondly. And then she added, "A twinkle that dazzled so you couldn't see his failings until he had hightailed it out of town."

"What do you mean?"

"Being with Augustus was like existing inside a bubble: magical and perfect. And then he'd disappear, and you'd be left cleaning up a soapy mess."

Despite being a self-styled bachelor, in his twilight years Augustus found himself father to three daughters from three very different mothers. His role in their lives was for the most part transient. But for four weeks of every summer, he would have his daughters to stay with him at his flat above North Novelties & Curios.

"That must have been confusing when you were kids," Joe said, up to his elbows in floral arrangements.

"Not really. You don't question that stuff when you're little. That was just how our family worked." She thought for a moment. "I think I naturally felt it a bit more than my sisters, because they lived in different parts of the country, so for them it was another holiday event like Christmas or Easter. But I lived in the same village as my dad and still only had the same level of contact as they did. We had those four blissful weeks a year and then next to nothing."

"Isn't that a bit . . ." He hesitated as though trying to find a word that wouldn't be disrespectful to the dead man in the picture beside him. "Cruel? To withhold love like that?"

Maggie's old defenses—spring-loaded and activated if touched—jerked up. "He loved me. He was away most of the time, so it wasn't like he would see me on the street and blank me. I think in his own way he was trying to keep things fair between the three of us." She chewed the inside of her cheek as she remembered how Simone and Star were so jealous of her living in the same village as their dad. "To this day they don't believe that Augustus was as absent for me as he was for them." *Or how much more his absence stung*, she didn't say. How it crushed her to see the light on in his window and know that her dad was just across the street and yet completely unattainable; it was a tough lesson in emotional self-sufficiency she'd had to learn far too young.

Joe was looking at her like he'd just read a transcript of her thoughts. But he was wise enough to steer the conversation away.

"And your mum?" he asked. "How did she feel about handing you over to your dad for a month every summer?"

"I think she was pleased that I got that quality time with him, even if it was only for a few weeks a year. She used to say she saved up all her boring jobs, like sorting out the accounts and deep cleaning the house, for when I wasn't there. But she went away too, to visit her sister and see old friends. It was a nice break for her. She was a single working mum; how many get a month off a year?"

"You mean to tell me Verity's dad doesn't take her on holidays?" he asked with mock innocence.

Maggie snorted out a laugh and reached across the flowers to swipe at him. She had two children: Patrick, who had turned twenty in the summer, and ten-year-old Verity. Verity's dad— an attractive, unreliable man with a host of emotional hang-ups—had left the scene before Maggie's baby bump was even showing. Theirs had been a short-lived relationship of pure convenience. She might have been desperate enough to have sex with him, but she wasn't stupid enough to think he was partner or parent material. She'd told Joe all this months ago in a "full disclosure" heart-to-heart, which she'd assumed would have him running for the hills. It hadn't.

"And your mum and Augustus never tried to make it work between them?" Joe asked. "They surely must have thought about it, living in the same village."

"Mum never really talked about it. I think she came here originally with the intention of them making a go of it. Only when she finally tracked the elusive Augustus North down to Rowan Thorp, by this time eight months pregnant with me, it was clear he was not a man to be tied down."

"Jesus," said Joe, and then looked over to the altar and added, "Sorry, your godliness," before turning back to Maggie. "She must have been gutted."

She pulled a face. "I honestly don't think she was that sad about it. I don't want to blow my own trumpet, but she got me out of their brief affair, and that was enough. Mum was forty-five when she met Augustus at the Somerset County Fair. She'd given up hope of ever having kids; she'd tried in both her long-term relationships and it simply hadn't happened. Then suddenly she meets this randy older guy and gets pregnant. She told me once that coming here was like a formality, like she had to at least see if he wanted to do the traditional thing. But he didn't, and she was okay with that."

"She stayed here anyway, made a life for you both."

"She fell in love with Rowan Thorp. It was a great place to bring up a kid. And I think she wanted me to at least have a chance at a relationship with my dad."

The guilt crept over her like it always did and she breathed deeply in the hope that it would pass. She had been a nightmare teenager, a caged snarling animal, stifled by the tiny village and angry at her mum simply for being her mum. At seventeen she ran away to follow her then childhood sweetheart—it didn't last long—to Liverpool. As an adult and a parent, Maggie could imagine vividly how frantic her mum must have been. How heartbroken. That was when the first cancer came. She rubbed her hand across her forehead and tried to swallow down the sticky regret that was climbing up her throat.

Joe was there in a second, arms wrapped around her, holding her close. He couldn't know what she was thinking, but that didn't matter; he knew enough of her to know that she needed to be held. She let herself melt into him. His steady heartbeat was a map guiding her back to the present, and at the moment she didn't care if anybody came in and saw them. Joe was her employee and friend; it was perfectly natural that he should comfort her.

"What is it about funerals that thrusts all your previous failings into sharp relief?" she asked, forcing levity into her voice.

"It could be the sudden facing of our own mortality. But it's more likely the worry about what people will say about us in their eulogies."

She snuffled a laugh into his jumper.

"I like to think whoever gives mine will let the congregation know that I was really good in the sack," Joe went on.

"I don't think you're allowed to say that kind of thing in church."

"You did read those condolence cards, right? Pure smut."

"Yes. They very much embraced the sexual revolution."

Now it was Joe's turn to laugh.

She let herself linger just a little longer in his embrace and then pulled away. "Come on," she said, bending to wiggle a giant bouquet of crimson gladiolus into place. "It's going to start filling up in here soon. I need to be at the door for the meet and greet."

"Will Simone and Star help you?"

She puffed out a sarcastic breath. "Like they've helped so far?"

"I see your point. I'll stand with you, then. I know I never met your dad, but you shouldn't have to shoulder it all on your own."

As the only one of Augustus's daughters who lived in Rowan Thorp, it made sense that the bulk of responsibility for dealing with their father's death and all arrangements thereof had landed with her. Though she suspected that even if she'd lived in the Outer Hebrides, she would still be bearing the largest weight.

2

THE NOTE IN Augustus's pocket had included an addendum, which requested that everyone at his funeral wear brightly colored clothes for the occasion. His wishes were enthusiastically adhered to, mostly by the female mourners. Eccentric women of a certain age wore their hair in various rainbow hues and had eyebrows drawn on with unsteady hands; when a breeze blew through the chapel a sea of multicolored kimonos billowed up and flapped like rows of Tibetan prayer flags. Anita—who worked in the local council office and had helped Maggie with the spools of red tape that followed death—had been struck down with a migraine brought on by the clashing colors and psychedelic patterns. Doreen—dedicated member of the Cussing Crocheters of Rowan Thorp—said she'd not seen anything like it since taking LSD in the sixties.

The church where Augustus's humanist funeral ceremony was held was standing room only. The crowd spilled out onto the lawns in front of the church, and speakers were hastily erected so that the people outside could hear. St. Swithun's formed the head of a medieval triangle of buildings in the village, the Rowan Tree Inn and the Stag and Hound Tavern—the two village pubs—making up the other two points, with a largish patch of green in the middle of the triangle. This area was known locally—possibly blasphemously, but it had stuck all the same—as Holy Trinity Green because you could walk out of the church and straight into either pub for a pint. Many of the mourners that day took advantage of this auspicious proximity and raised their glasses to their fallen friend, getting merrily sozzled during the service, just as Augustus would have wanted.

"Shouldn't we be sitting with your mum?" Evette whispered. The service had not yet begun, but people were taking their seats in readiness. Simone had guided them toward a pew away from *all* her relatives.

Simone shook her head. "I did ask, but she said there was no need. I think she's enjoying the attention."

"I'm not sure Rene likes sharing the spotlight with Star's mum," Evette noted.

Simone smiled sardonically. Rene and Star's mother, Perdita, had a pew to themselves, a little distanced from the rest of the mourners, singled out in a kind of hierarchy as the chosen few who had birthed Augustus's children. Other than both having procreated with Augustus, the two women had absolutely nothing in common. To try to make conversation would have been futile, so neither tried.

"I don't think I've ever seen so many eccentrics in one place. I've never been able to get my head around your mum and your dad together. Poor Rene sticks out like a sore thumb."

"It's not like they ever had a relationship," said Simone. "I was the product of an 'ill-conceived affair.' One for which she was left to carry the *burden*."

Evette winced. She of all people knew the long-term effects

that Rene's careless words had had on her daughter. Rene didn't speak from a place of meanness so much as a brutal honesty; hers was a tongue sharp as a cracked lemon sherbet, and her only daughter had inherited it. Rene, by her own admission, was simply not the maternal type. So, while she took great pains to ensure that her daughter was well taken care of, emotionally she just didn't have that motherly softness in her parenting toolbox. When Simone had read *Great Expectations* at school, she felt she had found a kindred spirit in Estella.

"Except for one whole month of every summer," said Evette. "That's more than most mums get off a year."

"My mother *lived* for the summer. She took herself off for luxury vacations somewhere hot and fabulous."

"I'm surprised she didn't object to letting you stay with your sisters."

"What, because she's such a snob?"

"Well, yes. I mean, I'd have thought it would have rankled her to have you mixing with his other illegitimate children."

"Not enough to keep her from her holidays." She felt bad as soon as she'd said it.

Rene was by no means a bad or selfish mother, and Simone would be lying if she said she hadn't got a kick out of having the most glamorous mum at the school gates.

The air in the church was thick with the scent of flowers, which almost masked the underlying smell of old varnish, damp stone, and mothballs.

"It was really quite modern, when you think about it. To have such an open approach to the blended family dynamic. Fair play to all the mums and your dad. And you got to spend quality time with your dad and sisters. I love it when you talk about your summers; it always reminds me of an Enid Blyton novel—without the xenophobia and sexism, obviously. Ice cream for breakfast, climbing trees, sleeping under the stars. It's the childhood most of us wish we'd had."

"Nothing's free, though, is it?" said Simone. "There's always a price to pay."

Despite their more recent estrangements, she couldn't deny that she had perfect memories with her sisters in Rowan Thorp. Their summers genuinely were halcyon days. It was a children's paradise, mostly because their father was himself a glorified child. For Simone, those summers had been the complete antithesis of life with Rene.

A committed career woman with no time for husbands or children in her life, Rene had been an art dealer, sourcing rare pieces for her wealthy clients. What she found on one fateful expedition to the Loire Valley forty years ago was a fifty-six-year-old lute player with a twinkle in his green eyes that made her forget all about the Rococo canvas she had been commissioned to find. She left France carrying rather more with her than she'd expected.

Simone studied her mother. Time had done nothing to soften her straight-backed haughtiness. In contrast to the rest of the mourners, she wore a chic vintage Chanel skirt suit and an expression that dared anyone to approach her.

"Perdita is exactly as you described her," Evette said with a giggle, changing the subject. "Right down to the floral head wreath."

"And all these years you thought I was exaggerating."

In addition to the wreath, Star's mum wore a floor-length velvet cloak embroidered with gold stars and moons. She wept openly despite Rene's evident scorn.

"And how did Perdita meet your dad? I don't think I've ever asked."

"It may surprise you to learn that Perdita was a leftover flower child from the sixties, drifting from commune to commune," she said dryly.

"No." Evette dripped sarcasm. "You don't say."

"They met at a Beltane festival in Ireland and wham, bam, thank you ma'am, nine months later Heavenly-Stargazer Rosehip was born in a yurt on the Isle of Man."

"Does anyone ever call Star by her full name?"

"Only Dad. Or us when we wanted to annoy her."

"It's much easier to see the appeal between your dad and Star's mum."

Simone pressed her lips into a thin line. "She's as ridiculous as her daughter."

"Your sister."

"Don't remind me."

Above their heads, electric heaters fastened to the stone pillars glowed orange but did little to heat the drafty church.

"You know, Star most probably had as difficult a childhood, being dragged from pillar to post, as you did being forced to strive for excellence. They were both extremes in their own way. I really do think that if you could acknowledge that, you might find you have more in common with Star than you think."

"No amount of your well-meant therapy will make me believe that Star and I are kindred spirits."

"Please just try to be friendly. If not for your dad or Maggie, then for me."

All around them, long stained-glass windows depicted vivid tales of saints and sinners. *Is it unholy to feel so much spite in a church?* she wondered.

"It's because of what she did to *you* that I don't have anything to do with her," Simone grumbled.

"I didn't ask you to cut Star out of your life. She made a terrible error of judgment, for which she took full responsibility. Maybe today is the right time to let it go."

Simone smiled at her wife and took her hand. "Maybe," she said, knowing full well that she would do nothing of the sort. But she didn't want to fight with Evette, not today. Things were hard enough at the moment. "I love you."

Evette cupped Simone's face in her hands. "And I love you."

Simone put her arm around her wife and reveled in the comforting reassurance of Evette scooching in closer and resting her head on her shoulder. Guiltily, she thought it was a relief to have mourning to eclipse their own problems.

MAGGIE HAD FINISHED settling an elderly magician in a top hat into a pew beside a man dressed in chain mail when her son, Patrick, met her in the aisle. He put his arm around her.

"You all right, Ma?" he asked.

"Yes, love, I'm fine, don't you worry about me. I've saved you a seat next to me and Joe."

"I don't really know why Joe's here; he didn't even know Granddad. He could have stayed behind and opened the grocer's."

Patrick was wary of her friendship with Joe, though he'd never said as much. She suspected he thought Joe might be using her somehow. If only he knew.

"He's here as my friend. And as for opening the grocer's, look around, all our customers are here."

Patrick's eyes swept the room. "Blimey, you're not wrong."

"Go and sit down, I'll be over in a minute."

It took some fancy footwork to avoid standing on the cloaks of the Druids who had congregated in the north transept, but she made it over to Simone and Evette without event. Artemis trotted along beside her. Nobody batted an eyelid at a cat wandering the church; where there were Norths, there was Artemis.

"Everything okay?" she asked.

None of the mourners appeared to be using their "inside voices," and the din echoed around the vaulted ceiling.

"You look like a children's TV presenter," said Simone.

Maggie had found a pair of bright green dungarees with a dancing elephant print online and thought they'd be just the ticket.

"I think Dad would have liked them." She grinned.

"I think so too." Evette smiled.

"You haven't seen Star, have you?" she asked, checking her watch. "I don't want her to miss the service."

"You didn't expect her to be on time, did you?" Simone sneered.

"We've been watching the awkward dowagers at the front of the church," Evette blurted loudly, to hush her wife. She nodded toward Rene and Perdita. Perdita's sobs were growing ever more exuberant to be heard above the noisy crowd.

Maggie laughed, but it was half-hearted, and Simone guessed she was thinking about her own mum. Lilibeth had died almost ten years ago, but that didn't mean it wasn't hard for Maggie to see Rene and Perdita without her.

"Without Lilibeth here as the glue, they've literally got nothing to say to each other," Simone said, trying to make her voice softer. "Your mum was always the middle ground between them.

She'd have made a good diplomat." It struck her that Maggie played a similar role between her and Star; without her, the sisters were worse than strangers.

"I think Mum would have loved all this." Maggie smiled as she surveyed the packed church.

"Though not, perhaps, as much as Perdita does," Simone added archly, just as the woman in question threw her arms toward the heavens and began to wail "*Why?*" while Rene looked on in appalled silence.

Heavenly-Stargazer Rosehip made it to the church just in time for the organ to strike up and the congregation to pipe down. For the first time in many years, all three North sisters were under the same roof, a fact which did not go unnoticed by the residents of Rowan Thorp.

Doreen turned to the woman dressed as Carmen Miranda to her left and said, "Can you feel it? That prickle in the air? Mark my words, there's a storm brewing and it's coming from the *North*." She waggled her eyebrows at the woman with fruit on her head and pulled out her crochet, chuckling to herself as she did so. "Things are about to get interesting."

3

MAGGIE AND JOE slipped into an alcove behind the church away from the crowd. Maggie leaned back against the cold stone wall, not caring that the damp was soaking through her clothes. She welcomed the cool, needed something to take her mind off the day.

The service had ended to the sounds of R.E.M.'s "Shiny Happy People" blasting out of the speakers. It wasn't customary for funeral services in the village church to end with dancing in the aisles, but this hadn't been a customary funeral. The impromptu Morris dancing troupe in the vestibule had also come as a surprise.

In a few minutes Augustus's coffin would be carried to his final resting place in the North family plot at the far corner of the graveyard. The mourners spilled out of the side doors of the church and were joined by those who had been standing on Holy Trinity Green.

"How are you holding up?" Joe asked.

"Okay, I think. I'm looking forward to it all being over."

"At least Star and Simone are keeping away from each other."

"Those two cat-fighting is the last thing I need."

"They wouldn't, would they? Not today."

"Ah, I forget you haven't seen them together. Trust me, a little thing like our father's funeral isn't enough to keep them from fighting. One sideward glance would kick things off."

Joe pulled a hip flask out of his inside pocket and held it out to her.

"It's a little early for me," she said, looking down at it. *Since when does Joe carry a hip flask?* Maybe that was the thing that was wrong with him—he was a secret alcoholic. Lord knows she hadn't been able to find anything else to fault him on, other than his age, but neither of them could help that.

"It's not booze," he said.

"What is it, then?"

He smiled that smile that lit something inside her and made her feel much younger than her forty-four years.

"Tea." He grinned. "Good, strong, hot builders tea."

Maggie almost snatched the hip flask from him and sighed as she took a long, deep swig. "You are too good." She smiled as she handed him back the flask.

"Then take me off the market."

She looked up at him. His face was serious. "What?"

"I realize my timing's off, and standing in a graveyard in the rain hiding from your family isn't exactly moonlight and roses, but I am serious about you, Maggie, about us. I don't want us to be a secret anymore. I know you don't like me saying it, but I love you and I want everyone to know it. I don't want to keep hiding."

She rubbed her face with her hands. "Joe, I can't do this now."

"Then when?"

"I don't know. But not at my dad's funeral."

"I'm not asking for a blood sacrifice. I just want to be able to hold your hand in public. I wanted to be able to put my arm around you today to comfort you, without you shrinking away from me. I want us to make plans and get excited about the future, instead of this limbo."

She would have liked to argue that she would never "shrink away from him," but he was right, she would. She had self-imposed rules for her and Joe; they were friends with benefits, nothing serious. She was never meant to have fallen for him, but how could she not when he was so thoughtful and funny and kind? He was also six feet three inches of pure outdoorsy man, dirty-blond wavy hair almost down to his shoulders, and four-day beard with just the right amount of scratch when he kissed her collarbone. He ought to work on a cattle ranch or as a surf instructor on the Cornish coast with those looks; he had no business being this sexy in the greengrocer profession.

"Why can't we stay as we are?" she pleaded.

"Because I don't want to be your fuck boy."

"You're not. You mean a lot to me."

If she told him the truth—that she was holding back for his benefit—he would only argue with her. He believed he loved her now, but what about down the line when the age gap between them really began to show? What about when he realized that being with her would mean giving up on a family of his own? He would make a wonderful father. What right did she have to deny him that? Her baby days were over. She didn't want more kids. She had to protect them both from heartbreak down the line. And losing Joe *would* break her heart, so it was better to never have him at all.

"But not enough for you to be with me in public." Joe's expression was one of genuine puzzlement.

"It isn't you . . ." she started. *I am saving you from yourself!*

"Yeah, yeah, I know, it's not me, it's you."

"But that's the truth! Please don't be cross with me."

Joe rubbed his hand through his hair and sighed, then pulled her into his arms. "I'm sorry, I'm being a selfish idiot. This isn't the right time. I didn't mean to make today even harder for you. I guess I let the whole 'life is short' thing overwhelm me."

Maggie buried her head in his chest. "Funerals can have that effect." Her voice was muffled by the knitted jumper he wore under his jacket.

"You looked so lost in the church. I wanted to comfort you, my arms were literally aching to hold you, but I knew I couldn't. Why are we wasting time? We could die tomorrow!"

"Morbid."

"I don't want to have regrets. I want to build a life with you."

"You want to commit to a woman who wears elephant dungarees to a funeral?"

"I wouldn't be seen dead with a woman who *didn't* wear elephant dungarees to a funeral."

Maggie breathed in the smell of him. He smelled like line-dried washing and fabric softener. Oh god, what was she going to do? Dearest lovely Joe. If only he was ten years older, or she was ten years younger. It couldn't work. It simply couldn't. And her brain was too damn full to take on extra complications. Why couldn't they just stay as they were? She nestled in further, feeling his warmth envelop her.

"There's such a lot happening at the moment, what with my impending homelessness and unemployment. And dad dying. My world feels like it's imploding. I just . . ."

"Shhhh," he soothed, kissing her head. "I'm sorry. Forget I mentioned it. I am here for you, however you need me. No conditions."

"I don't deserve you."

"I'm not that good."

"You are, you know." She felt him smiling. When Joe smiled, it was like the very air around him changed and the world became a little warmer. She allowed herself to bask for one more moment. "We'd better join the throng; I need to be there when he's interred."

They left their quiet alcove and fell in with the crowd.

"Will you tell your sisters about the eviction?" Joe asked.

"Why would I?"

He changed the subject.

"Belinda did well to keep God out of the service," he said as they followed the slow procession. "No mean feat for a vicar."

Belinda was vicar for the parish of Rowan Thorp: a gregarious woman of ample cleavage with a ring through her nose and a laugh like Sid James. She was rumored to wear leather trousers beneath her cassock in winter.

"She's been brilliant. It's not easy to write a eulogy for a father more devoted to the open road than his children." There was no malice in her voice, only a sad resignation.

Joe reached for her hand. She felt his warm fingers lace through hers and squeeze. She smiled up at him, gently freed her fingers, and drove her hand deep into her coat pocket. The flicker of hurt across his face sliced through her, but it was better this way; she wouldn't give him false hope.

The grass was spongy and slick with mud as they trampled the rest of the way in silence. The hole in the earth ahead of them yawned black and hungry, and neither the muddied Astroturf sheets around the opening nor the flowers strewn atop it lessened the ugliness.

* * *

STAR HAD NEVER seen so many velvet cloaks in one place, which was really saying something. The little churchyard at St. Swithun's resembled a wizarding convention as the funeralgoers clustered to watch Augustus's environmentally friendly cardboard coffin being lowered. Despite her sadness, she was relieved when it touched down in one piece; she had been worried that the heavy rain would break down the cardboard's integrity.

Though technically surrounded by her family, Star felt very alone. Perdita hung on to a man in a Viking costume, complete with horned helmet. For all her histrionics, she knew her mother was enjoying herself. Simone *still* wasn't speaking to her, and if she couldn't put her grievances aside on today of all days, then Star held out little hope of a reconciliation in the future. And Maggie was being Maggie, organizing her corner of the world and everyone in it. She had greeted Star with a hug and checked on her several times since, but it felt perfunctory, as though she was yet another item to be ticked off Maggie's to-do list.

"You all right there, Star, love?" asked Betty, stepping forward and throwing a clod of earth from the pile onto the coffin before turning to look at her. Betty was a keen member of the Women's Institute and a doyenne of Rowan Thorp and was never so formidable as in a crisis. She'd known the sisters all their lives.

"I think so. Why do you think he never stuck around?"

Betty sucked in a breath as she deliberated. "Ants in his pants, I suppose. You ought to know all about those. Of the three of you, you're the most like him."

"My roams are more circumstantial than Dad's were."

"Well, I suppose that's to be expected. You've never had the chance to let your roots grow."

"If I had children, I wouldn't *want* to leave them behind. I'd never make them feel as though they weren't enough to make me stay." Her voice sounded more forceful than she'd intended.

"Is that how you feel, duck?" Betty's voice was kind.

Star's sniff was partly to stifle her tears and part derision. She forced a laugh into her words. "I think the evidence is irrefutable." She looked over at her mother in time to see her kiss a rose and drop it into the grave while the Viking held her firmly by the waist. "I'm easy to discard."

"We'll have none of that nonsense, my girl." Betty's voice was sharp. "Some people are like sharks; they can smell low self-esteem a mile off. You need to stop attracting the sharks."

"Easier said than done."

"That man of yours still in prison?"

"Stu's not my man anymore, but no, he got out a couple of weeks ago."

"You keep away from him. He'll drag you down with him."

Star nodded. She didn't mention that despite trying her hardest to keep away from the man in question, he had found her and was not taking kindly to being dumped. Stu—her ex-boyfriend, a drug addict, and a terrible house burglar—was the reason Simone no longer spoke to her.

"Right, I'm going to shoot off and start laying out the buffet," said Betty, and she began to push her way back through the crowd jostling for a ringside spot. "Chin up! Be the architect of your own destiny!" she called back.

The rain picked up, huge drops sploshing down onto the muddied cardboard.

"Bye, Dad," she said under her breath. It didn't matter that throughout their childhood, the North sisters only spent four weeks of the year with their father. It didn't matter that as each of them reached adulthood Augustus had all but disappeared from their lives like emperor penguins leave their young after the winter. She would miss him still.

At thirty-eight, she was the baby of the family, and she was never allowed to forget it. Admittedly she was up against Simone, a qualified, well-respected physiotherapist, and Maggie, single mother of two who ran her own business and was top level at adulting. How was she supposed to compete with that? *No.* She corrected herself. *That is the wrong attitude. Let this be the catalyst. From this moment, I turn things around. I will be the architect of my own destiny. I will hold down a job and buy houseplants, which I will not kill. No more trying to fix broken men, no more picking up the guy in the bar least likely to have his own flat or job. From now on I am only looking for proper grown-up men who can appreciate that I am a proper grown-up woman, with a potential to own plants.*

She looked up to find a man, dressed in a brightly colored harlequin costume and holding three juggling clubs, looking at her from the other side of the grave. A black mask covered the top half of his face, but his grin was pure sexy wickedness. *Oh, hello!* Her heart skipped a beat. She smiled back at him. Maybe tomorrow was the right time to put her new plans into action.

4

THE WAKE WAS held in the Stag and Hound, where the deceased's numerous former lovers shared stories of making love with Augustus on mountaintops, riverbanks, forest floors, behind waterfalls, and in one instance a disabled toilet at Butlin's in Skegness. Tales of their father's conquests became more graphic as the sherry consumption racked up. Maggie, Simone, and Star could only grimace and keep the women topped up with vol-au-vents—courtesy of Betty's café along the high street—and pray that the nightmare would end soon.

Betty buzzed about now, clearing plates and slapping the hands of those who thought double-dipping was acceptable.

The male mourners were as unconventional as the female. Never had so many pagans, Wiccans, and mystics descended upon one small village in such great numbers. They cheered as they rambunctiously retold stories of Augustus's adventures and his many brushes with danger. Some drunkenly read out poems and odes to the Wizard of Rowan Tree Woods.

Many a bushy eyebrow was raised in flirtation, and copious eyelashes fluttered in return. If being horny was catching, the Stag and Hound was experiencing a serious outbreak.

Wedged between the jukebox and the trivia machine, Star was locking lips with the handsome harlequin, who turned out to be a Transylvanian juggler named Florin. She had already declared herself to be madly in love with him to Maggie while they were cutting the quiches for the buffet.

Simone looked on with something akin to malicious delight. "This is a funeral, not a pickup joint," she sneered.

"Don't be such a snob," Evette admonished playfully.

"I think Dad would be chuckling his socks off that Star got lucky at his funeral," said Maggie. "People handle their grief in different ways. This is Star's way."

"Well, you would approve, wouldn't you?"

"And what's that supposed to mean?"

"I just mean you're more open about that sort of thing."

"What? Sex at funerals?"

"No, just, you know."

"No, I don't know, please enlighten me."

Simone gave her a haughty look.

"I've seen the way you look at Joe. I've seen the way he looks at you. It's obvious there's something going on with you two."

"So what if there is? Are you slut-shaming me?"

"No. I'm saying that you both lean toward imprudent partners."

Maggie was saved from further offense by her children arriving; she cast a disgruntled glance in Simone's direction as she walked away.

"Why do you do that?" asked Evette.

"What?"

"You barely see Maggie from one year to the next, and then as soon as you're in a room with her you insult her."

"I did no such thing!"

Evette shook her head in exasperation. "You tell me you wish you and she were closer, and then when the chance arises you push her away."

Simone shrugged. Sometimes she wished her wife was less observant. The truth was, she did want to be closer to Maggie, but the distance between them had grown so steadily over the years, she didn't know how to bridge the gap.

"And as for Star," Evette went on, without waiting for Simone to reply, "that business has gone on for long enough. I know Stu stole from you too, but I lost family heirlooms in the robbery and if I can lay my grievances to rest, then so can you."

"You might have forgiven her, but I'm not done being angry yet. She allowed her junkie boyfriend to violate our home." She felt Evette's hand on hers.

"I think we both know that you're using Star as a convenient vessel for the real source of your pain."

Simone shot a glare at her wife and automatically held a hand to her stomach but said nothing. There hadn't been words invented yet that would adequately describe the feelings raging inside her, and no matter how much her wife cajoled, she couldn't bring herself to use the words that *were* at her disposal. She didn't know what would happen if she did. *No stress*, she told herself, taking a deep breath as she prayed silently to the universe that this one would stay cozy inside her.

"MAMA, ARE THESE people from Hogwarts?" asked Verity, looking around the pub in wonder.

"No, darling. These are Granddad's friends."

"Are you doing okay?" Patrick asked. "Is there anything you need me to do?"

Maggie's heart swelled with pride. He was such a good boy. She corrected herself—he was such a good *man*. His dad would have been proud. Patrick was a year old when Josh, his dad—and love of her life—had died, leaving her a widow at twenty-six. Patrick looked a lot like his dad, the same dark mop of unruly hair and square jaw, same build even—not especially tall but wiry—but his big round eyes were all Maggie; he'd inherited the North green eyes, as had his sister.

"I'm fine, darling. It's gone as well as I could have hoped. Your granddad would have enjoyed it."

"What about the aunts? Have they helped out at all?"

"Um, yes, they helped lay out the buffet."

"Wow. Thank god they came."

"Thanks for looking after Verity."

Patrick waved it away. "The old folks are really celebrating, huh?"

Maggie let her gaze follow his around the room. At least twelve couples—at a cursory glance—were very publicly making out: some on the dance floor, others sitting on laps. One couple had laid their dentures on beer mats, the better to snog.

"Maybe you should take Verity home," she ventured.

"Yeah," he agreed warily. "I think you're right. We can't ever unsee this."

With Verity protesting, Patrick ushered her back out of the pub. Maggie waved them off and slumped down in a chair. Joe came over and sat beside her.

"You made it through the day," he said, handing her a glass of wine.

"Unfortunately, it isn't over yet." She took a sip and briefly closed her eyes as the smooth liquid ran down her throat.

"Randy devils, aren't they?" Joe observed.

"I feel like an ineffectual chaperone at a school disco."

"I guess they're grabbing their moments while they still can."

"It's not only moments they're grabbing."

"I'm sorry about earlier. I feel like I ambushed you. I got swept up in all *this* and blurted it all out like a dumb teenager. I'm sorry if I made your day even harder."

Her heart squeezed. Perhaps if she wasn't in quite so much danger of being incurably in love with Joe, she could go along with his wishes. But the stakes were too high for her to risk either of their hearts.

"You didn't make it harder," she reassured him, smiling. "You are more than I deserve."

"I disagree." He looked at her so earnestly that her breath caught, and she had to look away. She really should have read the small print in the "friends with benefits" manual. It might work as a concept, but the reality of having a fulfilling sex life with your best friend—and employee—was that all the things you already admired about them became heightened and more intense, while the bonds of your friendship became more vulnerable to stress fractures.

"My sisters have managed to avoid each other all day, which is something to be thankful for," she said, moving to safer topics.

"They seem nice. Individually, that is. You described them well; I recognized them instantly. Obviously, the green eyes were a giveaway."

Simone was tall and athletic; she'd been on the rowing team at university, and Maggie always thought that her upper body strength must be a boon in her profession. She had an aquiline nose and a full mouth, which along with her excellent posture gave her a regal air that caused catcalls to dry and shrivel in throats.

Star, by contrast, was waiflike in appearance. To Maggie's mind she looked constantly like she needed to eat a pie or six, even though Maggie knew she ate heartily. She was beautiful in a beach-bum way; her skin held its tan year-round and her sun-bleached eyebrows matched her hair. She would fit in well with the Florida surf set; her hair was a permanent tangle of salt-sprayed waves, and her blond eyelashes were long and thick. She had a wide smile that beguiled men and women alike and had no doubt got her out of and into any number of tricky situations.

If Maggie was pushed to describe her own looks, she would say farmer's wife chic. Her skin was pale and freckled all winter, but at the first hint of sun she would tan to the color of a leather satchel, a throwback from her mother's Greek heritage, and her freckles would darken to form constellations over her nose and cheeks. She kept her thick curly hair—liberally streaked with gray—chin length for practicality, often pinning back the sides with Verity's glitter clips, not that this stopped it from constantly dropping over her eyes. Though she was fit from hard work she lacked the lean athleticism of Simone, and no one in their right mind would ever describe her as waiflike.

"Ah, yes," Maggie said knowingly, "the famous *North green eyes*. I used to hate it when I was growing up, always being referred to as one of the *North girls* or the *North sisters*. I think that's partly what I was trying to run away from when I left the village. I always felt like I was trying to live down a reputation that didn't belong to me."

"But then you came back, *and* you never left."

"I only came back to look after Mum when she got sick again. I'd never intended to stick around. But when I got here, I don't know, I felt differently about the place. All the things I'd run away from suddenly seemed like reasons to stay. Plus, it's a nice place to bring up kids. It was hard being a single mum in the city; here I already had friends, people who would look out for us. Who wouldn't want that?"

"I get it. Not the single parent bit. But I understand the appeal of belonging to a community. I felt it the moment I moved in to the pub."

Joe had arrived in Rowan Thorp a little over a year ago, having applied for the greengrocer's assistant job in Maggie's shop that he'd seen online. He took up lodgings in the Rowan Tree Inn and had been assimilated into the Rowan Thorp community in record time. Usually, true acceptance took at least a decade or a familial tie to the village; Belinda had been *the new vicar* for seven years. It didn't surprise her, though; Joe had a magnetic personality and anyone in his radius became as metal filings.

"And here I was thinking it was the glamour of working with fruit and veg all day that kept you here." She smiled.

Joe had previously worked in marketing, but he'd become disillusioned in his last job and decided he needed to "get out of the rat race." On numerous occasions since, she had found herself gleefully thinking, *Of all the grocer joints in all the towns, in all the world, he walks into mine.*

Across the room, Star and Florin had taken a break from heavy petting to help Ryan, one of the owners of the Stag and Hound, extract Perdita and the huge spliff she'd just lit out of the pub before he got fined and she got arrested. Mourners shuffled hopefully out of the pub, following the plumes of weed smoke.

"Looks like the party's moving outside." Maggie laughed. "Dad would've loved that. I wish you could have met him. He had this aura of pure jolly mischief. He was . . . impish, even in old age. I think the world has lost some of its magic with him gone."

But if anyone had been under the impression that Augustus's funeral marked the end of his mischief, they would have been mistaken. A few weeks later, after the mourners had fled and life in Rowan Thorp returned to its dull convention, three solicitor letters in stiff white envelopes landed on three very different doormats, and three very different women picked them up.

5

MAGGIE LOOKED UP and smiled as Joe placed a mug of coffee on the table and shifted a crate of cauliflowers onto the floor. He walked around behind her, lifted her fading auburn curls off the back of her neck, and laid kisses along her skin.

She melted. The brush of his lips sent the sweetest thrill down her spine, which blossomed into a warm honey caress and kept on going. Even as she told herself again that she had to put a stop to whatever this was, that she had no business having hot passionate sex with this younger man, she knew her body would betray her.

In her opinion her breasts had always been too droopy, and her bottom was the shape of two Comice pears sat side by side. Her body was etched with a silvery mass of stretch marks flowing in streams and rivulets over her stomach and thighs, the topography of having grown two humans. For years she had hidden her body in the darkness during sexual encounters, embarrassed by its many imperfections. But Joe was a lights-on man, something that had taken her a while to get used to. He had traced her stretch marks with kisses like they were something to be worshipped and reveled in her softness.

"Is Patrick home?" His voice was low, teasing against her ear.

Oh, how she wished just at that moment that her eldest child wasn't lurking in his bedroom. If only she had the kind of son who liked to go running first thing in the morning. But alas, Patrick was a perfectly normal university student, who liked to sleep late when he was home for the holidays.

"He's in bed," she said, taking some pleasure from Joe's obvious disappointment.

"Maybe if we're really quiet I could take you on the worktop?"

She laughed. She was not about to sex up her kitchen worktop; she'd done her food hygiene course and that kind of thing was frowned upon.

"I'm afraid you'll have to settle for tea and biscuits this morning." She smiled as he took the seat he'd cleared for himself.

"Tea and biscuits come a close second." He grinned at her. "What's that?" he asked, nodding toward the letter laid open on the table, three satisfyingly sharp creases preventing the thick paper from lying flat.

She rubbed her eyes and dragged her palms down her face. My god, she was tired. *Look at him sitting there all gorgeously ruffled like he's just jumped out of a hayloft.* She looked down at her dungarees, the inner thighs of which were wearing thin— the curse of the ample-thigh rub—and saw one of the cuffs on her jumper was beginning to fray. For the hundredth time, she wondered what it was that Joe saw in her.

"It's a letter from my dad's solicitors," she said, nudging the letter with her finger as though afraid it might bite.

"Augustus had a solicitor?"

"Who knew? It's Steele & Brannigan, on the high street.

They kept that quiet; I've known Vanessa Steele for years and she never said a thing, not even at the funeral."

"I don't suppose she could, client confidentiality and all that."

"It turns out he had a will, which is news to me. My sisters and I have been summoned to hear the reading of it on the third of December."

"Maybe he was a secret millionaire." Joe raised his eyebrows.

"I think that's called *very* wishful thinking." She smiled ruefully. It would take more than wishing to sort out her financial problems. It would take a miracle. Her landlord—Gareth Gilbert of Gilbert & Marks Holdings and Lettings—had been trying to get her out of the greengrocer's shop and the maisonette above for the last couple of years. She had managed—just—to meet his rent hikes, designed to force her into moving. But six weeks ago, he'd pulled out the big guns and served her an eviction notice. Her home and business, which had been her mother's before her, was to be converted into a boutique hotel, and she and her two kids would be homeless by the end of January.

She ought to have begun packing by now, dismantling the life they'd built here for the last decade. But she hadn't told the children; she didn't want to ruin Christmas for them. She'd simply boxed those worries up and stuffed them down with all her other anxieties. She didn't have time to be homeless!

The eviction wasn't the only thing haunting her, though. She hadn't expected her dad's death to hit her as hard as it had. Sure, she'd not seen him for five years before he died, and even before that, she could count on one hand the number of months he'd spent at home in the last decade. And yet his death had left a hole in her heart she could swear she heard the wind whistling through.

"Mags?" Joe brushed her arm, and she snapped back to the present.

"Sorry. Miles away." She shook herself. What had they been talking about?

"Do you think your sisters will come to the will reading?" He asked.

She sighed. Another complication. "It doesn't look like they've got much choice. Steele & Brannigan have been instructed to tell us that the will cannot be read unless all three of us are present."

Joe raised an eyebrow and quipped, "That'll please Simone no end."

THE LETTER DROPPED onto the doormat just as Simone was grabbing her keys, ready to head out of the door. She was running late because she had started her period, early this time, and then spent ten minutes crying and another ten fixing her makeup, and now she was late. Her last two rounds of IVF had been unsuccessful—as had the two before that—and now she was out of time and out of money, and every period felt like a betrayal, her body mocking her for being unable to fulfill the task that millions of women all around the world seemed able to manage with ease. She had turned forty this year, still "vibrant" according to *Cosmopolitan* magazine, although the eggs collected during her last retrieval might beg to differ.

"Was that the post?" came Evette's voice from the kitchen.

No, Evette, that was the sound of my leg dropping off. Of course it's the bloody post! She took a deep breath. "Yes," she called, holding back the scream that lived in her throat. When had she become this rageful person?

Evette strolled into the hall, a piece of toast in one hand. She took another bite. "Anything for me?" she asked.

Evette was petite, with short blond hair that kinked in all the wrong directions and eyes so blue that even after thirteen years together, Simone still wanted to dive in and swim in them. They were opposites in almost every way. Simone was tall with poker-straight black hair, dark skin, green eyes, and a determination that until very recently had seen her achieve every goal she'd set her sights on. By contrast, Evette was relaxed, friendly, and open in a way that endeared her to everyone she met. Lately Evette's sparkle had dulled to a matte finish, and Simone was painfully aware that she was probably the cause.

Even someone as patient and gentle as Evette could only take so much. They had known the stats, the success and failure rates when they began the process, but nothing had prepared them for the way the disappointment would crush them. IVF chipped away at their united front, splitting the rock they'd built their lives upon in two.

Every loss had stripped away more of Simone's spirit until she was a walking wound, raw inside and out, and even kind words burned.

She dealt with her grief by bottling it and venting the excess pressure through anger. When Evette wanted to talk, she shut her down. When she expressed her need for closeness, Simone was an iceberg. Little by little, she had driven away the person she loved most in all the world, ruthlessly mining her sparkle until her wife's reserves had finally run dry.

Simone picked up the expensive-looking envelope. "It's for me," she said, carefully running her finger beneath the self-adhesive strip and pulling the missive free. She swore as she read the contents.

"What is it?" asked Evette, still crunching her toast. Simone tried not to care about the crumbs dusting down onto the hall carpet.

"It's a solicitor in Rowan Thorp. I've been summoned to hear Augustus's will being read."

"That's a bit old-fashioned, isn't it? I didn't think gathering for will readings was a thing these days. How very Agatha Christie! Rather intriguing, isn't it?"

Simone was frowning at the small print. "Doesn't look like I can get out of it."

"Surely you would *want* to go?" said Evette, her head quirked to one side.

"Why?" She was sure these formalities could be done via email, or Zoom if Vanessa was going to be really picky.

"Don't you want to hear your dad's final words?"

She sighed. Of course she did. Augustus hadn't been a traditional parent in any sense of the word, but he was kind and she had loved him and now he was dead. The problem here was that she was already replete with sadness and if she let in the loss of her father as well, she might lose the control she'd fought so hard to maintain.

Instead of telling Evette the truth, she rolled her eyes. "My father never said a sensible thing in his life."

"For your sisters, then." Evette searched her face as though trying to find her wife hiding behind the eyes of this imposter.

She gave a derisive snort. "I don't have much choice, do I? I'll book a room at the pub we stayed in for the funeral. I only need to be there for one night."

Evette fell quiet and then said, "Maybe you should look at doing an Airbnb; there's plenty of little holiday cottages around there. You could stay a bit longer. Have a little break."

"What do you mean stay a bit longer? A little break from what?" She could feel the dread rising up into her throat, cold and thick. She swallowed and waited for the blow that she'd been dodging for the last six months.

"A little break from us," said Evette gently, tears brimming. "If we don't have some time apart now, I fear we'll be looking at something more difficult later." She reached up and rested her palm softly against Simone's cheek. "I don't want that."

"We promised this wouldn't break us," Simone challenged.

Evette smiled sadly. "That was before we knew how hard it would be. For me, Simone. Take a break."

STAR BUMPED THE drawstring laundry bag down the stairs and rested it against the bulging rucksacks, the battered pull-along carryall, and the scuffed guitar case: her worldly belongings.

"I am sorry." Mr. Cavell looked pained, and for a moment Star wondered if he was going to cry.

"It's okay," she soothed. "I completely understand."

"But I have other tenants. The noise. The shouting. The older residents are frightened."

"Honestly, Mr. Cavell, it's okay." She gave him her most reassuring smile. She'd never been evicted with so much remorse. And she'd been evicted a lot.

She'd been renting a nice room, one of the better places she'd lived in, in a tall Victorian mansion house share in Bradford. There were twelve other tenants in the building; some of them had bedsits, and others, like her, had rooms with shared bathroom and kitchen facilities. She had enjoyed a peaceful existence in this place; she got on well with the other residents and nobody tried to sell her drugs or get her into bed. Unfortunately, Stu wanted to rekindle their relationship and living arrangements.

"How did a nice girl like you get mixed up with a man like him, anyway?" asked Mr. Cavell.

Star liked the way that Mr. Cavell always referred to her as a "nice girl" even though she was thirty-eight. She still felt like she was twenty—Simone would say she behaved as though she were twelve—and she didn't look a day over twenty-five; she was like her dad in that way, never looking her age. She huffed out a sigh.

"Because I never learn. And because I thought that if I could make Stu happy enough, he wouldn't need to use drugs to make himself feel better."

The way Mr. Cavell looked at her then made her realize why he thought of her as a girl.

She slapped her forehead and shook her head. "Trust me, when I say it aloud, I realize how stupid it sounds."

"And why did he go to prison?"

"That's a longer story." She smiled sadly.

"Cup of tea before you set off?" He smiled hopefully and pushed open the door to his ground-floor flat. Gossip was Mr. Cavell's lifeblood. If she told her landlord about her disastrous relationship with Stu, it would be all over the building by the end of the week. But what did it matter? In an hour she'd be gone, and if gossiping gave the lonely old man an excuse to talk to people, then who was she to deny him some juicy tidbits?

"Why not?" She smiled.

On the other side of the glass of the communal front door, the red-jacketed postman was trying to force all the post for the building through the letter box at once. The bundle landed with a thud in a crumpled heap on the welcome mat. Star gathered it up and placed it on the shelf by the stairs; some of the elderly residents had trouble bending down to get their post.

"Ooh, look!" she said, delighted to find a letter addressed to her. She didn't often get mail. "Just in the nick of time too." She left her belongings in the hallway and carried the letter with her into Mr. Cavell's flat.

Mr. Cavell set the tea tray down on the small coffee table between two armchairs, which smelled like stale cigarettes and dust, and settled down on the one opposite Star. One of the quirks she had inherited from Augustus was a need to seek out at least one piece of magic in every place she found herself. The flat was run-down; the furnishings bore the mustard and burnt sienna shades of the 1960s, which was probably when it was last decorated. But on the wall above the faux stone fireplace was a massive blown-up photograph of Dave Grohl with his arm around Mr. Cavell, who was making a "rock on" gesture with his arthritic fingers. She smiled contentedly; there was her magic.

"So," he started, his gray eyes twinkling as he bit into a digestive biscuit, "tell me everything." Mr. Cavell leaned forward in his chair eagerly. He reminded her of an old tawny owl.

Where did everything *begin?* she wondered.

"The thing is, Stu has a pretty serious drug habit, as you've already guessed. He has to use several times a day to function. About three years ago, things got bad. We were living in Bristol then. He was stealing money from me, and I knew he was stealing from his mum, but Stu is not an easy person to break away from." What she meant was that she was a soft touch and he was a master manipulator. "When I had no money left, he broke into the café where I worked, one night after everyone had gone home, and stole the takings. That was the last straw for me, so I broke up with him. Love isn't always enough, as it turns out. He was already on probation, so he got sent down for two months and I lost my job, which meant I lost my flat. But it gave me the excuse I needed to not be there when he got out."

"Good gracious me." Mr. Cavell was riveted, and she couldn't help smiling. "But you said he only went to prison for two months?"

"That time, yes. I went to stay with my sister Simone and her wife in Greenwich for a bit while I got myself together. Only when Stu got out, he came and found me."

"All the way from Bristol!" he exclaimed.

"We'd been to visit my sister once before, so after having no luck in Bristol, he must have guessed I'd be there. He'd already tried my eldest sister in Rowan Thorp."

"And then what happened?" His biscuit arm was suspended halfway to his mouth, his crinkly face enraptured.

"He turned up when Simone and Evette were out for the evening. I'd say with hindsight, he'd probably waited for the right moment."

Mr. Cavell gasped. "What did you do?"

"I told him we were over, for good, and that he had to leave. I didn't even let him in, kept him on the doorstep. Eventually he got the message and said he would go but that he needed some cash, and could he use the toilet before he caught the coach."

Mr. Cavell clapped his hands over his mouth, the biscuit dropped onto the plate. Clearly he had better foresight than she did.

"I only let him in for five minutes. He used the toilet while I got him some cash from my bag, and then I chucked him back out onto the street. But when Simone and Evette got back from their night out, they found that Evette's jewelry box had been ransacked and the holiday money Simone had been saving was missing."

Mr. Cavell shook his head sadly.

"He got caught the next day trying to pawn Evette's grandmother's engagement ring. He got sent down for two years, and my sister hasn't spoken to me since."

"But it wasn't your fault! You were hoodwinked. That scoundrell!"

"I let him in when I should have known better. But I felt sorry for him. He's not violent or anything, he's just troubled and addicted and it makes him do bad things. Anyway, you know the rest because you've seen. He doesn't seem to understand that we're over. It's like he thought we were on a hiatus while he was in prison and now that he's out he thinks we'll get back together."

Stu's tearful drunken wailing in the communal hallways, not to mention his relentless banging on her door the last two months, had resulted in numerous police calls and her current eviction.

Star had always been attracted to troubled souls, unable to resist sad puppy eyes, even when they were attached to a manipulative scoundrel. But even she had her limits.

Mr. Cavell was wringing his hands. The furrowed crease above his nose was in danger of consuming his eyebrows. "Where will you go?" he asked.

"Oh, don't worry about me. I've got friends who will put me up for a while."

She didn't know where yet, but she'd figure it out. She always did. As she went to stand, she remembered the letter. She tore it open and smiled. Now she had a destination.

"Are you *sure* you have somewhere to go?" he asked, pulling nervously at his knitted sweater-vest.

"Absolutely." She smiled at him. "You don't need to worry about me. The universe has provided."

By which she meant her big sister Maggie would put her up for a few days while she got her shit together and they dealt with the will. Suddenly the day had gotten a lot brighter. Mr. Cavell waved her off as she dragged her possessions up the street toward the train station. Rowan Thorp had been on her mind ever since the funeral and now she had an excuse to go back.

6

ROWAN THORP WAS a pretty village in the southeast of England surrounded by rolling hills, fields, forests, and other pretty villages that dotted the countryside like they'd been dropped fully formed into the landscape.

Once a bustling village with its close proximity to the river, farms, and orchards, Rowan Thorp had been a destination for traders and travelers alike. Over time it became less of a hub for merchants to sell their wares and more of an afternoon escape for city folk in need of a slower pace, some window shopping, and a cream tea.

The high street was a harmonious muddle of Georgian, Tudor, and Victorian architecture—stout, bent, tall, gabled, thatched, stone, and beam—a visual history giving voice to the ghosts of the past. Most of the houses and all of the shops were already decorated for Christmas even though it was only December third. Voluptuous wreaths of holly, ivy, and eucalyptus hung from front doors; candles stood in windows; and twinkle lights flickered from beneath frosty thatched roofs.

The Stag and Hound had erected a huge fir tree in their front courtyard, which was mirrored by the Rowan Tree Inn. Both trees were festooned in matching multicolored fairy lights of blue, red, amber, and green, hues so happy that just looking at them could warm the chilliest of cockles.

Set back a little between the two pubs, the spire of St. Swithun's—the tip of the Holy Trinity Green triangle—punctured the forget-me-not-blue sky. The sun was impossibly bright, and the ice crystals on the paths and grass verges glittered beneath its dazzling gaze.

THE OFFICES OF Steele & Brannigan Solicitors were a mixture of generic workplace carpeting and gray filing cabinets mixed in with some rather nice dark wood antique furniture. Behind her leather-topped mahogany desk, Vanessa Steele regarded the three sisters above her tented fingers.

Though she naturally saw more of Maggie these days than the other two, they had all spent their childhood summers getting into trouble and had been generally regarded by the villagers as a nightmare. She had known what to expect this morning—she had cleared her schedule in anticipation—and they didn't disappoint. Vanessa sat quietly, waiting for the sisters to finish bickering.

"I only asked why, if you arrived last night, you didn't come and see me?" Maggie asked. "I could have made you dinner."

"I needed time to prepare. Mentally. You know I don't function well in off-the-cuff situations. I don't like having things sprung upon me and by the same token I don't spring myself on other people," said Simone. "Most people would appreciate that courtesy."

"I'm not *other* people. I'm your sister."

"Why are you making a big deal out of this? I had a long

journey and I simply wanted to get settled in at the cottage and acclimatize myself to this"—she flapped her hands to encompass the room and everyone in it—"situation."

"Maggie's right, it wouldn't have hurt you to pop in and say hello," Star butted in.

"Yes, well, I had a feeling *you* might be there, and I wasn't in the mood for playing 'happy families.'"

"When do you *ever* play 'happy families'?" Star retorted.

Maggie was seated between Simone and Star in her usual capacity as the bland filling in the sister sandwich, caught between slices of sourdough Simone and brioche Star. In this analogy Maggie imagined herself to be something neutral, poached chicken breast or mild cheddar maybe.

Already she was getting a tension headache. She'd left Joe and Patrick to run the grocer's, but there were still at least twenty things that needed doing today rolling around in her head. Hovering on the periphery of every conscious and unconscious thought was her eviction notice, squatting in her mind like a spider in the corner of a room. She looked up and saw her friend's expression. She nudged Star and Simone, nodding toward Vanessa, and the three fell silent.

Vanessa smiled calmly and began. "First of all, I know we spoke at Augustus's funeral, but I would like to offer my condolences to you in my official capacity as your father's solicitor. Secondly, thank you for attending this meeting."

"Did we have a choice?" Simone asked.

"There is always a choice." Vanessa smiled. "And your decision to be here will make this process easier and faster."

"What process are we talking about exactly?" Maggie asked.

"Have any of you been into your father's shop recently?" Vanessa inquired.

"I stayed at the flat last night, but I didn't venture into the shop," said Star. "Wasn't quite brave enough to go in by myself; all that taxidermy gives me the heebie-jeebies."

"You slept at Dad's?" Simone asked with something like surprise on her face. "I thought you would have stayed at Maggie's."

"I offered, but she would have had to share a room with Verity."

"I didn't mind that. But if I'm going to be staying for a while, it makes sense for me to not be under your feet."

"By that, I take it you're unemployed and homeless *again*?" Simone drawled.

"It's really quite something how you manage to sound both weary *and* scathing," snapped Star.

"What can I say? You make it easy."

Star threw her arms in the air and flopped back in her chair dramatically. Maggie gave Vanessa what she hoped was an apologetic smile.

Vanessa cleared her throat and continued. "Well, as you know, Augustus was a collector . . ."

"A human magpie, more like," said Simone.

"Yes. Well. Over the years, your father had an agreement with us that he would send artifacts from his travels to us, and we would store them in the shop."

"The shop that was never open because he was never in the country," added Maggie.

"Quite," Vanessa agreed. "He continued to do this right up to his death. The last items we received arrived just three days before we learned of his passing."

"What kind of items?" asked Simone.

"To be honest, I don't know. We merely took delivery of the

crates, and your father would sort through them when he re-turned. Of course, this last time he never did."

"So, five years' worth of deliveries are still boxed in the shop?" asked Maggie.

"That is correct." Vanessa nodded.

"But why do it?" asked Star. "I never understood it. Why collect all those pieces when he was never around to sell any of them?"

"Maybe he was *actually* a magpie in human form," joked Maggie.

"Maggie, you could romanticize a turd," said Simone. "The man was a hoarder, and the only way he got away with it was under the guise of being a shopkeeper."

"I think," Vanessa interrupted, "although nobody can be sure, that he was building you a nest egg."

"Of junk," added Simone.

"I am assuming that Augustus believed at least some of his collection had a market value, because he instructed us to em-ploy the services of an appraiser from Sotheby's to catalog the shop for you. The appraiser ought to be arriving today."

Maggie gasped. "Sotheby's? How much is that going to cost us? I more imagined us all chipping in for a man with a van."

"The appraiser's services have been paid for in advance by your father and there are adequate funds put aside to cover the duration of his stay. The appraiser is working on your behalf, so please feel free to be as involved or not as you wish in the process."

"I'm getting the feeling that Dad wanted us to be involved," said Maggie.

"I would have to agree with you," Vanessa replied. "As you

probably know, reading a will out like this is highly unusual; in fact, this is the first one I've ever had to do. It was much more common in my grandfather's day."

"Typical Augustus, ever the showman," said Simone dryly.

The blinds at the large windows were pulled down low, presumably to prevent prying eyes, as if that would stop the Rowan Thorp hotline from buzzing. The winter sun shone through the fabric, bathing the office in a pale primrose haze. In her own way, each sister steeled herself for what their father planned to pull out of his hat next.

Vanessa cleared her throat. "Before we begin, I should warn you that your father wrote certain caveats into his will, which are nonnegotiable."

Maggie felt Simone stiffen, while her own shoulders sagged, and Star perked up.

"Caveats?" Simone asked, rather more sharply than was necessary in Maggie's opinion.

"Yes." Vanessa remained unflustered. "They are . . . somewhat unusual."

"Classic Dad." Star sounded delighted.

With another look at each of the sisters, Vanessa unfolded a sheet of thick cartridge paper and began to read.

To my three daughters, if you are reading this, then I am dead. I don't believe in regret, but if I had one, it is that we were not perhaps as close as we might have been. The blame lies solely with me. It is my greatest wish that you—Marguerite, Simone, and Heavenly-Stargazer— forge the relationship with one another that I was unable to have. Together you are a force to be reckoned with. Each of you has a gift that brings strength to your sisters,

*and I hope in death to do what I was unable to in life: to
rally your hearts and spirits and rekindle the sisterly
harmony you enjoyed as children.*

*To you, my three daughters, I bequeath all my worldly
goods and my estate in its entirety on the understanding
that you complete two quests. For the first, you will be furnished with instructions by the good solicitors of Steele &
Brannigan. It's just a bit of fun to get you working as a
team in order to be ready for the second quest, which is to
reinstate the traditional winter solstice celebration to the
village of Rowan Thorp. I mean for this to be done
properly. The whole village must be invited and encour-
aged to join. You will find much of what you need to know
by speaking with those who remember the old ways. As
for the finer details, well, those are to be found by completing the first task. Should you, for whatever reason, be
unable to accomplish this task, my estate will be divided
up and donated to various listed charities in an alternative codicil. Should any one of you decide not to partake
of the quest, the above codicil will be activated. The only
way to claim your prize is to work together.*

Bonne chance, mes bébés des bois.

Vanessa laid the letter on the desk and unfolded another piece
of paper, but before she could read it, Maggie held up her hand.

"I'm sorry, what? He wants us to reinstate the winter solstice
celebration?" she asked. She could feel her anxiety sitting in her
throat like a dry potato chip.

"Yes. Your father has set aside a small cash fund to help with
any costs incurred, which you may draw upon from this office."

"How much is *small*?" asked Simone.

"I'm afraid I am not at liberty to discuss that at this time. However, if and when you need to dip into it, Augustus has asked that you put your request in writing and someone here will see that you are credited."

"Well, that's something, I suppose," said Maggie. "I am not a person who has the luxury of *disposable cash*."

"Was that aimed at me?" Simone snapped.

"What? Why would it be? Jeez, you're so tetchy all the time!"

"I don't have *any* cash, disposable or otherwise," Star chimed in.

"Well, there's a surprise. Maybe you could get one of your boyfriends to steal you some."

"That was uncalled for," Maggie reprimanded.

"The point being!" Vanessa spoke over them. "Your father has put measures in place so that none of you should be out of pocket financially. Your time is another matter, and one that I'm afraid I can't help with."

"What the fuck even is a winter solstice?" asked Simone. "I've heard the term, obviously, but what *actually* is it, like some chanting around a bonfire or waving sage around? Animal sacrifice or some shit?"

"Why must you always look down your nose at anything that doesn't fit with your own personal beliefs?" Star snapped uncharacteristically. Simone remained unabashed. "Just because *you* don't understand something, doesn't make it *shit*!" she went on. "The winter solstice marks the shortest day and the longest night of the year. It signifies the beginning of winter, but also it marks the point at which the days will begin to get longer again. For centuries, communities have made an event of the winter solstice by giving thanks and celebrating the light soon to return."

"Of course our little resident hippie would know what a winter solstice is." Simone smirked.

"It's a natural science event based in astronomical fact, not made up by anyone, 'hippie' or otherwise." Star rolled her eyes.

"At least one of us knows something about it," Maggie said diplomatically before turning back to Vanessa. "Are you sure he wants us to *actually hold* a winter solstice event? Could he have been speaking metaphorically?"

"I'm afraid not. Those are his *actual* wishes, yes." Vanessa looked apologetically at the three women.

"*Wishes* we couldn't ignore if we wanted to," said Simone. "He's got us over a barrel."

"Cheeky old bugger," Star mused.

"I haven't got time to be chasing around the village trying to organize a festival." Maggie felt the weight of all her responsibilities pulling her under. How on earth was she going to fit anything else onto her plate? Any day now, Verity was going to come home from school with details of the Christmas play costume, which Maggie was required to make; the orders for Christmas veg boxes and Christmas trees were coming in thick and fast; and oh yes, she also had to pack up their whole life and magically pull somewhere out of her arse for them to live.

"You're not the only one with a busy life," Simone snapped.

"I didn't say I was. But we all know who this is going to fall to, don't we?"

"Oh, here we go with the martyrdom."

"I'm not being a martyr, I'm stating fact. You were both demonstrably absent when I was organizing the funeral."

"I wondered how long you'd hold that against me."

"It was only three weeks ago! You have *no idea* what I'm dealing with right now."

"Well, I'm sure you'll do what you always do and tell us all about it after you've dealt with it so that we can do nothing but feel guilty."

"You are a piece of work, Simone, do you know that? Jeez! If they gave out certificates for being bitchy . . ."

"I think it might be quite fun," piped up Star.

"Of course you do, you've got nothing better to do with your time than flit about." Simone's sarcasm was scathing. "You've turned being irresponsible into an art form."

"Don't pick on her. Being miserable doesn't give you the right to be mean."

"Okay, take Star's side, like you always do."

"That's simply not true, is it, Simone? I'm as bloody Switzerland as they come, but you make it very difficult sometimes." Maggie was trying to keep her cool, but this was a lot to take in and Simone was not helping.

"Ladies, if I might be allowed to continue?" Vanessa appeared unruffled by the outburst; she had long been impervious to their bickering.

The sisters sat chastened.

"Sorry, Vanessa," Maggie said, and her sisters followed suit, mumbling their apologies.

"I know this is a lot for you. But we *are* dealing in legalities here, and as a solicitor, I can serve you better if you let me do my job. These are the instructions for the first task." She waved the unfolded paper and began to read.

"My girls, listen closely to what the nice solicitor is reading."

Vanessa looked up pointedly.

"Hidden within North Novelties & Curios are thirty-two Monopoly houses. Working together you must find all thirty-two and present them to Steele & Brannigan. Upon receipt and verification,

you will be presented with the key to a lockbox that holds the deeds to the building, land, and the woods, and a comprehensive ledger containing details of every item in the shop, as well as details that will help you in your winter solstice endeavors . . ."

"Easy," said Simone. "I'll drive over to Lakeside now and pick up a Monopoly game. Job done. We'll give you the houses, and you can hand over the key."

"Good idea." Maggie patted her arm. "We can come with you."

"I could do some Christmas shopping," added Star.

"Ahem."

All eyes turned back to Vanessa, who cast her own back down to the paper and continued to read.

"And before one of you—probably Simone—gets any ideas about simply purchasing a fresh game of Monopoly . . ."

Simone shook her head, her mouth pulling between a pout and a smile. Star chirruped out a giggle, and Maggie grinned at their father's uncanny ability to pin them even from the grave.

Vanessa continued, *"You should know that I have customized each house in some way, details of which are inside a sealed envelope"*—Vanessa held up said envelope while continuing to read—*"which is only to be opened upon receipt of all thirty-two houses, whereupon they will be marked off against written details of my customizations. Happy hunting, my babes of the woods. May Artemis watch over your endeavors!"*

"Crafty old fox." Maggie sighed. "Does he mean Artemis the Greek goddess or the cat?"

"Both, probably," said Simone. "Can't be the same cat from when we were kids, can it?"

"It looks the same." Maggie shrugged. "Answers to the same name."

"To be fair, a stray will answer to any name if you feed it," said Vanessa.

"But to have the exact same markings?" Star was incredulous.

"Well, I remember her from when I was maybe three years old, which would make her over forty, which is impossible."

"Dad said she came with the shop," said Star.

"So that would make her like seventy years old?" Simone balked.

"That's assuming she was a kitten when Dad inherited."

"Maybe this Artemis is like the original Artemis's great grandchild," Star suggested. "She slept on the end of my bed last night."

"Did you sleep in our old room?" Simone asked.

"Yeah. It felt too weird to go into Dad's room. It's just the same in there, you know, still the old daisy wallpaper."

"That was faded even when we were little," said Simone.

"Except behind the armoire, where it's all still like new. It's like a time capsule. The same patchwork quilts on our old beds. Remember the rag rug?"

"Where Dad used to sit cross-legged and read us bedtime stories." Maggie smiled. If nothing else, Augustus had made great readers out of his daughters.

"Wasn't it dusty?"

"I go in every couple of weeks and give it a once-over," said Maggie. "And I changed all the bedding yesterday; I had a feeling Star might end up staying."

"Witch." Simone smiled.

"Takes one to know one." Maggie grinned back.

"You ought to hire a cleaner to go in once a month to save you having to do it," Simone offered helpfully.

"Like I can afford a cleaner!" It irked Maggie that things like keeping their dad's flat in good order was something her sisters didn't even have to think about. It wasn't their fault, but neither was it fair.

"Did it feel odd sleeping in the flat?" Simone asked. "Was it spooky?"

"Not spooky. Nostalgic maybe. But then I spent a lot of time there on my own, if you recall. Maggie said you've rented the Dalgleish cottage. What was that like? Old memories of snogging Kelly?" Star grinned.

They used to play with Mrs. Dalgleish's daughter, Kelly, when they stayed in Rowan Thorp for the summer. Kelly was Simone's first-ever kiss.

"What about you?" Simone countered, blushing. "I saw you out of the window last night, in Troy's car. Did Antonia know?" She made it sound like an accusation.

Troy and his wife, Antonia, owned the Rowan Tree Inn.

"Spying, were you? Troy very kindly picked me up from the station last night. Don't make it sound seedy."

Troy and Star had been summer sweethearts in their early teens, but it had fizzled out quite naturally. He'd been a good friend to her when she'd been in desperate need of one and they'd remained close into adulthood. Star was also friends with Antonia and was a firm favorite with their children.

"You started it." Simone pouted.

"I made a joke. You made an accusation."

"And also, I wasn't *spying*, I just happened to be looking out of the window as you drove past."

"All right!" Maggie interjected. "Dad's forcing us to work together and it's going to be a bloody nightmare if you two keep bitching at each other. So grow up and suck it up." She let out a shaky breath. Confrontation wasn't her forte, but her nerves were already stretched too thin.

"Dad's really done a number on us, hasn't he?" Star dropped her head onto Maggie's shoulder.

"Doesn't look like even death can put a stop to his shenanigans," Simone agreed.

"It's nice to be called 'babes of the woods' again," Star remarked sentimentally. "Do you remember?"

Maggie covered Star's hand with her own. "I remember," she said, and was surprised to feel Simone's smooth fingers curling around her other hand.

"Me too," said Simone.

"WELL, THAT'S ALL of it," said Vanessa, slipping the papers back into a folder and laying her palms down flat upon it in the universal gesture for "we're done here, folks." She looked at each of them. "Any questions?"

"Apart from 'what the hell?'" asked Simone.

Vanessa laughed. Now that she had removed her metaphorical solicitor's hat, she seemed to relax. "Yeah, apart from that. It's a lot to take in. We've never had a will quite like it."

"But when did he hide all the Monopoly houses?" asked Maggie.

"According to my dad, he's been hiding them for the last fifteen years, but he only delivered the instructions to us just before he left for his last trip. Was Monopoly a game you used to play together?"

"Not religiously, no. We probably played it a couple of times each summer," said Maggie. "On a picnic rug spread out under the trees."

"Dad said it would teach us about the transience of material things," Simone chimed in.

"Which I'd always thought was a little hypocritical given that the building he owned had been in his family for generations," said Star, which earned her a hearty agreement from Simone before she seemed to remember that she wasn't technically speaking to her and sat up in her chair, scowling.

"It was one of the few games he played with us, that and hide-and-seek," said Maggie. "In fact, didn't we hide the pieces once because we didn't want to play?"

Augustus had done his best, but his talents were better suited to setting up magical adventures and scavenger hunts for the girls to go on—at which he excelled—than actually spending time with them. Once a whole miniature porcelain tea set appeared in their tree house, alongside tiny jam tarts and cookies, apparently left by the fairies. Another time the pixies left clues to buried treasure written on rice paper—which the sisters had to eat immediately to prevent the pirates from finding the treasure before them. Augustus was a brilliant activities captain; it was too bad, Star thought sadly, his one-on-one relationships weren't adventures.

"Yeah, we did. I think we wanted him to play hide-and-seek again," Simone said, pondering. "It was too hot for concentrating on board games, and we started acting up."

Star gasped. "Oh my god, we totally did, I forgot about that. We scattered the Monopoly pieces all over the woods and then couldn't remember where we'd hidden them."

"Yes!" Maggie laughed. "It was a vintage edition as well."

"Augustus North: The Revenge," said Simone dryly.

Vanessa smiled and nodded at their remembrances. "Didn't I come to help?" she asked.

"You did. I think you stayed for a sleepover."

"Yes, that's right, it *was* that night. We stayed in the tepee in the back garden."

"It was the only time I ever remember him being even remotely cross with us," said Star.

"And even then, he was only mildly perturbed. I don't think he had the anger chip," Maggie agreed.

"That's rather nice, really, to have a parent who never gets angry," Vanessa mused.

They were all quiet for a moment, and Star wondered if maybe Augustus's plan wasn't quite so silly after all. Already they'd found a common ground that had been notably absent for the last few years.

"Well, whenever you're ready, you've each got a key still?"

The sisters nodded.

"Good. I've got spares if anybody needs them, but otherwise you can start whenever you like. But you must work together. That stipulation was very clear. Good luck!"

7

IT WAS UNANIMOUSLY decided—a miracle in itself—that Maggie, Simone, and Star should go straight to their father's shop and make a start on finding the Monopoly houses.

"Didn't you go into the shop when he died?" asked Simone as they hovered around the door. Maggie held the key but was struck by a sudden reluctance to push it into the lock, as though once she turned the key there would be no turning back.

"Why would I? I only needed to get into the flat," she replied, as though rebutting an accusation.

"You weren't tempted at all? Even just to look around?" Simone pressed.

Maggie tried to articulate her feelings. "You know the old question 'If a tree falls in the woods and no one is there to hear it does it make a sound?' Well, that's how I've always felt about the shop when Dad wasn't here. As though it doesn't exist without his presence, or it does exist but it's an empty shell, dead and blackened."

Maggie waited for Simone's derisive laugh, but it didn't come.

"I actually know what you mean." Simone nodded. "I kind of

feel the same way about the flat too; that's why I was surprised you stayed there by yourself, Star. I'm not sure I would have."

"The flat's different," Star said. "It feels like home—to me anyway. It was the only place in my life that remained constant." The wistfulness in her tone didn't go unnoticed by her sisters.

The flat above the shop could be accessed by a separate entrance, via a wooden gate built into the Tudor limestone wall that faced the high street. The North land in its entirety—including the building, gardens, and extensive woodlands—was enclosed within ten-foot-high walls. Those high-security walls had granted the sisters much freedom growing up, lending them ten and a half acres to play in. How could it not feel like an enchanted place, insulated from the world outside, surrounded by ancient trees and lawns that stretched out like daisy-covered carpets? Even the shop had felt charmed, with hidden panels in the walls and shiny things glinting out from every surface.

Maggie was still holding the key to North Novelties & Curios, as though hoping someone would take it from her, but neither of her sisters seemed inclined to do so. The blinds were fully down at the windows and thick cobwebs had layered in the corners of the frames; black bodies of cocooned insects were suspended in the voluptuous froth of white. On the outside, most of the paint on the frames and sills had flaked off, and what remained was brittle and bubbled. The overall impression now was more haunted than magic.

"When *was* the last time you went in?" Simone asked.

Maggie thought back. "Before the last time he left, so five years ago, I guess. Verity had been five when he'd taken off, she'll turn eleven in the spring. She hardly remembers him; it's a shame, really. I would have liked the kids to have known their grandfather better."

"It isn't your fault that they didn't. That's on him."

"How about you?"

"When was I last at the shop?" Simone asked, and Maggie nodded. "Christ knows. Verity's baptism maybe?"

"I'm looking forward to having a good snoop around," said Star, a look of glee on her face.

Simone chuckled. "Now that it's daylight and you've got both of us with you, you're feeling brave."

"Exactly."

"I feel stressed just thinking about the disorder inside. It was fun when we were kids, but that's because it wasn't our shit to deal with."

"Well, you'd better see if you can score some Valium to calm you down, then, because we've got no choice now. The old codger's going to make us sort through all his crap whether we like it or not," said Simone dryly.

"It's going to be even worse if he's been sending his finds back from his travels. We'll have to go through all that junk as well."

"Let's concentrate on finding the Monopoly houses first."

Artemis hopped up onto the window ledge and rubbed her head against Maggie's hand, purring and nudging her to turn the key.

"Right!" she said, gathering herself. "We're going in."

THE SHOP WAS long and narrow, reaching so far back that the daylight was lost to cave-like shadow by the time it reached the end. The space was unnervingly cluttered, the kind of place that could only fit one person in each aisle at a time. Not that they much resembled aisles in the traditional sense; there wasn't a straight line in the place. Instead they meandered lazily, curving in on themselves like a maze made of head-height bric-a-brac instead of hedges, so that every now and then you'd find yourself at a dead end and have to shuffle back out the way you'd come. The floor was original flagstone, worn smooth over time but still uneven enough to cause the freestanding shelving units to list alarmingly. In places, faded rugs laid threadbare and footworn.

Then there was the snarled-up mass of merchandise itself. A porcelain figurine inside a yellow diving helmet behind a cow-shaped butter dish, draped in a silk scarf, beside a 1939 hardcover edition of *Macbeth*, which lay beneath a wooden mouse . . . and so it went in an eclectic jumble of items so tightly packed it was hard for the eye to single out one object from the next. Much of the tangle seemed to defy gravity as it teetered precariously on the shelves without falling.

At the back of the shop, behind a mahogany-and-glass display unit, which looked as antique as the brooches and pocket watches it housed, was the wall of clocks. Each one's hands had stopped at exactly seventeen minutes past three.

"What time did Dad die?" asked Star, as the three sisters stood looking up at the wall of silent timekeepers.

"Don't even start with your nonsense," warned Simone.

"What?" she asked innocently.

"You're going to suggest that all the clocks stopped at the time he died, aren't you?" said Simone.

"Well, even you have to admit, it's a bit spooky," she retorted.

"Romantic as that idea is, Star, I'm afraid those clocks probably wound down a week after Dad left for his last expedition," said Maggie kindly.

"I'd hardly call our father's wanderings 'expeditions,'" said Simone.

"Why not?" asked Maggie. "He was exploring in his own way. He's a lot better traveled than I'll ever be."

"Yes, but at what cost? He barely even knew his own children." Simone's expression was petulant.

A knock at the door prevented further quarreling, though Star knew it would only be a temporary ceasefire. She began to wend her way down to the front of the shop, her sisters trailing behind her.

A smart-suited man with a trepidatious expression was peering in the window of the door, his hands on either side of his head to shield his eyes from the light outside and better see into the gloom of the shop. He flustered, embarrassed, when he saw Star and quickly moved away from the window, pushing up his glasses and picking his briefcase up off the ground. He seemed familiar to her, though she couldn't place him.

"Can I help you?" she asked as she pulled the door open, the airflow causing several wind chimes hanging from the ceiling beams to tinkle daintily.

"I hope so, yes." The man smiled nervously. "I stopped in at Steele & Brannigan, and they told me you were all here. I'm the appraiser from Sotheby's. Duncan. Duncan Steadman, pleased to meet you."

He held out his hand and she shook it. His fingers were long and thin, like a pianist's or an artist's, and warm as they wrapped around Star's own hand. Suits—as a type of man—had never been her cup of tea, but there was something about him. She found herself both intrigued and soothed by his gentle manner.

"You are very welcome indeed, Duncan Steadman. We need all the help we can get sifting through this mess," said Star

"I can't wait!" said Duncan, sounding like he absolutely meant it. "The North account is the stuff of Sotheby's folklore.

I put myself forward as soon as I heard they needed an appraiser to come down." He faltered and looked suddenly shamefaced. "I'm so sorry, that was thoughtless. I'm sorry for your loss. Your father was a legend in the office."

She had so many questions about Duncan's statements that she didn't know where to begin.

"How did you know he was our father?" she asked.

"You have the North eyes!" he said eagerly, like a pupil confident of his answer in class. Suddenly she knew where she'd seen him before.

"We met on the train yesterday afternoon. Kind of. We didn't actually speak. You were knitting."

Duncan's expression seemed at once both delighted and shy. "Yes, I remember you. It never occurred to me that one of the North daughters might be on the train."

She had almost given up hope of discovering any magic on the overcrowded commuter train, when a man in a suit, walking so stiffly his trousers might have been made from wood, had got on at London Bridge station. He stashed his immaculate Ted Baker suitcase in the overhead rack and sat awkwardly in the chair opposite her. She had been struck by the Clark Kent air about him: handsome in an uptight, probably-starched-and-ironed-his-socks sort of way. He had close-cropped curly black hair and a precisely trimmed beard, sharp and angular like his jaw. When he'd opened his briefcase with two neat clicks and pulled out some knitting, she had smiled to herself, satisfied she had found her magic after all.

And now he was standing in North Novelties & Curios, and she realized she'd been holding his hand far longer than was necessary. She smiled shyly and released him, stepping back and knocking into a shelf, causing three hundred items to rattle in protest.

She did a brief internal assessment to try to decipher this peculiar feeling and the only word she could come up with to describe it was *glittery. Holy crap, what's happening to me?*

Maggie, smiling, stepped forward briefly to shake Duncan's hand before stepping back to make room for Simone.

Simone glided into the now-crowded shop entrance and held out her hand. "In case you didn't already guess, I'm the third sister, second if you're going by age."

Duncan looked a little overwhelmed. "Like I said to your sister, I am so excited and honored to be here," he gushed.

"What did you mean by 'the North account'? And why is it legendary?" Maggie called over from her position next to a complete skeleton on a stand, whose name, according to his label, was Cuthbert.

"Oh, well, the North family have been buying and selling through Sotheby's ever since Patience North approached us when we started business in 1744, and we've had dealings with every owner of North Novelties & Curios since. Did your father not tell you?"

The women shook their heads.

"I see. I mean, I just assumed . . ."

"What makes it the stuff of legend?" asked Simone.

Duncan pushed his glasses up his nose for the second time in as many minutes. "We, that is, the collective and historical 'we,' have always wanted the chance to root around in the shop. Our dealings were only ever to do with specific items; the North family have always been very private about their collectibles, but everybody knows that this shop is a historical treasure trove."

"'Historical treasure' as opposed to actual treasure worth real money," interposed Simone.

"I'm quietly hopeful of both." Duncan did indeed look hopeful; in Star's opinion he resembled Charlie Bucket upon finding the golden ticket.

"Really? I guess we should check that our insurance is up to par," Maggie considered out loud.

"Oh, I'm sure it is. Your father was meticulous about that sort of thing."

"Are we talking about the same man?" asked Simone. "I can't imagine him being meticulous about anything."

"I have all his documents with me. You're welcome to look through them. He ensured that his certificates of authenticity were in order and insured certain items accordingly."

"Good lord." Maggie looked bewildered. "I'm beginning to think our father had multiple personalities."

"I don't suppose he sent you stock sheets, did he?" asked Star, looking up and down the crowded shelves. "Any clues that might make it easier to sift through this lot?"

"Unfortunately not," said Duncan, though his expression said that he felt there was nothing unfortunate about it at all. "But we are given to believe that some of the items here were antiques when Patience purchased them, and to our knowledge, she never sold them on. If you have any more questions, please feel free to ask me. I will keep you fully updated as I go along. After all, this all belongs to you now."

The women looked about them with expressions that ranged from intrigued to exhausted.

"I have a question," Star piped up.

"Of course, fire away."

"What were you knitting?"

She had the pleasure of seeing him look bashful. *Definitely Clark Kent!* she thought dreamily.

"I'm making my niece a unicorn jumper for Christmas. Although at the rate I'm going she'll be getting it for Easter."

"How lovely," said Star. Her glittery feeling was dangerously close to going full snow globe.

She saw Maggie cast a look at Simone, who rolled her eyes in response, and Star wished her face didn't betray her every thought and emotion. Maybe she could use this enforced togetherness to try to harness some of Simone's poker-faced attitude.

"Are you going to travel in every day all the way from Tunbridge Wells?" Star continued, and then, turning to her sisters, she added, "He got off the train at Tunbridge Wells. Don't you think it's funny that we were on the same train?"

"Hilarious," said Simone.

"I'm staying in Rowan Thorp, at the Stag and Hound while I look for somewhere to rent; this job is liable to take a couple of months at least. But I visited my sister in Tunbridge Wells yesterday."

Star could not seem to wipe the smile off her face and was painfully aware of the side-eye she was getting from Maggie and Simone.

"Well, we better start sifting through all this mess," said Maggie, looking around at the cluttered shelves.

"Oh, this isn't mess," said Duncan enthusiastically. "This is history. Do you happen to have your father's ledger to hand?"

"Ah, slight problem there," Simone interjected. "Our father thought it would be amusing to hide it."

"But as soon as we find it, it's yours," Star added.

She'd always been a believer in coincidence. The world turned on it: one random event colliding with another to create a perfect storm. Could these be the first rumblings of her own perfect storm?

8

DUNCAN WAS KEEN to begin work right away. After stashing his briefcase in the drawer of a Queen Anne sideboard beneath the wall of clocks, he began moving slowly along the aisles, picking up seemingly random items and jotting notes down in his notebook before replacing the objects exactly where he had found them.

The North sisters' approach to the shop's contents was less exacting. Boxes were rifled through, jugs and vases upturned, drawers ransacked as the quest to find thirty-two Monopoly houses began in earnest. It felt like an overwhelming task.

"This is the proverbial needle in a haystack." Maggie had her hands clasped on top of her head, seeds of defeatism already germinating.

"A wooden house in a junkyard," Star agreed.

"Thirty-two of them," added Simone. "That's practically a housing estate."

"Would you like some help?" Duncan asked, glancing up from a black bangle, which he advised was a Whitby jet Victorian mourning bracelet.

"No, you're all right, you stick with your antique hunting, see if you can find us something worth cold hard cash in this hell-hole," Simone replied.

Duncan looked pleased; it was clear that all he wanted to do was get down and dirty with Augustus's novelties and curios.

The shop was well and truly living up to its name. All day long the bell above the door jangled as a stream of helpful—nosy—villagers came in bearing gifts of cakes, biscuits, thermoses of tea and coffee, and advice. With the place having been undisturbed for five years, it was understandable that its opening should incite curiosity.

"I can smell the dust," said Betty as she laid a tray boasting four takeaway coffees onto the fold-down door of a 1950s cocktail cabinet. Maggie held her hands up to show that her fingers were black with the stuff, and Betty screwed her nose up in distaste. "Monopoly houses, you say?"

"Yes." Star peeped through a gap in an aisle. She had cobwebs in her hair. "Thirty-two of them. Any ideas?"

Betty put her hands on her round hips and surveyed the shop. "Instrument cases," she returned with certainty. "Your father was a musical man, and I'll eat my apron if he hasn't hidden at least one of them in with an instrument."

"Bloody hell, Betty, I think you might be onto something there." Simone was clearly awed. "Right, change of plan. Let's be focused in our ransacking. Concentrate on anything that looks like a music case."

Betty left with a satisfied air; no doubt she would have a waiting audience in the café keen to hear about the task Augustus had set upon his daughters.

Once the sisters had homed in on specific targets, the search began to feel less chaotic. Suddenly battered and peeling instrument cases of all kinds were falling into relief among the jumble.

In just twenty minutes, they unearthed a saxophone, a modest lute collection, panpipes, bongos, a French horn, a zither, a piano accordion, and a glockenspiel.

"I've got one!" Maggie shouted, plucking a tiny red wooden house from the blue silk lining of a lute case.

"Woo-hoo!" Star threw herself at Maggie as though she'd just scored a goal at Anfield Stadium. "Betty was right! Well done, Maggie-Moo!"

"One down, thirty-one to go," said Simone.

"Don't you see?" Star asked, one arm still draped around Maggie's neck. "Betty was right. It isn't random. This means that Dad hid the houses in places of significance to him, things that meant something to him, like the lute."

Simone nodded. "Okay, okay, we can work with this. We just need to think about the things that were important to him. What did he like? What were his hobbies?" As she spoke, she clicked open the clasp on a zither case. Her mouth lifted into a smile. "Found another one." She raised the small green house to show them.

"Good work!" Maggie wove along the crowded aisle and high-fived her.

"Oh, yay, well done!" Star called across, but stayed where she was.

It was obvious that she was holding back, and her evident hesitancy pulled at something in Simone's chest. Would she have welcomed a hug from Star? Absolutely not. But did she feel a twinge of sadness that her sister was too wary to even try? Yes, it appeared that she did.

"Right, we're on a roll now. What else did Dad like?" asked Maggie.

The rest of the instrument cases bore no fruit, but they

remained buoyed by the fact that they'd cracked Augustus's methodology.

"Traveling?" Simone began.

"Bric-a-brac," Maggie said, and then checked herself as she took in their surroundings. "Although that's not going to narrow it down much."

"Sex!" trilled Star, just as Miss Eliza Radley—formidable spinster and techno-wizard of the Rowan Thorp chapter of the Women's Institute—walked in. She'd been a teacher back in the day and had taught many of the residents in the village. Despite having retired thirty years ago, she was still universally addressed as Miss Radley.

"Gracious!" squeaked the tiny, wizened woman. She took a moment to clean her steamed-up pince-nez attached to a delicate gold chain and adjusted them back onto her nose. "Looks like I've arrived in the nick of time. What about sex?"

"We're trying to think of things that our dad liked." Simone had a feeling that by now Betty would have informed most of the high street of their quest. She was right. Miss Radley nodded her instant understanding.

"I see. Yes. Augustus certainly did like sex. He was very good at it too. Cunnilingus was his specialty."

At the back of the shop, they heard the sound of coffee being spat out violently and Duncan choking. Star clapped her hands to her mouth to hold in her laugh, but Maggie was unable to stop a guffaw escaping her.

"That's a touch more information than we would have liked, but thanks for the input, Miss Radley." Simone managed to keep a straight face. "Not sure there's too much pertaining to oral sex in the shop, though. And if there is, I'm not sure any of us are mentally equipped to tackle it right now."

"No. I understand. Young people are strangely frightened by the sexuality of their elders. Odd when you think about it; after all, we were doing it first—copiously."

The North sisters' mouths hung open.

"Oh, he did also like horses," Miss Radley continued. "Before he got the new van, he had a horse-drawn caravan. He was terribly fond of them. Shire horses, they were, used to graze on Holy Trinity Green. They died of old age, and Augustus donated them to Port Lympne zoo to be fed to the tigers. So much nicer than being turned into glue, don't you think?"

"I didn't know that. Thank you, that's very helpful. I've seen a few horsey things about the place." Maggie smiled. Miss Radley gave a sharp little nod and began to shuffle about the shop. "Is there anything we can do for you?"

"No, thank you, dear."

"We're not actually open," Simone added, which earned her a sharp look from Maggie.

"Oh, that's quite all right, I'm not looking to make a purchase. Simply browsing. I don't suppose he ever joined the digital revolution and got this lot on the computer?"

"No, unfortunately not." Simone was following the lady around, making shooing gestures behind her back.

"I kept offering to teach him how to use spreadsheets, but he was very reluctant; a lot of people his age are, you know." Miss Radley was ninety-three. She stopped suddenly and Simone almost stepped on her. "There! Up there behind the monkey with symbols, next to the cannonball."

Simone followed the bony pointing finger to the top shelf, where a thickset china shire horse reared up from its base. She pulled a set of wooden steps over and used them to carefully bring the horse down.

Miss Radley clapped her hands in delight and pushed her pince-nez back up her nose. "That's it!" she trilled. "It used to be filled with a very expensive aged whiskey, but Augustus never could resist a good thing. We polished it off one night, naked under the stars. Unscrew the head, dear," she instructed.

Simone did as she was told. The horse's head came off easily, and at Miss Radley's urging, she tipped the heavy body upside down over the old woman's cupped hands. Something solid clattered down through the china body and a red Monopoly house dropped into Miss Radley's wrinkled palms.

"That's amazing!" Star was delighted. "How did you guess there'd be a house in there?"

Miss Radley handed the house to Simone and dipped her head from side to side like a small bird. "Hmmm, just a little hunch. He was a sentimental soul. To know your father was to love him."

"What if we didn't really know him?" asked Maggie.

"Oh, I think you'll be surprised." The tiny woman smiled, her sharp eyes almost disappearing behind her crinkly paper cheeks. "Now about my finder's fee."

"Your what?" asked Simone.

"My reward for leading you to the house. I don't want money, but I am led to believe that you, dear, are a physiotherapist, and I've got this bother with my neck."

Simone held her hands up. "Oh, no, I'm afraid I can't. You'd need referrals, and I'm not registered here . . ."

"Oh, silly nonsense, all I need is a little massage, just to loosen things up. Call it a friendly rub, no need to be official. It will be the work of moments for someone with your magic touch. Come along, we can use the kitchen. No peeking, young man!"

Duncan bent his head determinedly to his work. Miss Radley began to peel off layers of clothing as she doddered out toward the kitchen. Simone followed behind, shaking her head.

Ten minutes later, after some mumblings behind the closed door and some appreciative squeals, Miss Radley appeared—fully dressed—with Simone close behind.

"That was just the ticket. You are a marvel, dear. It's a pleasure doing business with you. I'll be off now; I'm running an online seminar this afternoon on how to make last-minute mincemeat."

And with that she tottered out of the shop.

"I could be wrong," Simone said, looking after her, "but I think I just bartered my professional skills for a Monopoly house."

"Welcome back to Rowan Thorp." Maggie grinned.

AT HALF PAST five, Simone excused herself from the shop and headed back to the cottage to call Evette. She let herself into the place that was to be her home for the foreseeable future and poured a glass of wine from the bottle she'd opened last night when she'd stolen unnoticed into Rowan Thorp.

The cottage was much like she remembered it, a mix of tasteful chintz and whitewash with exposed black beams in the ceilings and roughly textured plaster on the ancient walls. Mrs. Dalgleish had gone to stay with her daughter, Kelly, in Canada and wouldn't be back until the spring. It was a happy chance that Simone had found the place for rent on Airbnb.

A picture of Kelly smiled out at her from a frame on one of the bookshelves. She was a nurse practitioner now and mother to three boys. Another mother. It was inescapable; the reminders

were everywhere she looked: pregnant women, women with babies and children, in the street, in shops, on the TV. It was a
deep scratch that was never closed long enough to heal over, and
every baby bump was a saltcellar pouring into the wound.

Evette answered on the second ring.

"Hey, you." She was out of breath, but she sounded pleased
to hear from Simone.

A pang of homesickness threaded itself through her rib cage
and pulled corset-tight. "Hey. Did you just get in?"

"Yes, I literally just dumped the shopping down when you
called. How are you doing? Tell me about the solicitors' and
don't leave anything out."

Simone plopped down onto the cottage-style sofa, glass of
wine in hand, and filled her wife in on the day's events. They'd
only managed to find four Monopoly houses, but that wasn't
surprising given how many distractions they'd had to contend
with throughout the day.

"You need to give Star a break," Evette said when she'd finished.

Simone growled in frustration. "She's so irresponsible. She
needs to learn that she can't just float through life."

"And you need to learn to let stuff go."

"By that do you mean having a baby or our relationship?" As
soon as she'd asked it, she wished she could suck the words back
down. What was this urge to constantly pick at the scab instead
of leaving it be?

"That's not what I meant." Evette's tone cooled instantly.

"What does being on a break even mean?" She shook her
head in despair. It was like her mouth had a will of its own. Her
pain was magma looking for cracks through which it could spew
out and incinerate everything it touched. "Why am I in exile?"

"I'm not doing this with you."

This was the voice Evette used with clients on the phone: patient yet unyielding, refusing to be drawn in. Simone's anger spiked.

"Not doing *what*?"

"I'm not explaining a concept that you already understand simply because you refuse to accept it," her wife responded with well-practiced calm.

"But I don't understand it! That's just it. The reason we started trying for a baby is because we love each other so much that we wanted to share our love with a family. And now suddenly trying for a baby is a reason for us to be apart?"

"I get that this is hard for you. It's hard for me too. We need to decide, if having kids isn't in the cards for us, if we can still make it as a family of two. At the moment, I'm not sure we can come back from this sense of malcontent hanging over us." Her voice cracked, and Simone couldn't help the split-second of sick satisfaction she felt at having elicited it. She needed to know that Evette was as devastated as she was.

"You haven't had to come back from anything! You haven't been through the injections and the hormones and the indignity and the knowing that something alive is inside you only for it to not . . . be anymore." Suddenly she was rinsed out. Her anger was like a back draft exploding outward and then sucking back in, leaving her spent and regretful as the heavy awareness that she had doomed yet another conversation draped itself across her.

"You be the one to try next," she said now, idly watching a squirrel dash up the Christmas tree outside the butcher's shop. "You're younger than me, maybe it'll work better with you."

"My darling, think about what you're saying. We've discussed this countless times. I don't feel the same physical need as you do to carry a child. The biology of our family simply isn't important to me in the way it is for you."

"That doesn't mean you shouldn't try." She was annoyed by her own petulance.

Evette as always remained calm and irritatingly reasonable. "Let's say for argument's sake that I agreed to try, and I fell pregnant. How would you feel? What would that do to us?"

"We'd be a family, I'd love it!" Simone felt hurt by her wife's assumptions.

"That you would love the baby is not in doubt. You will be a wonderful mother. But what about your feelings toward me? Would you be able to forgive me, knowing that I had been ambivalent about carrying and yet *I* was the one who managed to get pregnant?"

"It would still be our baby, I wouldn't care." She squeezed her eyes tight to stop the tears from escaping. The ugly truth was that she *had* thought about it, and she *did* wonder how she would feel if Evette did what she couldn't. Would her sense of inadequacy eat her alive? She repulsed herself. Her insides burned with shame at her own traitorous thoughts.

"Don't lie, Simone, not to me." Evette's voice was gentle, full of love. Of course, her wife knew her innermost secrets; she knew her better than anyone.

"I don't want to feel this way."

"I know."

"What are we going to do?"

"I am not going to have IVF. Not because of you. Because I don't want that experience for my body. I've made my decision. So, if it's what you want, we'll save up for one more try for you.

And in the meantime, I think we should start the adoption process."

Adoption had always figured in their family planning; ideally, they would have one child biologically and one by adoption.

"Okay." Her voice sounded small to her own ears. "Let's look at adoption. I need to think about the IVF, whether I want to try again, I mean."

"Take some time. Did you hear back from your work yet?"

"Yes, I spoke to someone in HR earlier. She was *annoyingly* understanding. They've offered me a year's sabbatical."

"That's great. So use this time. Throw yourself into your dad's challenges. Let yourself grieve."

Her gut reaction was that she didn't have the time to take a break or to grieve. Every moment she wasn't doing something to make herself a mother was a moment wasted. But she knew Evette was right.

"It feels fraudulent to grieve for something I've never had," she said, and it was the truth; she felt constantly heartbroken while equally feeling she had no right to it.

"You've lost promises of babies. You are not a fraud, and you are allowed to grieve for what you've lost and what could have been."

"Trust me to marry a counselor."

Evette laughed softly. "You should take my advice, I'm fully qualified. I've got certificates, I'll have you know. I don't just counsel any old wife for free. Talk to your sisters. You need them more than you think." Simone doubted that very much. "I've got to go. I've got a client."

"I love you." Simone's desperation was thick black tar. Why hadn't there been better words invented? That overly used phrase was surely an insult to what she felt for her wife. "I love you so much."

"I know. I love you too," Evette replied, the fatigue evident in her voice.

Their arduous journey toward a family had changed their relationship. It overshadowed everything. They'd had to stop socializing because Simone couldn't bear the inevitable questions about how "things" were going. They didn't talk like they used to because her mind was consumed with thoughts she couldn't express. And their once-active sex life had become almost nonexistent.

They held on to the call for a minute more in silence, just breathing together. And then the green phone icon changed to red, and Evette was gone.

Simone could feel her throat closing, clogged up with all the emotions that she didn't seem able to express in a safe way. Instead, her hurt seeped out as snide, hateful remarks that half the time she didn't mean, while all the time the lump in her throat seemed to grow bigger. She could feel it, a physical as well as a metaphorical thing. When it had first started happening six months ago, she was convinced she had a tumor, but her doctor had diagnosed stress reflux and prescribed antacids. He told her she needed to learn to decompress. Her stress was literally choking her.

She could see into the sitting room of the cottage opposite her: a boy and girl were decorating a Christmas tree in the bay window. Outside, fairy lights wound around a potted bay tree shivered in a wintry breeze. She sipped her wine and sighed.

9

MAGGIE BIT HER lip to stop from crying out and collapsed onto Joe's naked chest. She rested there, spent and loose limbed, both of them breathing heavily. Joe kissed her neck and held her tightly, absorbing her shock waves as they lay tangled together in her bed.

"Can't they start without you?" he asked.

It was Tuesday evening, and the very last thing she wanted to do was go out again after a long day at work, but go out she must.

She basked in his arms, relishing the warmth of his skin, his smell, the taste of him. If only she could simply enjoy this for the fantastic sex it was.

"No. I wasn't around for most of the day, I need to make an effort."

Yesterday had been full-on. Between her dad's surprises at the solicitors' and the enforced proximity with her sisters hunting for Monopoly houses, she had devoted the whole day to North family matters. Today she had begun to adjust her daily routine to make room for Augustus's demands alongside her ongoing commitments. Unlike Star and Simone, she was not on a hiatus from life. She still had a business to run and a child who needed dropping off and picking up from school and feeding and helping with homework.

Patrick was meeting friends in Tenterden, and Verity was tucked up in bed, fast asleep, exhausted after practicing her lines for the school Christmas play—*A Christmas Carol*, in which she'd been cast as a pomegranate.

Maggie had not intended to end up in bed with Joe this evening, but where Joe was concerned, she didn't appear to have any willpower. It had reached the point where all he had to do was look at her a certain way, and she could practically feel her knickers sliding off of their own accord.

"Couldn't you just stay a little bit longer?" he asked as she began to unwind his limbs, which held her in a very comfortable cage.

She smiled. If only. "As tempting as that is, we only found four houses yesterday. The sooner we find the rest, the sooner we can get things moving with the appraiser and get this shit sorted."

Her knees were locked up from having straddled Joe, and they each let out an alarming crack as she carefully straightened them. *Jeez, when did I get so stiff?* she wondered. It was an effort not to make ungainly *oof!* noises as she hobbled about the bedroom. Another point against them: he was yet to reach the age where every joint seemed to have something to say about being asked to perform its basic functions. These days her neck, shoulders, elbows, ankles, and knees clicked when she got off the sofa, as though tutting at being disturbed.

"Such a ruthless businesswoman." He was watching her, one arm behind his head. He looked delightfully ruffled and Maggie couldn't help staring as she wriggled into her jeans. The moonlight shone in through a gap in the curtains, casting a sliver of light across his body. Her heart beat faster. She felt as though every cell in her body was reaching for him, yearning for him. She swallowed her feelings.

"I think we both know that's not true." She smiled. "Are you sure you don't mind holding the fort while I'm gone?"

"Of course not." He raised an eyebrow and added archly, "Although if you were to make an honest man out of me and let me move in . . ."

This was a joke that had started when they'd first begun sleeping together (the convenience of having a live-in lover, etc.), but like their feelings, the joke had gathered weight as time went on and now it had become a code for the elephant in the room.

"You forget, I'm being evicted. What would be the point of you moving all your stuff in, only to shift it all back out again?" She tried to play along, but it felt forced, tender, like pressing on a bruise.

"I'd settle for a sleepover." He was negotiating.

"Too complicated."

"Even if I sleep on the sofa?"

"You live five minutes up the road. What possible reason could I give the kids for you needing to sleep on the sofa?"

"Patrick knows about us, you know. And it's pissing him off that we aren't coming clean about it. He thinks I'm using you, and I don't want him to think that; it isn't fair."

They'd left the protective circle of the joke, and she felt her familiar fight-or-flight response rising.

It would be easy to give in. Maybe for a couple of years they'd have a good run, but you could only keep reality at bay for so long before it comes knocking. Her reality would be HRT and graying pubic hair, while Joe's would be missing his chance to meet a woman who could give him children. She didn't want this wonderful man stuck with an aging greengrocer with thighs powerful enough to wear holes through industrial-strength denim.

Besides, there was more at stake than her own feelings. She wouldn't allow Verity to give her tiny heart to a father figure only to have it broken when he inevitably realized his mistake and left.

"I know this is hard for you and I *am* sorry. But things aren't simple for me. I can't afford to make rash decisions, and now is *definitely* not a good time for me to be considering any more life-changing choices."

Joe pulled on his T-shirt and climbed out of the bed. He straightened the sheets with undue attention, erasing the evidence of their lovemaking.

"I'm starting to wonder if it'll ever be the right time to talk about us," he said quietly. He appeared crestfallen, without anger or malice, only a sadness of Maggie's making. She felt it like a rock sitting in her stomach.

"We'll talk soon, I promise."

"*We* shouldn't feel like something else that needs to be ticked off your list or an extra burden you need to deal with." He was shaking his head as he buttoned his jeans.

She pulled her socks on, hiding her face. "It doesn't," she said. "I don't feel that way. I just. I don't see how *this* can work in reality."

"We've got something, Maggie. Something special, something not many people get the chance to experience. Or at least we could have . . ."

He left the sentence open-ended for her to fill in the blanks:

we could have if you weren't so terrified of commitment is what he'd left out. And he was right.

"Soon," she said, shaking her head upside down to de–sex hair her hair. She stood back upright. "Soon. I promise. Please don't be cross."

He walked around the bed and took her in his arms. "I'm not cross," he soothed. He left it for a beat and then added with a smirk in his voice, "I'm just disappointed."

She blustered out a laugh and slapped his chest. "Are we good?" She looked up, and his warm eyes smiled down at her.

"We're good."

"I—" She stopped herself. "You are important."

He kissed her so tenderly that her heart cracked twenty ways, and she kissed him back, hoping her lips could express all the words she couldn't speak out loud.

As she pulled the front door shut behind her, she took this latest nugget of guilt and tossed it onto the mountain of anxious feelings that she hauled behind her like Santa's sleigh.

10

THE ROWAN TREE INN was lively for a Tuesday evening. The festive three-course set menu was in full swing, and businesses as far away as Tenterden and Tunbridge Wells had booked in for their staff Christmas meal.

Someone had painstakingly pinned hundreds of brightly colored baubles on ribbons to the ceiling beams and wrapped every picture frame with tinsel. Long strings of multicolored fairy lights ran above the bar and icicle lights dripped down the walls. The festive aesthetic was 1970s disco, with a whisper of drag.

Star had eaten her discounted dinner (perks of being mates with the owners) at the bar so that she could talk to Troy while he worked. Artemis had taken to following Star wherever she went and was now curled up in front of the log fire with an elderly Labrador.

"It doesn't weird you out sleeping in your old room?" Troy asked.

"It did a bit, but I'm no stranger to laying my head down in weird places." She grinned to hide the truth. She had been hit with such powerful nostalgia and melancholy that she had almost buckled at the knees when she'd stepped into the bedroom two nights ago. She had not expected the wave of longing for her childhood to sweep over her with such ferocity.

"Still the Rowan Thorp wild child." He chuckled.

"You know me." She forced the smile that was expected of her.

Throughout her twenties she had worn her transience with pride, but now in her late thirties, it had worn thin. Troy saw through her instantly.

"What is it?"

She chewed her lip as she tried to articulate her feelings. "I've always been a wanderer, like my parents. I also know from bitter experience that I am not cut out for any kind of office work; I haven't got the stamina. But at the same time, I'm desperate for routine. And honestly, for the roof over my head to stay the same for more than a few weeks at a time. Is that terrible?"

"To put down roots? No. I'm hardly one to talk, am I, Mr. Married with Kids? I moved back to the place I was born to bring up my own family—how's that for ready, steady, boring?"

"Is it boring, though?" she challenged knowingly. He tried to play it down, but she knew how happy he was.

He laughed. "No, not even a little."

"You see!" She pointed at his smiling face. "Contentment, that's what my heart wants."

"Then find somewhere you like and dig in, get settled. It's not that hard."

"I don't know how. Every time I try, I mess it up."

Troy raised his eyebrows. "You need to start by shaking Stu off once and for all," he said in his most teacherly voice.

Antonia came in through the door to the side of the bar. A toddler on her hip, a baby bump, and Mica, newly five years old and impossibly gorgeous in Paw Patrol pajamas and slippers.

"Oh no, are you talking about the dreaded Stu?" Antonia gave a Mona Lisa smile.

"Only in the past tense," Star replied, kissing Antonia on both cheeks and lifting Mica up onto her lap, where he began to make his toy dinosaurs dance across the beer mats.

"I'm glad to hear it. How's it going with Maggie and Simone?"

"Maggie is her usual 'mother to all' self, and Simone is being forced to speak to me."

"That's progress," said Antonia.

"Yeah, it only took Dad meddling from the grave to make it happen."

"What about that appraiser down from the city?" asked Troy.

To her horror, she felt her cheeks get hot. "He's nice. He seems to know his stuff, which is what you want from an appraiser, I guess."

Antonia and Troy shared a look, and Star suddenly felt her capacity as third wheel. She wondered what it would be like to know someone so well that you could communicate by looks alone.

BY 8 P.M. she was back at the flat. She flumped onto the sofa with Artemis to wait for Maggie and Simone to arrive. She was feeling things she hadn't expected and wasn't sure where to put them all. Last night after leaving her sisters, she had been overwhelmed by a silent vortex of emptiness. Her dad was gone. After a lifetime of absenteeism, she hadn't expected his death to feel so very different. But being surrounded by his things had brought home to her that he wasn't ever coming back. It was like having her insides sucked out at high velocity as the reality of his new, permanent absence caught up with her.

This building and its land contained all her happiest memories. She had had magical times in this place with her sisters. Long summer nights too hot and sticky for sleep when they would stay up telling stories or talking about their home-lives. Often, having found their beds empty in the morning, Augustus would find them sleeping on cushions in the tree house.

When both her sisters had grown too old for summers in Rowan Thorp, and it was just her turning up on the doorstep with her bags at the beginning of the summer, that had been hard. Missing them was an overwhelming ache, enduring and unceasing. No one would accuse Augustus of being even remotely reliable or responsible, but he had been there during the times when her loneliness was a monster with gnashing jaws trying to swallow her whole.

She conceived her grief now as a body of deep dark water. Where last night it had been a roiling storm, this evening her sadness lapped gently around her, unobtrusive and perpetual. Now it had arrived, she had the feeling it would be her long-term companion.

Desertion had its own scent. It was a sad smell, the miasma of abandoned hope hanging in the stale tang of still air and the powdery chalkiness of cold walls. This place needed people; Star could feel its hunger in every armchair, mug, and cushion. She recognized the feeling in herself, the wanting.

Closing her eyes, she breathed slowly in and out, acknowledging each emotion in turn and practicing her gratitude. Something skittered against the front room window, shocking her out of her meditation. The noise came again, and she looked to the window in time to see a handful of shingle, illuminated in the glow of the streetlamps outside, click-clack against the glass.

As the panic rose up, a familiar dread dragged downward. *Not again. Please not again. Not here.* Her palms were clammy as she moved cautiously to the window and looked down onto the street. *It couldn't be. Could it?* But it was. Standing beside a thick-trunked horse-chestnut tree with a fistful of shingle clearly sourced from the communal planter on his other side was Stu. He grinned when he saw her and let the shingle drop onto the pavement.

"Star!" he shouted. "Did you really think I'd let you get away?"

She pressed her forehead to the cold glass and breathed deeply to calm her racing heart. At what point did an ex-boyfriend evolve from extravagantly heartbroken to stalker? Her impulse was to stuff her things into a bag and run away. With her heart pounding, one thought shouted louder than all the rest: *Simone is going to freak out.* She couldn't, after the tentative steps they'd taken over the last couple of days, risk losing her sister forever. Because in what world would Simone not see this and think she was in league with Stu?

"Shit! Shit. Shit. Shit!"

She unpeeled her forehead from the glass and yanked up the sash window. She was notoriously bad at confrontation, so she focused hard, channeled her inner Simone, and prepared to get snippy.

11

SIMONE SAT IN the bay window seat looking out onto the dark street. She'd spent another day in the shop with Star and Duncan, sorting through old crap and looking for Monopoly houses. Maggie had been largely absent today, and without her there to referee, Simone had found herself biting her lip repeatedly to keep from starting an argument with Star over something and nothing.

Maggie would knock for her soon and they would spend the evening back in the shop in continuance of the search for the small wooden houses, which were fast becoming another bane of her life.

The cottage was situated on the bend of Rowan Thorp's high street and afforded a view of the general comings and goings of the little village. Each time she looked out, more Christmas decorations had sprung up at windows and in gardens. Several of the houses now had snowflakes of various sizes projected onto their front walls. She wanted to feel snobby about it, but honestly she rather liked it.

She picked up the four little houses they'd found—put into her safekeeping as supposedly the sister least likely to lose them—and was about to grab her coat, when she heard shouting on the street and a loud banging on the front door.

She answered it and was grabbed at once by Maggie, who yanked her out of the house.

"Hold your horses!" Simone yelped, reaching back in and grabbing the bag containing bottles of wine she'd bought for the evening. "What's the emergency?"

"Come on!" Maggie shouted. "We're on standby in case Star needs our help."

"What?" she grumbled, pulling the front door shut and trying to unravel herself from her sister's grip. It was useless, of course; Maggie was strong as an ox. "What is going on?"

The shouts across the street began anew. Curtains twitched at windows.

"Stu's back!" Maggie hissed urgently.

The anger that simmered permanently in her stomach came to a boil. She let out a derisive sound. "Huh! Of course Star would invite him here. Why am I not surprised! They're probably going to loot the shop. I'm calling the police."

Maggie stamped her foot impatiently. Simone was the firecracker of the three, but when Maggie lost her shit, they paid attention.

"Listen to the shouting. Does it sound like Star is happy to see him?"

Simone stopped talking as they hurried along the road. She was right—Star was clearly not at all pleased. Righteous indignation stirred inside her. Sisters may be utterly vile to one another, but woe betide anyone else who dares to mess with them; it was a universal rule. She flexed her fingers. She pummeled her patients' locked-up muscles daily; she could pummel Stu's weaselly face with ease, and quite frankly, she'd been waiting for the opportunity.

North Novelties & Curios came into view. Stu swaggered about below like a reprobate Romeo, while Star hung too far out of the front room window, waving her arms about and hiss-shouting. Simone moved to confront Stu, but Maggie held her back in the shadows.

"Give Star a chance to handle it. We can jump in if things get tricky."

"Oh, Star couldn't handle kittens!"

"Let her try."

Stu's voice was getting louder, as were Star's whispered shouts in return.

"You can't be here!" Star's top half was bent in a right angle from the waist. "You've done enough damage as it is."

"I've paid my debt to society," he said petulantly.

"Sure, but I'm still paying for your misdemeanors. My sister still hates me. I've lost my job and my home because of you. This has to stop. I'm sorry, but you need to move on. We broke up three years ago!"

"You said you'd love me forever!" He was accusing now.

"That was before you broke into my work and got me fired and then stole from my sister's house. As abuses of trust go, that's a pretty big one!"

He waved his arm dismissively. "That was ages ago."

Star's mouth was open, and she was shaking her head as though she couldn't think of a response.

Stu filled the silence. "And anyway, she can afford it."

"That is not the point! You are not Robin Hood. And you certainly didn't nick that stuff to give it to the poor."

"I love you, Star! And I'm going to make you see that you love me too."

"We are over. You have to accept it. How did you even find me anyway?"

"Let me up and we can talk about it."

"No. You can tell me from there."

In the light from the streetlamps, Simone saw him grin boyishly in a way that he clearly felt would melt Star's heart.

"I tracked you. On your phone. And then I hung around and waited for you to show up. Plus, your surname is North," he said, gesturing to the sign plate above the shop. He looked pleased with himself.

Realization broke across Star's face. The look she gave Stu was clearly not what he had been expecting, and Simone felt a twinge of satisfaction as his hopeful expression faltered.

"You stalked me."

"It's not stalking—you up and left without telling anyone where you were going."

"That's because I didn't want you to follow me! I don't have to tell you anything because we are not together. You need to get that through your head. *We are over!*"

"Look, let me come up, we'll talk."

Back in the shadows, Maggie leaned in and whispered, "Got to give him points for perseverance."

"Can I punch him yet?" Simone asked.

"Give them another couple of minutes."

Stu's wail filled the air. "But I love you!"

"Whatever, this isn't love. I'm sorry." Her voice was pleading, begging Stu to understand.

In that moment, Simone could absolutely understand how her sister got into the scrapes she did. She was too nice for her own good. Peace, love, and understanding had their place, but sometimes a person simply needed to be told to swing their hook!

"What am *I* supposed to do now?" From his tone it was clear that this was not a rhetorical question.

"I don't know. I can't tell you what you should do. Quit drugs? That might be a start. But you need to go."

"And what if I don't?"

The pleading of a moment ago had morphed into something more menacing, and Simone felt herself clench.

"I'll call your probation officer," said Star. "I don't want to, but I will if I have to."

Simone could hear the hesitation in Star's voice and so, it seemed, could Stu.

"You wouldn't." His smile was cocky, as though this was a game they had played before, one which he was sure was going to end in very good makeup sex.

"I absolutely would. I mean it, Stu. I have tried to be kind. I wouldn't mind if it was only me you hurt, but you hurt my sister, you violated her home and her trust in me, and I'll never forgive either of us for that."

Simone felt her spine stiffen.

"What?" The cocksure grin was becoming a sneer. "You're choosing your stuck-up sister over me?"

Star leaned so far out of the window that Simone's heart gave a stutter of alarm.

"Every time!" Star hissed.

The boulder of resentment that Simone had been lugging about for the last two years suddenly felt like a pebble. Out of the corner of her eye, she caught Maggie watching her.

Stu rocked on his heels for a beat as though in shock and

then grabbed a fistful of shingle and hurled it up toward Star, yelling, "Don't you turn on me, you bitch! Who else is gonna want you—"

But he didn't get to finish his tirade because Simone had broken cover and was striding toward him with her arms swinging and Maggie half running to keep up. Stu, suddenly aware of the two women barreling toward him, one of whom he definitely remembered robbing and last saw shooting death stares at him across a courtroom, stumbled backward into the large concrete planter.

"What!" he quavered, trying to scrabble out of the planter. "What do you want?"

Simone reached him and bent over his cowering form. She could feel Maggie beside her, acting as adjudicator to make sure things didn't get out of hand, and she was vaguely aware of being grateful for her presence; left to her own devices she would very possibly crush Stu like the cockroach he was.

"I'm going to make this clear for you because I can see that you're having trouble understanding the word 'no.' Leave. My. Sister. Alone," she snarled. All the anger and hurt she kept dammed up was bubbling out of her.

"Or what?" There was no mistaking the crack in his voice.

"Or I will make you sorry. Unlike my sister, I won't hesitate to call your probation officer. In fact, if you don't leave Rowan Thorp right now, I'm going to call the police."

"And tell them what?" Stu was breathing fast; after his initial surprise his bravado was returning. Maggie piped up.

"And tell them that you are being abusive and harassing and stalking our sister." Maggie waggled her phone at Stu, close enough for him to see the numbers 999 and the green phone button waiting to be pressed. "I'll also add in 'disturbing the peace' and 'aggressive behavior.' Have you had an electric ankle tag yet? That could be next on your list of achievements."

Simone beamed at Maggie, proud. She stood up straight, allowing Stu the space to shuffle out of the planter, shingle skittering onto the pavement. He dusted himself off.

Up close, she could see the addiction that held him in its grasp. His eyes were bloodshot, darting too quickly from one thing to another, his movements jerky. She'd worked with addicts and ex-addicts, tried with physiotherapy to ease the ravages that the drugs had taken on their bodies. It wasn't only the damage done by the drugs themselves—bones that became chalky and fragile—but the lifestyle: bad diet, dangerous crowds, and rough sleeping caused skeletons to crick and crumble. It was a slow and painful way to kill yourself.

Simone the sister still wanted to knock seven bells out of Stu, but Simone the health-care professional knew that Stu had a hard life ahead of him and a short one if he didn't get clean soon.

"I'm only going to give you one chance. Just one. Go now and leave Star alone. Don't try to find her again, don't try to speak to her or contact her in any way. If you leave now, I won't take this any further, but if you don't, I will bring the full force of the law down on you. And next time you'll be banged up for a lot longer than two years." She pushed two twenty-pound notes into Stu's hand. "Train fare," she said, though they both knew that money was unlikely to ever see the inside of a ticket machine.

Stu took a few seconds to compute this information before nodding just once and shoving his hands deep into his pockets. He had only walked a few paces when he stopped and turned. "I do love her, you know."

"Then you need to leave her be," she said with as much firm kindness as she could summon. "You and I both know there's no future for her if she's with you. And I don't think you really want to drag her down where you're headed."

Stu's eyes darted between Simone and Maggie, his hands still in pockets, shoulders hunched forward as though walking against rain. He nodded again and walked away. They watched him until he rounded the bend in the high street and fell out of view.

Maggie rubbed her arm. "Well done," she said. "You handled that really well. Even though I could tell you wanted to chop one of his ears off and dance around him singing 'Stuck in the Middle with You.'"

Simone snorted a laugh, and when she breathed in the cold air felt fresh against her lungs, as though she'd been breathing shallow for the longest time. Star was standing on the doorstep of the shop, an oversized chunky knit cardigan wrapped around her. Simone marched over with Maggie a step behind.

"Block his number," she said without preamble. "And get *your* number changed. Fresh start." She made a shooing motion at Star. "Come on, in you go, you're heating up the whole village."

Star gave a small smile and turned into the shop, followed by her sisters.

12

"RIGHT, FIRST THINGS first. Wine. Let's find some glasses," said Simone, holding up the blue plastic bag containing the wine bottles. "We can rinse them out in the kitchenette. Second thing, what the hell was all that out there?"

Star swung her arms out from her sides and puffed out her cheeks in a gesture of flummoxed exasperation. "He just doesn't seem to get the message. I don't know how to make it any clearer for him."

"A restraining order?" Simone suggested. "What would have happened if we hadn't come along?"

"I'd have called the police. Or someone else would."

"And what if he'd got to you before they arrived?"

"He's not violent. Not to other people and never to me." She saw the incredulous looks from her sisters and added, "I know he has a temper; he shouts his mouth off and throws things, but the only person Stu ever hurts is himself."

"I don't know whether to believe you." Simone was shaking her head.

"It wouldn't be the first time."

Simone's head snapped up, and Maggie prepared to get

between them as mediator, but to her surprise, Simone said, almost defeatedly, "I know you didn't have anything to do with the robbery."

"Oh." Star looked as taken aback as Maggie felt. "Thank you."

"Promise me you have detached yourself from Stu once and for all. No going back because you feel sorry for him and no being charmed by his romantic histrionics; I know what you're like about wounded animals."

Star quailed beneath Simone's head-teacher tone. "I promise," she said in a small voice.

A moment followed during which any normal sisters would have hugged and broken the tension, but Star and Simone stood awkwardly like a couple of wallflowers at a school disco.

"Okay, let's find those glasses, shall we?" Maggie chivied. *Baby steps*, she thought.

Star managed to find two glasses hiding in the shelves, a pale pink champagne flute and an ornately cut crystal goblet. Maggie spotted an etched wineglass, yellowed with dust, and extracted it from an old shoebox filled with metal toy soldiers. Her eye fell upon a wicker basket full of tarnished cutlery and kitchen utensils, and she rummaged around until she found a corkscrew. She also found a red Monopoly house, which she held aloft with the corkscrew, standing on tiptoes and waving to be seen over the top of a shelving unit.

"Now we're talking," said Simone. "Bring it over."

Maggie sidled down a skinny aisle and joined her sisters at a mahogany sideboard on which the cash register—an antique in its own right—sat, dusty and sad looking.

With glasses thoroughly washed and wine poured, they began their search in earnest. Maggie had compiled a list of things Augustus had been fond of—though this wasn't easy since he seemed delighted by almost everything—and they used this as a rough guide of where they might focus their attention.

Star dusted off the gramophone, and soon the shop was filled with the tinny crackle of old jazz. Simone positioned the Calor gas heater in front of the sideboard and after a few minutes a gentle heat slowly wended its way along the aisles, warming the merchandise and awakening fragrances of old book bindings and beeswax polish. They worked as methodically as possible in the chaos, taking an aisle each, starting at the end nearest the front door and working slowly down. Their thematic approach to the search was short-lived as the sheer farrago of stuff overwhelmed them. Every trinket box was shaken, every watch, ring, and jewelry box was opened. Vases were tipped out and knickknacks rifled through. Artemis had a habit of leering unexpectedly out from the shelves or jumping up to inspect what they were doing. Maggie thought the cat gravitated toward whichever of them was about to find a house, but she dismissed the idea as nonsense.

As they worked, they called out the names of unusual items found.

"Ceremonial tribal staff!"

"Didgeridoo!"

"Victorian clockwork bird in a cage."

"China figurine of man sitting on a chamber pot!"

"An actual chamber pot!"

At the end of each aisle, they would refill their wineglasses before disappearing back into the mountains of jumble. Each Monopoly house they discovered received a cheer and a celebratory wine top-up.

By the time they had scoured the shelves, their hands were grey with dirt and dust and they were all three drunk as farts. It was eleven o'clock and even through her wine haze, Maggie was aware she would regret drinking when she got up at five tomorrow morning to receive the egg shipment. They had found twenty-six more Monopoly houses, which they added to the four they had found yesterday, making thirty. Only two more to find and they would have access to the ledger, which would help Duncan, the handsome knitting Sotheby's appraiser, make sense of the vintage mess.

"Where haven't we looked?" asked Simone.

"Ooh, the till!" yipped Star.

"You always loved that till." Maggie laughed. "You used to stand on a chair to play with it."

"Remember when the cash drawer shot out suddenly and knocked her clean off her stool?" Simone quipped.

"It's got such huge buttons; it looks more like a slot machine than a cash register." Star was already pushing down the stiff buttons, which clacked like typewriter keys, as she worked to find the one that would open the drawer.

"We haven't checked the kitchenette," suggested Maggie.

"Okay, you do the kitchen and I'll do the understairs cupboard," said Simone.

"Watch out for spiders," Maggie urged, just as Simone pulled open the cupboard door and a thick web plastered itself over her face. She screamed and fell over, and the others stifled their laughter.

Unsurprisingly, the poky kitchenette contained nothing you'd expect to find in a kitchen. One cupboard housed several small wooden and leather chests containing various war medals. Another was full of beautifully hand-painted tea caddies, with designs ranging from Chinese inspired to Victorian floral. Maggie painstakingly checked them all, sifting through buttons, ribbons, thimbles, and even a few gold teeth, which she didn't want to think too much about, but found no Monopoly house. A loud ting rang through the shop followed by a yelp from Star as the till finally gave up its treasures.

"I've got one!" she shouted jubilantly.

Maggie abandoned a cupboard full of painted canvases to join her.

"Good work," she said. "One more to go."

Simone backed out of the understairs cupboard and they rushed to divest her clothes and hair of cobwebs and dead spiders.

"We'll need to pull it all out and go through it if we're going to search properly. It is absolutely full of crap," she said, pouring them all more wine. "It's impossible to find anything in there, let alone a fingernail-sized house."

Star was tapping her chin. "Where else would an eccentric old codger hide a Monopoly house?"

"Has anyone looked inside the grandfather clock?" Maggie suggested.

They moved as one toward it, a little wavy for the wine. Simone turned the key and opened the door to the front of the old clock. The stilled pendulum felt like a metaphor for the shop. Aside from a surprised field mouse, who quickly scampered out of reach up into the workings, they found nothing of note.

Simone swayed slightly as she relocked the front panel, and Maggie giggled and helped steady her, though she was not much more balanced herself. They both jumped and turned as a loud *cuckoo, cuckoo, cuckoo* sound rang out through the shop. Star stood grinning beside the noisy clock on the wall.

"What are you . . ." Simone began, but her words trailed off when she registered that the twig, which repeatedly emerged from the clock, held a blue Monopoly house instead of a wooden bird.

"That's it! There it is!" said Maggie. "We've found them all."

"More wine!" shouted Simone.

13

AN HOUR LATER they were each slumped in chairs pulled from various parts of the shop and positioned around the glowing Calor gas fire, wineglasses in hand, three empty bottles lined up on the flagstones.

"You didn't drink at the funeral," said Maggie.

Simone shifted in her chair with an expression of deep discomfort, as though someone had waved something unpleasant under her nose. "No."

Maggie nodded and looked into her glass. "I'm sorry. That's shit."

Star looked between them, but neither elaborated. They were all really drunk. She was experiencing that stage of inebriation whereby she felt melded to the chair. It was one of those large wingback affairs, and she imagined she could feel herself seeping into the cracks in the leather like water.

"Am I missing something?" she asked. "Why is Maggie asking about you drinking?"

Maggie's eyes widened as though she just remembered something. "Bollocks, sorry, Simone. I forgot she doesn't know. Wine makes me stupid."

Star looked pointedly at Simone, who looked back at her, resigned.

"If you must know, Evette and I have been trying for a baby. And now my latest and possibly final attempt at IVF has failed." Her voice was matter-of-fact, but Star could see the pain in her eyes. "It would seem that I am unable to carry a pregnancy."

Suddenly Star's chair didn't feel so accommodating. She dared not blink in case the tears that blurred her vison spilled out. Simone wouldn't appreciate her crying, not when she was trying so hard to keep her own emotions trussed up. The least she could do was keep her shit together. They were so different, but she understood Simone. She always had. Simone felt things deeply; she was an empath in a suit of medieval armor.

"I'm sorry," she said when she could trust her voice not to wobble. "How long have you been trying?" She rested her head on her elbow on the chair's arm.

Simone sat rigidly on a vintage bistro chair. "Four years," she returned. Her eyes were closed as though she could pretend she wasn't having this conversation.

"Will you try again?"

Simone let out a long breath. "I don't know. We've used all our savings. And I've used up all of Evette's patience."

"You'll get through it," Maggie soothed.

"I'm not so sure. I'm not the best at opening up about stuff." She opened one eye and comically looked about, then opened the other.

"No shit!" Star quipped, and was relieved to get a smile back. Maggie snickered in her arts-and-crafts tub chair.

"It's just easier that way. I don't know what will happen if I let all this stuff out. Sometimes I worry that if I start crying, I might never stop."

"And what about Evette? Will she try?" Star asked.

Simone shook her head. "She wants a family, but it's never

been about the pregnancy for her. That's always been me." She was quiet, and Star could literally see her swallowing her feelings. "Perhaps I ought to consult with Perdita, maybe she could help me open up, do something to my chakras."

"Christ, no!" said Star. "Don't take lessons from her. My mother needs to learn to keep stuff *in*."

"At least she's open with you. My mum is a closed book. She is the consummate professional at all times; I am simply another side business in her portfolio," said Simone.

"My mum wasn't particularly open either," piped up Maggie, whose eyes kept drooping as though she was fighting sleep. "I mean, she was loving and everything, I have no complaints, but she was very private; feelings were improper. She never let on when she was hurting. It must have killed her when she moved here, and Dad didn't want to be with her, but you'd never have known it. She rallied—that was always her way."

"When I first told my mum I'd started having sex, she drew me diagrams so I could show my boyfriend where to find my G-spot," said Star. "*That's* openness."

"Okay, yep, that's waaay too open," said Simone, screwing her face up. "I'll stick with Rene."

"Oh my god, that's hideous." Maggie cackled. "I *never* discussed sex with my mum."

"Nor me with mine," said Simone. "When I told my mum I was gay, she told me not to make a song and dance about it."

Star spluttered a laugh. "What does that even mean?"

Simone shrugged. "Who the hell knows! I won't be like that with my children, child . . . if I have any."

"Maybe the sale of some of this crap will be enough for another round of IVF?" Maggie suggested.

"I'm not sure it would make any difference at this point."

Simone twiddled her wedding ring. "I've spent so long focusing on becoming a mother that I stopped being a good wife."

"Evette knows how hard this must be for you," said Star. "She's lovely. Far too nice for you." She poked out her tongue, and Simone smiled.

"Even Evette has her limits. Trust me, I have pushed all the way to hers and back again."

"That's why you've booked the cottage," said Maggie.

"Yeah. Evette thought some time apart would do us good. And if it doesn't, I guess I'll be moving in with you, Maggie."

Maggie laughed, but Star caught something behind it that she was too drunk to place.

"Or you could move in here with me." She grinned. "Roomies ride again."

"Absolutely not," Simone deadpanned.

There was a lull in the conversation as each sister disappeared into her own thoughts. The shop had its own set of noises: creaking pipes, the tick of the newly wound cuckoo clock, a dripping tap in the kitchenette, and the gentle hiss of the heater. It was all so familiar; this whole shop was a time capsule in which they were comfortably cocooned from the outside world.

"I've missed you two," Star said quietly. "I *do* miss you."

"I haven't been anywhere but here," said Maggie, a little defensively.

"But we've been distant, all of us have, emotionally I mean, as well as physically."

"That's true," Maggie agreed.

"I'm afraid the company you keep has a lot to do with that, Star." Simone raised her hands. "I'm not trying to start a fight, I'm simply stating a fact."

That stung, but she let it pass. "I hear you, but I don't accept that it's the only reason." Star kept her voice even. "We've been distant for years. I think it's partly because we were only ever summer sisters, and outside of here our lives were poles apart. But we're adults now, and I don't believe that our different up-bringings should make us irreconcilable. I'd like us to be, I don't know, full-time sisters. You're the only family I've got, apart from Perdita and, well, she's . . . flaky at best."

"I haven't got any family other than you two and the kids," agreed Maggie.

"You're right. We shouldn't take each other for granted," Simone began, and for a moment Star wasn't sure she'd heard correctly. "I adore Patrick and Verity and I've missed so much of their childhoods; I regret that. I haven't been a very good aunty. I'd like to think that if I do ever become a mother, my children will at least know their aunties."

"It is what it is." Maggie shrugged. "Anyway, you always send birthday cards. Unlike Aunty Star . . ."

"I'm not good with dates," Star protested. "But I always re-member Christmas!"

"You're not good at adulting—full stop." Simone sneered.

"Ah, but you included me in the 'aunties' for your kids, so you must think I bring something to the party."

"Of course," she replied with her usual abruptness. "I'll need to use you as an example of what *not* to become."

Star felt the gibe like a gut punch and her breath caught.

"I'm kidding! Don't give me those Bambi eyes. You're family, of course I'll want my children to know you. Even if I don't always like you very much, I do still—well, obviously—of course I love you, stupid girl."

Star was so relieved she burst into tears.

Maggie rolled her eyes. "You know, Simone, you really need to work on your interpersonal skills," she chided. "You're the only person I know who can make 'I love you' sound like 'fuck you.'"

Star wiped her eyes and heaved herself up out of the chair. "For the record," she said, sniffing, "I love you too." She wandered unsteadily to the sideboard and disappeared down behind it, then reappeared holding aloft an unopened bottle of honey-infused Scotch whisky like it was the Olympic torch. "I found this earlier." She grinned lopsidedly and waggled her eyebrows. "I don't think Dad would mind."

Her sisters clapped and whooped in response.

14

THE SHOCK OF her alarm going off at seven thirty had caused Simone to reach over the side of the bed and throw up into a floral chamber pot, which she vaguely recalled bringing home from the shop last night . . . or rather, this morning. Why had she thought drinking whisky after all that wine was a good idea? *What day is it?* she wondered, trying to count back to when she'd arrived. *This place is like the Bermuda Triangle.* She retched again. *Time has no meaning.* She breathed slowly in through her nose and out through her mouth. *Wednesday,* she concluded. The act of thinking had exhausted her.

She rolled back onto the bed and covered her face with her arm. It felt as though an invisible entity was using a tin opener to prize open her skull. She was dehydrated. She imagined herself like one of those sea sponges stranded on the beach when the tide's gone out, brittle and parched as the sun beats down on it. The duvet was stifling her, so she kicked it off and then regretted the movement as waves of sickness rolled over her. Evette always made her drink a pint of water before bed after a night out. But Evette wasn't here.

The thought of her wife stirred a hazy memory to the surface, and she pulled her phone out from beneath the pillow, where she had stuffed it after turning off the alarm. A notification citing seven missed calls in the early hours and a message from Evette flashed across the top of the screen and Simone grimaced.

> Sorry I missed your calls at half one and two
> o'clock this morning. I was, as most normal
> people would be, asleep. Your two fifteen call,
> however, did wake me.

"Oh, bollocks," she sighed. Evette was a wonderful woman but a horror if she didn't get enough sleep.

> I called you several times, worried that
> something had happened to you, and when
> you didn't answer, I called Maggie. She didn't
> answer either. Eventually I tried Star, who did
> pick up, and she told me you were drunk. So,
> thanks for that. I hope you drank some water
> before you passed out. I've got clients booked
> in all day, so I'll call you later. x

The single kiss at the end of the message did not go unnoticed. *Cheers for that, Star, you snitch!* she thought, but what else could Star have said, really?

Tentatively she lifted her head off the pillow; the room was shuddering but not wholly spinning. That was something at least. A cotton tote containing thirty-two tiny wooden houses on the dressing table reminded her that she had a meeting at the solicitors' this morning. Vanessa had booked them in for what she called an "informal catch-up," by which Simone hoped she meant "free of charge."

The first muted rays of morning eked in through the gap in the curtains and she steeled herself to get up. Today would require coffee and carbs—fried where possible. She was glad of the claw-foot bath in the ensuite; a good long soak was the first order of the day.

"WEEE *WISH* YOU A MERRY CHRISTMAS, WE *WISH* YOU A MERRY CHRISTMAS, WE *WISH* YOU A MERRY CHRIST-MAS AND A *HAPPY NEW YEAR*! AWAY IN A MANGER, NO CRIB FOR A BED, THE LITTLE LORD JESUS LAY DOWN HIS SWEET HEAD!"

"Jesus, Mother Mary, and Joseph. Verity, light of my life. I will give you five pounds if you'll just stop singing." Maggie's breakfast of black coffee and paracetamol was threatening to return. She couldn't remember when she'd last had a headache this ferocious. She laid her forehead on the cool wooden table and prayed that the room would stop spinning.

"But, Mama, I have to practice for the school play. I'm part of the fruit chorus."

"Can you practice in your head? Please? Just for this morning?"

"No, Mama, Miss Baker says we have to project our voices. Like this: LITTLE DONKEY. LITTLE DONKEY!"

Maggie felt, rather than saw, Joe come into the kitchen; he went back to his room at the pub every night and arrived back at her place early each morning. She was always keenly aware of his proximity to her; even now as she felt barely human, her body was alive to his presence.

"How you doing, sunshine?" He ruffled her hair on his way to the coffee machine. She remained face-planted to the table. "Good morning, Verity. Lovely singing. Excellent projection."

"Thank you, Joe. Shall I sing you the new song we've learned? It's called 'The Holiday Frog Hop.'"

Maggie groaned.

"I tell you what, let's leave that one for later," he answered diplomatically. "I think right now you'd better get dressed, unless you want to go to school in your pj's and lion slippers?"

"Can I?"

"No," Maggie mumbled. "We're leaving in ten minutes."

Ordinarily Maggie would have been up at 5 a.m., taking produce deliveries from local farms and putting together orders for the various businesses and households she supplied. But not this morning. She had stumbled home in the early hours, tripping over the rug and clumsily attempting to seduce Joe before collapsing on the sofa, which is where Joe found her—when he'd let himself back in this morning—fully clothed, lying in a wet patch of her own dribble that had left a dark stain on the cushion and caused the hair on one side of her head to stick to her face.

With Verity gone to get dressed, she asked, "Last night, did we?"

"That'll be a hell no." He laughed softly. "You were in no fit state. I tried to get you to go to bed before I left, but you insisted that you were quite capable of doing it yourself."

"Oh god. Thank you for babysitting."

"Anytime. Did you remember you've got a meeting at the solicitors' this morning?"

"Just kill me."

"Come on, party girl." He helped her up and ushered her

gently toward the bathroom and left her to shower away her shame. She felt so ill she couldn't even feel embarrassed. She had the sensation that she had been stuffed into a hamster ball and kicked around for four hours. She wondered if her sisters felt as bad as she did. She really hoped so.

STAR STRETCHED OUT on the carpet and reveled in her Savasana at the end of her yoga session. She let her body relax and her mind drift to a place of peace. Though she didn't practice nearly as much as she should these days, she always did it after a night's overindulgence. She didn't suffer from hangovers per se, but alcohol always left her feeling tense and groggy-headed the next day.

Slowly she brought herself back to the present. Her thoughts regathered like spun sugar strands in a candy floss machine and she recalled her conversation with Evette in the early hours of this morning.

She had always liked her sister-in-law, the yin to Simone's yang; they complemented each other. Some people were better together than apart, and to her mind Simone and Evette were the former.

Still, she was surprised to get a panicked phone call from her in the middle of the night. She was even more surprised when Evette stayed on the phone and confided in her about their problems. She had wondered if she ought to try to close down the conversation, if it was somehow disrespectful to her sister to be listening to problems that Simone herself would never have divulged, especially not to Star. But the words torrented out of Evette like she'd spent too long trying to plug the dam and the force of it had finally become too great. Perhaps she needed, Star reasoned, to speak to someone who knew and loved and understood Simone, like she did.

It would be easy to feel annoyed at Simone's closed-book approach to life; it felt to Star like wanton self-destructiveness to internalize feelings that bred toxicity rather than air them and remove their power. Being aloof didn't do her any favors, especially when people assumed that her attitude was born out of conceit rather than caution.

It was strange. She had always viewed her sisters through a lens of capability and infallibility. But now she was beginning to realize that neither of them had all the answers and that their shit was far from being together, and that frightened her; surely somebody had to be in control? Because the alternative was that *nobody* knew what the hell they were doing and where did that leave *her*?

She stood slowly and began to dress, looking out over the garden and the woods beyond as she did so. A low mist hung over the land like yards of silver tulle. Perhaps it was a good thing that the scales had fallen from her eyes, because now she would have to woman up and become her own fallback, and maybe in the process become someone her sisters could lean on too.

15

VANESSA WAS—AS SIMONE had hoped—surprised when they handed over the tote bag containing the Monopoly houses later that morning. She dutifully verified each house against Augustus's list and passed Simone a small, tarnished key on a piece of brown string in return.

"According to his notes, everything you will need to re-create the winter solstice celebrations of years gone by is waiting for you inside the strongbox."

"And where is the strongbox?" asked Maggie.

Simone was pleased to see her sister looked as green as she felt. Star, however, was annoyingly chirpy.

"I don't know. You didn't come across it during your house hunting?"

"We came across plenty of things. What does it look like?" asked Simone.

Vanessa shook her head and shrugged. "I can't help you, I'm afraid; I've never seen it. All I can tell you is what your father wrote in his instructions: that it was to be found somewhere on the property."

"We'll find it," said Star brightly as they got up to leave.

"I'm afraid you may be beset with visitors today. Just thought I'd warn you."

"Why?" asked Simone.

Vanessa pursed her lips. "The fracas outside North Novelties last night didn't go unnoticed. Maggie can tell you that the speed of gossip in this place is faster than the broadband."

Simone tsked. The mere memory of Stu irritated her, and she gave her sister an accusatory side-eye. Vanessa continued, "And yours and Maggie's three a.m. rendition of 'All I Want for Christmas' along the high street wasn't missed either."

"Ha!" Star burst out, looking smugly at Simone. "Now we're even."

Simone scowled at herself; she'd forgotten about the singing.

"Gerry Myers said it sounded like the screams of foxes mating," Vanessa added.

Maggie, still green, laughed weakly. "I'm rather offended, I thought we were quite good."

"I nailed those high notes," Simone added.

"You did! If Simon Cowell doesn't come in today and beg to represent you, there's no justice in the world," Star agreed.

"I NEED TO go back to the grocer's," said Maggie as they wandered out onto the high street. "I'll come over in a bit."

"No hurry," Star replied brightly. "We can make a start, can't we, Simone?"

"I won't be long," Maggie assured them. "I just have to make sure Joe's okay."

"Sure." Star winked. "Make sure he's *okay!*"

Maggie raised her arms. "I don't even know what that means," she said, turning and walking toward the grocer's.

"Come on, then, let's crack on. We might even find the strongbox before Maggie is finished with Joe."

"Do you have to be quite so cheery?" Simone asked, wincing. "Your voice is like knitting needles being poked into my ears."

Star was unperturbed by her sister's mood. "Ooh, speaking of knitting needles, I left the key to the shop in the hanging basket for Duncan. He's so nice, isn't he? And so clever! Imagine knowing so much about antiques; it's such a broad subject. He must have a brain like an encyclopedia. Not like me, scatterbrained and clueless."

"You are neither of those things, you simply choose not to apply yourself. He does seem very nice. Will the juggler be jealous of you making gooey eyes at the appraiser?"

"The juggler? Oh, you mean Florin. No, he's back with the circus; we decided to just be friends. I didn't want a long-distance relationship, and he's got an on-off thing going with a unicyclist."

"I am baffled by your life."

"Thanks."

"I need fried food and lots of it. I'm heading to Betty's. You coming?"

"No thanks, I already had a green smoothie."

"That sounds disgusting."

"It was."

They parted ways, and Simone followed the scent of bacon down the street like a woman possessed.

STAR PUSHED THE door open, calling, "Hello! Duncan, are you here?"

"Good morning!" came a deep voice from the back of the shop.

"It's only me, Star. So, apparently the strongbox, which is somewhere on the property, holds your ledger and the answers to all our questions."

She heard Duncan laugh softly. "Like an oracle?"

"Yes, though it only answers questions in relation to the winter solstice."

"Shame," came Duncan's disembodied voice. "A box that contains the answers to *all* questions would be worth a lot of money."

She found him sitting in the same cracked leather armchair that she had been slouched in last night. He was turning a rather pretty glass vase carefully in his hands. A pair of reading glasses balanced low on his nose. His suit was neatly pressed, jacket buttons undone to reveal a crisp white shirt and a tie so tightly knotted, it made Star pull at the neck of her knitted rainbow sweater. Duncan was the studious type. He probably called his mother regularly and took flowers whenever he visited his nan. He would likely never have lived in a squat or taken drugs or been cautioned by the police for chaining himself to a tree. One thing she knew for sure: he was out of her league.

"This is Lalique," he said, continuing to admire the vase, as though this should mean something to her.

"Is that good?"

His lips twitched as though he wanted to smile. She could feel him taking the measure of her. "It is good," he replied. "Lalique glassware is very sought-after, especially antique pieces like this."

"Cool." She wanted to ask how much it was worth but didn't want to seem crass. Luckily, Duncan was pleased enough with his find that he volunteered the information.

"This piece would probably fetch around six hundred pounds at auction, more if you had the right collectors on the day."

She swallowed hard and tried to look casual and wondered if they had any more Lalique glass hiding in plain sight. Her mind rewound to the old glasses they'd used to throw back whisky shots last night and she hurried into the kitchenette to rinse them out.

"Is there anything you'd like me to do to help?" she called as she sloshed soapy water around the sticky remnants of last night's frivolity.

"Um, well, I suppose you could gather together any pieces you know to be collectors' items."

That rather stymied her offer since she really had no idea what was worth collecting; it all looked old and a bit grubby to her.

"I don't think I'd be much help in that department," she admitted as she dried the glasses. "But I am excellent at cleaning silver. My dad used to get us to do it when we were kids. It's surprisingly satisfying."

"That would be helpful. I'll need to photograph everything for my records, and it would be better if things were clean."

"Good." She was pleased. "That's good, I like a purpose."

When she returned to the shop floor carrying a tray with the glasses on, Duncan held out a loupe hanging from a length of thin black cord toward her.

"So you can check for hallmarks," he qualified. "Do you mind?" He gestured that he should put it over her head.

"Not at all." She placed the tray down. Her stomach tightened.

Gently he placed the loupe around her neck, as though awarding her a medal. Their eyes met, and Star felt a frisson between them. The barest brush of his fingers on her neck thrilled her to goose bumps and she knew she was blushing. She was suddenly very aware of her own breathing. He took a step back and she pulled her long hair free of the cord.

"Thank you." She smiled, feeling overly warm.

"If you like, I can teach you how to read hallmarks to tell the age of an item," he ventured. "That would be really purposeful. But only if you want to."

"Yes, please!" Realizing she was gawking, she proffered the tray toward him.

"Could these be Lalique?" The word sounded too fancy on her tongue.

Duncan studied the glasses in turn. "No. Not Lalique. This one's rather nice. Georgian. Would probably go for about twenty pounds, a lot more if it's part of a set. This one is handblown— pretty but not worth much, and this one looks like it was made in the eighties."

"The 1780s?" she asked hopefully.

He cleared his throat and laid the tray on a side table. "The 1980s." He must have seen her face fall because he added, "It's still vintage, though. There's a huge market for vintage."

"The 1980s is vintage? That can't be right, I was born in the eighties and I consider myself as only at the beginning of my voyage to female enlightenment—I can't be vintage!"

Duncan chuckled, whether *at* her or *with* her she couldn't be sure. He looked uncomfortable in the large chair, as though he was both too big for it and at the same time being swallowed by it. He went back to making notes about the vase, picking it up, turning it, and then resting it back on the table and making more notes.

"How long have you been an appraiser?" she asked, perching herself on the chair next to him. The chairs were still arranged as they had been last night; the smell of burning dust from the gas heater lingered.

"Well, I studied for my master's at the Sotheby's Institute of Art and from there I was taken on by Sotheby's. I've been in this role for about ten years."

"I can't imagine being so qualified."

"That's a strange thing to say."

"Is it?"

"Most people are qualified in something, aren't they?" He looked up from his notes.

"I'm not. I mean, I've worked in lots of different jobs, but I don't feel particularly qualified for any of them."

"There's a lot of training for this work, and you pretty much never stop learning, which works for me because I get bored quickly."

"Do you?"

"Does that surprise you?"

"Well, I get bored quickly too, only *I look* like the type of person who would get bored quickly."

"And what do I look like?"

"Someone who enjoys concentrating."

"So . . . boring."

"Not necessarily."

Duncan frowned. "I'm giving off *concentration* vibes. I mean, that's not exactly setting the world alight, is it?"

"Trust me, burning your world to the ground is not as exciting as it sounds."

"Are you speaking from experience?"

"Maybe." He was looking at her in the same way he had been studying the vase. She didn't know if she liked being appraised. "You come across like someone in control of their destiny."

"Are any of us in control of our destiny, really?" he asked.

"Maybe not, but you seem like you'd have a better chance of choosing your own fate than most."

"Thank you, I think."

"What happens if you get bored?" She was curious.

"What do you mean?"

"Do you go wild and tear up the town, or do you flop about like a slug?"

"I don't know that I do either. I get restless, I suppose. That's why I knit; it occupies me. What do you do?"

"I make unwise choices," she said, and was rewarded with him raising a quizzical eyebrow. "But I'm trying to make changes on that front. I'm trying to be less impulsive, to stick at things rather than moving on when they get tricky. Would you teach me to knit?"

"Yes, if you'd like."

"Thank you, I would like. That's two things you're going to teach me, now we need to think of something I can teach you."

Duncan smiled. "Perhaps you could show me how to look less like my superpower is concentration."

"Perhaps," she replied, though she was beginning to hope that some of his focus would rub off on her. "Right, well, I'm going to start hunting for a strongbox."

"I thought you were going to clean the silver."

"Oh, yes. You see, short attention span. When I'm bored of looking for the strongbox, I'll clean the silver."

"Deal." Duncan smiled at her, and she returned it. They stayed that way for just a little too long, as though they each had an inkling that they'd found a friend.

16

THE GROCER'S WAS quiet when Maggie got back from the solicitors'. Joe was creating a bounteous display of fresh produce in the window. He smiled knowingly when he saw her.

"Still suffering?" he inquired.

"I think it was the whisky that pushed me over the edge. I may never be the same again."

"The shop's been very busy. Lots of people popping in for 'just a few bits' and 'just wondering what that business was about outside North Novelties & Curios last night.'" He gave her a wry smile. "And apparently there were 'high spirits' in the early hours."

She grimaced. "My singing voice has been likened to mating foxes."

"I'd have gone with coyotes myself."

She laughed half-heartedly.

"How did you get on with Vanessa?" he asked.

"We gave her the houses; she gave us a key to an elusive strongbox. God, I feel like death."

"What if there was something I could do to take your mind off it?"

She managed a half smile. "I'm not sure I'm up to it."

Joe put the parsnips down, flicked the sign on the door round to *Closed*, pulled down the blinds, and latched the door. He walked determinedly toward her. Instinctively she took a step backward and found her back against the wall. She ought to at least attempt to protest that it wasn't good business to close the shop willy-nilly and she really did feel dreadfully hungover, but those thoughts were fleeting, and her body was already in full agreement with Joe's plan. Her pulse spiked; she squeezed her thighs together in delicious anticipation. He had that look in his eyes, the flash of something dark that took her breath away and brought heat to her cheeks. It was a look that made her forget everything.

"Sometimes," he said, his voice low as he took her by the wrists and pulled her arms above her head, "you need to counteract one strong feeling with a more powerful sensation to cancel it out."

"HOW'S YOUR HANGOVER?" he asked, his face buried in her hair.

"Cured." Maggie smiled dreamily.

He pulled away, sweeping her curls off her face and tracing his finger along her jaw. He kissed her softly, his sweetness returned. Maggie enjoyed all the sides of Joe. The attentive, tender lover and the one who could apparently shag a hangover right out of her.

As they put themselves back together, she knew that her cheeks were red from more than just the exertions of the last fifteen minutes. She was embarrassed at her own wantonness. It had been a long time since she'd been so brazen, maybe not since Josh. With Joe, she felt able to embrace all the facets of herself, not just the parts she felt were palatable to others, and that notion both pleased and frightened her at the same time.

"I'm glad you're feeling better," he said sheepishly.

"You can't buy *that* remedy at the pharmacy." She couldn't suppress her smile. "Is it a tried and tested treatment?"

His laugh was soft and low. "A gentleman never cures and tells."

"Fair enough." The sharp scratch of jealousy caught her off guard. She had no right to it.

"Would you like a cup of tea?" he asked.

"No thanks, I only came back to see if you needed any help."

He raised an eyebrow at her, and she flushed anew. She cleared her throat theatrically.

"Anyway, you seem to be coping, so I'll get back over the road if that's okay, see if we can find this strongbox."

Joe moved toward her and kissed her lightly and the familiar war of emotions filled her chest.

THE MORNING SKY was dark and the rain seemed determined to find its way inside her coat, but the cold helped to crystallize her scattered thoughts on her way to the curios shop. Joe wanted a relationship. She knew all the reasons why it wasn't a good idea, but still, he wasn't making it easy for her. If she was being completely honest with herself, it wasn't only the age and baby thing that was holding her back. In her experience men always left, even the good ones. She'd loved Josh and he'd died; granted he hadn't done it on purpose, but he'd left her all the same and part of her would be forever broken because of it. There had been others over the years and always they left in the end. Even her own father was only ever a fleeting presence. Each man who left took a piece of her heart with them; some took a bigger slice than others. The truth of it was that what remained of her heart was fragile and she couldn't risk losing it. After all, life had taught her time and again that she wasn't enough to make a person stay.

17

WITH SIMONE AND Maggie having filled up respectively on carbs and orgasms, they joined Star back at the shop. They were standing in the kitchenette while Star made cups of tea. Duncan was still in the leather chair, working on his laptop.

"I saw Patrick in Betty's, looks like I'm not the only one nursing a hangover today," said Simone. "He looked *rough*."

"He's been catching up with his old friends while he's home from uni. He hasn't yet learned the art of moderation."

"Like mother like son," quipped Star.

"I get the feeling he's worried about you. He didn't say as much, but I got the impression he's not keen on Joe."

Maggie rolled her eyes. "Patrick is being overprotective. It would be sweet if it wasn't so annoying. Plus, I think there's some male rivalry there."

"Does Joe try to tell him what to do?" asked Star.

"No, not at all. He's really careful not to give Patrick any cause for alarm or animosity. Honestly the way Patrick speaks to him sometimes, I don't know how Joe holds his tongue; I wouldn't be able to. Unfortunately, despite Joe's best efforts, Patrick still feels threatened."

"He's just looking out for his mum," said Star. "I think it's a boy thing."

"I wish he'd realize that I don't need looking out for. I'm the parent. I'm not sure when this shift in our dynamic happened. Joe thinks he knows something's going on between us."

"*Everybody* knows, Maggie!" Star drawled. "You two are the worst-kept secret since Charles and Camilla's affair."

"Star's right," said Simone.

"Maybe, if this thing with Joe is something that's going to become serious, you ought to discuss it with Patrick, so he understands that Joe isn't a threat to your family dynamic."

"I don't know where it's going myself yet. Probably nowhere; there are a lot of things against us."

"Like?" asked Star.

"My age. His age. My precarious living situation . . ."

"Wait, what? What's precarious about your living situation?" Star asked, flicking the last teabag into a pot and handing out the steaming mugs. She'd had a feeling something was going on but couldn't pin it down.

Maggie seemed to deliberate and then said, "I might as well tell you. But the kids don't know yet, so keep it under your hats."

"Um, do I need to leave?" Duncan called in, embarrassed. "I don't want to intrude on a private matter."

"It's fine, Duncan. Everyone will know soon enough. I'm being evicted."

"What!" Star and Simone said at once. "Are you serious?"

"As a heart attack. The landlord is converting the building into a boutique hotel. I've got until January the thirty-first to vacate."

"Fuck!" said Star.

"Ditto that," added Simone. "How long have you known?"

"Since September."

"Why didn't you say anything?" Star held her hand out to Maggie, who took it.

"I was hoping I could turn things around. I've had meetings with a solicitor and with the Citizens Advice Bureau. And obviously I've tried to reason with the landlord. None of it did any good. He's not breaking any laws. I had my final eviction notice the other day."

"But you've lived here on and off for nearly thirty years. You took the tenancy over from your mum! Doesn't being a long-standing, rent-paying tenant count for anything anymore?" asked Simone.

"I guess the building is worth more with paying guests in it than a tenant. The *Observer* did one of their 'Ten Prettiest Villages to Visit' pieces awhile back, and Rowan Thorp was one of them; there's money to be made."

"Maggie, you have to tell the kids," said Star. "At least Patrick."

"I know, I know. It's just hard. I didn't want to worry them about something that might not happen. And then as I realized I didn't have a legal leg to stand on, their granddad died. I couldn't tell them then, could I? 'Hey, guys, guess what? Granddad's dead and we're homeless!' And now it's nearly Christmas. I want them to have a carefree Christmas in their home, without worrying that it'll be their last."

Star nodded. "I get it. I do. I just hope it doesn't come back to bite you in the arse."

Maggie rubbed her eyes. "You and me both."

"What will you do?" asked Simone.

"Well, I was hoping you both wouldn't mind if we moved in here, just for a little while, while I get myself sorted. It would mean putting off selling the place for a bit. Although I suppose we could put it on the market while I'm living here; there's no guarantee it would sell immediately anyway . . ."

"Take as much time as you need," said Star, and Simone nodded emphatically.

"To tell you the truth, I could use a bit more time to get my head around selling it," added Simone. "I know it's the sensible thing to do, but now I'm here again . . ."

"I totally get it," said Star, relieved that it wasn't only her who felt an attachment to the place.

From a practical perspective it was simply a building with some land and woods attached, a potential pot of gold that they all badly needed a piece of. But standing here together, ensconced in their familial history and shared memories, it was hard for the sisters to stay detached.

"I'll share Dad's bedroom with Verity, and you can stay in our old room. Patrick will be back at university by then, and hopefully by the next time he comes home I'll have something sorted."

"It'll be lovely to live together, even just for a little while," said Star.

"What about Joe?" asked Simone.

"What about him?"

"Come on, Mags."

"I guess he'll be unemployed. But he'll be okay. Troy's already offered him a few shifts in the bar."

"You never said anything to us for all that time, not at the funeral or when Dad died . . ." Star trailed off.

"We're not the kind of sisters who call each other up on a Sunday for a catch-up. We don't call each other—period. And it didn't seem like the right time to burden either of you. You've both had your own stuff going on."

"That doesn't mean we wouldn't have at least lent you a sympathetic ear," Simone protested. "Just because you're the oldest doesn't mean you have to be the mum. We're your sisters, we're both grown women, you should be able to tell us this stuff."

Star could see that Maggie was far from convinced by this statement, and she couldn't help feeling her own part in it. What reason would her sister have to confide in her? Over the years Maggie had bailed her out with bailiffs, helped her with rent, been her guarantor, loaned her deposits—which she'd rarely paid back—and both her sisters had tolerated her sofa surfing. It was exhausting to think about.

"We're here now," she said. "We'll help you in whatever way you need."

"I never thought I'd say this," Simone said, frowning, "but . . . what Star said."

It was the tiniest throwaway comment, but Star took it and banked it in the place in her brain where she kept meaningful things. Such an affirmation, even one as small as this, would have been inconceivable a week ago, and she wasn't too proud to take her micro-miracles where she could get them.

18

AT HALF PAST two the following afternoon, Maggie left her sisters to the strongbox search and went to pick Verity up from school. The sky was dark, the sun having been hiding all day, and a dogged mist ensured wayward hair and consistently damp clothes. It was Thursday already, three days since Vanessa had first told them about the winter solstice celebration. Time felt like a herd of buffalo barreling toward her at high speed, and she had nowhere to run.

Verity delightedly handed over a pattern for her Christmas play costume—courtesy of the PTA, who genuinely thought that this was helpful—and skipped off along the road, leaving Maggie wondering when in god's name she was going to have time to rustle up a pomegranate costume.

"I need to pop in to see your aunts. Would you like me to drop you at home with Patrick?"

"No, I'll come with you. I like the shop, it smells funny."

Star and Simone were no closer to finding the elusive strongbox than when she had left them, though they had unearthed a clay painted pot, which Duncan surmised could be Roman, a terrifying Mickey Mouse gas mask, and a set of brutal-looking pliers whose cardboard tag proclaimed them to be *Early Victorian Dentistry Tools.*

Verity was intrigued by Duncan, but her interest quickly wore off and soon her restlessness, which took the form of very expressive dancing, was in danger of causing a bric-a-brac avalanche.

"Shall I take you back home, sweetheart?" Maggie offered.

"No, I'll go and play in the fairy house."

"Okay, but your coat and gloves stay on and no bouncing up there. I know Joe fixed the boards, but it's been very damp lately, and the wood might be soft."

"Oh, Mama, you worry too much!"

Star guffawed.

"I worry so that you don't have to," Maggie replied. "Go on, off you go, I'll come find you in a bit."

The fairy house, as Verity called it, was in fact the sisters' old tree house, built by their dad and well loved by all their friends and both of Maggie's children. It was still pretty sturdy given that it was over forty years old, and Joe had given the whole structure an overhaul in the summer, which should see it through for the next few years. She experienced a pang of melancholy when she thought about it not being the North tree house any longer after the building sold. It would be the end of an era. There had been Norths on the property for almost three hundred years. Soon it would be just another photograph in an estate agent's window, an "investment opportunity" pared down to nothing more than acreage numbers and room measurements.

If there was one good thing to come out of her eviction, she decided, it was getting the chance to stay here in her ancestral home for one last time.

Duncan continued studiously with his work while the sisters pulled out furniture and delved into hidey-holes around him. Earlier in the day, he and Star had rescued a stout George II (according to Duncan) walnut kneehole desk from beneath a display of dead-eyed porcelain dolls and fashioned a workstation for him near the back of the shop. He now had room to lay out his laptop, notebooks, and magnifying and measuring equipment, which seemed to please him immensely.

By five o'clock, all they had to show for their search were dirty hands and aching muscles.

"I'd better get Verity in before she turns into an ice pop."

The garden used to be lit with fairy lights; now the decayed wires hung in sad loops from the skeletons of apple and pear trees that grew along the high stone garden walls. Augustus had made sure that his daughters could play out in the woods till late by hand-carving signs that read *This way home! This way to the tree house! This way to the Fairy Glade!* and nailing them to rowan tree trunks throughout the area. Winding through the middle of the garden was a stepping-stone path studded along each side with footlights, which Joe had put in during the summer. Maggie followed the path down to the end and stepped through a stone archway into the woods. Here too was Joe's handiwork. Following the original pattern left by Augustus, he had wired in new lights, which twinkled out from blackberry bushes and rhododendrons like golden fireflies and lent the otherwise dark woods a glowing warmth.

Her footfalls were dull against the soft mossy ground; only the occasional snapping twig gave her away. Above was the canopy of rowan branches with their bunches of red berries hanging down like Chinese lanterns.

"Verity!" she called as she rounded another twist in the path and saw the tree house lit up ahead. The word *tree house* suggested a kind of makeshift affair, but this more resembled a log cabin built across the boughs of two trees.

Verity came to one of the windows and peered out. "Oh, good, you're here," she said, as though she had been telepathically summoning her mother.

"It's time to go home, sweetheart, come down from there now."

"I can't go yet. I've lost my holly sticker down the back of the fairies' treasure chest."

"It's only a sticker, darling, I'm sure we've got some more at home."

"No, Mama, this one's special! Sameera gave it to me in class—it's the best-friend sticker! I can't lose it!"

Maggie knew better than to argue: you were never going to dissuade a ten-year-old of the power of best-friend stickers.

"Can you pull the fairy treasure out a bit so you can reach behind it?"

"No, it's too heavy. I think it's filled with magical golden goblets."

She sighed. Her daughter's imagination was a precious thing, but sometimes it could be a pain in the bum. Just the other day, a group of elves had supposedly moved into the fairy house and she'd had to supply them all with Hobnob biscuits. Now she was going to have to deal with fairy treasure if there was any hope of getting her daughter home this evening.

"Okay, I'm coming up."

She climbed the ladder set to one end of the tree house and crawled in through the small doorway. The room was just high enough for her to stand up, and she dusted her knees for what felt like the ninetieth time that day as she rose.

"Where's the fairy treasure?" she asked.

"There, under the reading bench. My sticker fell down the back when I was reading to a pixie."

"Uh-huh," said Maggie, crossing to the bench built into one of the walls beneath a round window. She bent down and peered underneath. "Oh!" Whether there was fairy treasure in it or not, there was indeed a chest under the bench. How long had that been there? Then again, how long had it been since she'd been in here? Reaching around it with both hands, she pulled. It was heavy, and for a moment she wasn't sure it would budge, but with another prolonged heave, the chest began to shift inch by inch until she had pulled it clear. Quick as a flash, Verity ferreted around behind it and emerged triumphant with her sticker, minus all its stick; Maggie would have to tape it to her school jumper tomorrow.

She looked down at the box and shook her head, half smiling, half mildly pissed off at their old man's wily sense of humor. This had to be it. He'd hidden the strongbox in their most favorite childhood place in the world. Of course he had. "You crafty old bugger!" she said under her breath.

"*Uh!* You said a swear!"

"Yes, I did. But in this case it's true, so it doesn't count. Your granddad was a crafty old bugger, which nobody can deny."

The box was too heavy for Maggie to manage on her own—quite how Augustus managed to get it up there in the first place was a mystery—but Duncan's wiry frame belied an easy strength, which meant she was able to lower the box down into his waiting arms. Star, Maggie noticed, couldn't take her eyes off those arms.

Once back inside the curios shop, she sat down, pulling Verity onto her lap, and Star took the chair opposite, leaning forward eagerly. Duncan stood on the perimeter, and they all watched with bated breath as Simone knelt before the chest and pushed the key into the lock. It fitted. The scrape of metal turning in metal was followed by a clunk, and the lid gave a little jump as the lock snapped open. Simone pushed the lid up and let it fall backward.

"That's not treasure! It's just old paper!" Verity was disappointed. Newspapers browned with age shouted Victorian headlines of the day beside old curly-edged notebooks. Maggie stole a glance up at Duncan, who was almost salivating at the contents; like her, he probably wanted to dive in and have a good rummage, but he kept a polite distance. When they unearthed the shop's ledger, a weighty tome with a cracked spine—as promised in Augustus's letter—Simone handed it up to Duncan, who took it as though she'd just passed him the Holy Grail. He retired immediately to his desk to look through it.

Looking incongruous against the backdrop of biscuity paperwork was an oxblood leatherbound photograph album. Simone looked up at her sisters, who nodded reassuringly that she should open it.

Star's hand flew to her mouth. Maggie too felt a sudden rush of emotion. Simone held the album steady and bit her lip to keep her emotions in check. Their younger selves stared gleefully out at them from the page. Three little girls, wild looking, like woodland nymphs, with flowers in their hair and clothed in cotton sundresses smudged with grass and blackcurrant stains. They were grinning at the camera, the sun's rays catching in their hair and casting a yellow film over the scene. Simone's jet-black hair was cut short, in contrast to Star's white-blond shoulder-length hair, while Maggie's curls were a thick magenta tangle to her waist. If their differing hair and skin tones had caused anyone to question their sisterhood, one look into those matching green North eyes would have set them straight.

She turned the page.

"I don't remember these," said Star.

"Me either," said Simone.

"But I can remember the feeling of it," Maggie added, and her sisters agreed. "Dad must have taken them."

"And then he took the time to put them all in an album." Star smiled.

"You look like me," said Verity, peering closer at a photograph of Maggie holding a plump pink-faced baby, Star, while Simone grinned like the proudest sister that ever was, Star's tiny hand clasped around her fingers. Looking at these photos, it seemed impossible to imagine the distance adulthood had brought.

"We were happy, weren't we." Simone was smoothing the bubbling cellophane over the photographs. "I forget that sometimes."

"I don't think it occurred to us *not* to be happy," said Maggie.

"I looked forward to the summer all year. It was my favorite time," added Star.

"Better than Christmas?" Verity asked, astonished.

"Better than anything," Star replied.

"Do you miss Granddad?"

"I do, very much." Star smiled sadly.

"He was one of a kind." Maggie's hair fell over her eyes and she tucked it behind her ear.

"It doesn't seem right that he's gone, does it? I didn't think I'd feel the lack of his presence in the world as much as I do." Simone was still kneeling by the box.

"That's just how *I* feel," said Star.

Maybe by sifting through the past they could find their way back to when they were summer sisters, and bring those lost parts of themselves into the present. It occurred to Maggie that for a man so invested in a life of free-spirited chaos, Augustus sure knew how to play the long game when it came to his daughters.

19

IT WAS FRIDAY morning. The night before, each sister had taken a pile of papers from the strongbox to look through. It had been an emotional evening. Old memories, old hurts, and old happy times swirled around them in a confusing jumble.

In the morning light, Star had her head bent over a collection of silver lockets and periodically looked up at the tablet Duncan had loaned her, to confirm the dates against a hallmark checker website.

The ledger was open on Duncan's desk, and he was prowling the shop looking for a pair of seventeenth-century shoe buckles, which had supposedly belonged to Charles the First.

"Are you starting from the first page and working through methodically?" asked Simone, who had left sifting through old winter solstice celebration menus and budgets to help Duncan's search.

"I am attempting it this way first, yes. If that doesn't seem fruitful, I will do it the other way: pick an item and attempt to match it to the ledger. Have you looked through it?" he asked.

"No."

"It's a bit . . . disjointed. I'd expected it to be laid out chronologically or alphabetically by item. Whilst it is alphabetized, it's organized according to where the items came from rather than what they are. Where space has run out for a particular letter, another page has been added in with glue. It's a little chaotic."

"Ah, much like the man himself."

"Oh, it wasn't started by Augustus. The ledger begins with notes from Patience North and has been carried on down the generations."

"So the buckles we're looking for came from where?"

"Abingdon."

"Of course. Absolutely no help whatsoever in finding the items."

"That is correct."

The door to the shop opened and Patrick walked in. "Patrick North!" Simone raised her hand in greeting. It still took her by surprise that he was a young man now. Seeing him at the funeral had been the first time she'd seen him properly in maybe five years. He looked like his dad, apart from the eyes of course.

Despite the sisters' difficult relationships with their father and, in more recent years, one another, they were all fiercely protective of their name. Maggie had kept the name North when she'd married Josh, and when Simone had married Evette, she'd taken the North name. Patrick and Verity were also Norths, as would Simone's children be, should she ever have any.

"Hi," he called, meandering through the aisles until he located them.

"Hey, Patrick." Star smiled up at him. "How are you?"

"Good, thanks," Patrick replied, letting his eyes wander over the crammed shelves. "You?"

"Not too shabby," Star replied.

Patrick nodded and murmured "good, good" but was too captivated by the clutter to start a proper conversation.

Duncan raised a hand in greeting. "Hello, we haven't been formerly introduced. I'm Duncan, the appraiser. You must be Maggie's eldest. I've heard a lot of good things about you. Great to meet you."

Patrick smiled warmly. "You too," he said. "Ma asked me to give you these," he said to Star idly, placing a bowl of fruit down on the desk. "She said to tell you she'll be over later to talk winter solstice plans."

"Cool," said Star, taking a bite out of one of the apples.

"I thought she was going to be here." Simone didn't like the petulant sound in her own voice. She took a breath. *Don't be stroppy. It is what it is. You have to be here, so suck it up.*

"The shop's busy, she can't get away." Patrick picked up a tiny model of a ship and studied it. Duncan came over.

"Trench art," he said, pointing at the model.

"Huh?" Patrick looked quizzically up at him.

"Crafts made by soldiers who were in the trenches or held as prisoners of war. Most war-related arts are given the umbrella term of 'trench art.' That piece probably originated from World War One. Soldiers used what they had on hand, bits of wood, bullet casings, that sort of thing."

"Wow, that's kind of chilling." Patrick frowned.

"I think it's kind of nice, art through adversity, et cetera."

"Sure, mate. This place is just mad, huh."

"That's an understatement," said Simone.

"I don't think Mum liked coming in here when Granddad wasn't around."

"It shows."

Patrick turned to look at Simone. "What do you mean?"

Star was glaring at her with bug eyes, clearly imploring her to stop, but she didn't seem able. She didn't want to be sorting through two hundred years of grimy old crap. She wanted to curl up in a ball and hibernate through till spring, and she wanted someone to blame for not being able to. Patrick was watching her, the tic at the corner of his eye said *Don't you dare!* and suddenly her blood was up.

"Only that the place is a mess." Her words were a challenge. "Everything's covered in dust. I thought since you only live over the road your mum might have tidied things up a bit before we got here."

"Simone!" Star admonished.

Patrick cocked his head to one side. "She's had a lot on her plate," he said, his stare flinty.

Oh yeah? she thought. *You want to see my plate? It's brimming over, sunshine!*

"Yes, well, we all have a lot on our plates now," Simone countered, motioning around the shop. "I'm not having a go, I'm simply saying, you know it wouldn't have hurt her to pop in and flick a duster around when she knew we'd all be having to go through this crap."

She watched as Patrick gently placed the wooden ship back on the shelf and turned his gaze on her, his jaw set. *Oh, crap.*

"Where were you?" he asked. "When the funeral needed to be arranged?"

"Don't get defensive, Patrick. I helped out on the day. But as far as organizing the rest of it, I live miles away, and your mum lives right here. It was a lot easier for her to sort it out than for me to try and do it from Greenwich."

"You do know Granddad died on a mountain, in a van, in Italy? Yeah? Do you know how stressful it was for Mum to get him repatriated? I was coming home every weekend to help out because she was trying to organize the paperwork, which was a minefield by the way, and arrange the funeral and run the grocer's and look after Verity. All you had to do was turn up on the day and eat vol-au-vents. I thought she was going to have a nervous breakdown. I don't know what would have happened if Joe hadn't been around and he's practically a stranger."

"Hardly a stranger," Star interjected.

"Not family, though, is he? It's not his business."

"What's your problem with Joe?" Simone asked. "You ought to be pleased your mum's got someone to help her out."

"Why? Because it makes it easier for you to shirk any responsibility?"

"Don't speak to me like that," Simone snapped.

"Why not? Where *have* you been? You certainly haven't been down here for years. I'm surprised you even know who Verity is! So don't chat shit about my mum not 'flicking a duster around' when you abandoned us a long time ago!"

"That is not fair!"

"No, what's not fair is my mum trying to make everything easier for everyone else all the time, and the people she tries hardest for not even noticing."

Guilt slithered in her stomach. What was she doing? It was as if the devil on her shoulder had punched the lights out of the angel on her other shoulder, and now she only had one voice in her head. She took a breath. This was ridiculous. The last thing she wanted to do was fight with her nephew.

"Listen, Patrick . . ."

"No," he said, shaking his head. "I don't think I will."

He walked deliberately out of the shop, leaving Simone wondering how she'd managed to screw things up quite so spectacularly.

"You really upset him, Simone, slagging his mum off. You know how protective he is."

"That wasn't my intention, obviously. Shit."

"Aren't you going to go after him, then?" Star asked.

"Should I?"

"Yes!" She nodded emphatically. She snatched up her phone and fired off a text.

"I don't even know where he's gone. I can't exactly go over to Maggie's and ask if I can speak to her son to apologize for slagging her off."

"He's right," said Star. "We should never have left everything to Maggie to sort out."

"I didn't realize it had been such a hassle." She was on the defensive again.

"Really? I think we did. We're just used to her sorting everything out for us. Doesn't paint us in a very favorable light, does it?"

Star was right. Simone had known full well she should have helped Maggie, but she was so overwhelmed with her own emotional trauma that she'd let her sister carry it all. She'd told herself that if Maggie needed help, she'd ask, knowing full well that her sister would rather die of exhaustion than bother anyone. *Like hiding your eviction from everyone so as not to burden us. Oh, Maggie!*

"Shit, shit, shit!" Simone twiddled her ponytail, a nervous habit.

Star's phone pinged. "He's at Betty's," she said.

"Was that him?"

"Yeah."

"How have you got his number?"

"I asked for it at the funeral. I'm trying to be a less crap aunty."

"Oh, bollocks to everything!" shouted Simone, grabbing her coat. "I'm going to Betty's!" She slammed out of the door and then slammed straight back in again. "And you're coming with me!"

PATRICK WAS SAT at a table in the window with a mug of something covered in a spiral of squirty cream. He was scrolling through his mobile phone and didn't notice Star and Simone arrive until an aunty-shaped shadow fell across the table. He looked up.

"Oh god, what?" he sighed. "Are you here to berate me for disrespecting my elders?"

"Elders?" Star sucked in a breath. "Low blow, Patrick."

He smiled despite himself.

"Can we sit?" Simone asked. She was aware she needed to tread carefully here.

Patrick gestured at the chairs opposite him, and they sat down.

She took in a deep breath and slapped gaffer tape over the devil on her shoulder's shouty little mouth. "I'm sorry," she said. "Maybe I've taken your mum a bit for granted. I didn't mean to criticize her. But you know, she isn't perfect either." *You couldn't help yourself, could you!*

Star rolled her eyes.

"I never said she was," said Patrick. "But she's always been there for both of you, and when she needed you, you were nowhere to be seen." Simone spluttered, offended, but Patrick carried on. "You might have forgotten, but I haven't. I remember being lifted out of bed in the middle of the night and driven halfway across the country because you'd been arrested." He looked at Star, as did Simone.

"It was a protest thing." Star waved it away. "They wanted to build a housing estate on an ancient woodland."

"Mum bailed you out," said Patrick.

"She did."

"And what about when you got cold feet before your wedding?" He looked accusingly at Simone.

"I know, I know, I called her, and she came running." She had panicked that Evette was too good for her two weeks before the wedding. Maggie had talked her down, assured her that Evette could see all the good things Maggie could see too, and a hundred more.

"And where were you when Grandma Lilibeth died? Or when we were moving, and Verity was a baby? Where were you?" He was trying not to shout, but it was clear that there was a lot of backed-up resentment. People always underestimated children, thought they didn't pick up on things, but they did, and then they grew into adults who remembered. Maggie may have allowed herself to be taken for granted with good grace, but her son had clearly been keeping score.

"I came to the funeral," Simone said weakly, and hated herself.

"Yeah, you're good at that. Turning up when all the work's done."

"I have a busy life . . ." She sounded pathetic even to her own ears.

"And Mum doesn't? Just because she isn't a physiotherapist or a psychologist doesn't mean you can look down on her life.

It's not less important than yours. And she isn't your packhorse, you can't just dump all your shit on her and expect her to deal."

"Wow, don't hold back, Patrick," said Star.

He took a deep breath and scratched his hands through his messy hair. He looked out of the window, and Simone watched his fists clench and unclench.

"You're a good son. Your mum is very lucky to have you. I'm sorry we weren't here."

"Ahh, do you know what, this isn't all on you. I'm off-loading my own guilt." He looked from Star to Simone, and she knew this was her moment to break new ground.

"What do *you* have to feel guilty about?" she asked.

"Being away at uni, and not wanting to come back here to live after I've got my degree. I'm moaning at you for being distant when I'm planning to desert my family."

"Your mum doesn't expect you to spend your whole life in Rowan Thorp," Star said, laughing. "She wants you to get out in the world and build a life for yourself, independently of her. Trust me, you're not deserting her; all she's ever wanted is to give you the tools so you can set out on your own. I'm not saying she won't miss you, but she'd be devastated if she thought you hadn't pursued your dreams because you were worried she needed a babysitter."

"How can you be so sure?"

"Because that's exactly what she said to us when we were your age," said Simone.

"Big sister wisdom with no psychology degree," Star added.

"I'm sorry I snapped at you." Patrick trained his bright green eyes on Simone. "Mum and Verity are all I've got, you know, they're the only properly solid things in my life. Everyone else is just, well, transient."

Wow, that stung. Would she want *her* children to feel that their family was transient?

"Okay, that's not good," she began. "How about this? We"—she looked at Star before carrying on—"we will try to use this enforced time we've been given to build some new bridges between our family. And that way we'll always have a path back to each other."

"I'd like that." Patrick smiled tentatively. "Can I ask you something?"

Star and Simone nodded.

"Has Mum said to you she's worried about anything? Other than Christmas, work, and the whole organize-a-massive-festival-in-record-time thing? I feel like she's even more stressed than normal."

Star, who found it impossible to lie convincingly, bit her lip and looked wide-eyed at Simone. It wasn't their place to tell Patrick about the eviction but equally his asking about his mum made things awkward when they knew that losing the greengrocer's and the flat above was foremost in Maggie's mind.

"We will keep a close eye on your mum." Simone used her best comfort voice, the one she used on her patients. "Don't worry."

THEY LEFT BETTY'S with takeaway coffees and a lot to think about.

"You know, you should go into politics; you did a great job of not actually answering Patrick's question." Star nudged Simone gently.

"Politics would be a breeze compared to this family."

20

"OOOEE!" SONJA MOORHEN—chairwoman of the Rowan Thorp Historical Society—pushed her way into the greengrocer's, her arms full of books. As a historian, her to-be-read pile was never-ending, and she always appeared to be carrying some of it with her.

The weather seemed to have decided today was the day to really get winter started and had taken great pains to slather the whole village with ice. Now, at half past four in the afternoon, it was beginning to add another frosty layer, and Sonja was taking no chances dressed as she was in full arctic attire, including padded trousers.

Maggie's shop was light and airy, with exposed brick walls, a bright white ceiling between the black beams, and a cobblestone floor. Floor-to-ceiling Georgian kitchen dressers lined the walls. The topmost shelves housed vestiges of the shop's history—old weighing scales, weights, earthenware jars and pots—while the rest were lined with bowls and baskets of fresh produce. At the bottom, the cupboards were left open to reveal sacks of potatoes and deep wicker baskets full of root vegetables, artfully arranged to look as though they were spilling out of the cupboards and lending the place a sense of abundance. Bunches of bay, rosemary, and curry leaves hung from drying racks, while tenderer herbs ballooned out from tall jugs on the sideboards. The only warmth came from a small fan heater, which Maggie used to defrost her hands at regular intervals.

Maggie was refilling the stock. The sudden drop in temperature had inspired half the village to make vegetable soup. She was piling parsnips into a wooden display crate while Joe was serving the last customer from the latest rush.

"Afternoon, Sonja! Making soup?"

"As a matter of fact, I am. Is that grocer's intuition?" She handed Maggie a list.

"Something like that."

"I'm not only here for shopping. I've been looking through my great-grandmother's almanac and journals about the winter solstice."

"Oh?" Maggie checked the list and filled Sonja's cotton tote accordingly.

"As part of the lead-up to the season, they would fill the trees with edible decorations for the birds and wildlife; lard and seed pomanders, dried fruit slices on strings, that sort of thing. It's all part of honoring the land, looking after nature so that nature will look after you. Is that helpful?"

"It is, thank you, Sonja. What a lovely idea." Her mind was suddenly whirring with possibilities. This could be the sisters' gateway to the community spirit their dad was trying to force upon them.

As soon as Sonja left, she messaged their newly set up "Summer Sisters" WhatsApp group.

Anyone found anything in Dad's papers about
decorating trees? Edible bird decorations?
Think we've just found our first event. Use the
woods? Get the church flower association
involved? What do you think?

SIMONE'S PHONE DINGED with a new WhatsApp message.
She saw it was from Maggie but ignored it; edible bird decorations could wait.

"I don't think I'd realized how jaded I am." She was lying on
the chintz sofa in the Dalgleishes' sitting room, a log fire crack-
ling in the hearth. On the other side of the road, a projector
Santa in his sleigh flew repeatedly across the front wall of number 62.

Evette chuckled lightly on the other end of the phone.
"You're not jaded, darling; you've had a lot of knocks lately and
it's set you back."

"I was looking at those photographs last night with Maggie
and Star and thinking, 'I was really happy.' How did I forget
that?"

"You buried it to make your home life easier."

"You mean how I used to pretend I'd had a less good time
than I did to avoid upsetting my mother." Even thinking about
her duplicity reawakened a crawling unease in the pit of her
stomach that as an adult she recognized as guilt.

"Bingo. I know she's your mum and I don't want to start a
fight, but boy did she do a number on you!"

"She's a realist, that's all." Simone could feel her spine stiff-
ening; she sat up and stretched. "She didn't believe in sugarcoat-
ing things simply because I was a child."

"From what you've told me, she showed nothing but disdain for your father or your sisters from when you were very young."

She couldn't argue with that. Some of her earliest sensibilities were of a war of conflicting internal emotions: to love her sisters was to hurt her mum and vice versa. The resulting self-loathing made her reactionary.

"It pains me to say it, but it rubbed off on me."

She remembered how close to the bone Patrick's earlier comments had grazed.

"Of course it did, you were a child. Children are malleable and impressionable—they look to their caregivers to set their moral compass. Her negative assertions colored your images of your family and made you feel guilty for enjoying your time with them. You were too young to go against the status quo, so you pushed your feelings down."

"Wow. Way to sum me up."

"Only with love, baby. Only ever with love."

Simone stood and began to walk between the sitting room and the kitchen and back again, like a cat in a cage that's too small. "I don't want to be an emotional fortress."

"So take down your walls. You've already begun with Patrick. Take those feelings forward. Every time you want to stump a conversation in its tracks, ask yourself why you feel defensive before you snap."

"Every conversation with my family makes me feel defensive!"

Evette laughed softly down the phone. "And what does that tell you?"

"That my family is annoying?"

"You know the saying 'You always hurt the ones you love'?"

"Oh, ick!" She totally loved them, and Evette knew it. God, she missed Evette so much. "I wish you were here." She sighed down the phone and flopped back into the dent she'd left in the sofa.

"And you know why I'm not."

"It is helping, I think, being away. I didn't think it would, but I've been so busy with Dad's nonsense that sometimes I'll go hours without thinking about baby stuff."

"And when you remember?" Evette pressed gently.

She closed her eyes and let her head fall back. The first millisecond always felt like someone had just thrown a basketball at her chest, knocking the air out of her lungs. Then the crawling disappointment slipped into the empty cavity inside her chest, snaking and twisting until she wanted to scream and keep on screaming.

Holding the phone between her ear and shoulder, she made tight fists of her hands, digging her nails into her palms harder and harder until the pain vanquished the threat of tears.

"It hurts," she said through gritted teeth.

"My love." Her wife's voice was tender. "I think it's going to feel like that for a long time."

"Aren't you supposed to tell me that it'll get better soon?"

"It's going to take as long as it takes. You are grieving, you can't rush it."

"Don't you miss me?"

"Yes. I miss you."

"Good."

Simone could sense her wife smiling and it brought her back to safer shores.

"Do *you* miss *me*?" asked Evette.

"Not so much."

She was rewarded with Evette's explosive laughter down the phone. "Cheeky mare!"

"Of course I miss you. You're my best friend. And I'm horny. The bed here is massive, it feels like such a waste."

"Well, we'll just have to make up for lost time when you come home, won't we?"

The smile in Evette's voice had grown, and Simone could swear she felt the warmth of it down the phone. Hope bloomed in her chest for the first time in months. She wouldn't have thought it this time last week, but it was good that she was here, it *was* what she needed. *Will wonders never cease?* she thought.

21

FOR FINE DINING and designer gin you went to the Stag and Hound, but for pub grub and dodgy jukebox tunes it was always the Rowan Tree Inn. The village had, as many had remarked before, the best of both worlds, and tonight the inn was a rowdy affair. Star caught Duncan smiling out of the corner of her eye.

"You're mocking me." She scowled. They were sitting in the booth farthest away from the busy bar.

"I promise I'm not. I've just never seen anyone make knitting look so complicated."

"I'm a left-handed woman in a right-handed world. In medieval times, I'd have been considered a witch."

"You are very bewitching." Duncan slapped his hand to his forehead. "I can't believe I just said that. Can we strike that from the record?"

"No," she said. "It's out there now. And besides, I like the idea of being bewitching. It makes a change from being scatterbrained or a loser. Oh man, I think I dropped a stitch." She handed her first knitting attempt to Duncan.

"Yeah, you've dropped more than one stitch here," he said, fixing it for her. "Why would anyone call you a loser?"

"Um, I have a habit of losing things: jobs, places to live, men . . ."

"Maybe you just haven't found anything worth keeping yet." He was looking at her with big brown eyes full of warmth, and she found it difficult to tear her gaze away.

He handed back the knitting, the dropped stitches now picked up. He'd had absolutely no qualms about teaching her to knit in the packed pub, which only made her admire him more. She had decided to start with a scarf, which was currently four inches long and growing steadily.

Earlier that day she'd paid a visit to the wool shop on the high street with him—many tongues had wagged—and under his supervision had chosen a multicolored double-knit yarn called "autumn woodland" and a set of needles.

Duncan was an excellent teacher all around; he'd shown endless patience and enthusiasm as he talked her through his processes for identifying Augustus's antiques. She wondered what else he could teach her.

He was undeniably handsome, and so very smart. Even now, in his downtime, he was wearing a shirt with a round-neck knitted jumper over the top and dark blue jeans. She had never been attracted to someone so formally attired. But she couldn't seem to keep her eyes off Duncan; small wonder she kept dropping stiches.

Her brain only allowed her fantasies to drift for so long before it reminded her that she wasn't good enough for the likes of Duncan. He was a kind man, and he was humoring her, as the client of his firm. This knowledge didn't stop her wanting to kiss him, but it made sure she wouldn't actually do it. Because why in the world would someone like Duncan look twice at someone like her? He had education coming out of his ears; she had none to speak of. No. He wouldn't be interested in her, not for anything more than a quick roll in the hay at least, and she'd been that girl too many times in the past. She'd rather be his friend than a fling to pass the time until a more fitting option came his way.

"Is Sotheby's happy with the reports you've sent back so far?" She decided that talking business was safer ground.

"They're delighted. It's really an honor to be able work on the North account."

"It seems funny hearing you call it 'the North account.' To us it was Dad's old junk shop."

"Your father collected some of the finest junk I've ever seen."

"I bet your family is proud of you."

"My mum is, but to the rest of the family I'm just the baby brother. I'm the youngest of five and the only boy."

"Wow, I bet you were well mollycoddled."

He laughed. "Yeah, very much so. I am also the butt of all jokes. But I don't mind, and I like being close to my nieces and nephews. It's good practice for if I ever have kids of my own."

"Is that something you'd like? To have a family?"

"I guess. Isn't that what most people want?" he asked.

"I'm kind of ambivalent for myself," she replied. "If it happens it'll be great, and if it doesn't that's okay too. But I've donated my eggs before, to a fertility clinic, so that someone with a greater desire than me to have a child can have the option." She wasn't sure why she was telling him this, but somehow it felt right to do so.

"Wow, that's . . . I'm a bit lost for words. That's a very altruistic act."

She felt herself blush at the praise but also like she didn't really deserve it. "It sounds more noble than it is. It was more . . . I don't know how to explain it. Have you ever just felt like something was the right thing to do? I had this strong sense of it, like I was moved to do it, so I did. I don't know." She hid her face behind her hair and picked at her nails, feeling exposed. "Maybe it's because my own lines are so blurred on the subject, I felt like I needed to balance the universe somehow?"

Duncan looked thoughtful. "It seems like an unfair burden to carry simply because you have a uterus. Nobody judges a bloke who says he doesn't want kids."

She was liking Duncan more and more. "It wasn't like that exactly; it was more like I was compelled by a higher force." She laughed at herself. "Simone would have a field day if she heard me talking about 'higher forces.'"

"I think it's easier for a man to be flippant about whether he wants kids or not because we don't have to go through any physical life-changing or life-threatening events to get there. If I had to actually grow the child myself, I'm not sure I would. I definitely wouldn't want to give birth." He shuddered.

"That's refreshingly honest."

"You heard me say I've got four older sisters, right? They have been meticulous in detailing their experiences of pregnancy and childbirth—no hemorrhoid, tear, or stitch was too much information," he said, smiling.

"I think that's just put *me* off!" She grimaced. "My dad was a wandering spirit; I think maybe I'm destined to be like him."

"But he did both, wandered and had children."

"Not so as you'd know it." She didn't like the taste of bitter on her lips. Augustus didn't deserve that from her.

"You didn't get on with him?" Duncan tipped his head to the side.

"On the contrary. I adored him. I wanted more of him, and he wasn't around as much as I'd have liked. But that's my bad, he was just being his authentic self. What about your dad? Are you close with him?" she asked.

"Ah, no, he left a long time ago. We don't have much contact. My mum brought us up single-handed. She's pretty amazing."

"I can imagine." She swallowed the urge to say something cheesy like *She must be to have raised someone like you* and said instead, "We didn't have much contact with our dad really either, although somehow it felt like more because we had one whole month every summer with him. And when you're a kid a month feels like a year."

"Didn't you miss your mum when you were here?"

Star thought about it. Had she ever missed her mum? "Not really. It was what we'd always done from when we were toddlers. Simone and Maggie might have missed their mums, but I was parented by a lot of people, really. We tended to move between communities, where everyone pitched in in terms of caregiving."

"Like communes?"

"Exactly."

"That's very cool."

"It's a more considered way of living. I think to outsiders it maybe looks irresponsible because there isn't the same impetus to own things or climb a career ladder, but it all depends on how you define responsibility. You could say that to live by borrowing only what you need from the world and returning it just as you found it is the *most* responsible thing you can do." She was used to automatically defending her lifestyle. People tended to get snarky if you lived in a way that challenged their own choices. Though she saw from Duncan's expression that she needn't have worried about that with him.

"You're not like anyone I've met before, Star North."

He was looking at her quizzically and she couldn't quite tell if it was a good thing or not. The warmth that spread through her felt very good . . . but that could just be the effects of the cider.

The bell at the bar tolled for last orders.

"I guess that's my cue to leave," she said, rolling her knitting up and putting it into her rucksack. "This must be a perk of living in a pub—you can simply stumble up to bed after last orders. Although, you'll have to stumble over to the Stag and Hound for *your* bed."

"I'll walk you home."

"That's just silly, I'm only up the road. I'll be fine."

"I'd like to, just the same."

His gentlemanly manners would be the death of her good intentions.

The rain had washed away the ice and the cobbled road glistened with the reflected red and green bulbs on the tall Christmas trees and the twinkling lights up and down the high street. The cold was shocking after the cozy warmth of the pub, and even now ice crystals were re-forming a slippery sheen on the street. She would be glad to curl up in her warm bed with her knitting and an audiobook . . . What had this village done to her? She smiled to herself. Whatever it was, she kind of liked it.

Duncan waited for her to unlatch the gate, and despite herself she couldn't stop the fluttery anticipation in her stomach; the *will he or won't he* feeling was a cross between excitement and nerves and needing a wee.

"Well, I'll see you in the morning." Duncan smiled. "Eight thirty, okay?"

"You know you don't have to work the weekend. I'm sure Sotheby's doesn't expect you to work six days a week."

He pulled a face like he was chewing a toffee. He looked embarrassed, which was the last thing Star wanted to make him feel.

"You are right, I am entitled to weekends off. But at the risk of sounding even more nerdy than I am, I'm having the time of my life in your dad's shop. I've never seen a collection like it. I can't wait to start work every morning."

The rain had become glitter in his hair, and his eyes sparkled in the fairy lights strung along the wall. His full lips looked like they would feel soft on hers. *Bloody hell, he's lovely! Stop looking at his mouth. Say something.*

"Well in that case, far be it from me to force a day of rest upon you. I'm looking forward to you." *Shit!* "To working with you. To the ledger. I'm looking forward to the continued deciphering of the ledger, with you."

"Me too, with you." He smiled.

Again, the sensation of wanting to kiss him swept over her, but she squashed it down and said, "Good night, then, see you in the morning."

He nodded. "Till then," he replied before turning and striding back toward the pub.

Star let out her longing in a low whistle and hurried into the house.

22

BY LATE AFTERNOON on Saturday the strongbox lay completely empty. The contents had been methodically examined by the sisters and classified according to their usefulness to the task at hand.

A clothbound scrapbook held a trove of winter solstice information, including the traditional drink served at the occasion—wassail—and lists of the kinds of foods to be served at the banquet, along with the route that the old processions had taken. It was an enormous task to master in very little time, but at last they were beginning to pull together, and their squabbles per day had dwindled to single figures.

Duncan was working at his desk. The loupe around his neck was almost a permanent feature, and was held so often to his eye it might have been a monocle. Already it was hard to imagine the place without him methodically perusing the aisles, his long fingers appraising its treasures.

A banging on the door so loud it made the windows rattle shattered their quiet contemplation.

"Oh god, it's not Stu again, is it?" Simone groaned. "I'm going to call the police if it is." She was a little ashamed that she was rather hoping it *was* Stu, just so she had an excuse to shout at someone.

"If it is, I'll call them myself," said Star. The words were tough, but Simone could see she was on edge, biting the skin at the side of her nail.

Maggie pushed herself up and made her way to the front of the shop, her sisters following behind.

She pulled the blind up and was greeted by Verity's cross little face scowling in at her. Maggie laughed and opened the door.

"Hello, my angry cherub, what brings you here?"

Behind her, Joe shrugged his shoulders. "She made me do it," he said apologetically. "She is *really* assertive."

"That she is," Maggie said proudly, and then turning back to her daughter's upturned face, she asked, "Okay, what's up?"

"You promised we would put the Christmas decorations up, Mama." Verity harrumphed and folded her arms, no easy feat in a duffle coat.

"And we will. But first I needed to take care of some things with Aunty Simone and Aunty Star."

Verity's fierce face was so sweet Simone could hardly bear it. She was much like Maggie in looks, thick auburn ringlets that stuck out at all angles and fell around her heart-shaped face. And those brilliant green eyes were all North family. Her heart squeezed. Would she ever get to be somebody's *mama*? Her body's treachery had caused her to hanker after all the things that most parents grumbled about: She wanted to be nagged by a tired child, to have her sleeve pulled constantly and her name called a hundred times a day. She wanted toddler snot wiped up her jacket and baby vomit down her top and she would *never* take it for granted. Was that so very much to ask?

Verity, meanwhile, was not to be appeased.

"Are you done with the aunts now?" Hands switched to hips like a mini Monica Geller.

Maggie raised a warning eyebrow, and some of Verity's bluster deflated.

"I just want to feel Christmassy," she said quietly.

Maggie pulled her into a hug. "And you will. Come on, then, let's go home." She looked around at her sisters. "Sorry, I did promise. I'll try and get over tomorrow to do some more sorting."

Verity pulled away from her and turned on her biggest puppy eyes. "Can the aunties come too? Please, Mama?" She peered around Maggie to Star and Simone. "Would you like to help us put up the Christmas decorations? It's so fun. Mama makes hot chocolate with sprinkles and freezer biscuits, and she always saves the biggest tree from the shop for us. Can they come, Mama?"

"Of course they can." Maggie smiled. "If they're not busy." She turned and smiled apologetically at her sisters. "There's no pressure. But you are very welcome."

Part of Simone wanted to run back to the Dalgleish cottage and hide under the bedclothes until morning. But a bigger part of her needed the comfort of being surrounded by her family. *Pull up your big-girl pants and make some memories with your niece*, she told herself.

"We'd love to!" she said, and was rewarded with Verity's beaming smile. "But I have a question: What are freezer biscuits?"

"I always keep a batch of uncooked biscuits in the freezer for fresh hot biscuit emergencies," Maggie answered.

"I can confirm they are excellent," added Joe. "Maggie's freezer biscuits are one of the reasons I stay in Rowan Thorp."

Star leaned over Maggie's shoulder and stage-whispered, "I bet I know what the other reasons are."

Maggie tried not to grin and shoved her sister off.

"And Duncan!" Verity piped up. "He needs to come too."

"Oh, darling, I'm not sure Duncan will want to help decorate our tree."

"Course he will." Star's face lit up. "Duncan!" she called to the back of the shop. "Grab your coat, we're going to Maggie's."

There was the scratching sound of a chair being moved and then Duncan appeared.

"That's very kind of you, but I've just found a rather interesting amulet that I think might be medieval . . ."

"Well, if it's been around for that long, it can wait until Monday," Star goaded. "And anyway, you've been working since half past eight this morning. Even Sotheby's appraisers are allowed to clock off at a reasonable hour on a Saturday."

Duncan looked a little awkward. "I mean, if you don't mind . . ." He glanced shyly at Maggie.

"Not at all." She smiled reassuringly. "You are very welcome. Come join us for some freezer biscuits."

"Right, that's settled, then. What are we waiting for?" Simone turned to Star. "Are you ready for some decorating?"

"I was born ready," said Star.

"Woo-hoo!" cried Verity, taking Joe's hands and dancing a jig on the spot. "Come on! We have to do it before bedtime."

Star locked the curios shop door, and they all headed across the street to Maggie's house.

"Remind me how old Verity is?" Simone asked quietly.

Maggie laughed. "She's ten with a stroppy age of fourteen."

"She's going to be a handful in her teens," said Star knowingly.

"She's a handful now!" Maggie countered.

"Maybe she needs a couple of aunties to help keep her on the straight and narrow," said Simone.

"Know where I can find any?" Maggie asked, one eyebrow raised.

"Simone, are you suggesting that I'd be a good influence on our niece?" Star was incredulous.

"A girl needs all the strong women she can get standing behind her." She winked at her.

"Amen to that," Maggie agreed.

The winter sun was setting, and within a very few minutes darkness would drop over the land like theater drapes. A freezing wind whistled along the high street, making the Christmas trees sway and the fairy lights dance in the gloaming. They picked up their pace and for the first time in years, Simone felt as though she might have her sisters back.

23

BACK AT THE flat, Maggie crawled into the roof space and—ignoring the bags of Christmas presents she had yet to find time to wrap—began passing the boxes of decorations back to her sisters. They in turn handed them to Verity, who was waiting impatiently in the sitting room, scissors poised to slice open the tape and reveal the festive treasures within.

Joe, Duncan, and Patrick extracted an enormous Norwegian spruce from the bucket of water in the garden and wrestled it up the stairs. Maggie heard them laughing (comradery born from trying to negotiate a seven-foot tree up the narrow staircase) and hoped that maybe the Christmas spirit would soften Patrick's prickliness toward Joe. She knew it came from a place of love, but surely anyone could see that Joe was a wonderful human . . .

While she busied herself, pulling out bags of frozen biscuits and laying them out on baking trays, Duncan came out to join her.

"Is there anything I can do to help?"

"No, you're all right. Have a little relax; you're always working."

"So are you," Duncan replied, and Maggie smiled at him.

"I guess we have that in common," she said.

"What's this?" he asked, leaning over the kitchen table, where several oddly shaped pieces of paper lay scattered over a considerable amount of crushed velour fabric in a striking shade of peach. He picked up a reel of hoop wire and studied it.

She let out a groan. "Verity's been cast as a pomegranate in the school play, and I'm supposed to be making her costume, but honestly I can't make head nor tail of it. Sewing is not my strong suit."

Duncan picked up the pattern instructions and began to leaf through the cut-out pieces of paper.

"Have you got a sewing machine?"

"My mum had one, it's in the attic, but I don't know how to use it. I was planning on cobbling it together with a mix of hand sewing and hemming tape."

Duncan pulled a doubtful expression.

"Please tell me if I'm overstepping the mark, but this looks pretty straightforward to me. I could have this knocked out in an hour or so if I could use your mum's sewing machine. Unless you *want* to make it?"

"Are you serious?"

Duncan appeared diffident. "I like sewing, knitting, anything crafty really. It wouldn't be any bother. I'm better at sewing than I am tree decorating." He smiled self-effacingly.

"You, my friend, are absolutely heaven-sent." Maggie slid the trays into the oven and set the timer for twelve minutes. "And you have earned extra freezer biscuits."

She crawled back into the roof space and dusted off the cover of her mother's old machine. When she returned to the kitchen, Duncan had cleared a space on the table and she dumped the heavy machine on it.

"There," she said, pulling off the case top. "Can you work with that?"

He gave it a quick once-over and nodded.

"My nan's got one just like it. Leave it with me." And with that he began pinning the paper shapes to the fabric and cutting them to size. Maggie laid a tea plate of hot biscuits beside him and left him to it.

"Anything you need—wine, cash, my eternal gratitude—you just let me know," she said, coursing with deepest relief that costume shaming would be one less thing she had to worry about.

"Do you realize this is the first time we've ever done this?" said Star, blowing on her hot chocolate.

"Well, we were *summer* sisters," agreed Simone.

"You mean you never spent Christmas together?" Verity looked appalled.

"Nope. We all had different mamas and lived in different parts of the country. We spent our summers together and the rest of the year apart."

"Patrick and I have different dads, only his dad is dead, and we don't know where mine is, so I guess it's kind of the same thing as you but different."

"My daughter, the straight shooter!" Maggie joked as she rested a holly-patterned serving platter piled with the rest of the hot Christmas biscuits on the coffee table. The sitting room looked like someone had ransacked Santa's grotto. Verity had tipped the boxes of decorations all over the floor "so they could see them better," and the carpet was now a swamp of tinsel and baubles to be waded through. *Dear god, I'll be hoovering up glitter till next Christmas!* Maggie thought as she surveyed the sea of spangle before her, and then she remembered that they wouldn't be here after next month, let alone next Christmas.

Nausea rolled through her insides and settled in the pit of her stomach, ominous and heavy like a concrete slab.

Verity frowned. "I wouldn't like that. I wouldn't like to only see Patrick in the summer."

"That's kind of how it has been since I started uni," said Patrick.

"Yes, but you come home for Christmas. I wouldn't like it if I didn't see you at Christmas."

"You'd better warn any future partners that all Christmases must be spent with your sister," Star said, and laughed as Patrick's eyes widened in mock alarm.

"And Mama and Joe," added Verity seriously. "All together forever."

All eyes flicked between Maggie and Joe. She shifted uncomfortably on the sofa while Joe busied himself with a knot in some fairy lights.

"Joe might have his own family to go to at Christmas," said Patrick.

"Joe is *my* family!" Verity protested.

"I am very happy that you feel that way, Verity," said Joe sincerely.

"Until he leaves," muttered Patrick. Maggie hoped Joe hadn't heard, but the pink tips of his ears suggested he had. To his credit, he said nothing. She felt a familiar twist of discomfort.

She had never expected that Joe would become so much a part of their lives. She could keep telling herself that her relationship with him was purely physical, but Verity was right: he had become like one of the family. Quite without anyone meaning for it to happen, Joe had become a paternal figure in Verity's life.

"You are going to be here for Christmas, aren't you, Joe?"

Verity was relentless when she got an idea into her head. Patrick's comment had clearly upset her.

Maggie suddenly felt like all eyes were upon her.

"I hadn't really given it too much thought, Verity," said Joe. "My mum and sister live in France, and I haven't seen them for a long time."

It was an answer of perfect avoidance and she was grateful for it.

"But, Mama, Joe *has* to be here for Christmas," Verity protested, as though it was entirely down to Maggie. What could she do?

"Joe is welcome to spend Christmas with us here. We'd love you to stay." She looked at him.

It felt like everyone in the room was holding their breath. Patrick looked away.

"Are you sure?" Joe asked.

"Yes." She smiled maniacally. "Yes. Absolutely."

"Yahoo!" Verity screeched and busted out a victory dance.

ONCE THE TREE resembled a tinsel hairball and all the freezer biscuits had been demolished, Simone went back to the cottage to call Evette, and Star took Verity up to bed with the promise of two stories. Joe helped Maggie to clean up the sitting room while Patrick washed up the plates and cups. The whir of her mum's old sewing machine was familiar, and it was good to hear the sound after all these years.

"Are you sure you want me to stay here for Christmas?" Joe asked as he swept biscuit crumbs into a dustpan.

"Of course. We'd love you to be here. So long as your sister doesn't mind."

"I feel like you were cornered into it."

"I only didn't ask before because I didn't want you to feel like you *had* to stay."

"I want to be wherever you are, Maggie. I don't know how many different ways I can say it."

She needed to change the subject. "How long has your sister lived in France?"

He shook his head. He knew what she was doing, but he went along with it and she was thankful. "About ten years."

"And your mum moved out to be with her?"

Joe paused. "It's kind of complicated. A couple of years ago, our family suffered a pretty monumental bust-up. My granddad had left equal shares in his business to my mum and her brother when he died. Then three years ago my uncle told my mum that he needed to borrow her shares to make a big business deal that would change all their lives. Just borrow them and then when the deal was done, he'd sign them back over."

"But he didn't?"

"No." Joe's mouth was a tight line. "He did not. He left my mum with nothing, and it's all legal and above board. Morally reprehensible but legally done."

"God, your poor mum."

"Moving to France made sense financially, since she wasn't getting any money from the business anymore."

"Were you close with your uncle? Before, I mean."

"Yes. I even worked for him for a time."

"Was that the marketing job that drove you to become a greengrocer?"

He laughed awkwardly. "It was."

He looked like he wanted to say more. She could see he was

steeling himself for something, but then Star wandered back into the sitting room, yawning.

"Looks like it's someone else's bedtime too." Maggie smiled.

Patrick exclaimed from the kitchen, and they all turned to see Duncan carrying in a flawless pomegranate costume, with little green leaves around the collar and the hoop wire sewn into the structure to create a perfect sphere.

"Oh my god! Duncan, it's amazing. Verity is going to be thrilled! I can't thank you enough. Can I give you some money for your time and expertise? Somehow freezer biscuits and hot chocolate doesn't feel sufficient."

Duncan smiled, looking down at the costume and not making eye contact with anyone as they each took turns to praise his sewing skills.

"Honestly, it was a pleasure," he said awkwardly.

Star was smiling hard, and Maggie noticed a look in her sister's eye, like she'd like to spread him on toast and eat him.

"Well, anyway, I'd better be off," Duncan said, looking as though the weight of compliments was crushing him.

"Me too," said Star a little too eagerly.

"I'll walk you back," Duncan offered.

"Thank you." Star gazed up at him adoringly.

At last you've fallen for someone deserving of you, Maggie mused, smiling at the two of them. *And it looks like he's equally smitten.* The idea made her feel deeply contented.

Patrick grabbed his coat and followed them out, headed to a party with a mate. "Don't wait up!" he shouted before pulling the front door shut.

"And then there were two," said Joe. He took Maggie by the hand and led her toward her bedroom and as always, she was powerless to resist.

24

THE DRIZZLE WAS freezing cold as Duncan walked Star home.

"Wouldn't it be quicker to go through the shop?" he asked, when Star steered them toward the gate in the wall like she had the night before.

"I don't really like walking through the shop by myself in the dark. I never did. I guess that sounds silly."

"Not at all. Some of those Toby jugs are pretty menacing." He grinned.

"I'm not keen on Dad's collection of taxidermy either, they're so creepy. He put a stoat in my room once to keep me company when my sisters were away. I was terrified all night! I was convinced I could see it snarling at me in the moonlight."

"That actually sounds truly frightening." Duncan chuckled. Unlike last night, this time he followed her through the gate and round to the door which led up to the flat. "It's the stuff of all good horror movies," he went on.

"Right!" She laughed too loudly to cover the beating of her heart. He was making it very hard for her to not kiss him. "I made Dad take it away, and he replaced it with some mangy old bear called Steph, or something like that, who looked much more friendly. He said it had been made for a prince and was gifted to him as a farewell token by a royal clockmaker in Geneva. But that could have been one of his tall tales; there were plenty of them."

"Could it have been called Steiff rather than Steph?" he asked.

He had a twinkle in his eye that Star had noticed he got whenever he found something really crusty looking in the shop. She loved seeing Duncan's excitement. He could see magic where others saw trash. She had begun to hope he might look at her like that one day. She stuffed the feeling down.

"Yeah, that was it," she said. "It was called Steiff bear. It was properly ancient."

"Is it still here? In the flat?"

"It is. Do you think it might be worth something?"

"Could be. If it is a Steiff bear, they hold their value. It would be even better if there was some proof of provenance."

"If there is, it'll be in that pile of papers next to your desk," she said. "I'm glad I didn't throw old Steiff out now. I gave him a good old damp dust the other day and sprayed him with body spray to freshen him up." She noticed Duncan wince. "You can come in if you like, and I'll show him to you now." *What are you doing?* she warned herself. *Do not invite this nice man into your bedroom!* But she didn't want this evening to end; she enjoyed his company and she would've liked to have it for a little longer this evening; it was a Saturday night after all.

Duncan pulled his coat collar up and became interested in a hanging basket full of long dead stems. "Oh, thanks, but no, I'd better get back to the Stag and Hound."

She tried not to feel rebuffed. He must have seen her face

fall, because he countered, "But I'd very much like to see it on Monday when I'm back at work."

Stupid Star, he's reminding you in his own sweet way that this is just another job for him, she thought. This was just like her, always hoping for something more than she deserved. She had nothing to entice him. She moved from place to place leaving no real trace of herself behind. Sometimes she felt like a ghost of a person, a fleeting presence to the people she met, soon to be forgotten. Perdita had always told her that being tied to any place or person was practically imprisonment. But if you had no ties at all, what was to stop you from disappearing without a trace?

After several blind stabs at the keyhole, she opened the door and flicked on the hall light. Stepping inside the threshold she turned back to Duncan standing on the doorstep.

"Well, thanks for walking me home. And thank you for making Verity's costume. That was really sweet of you, and I know it means a lot to Maggie."

"I enjoyed it. And the freezer biscuits."

They stood smiling at each other, not quite sure of the appropriate way to part.

"Well, goodbye." Duncan took a step backward.

"Goodbye. See you Monday."

She was holding on to the side of the door, ready to close it, when Duncan stepped toward her and bent to kiss her cheek. His lips were soft, and he smelled of aftershave and cinnamon biscuits. Then just as quickly, he turned and walked to the gate without looking back, closing it behind him. Star stood in the doorway wanting to preserve the moment just a little longer. She bit her lip to keep her smile under control. This wasn't how her encounters with men usually played out. Typically, men were greedy for her, wanting all of her at once, not thinking she was worth waiting *for*. To be fair, she'd never really cared to mind; she enjoyed sex and had always been happy to embrace that side of herself. She wondered now if perhaps, though fulfilling on a physical level, her consistent acts of spontaneity had become a bit boring.

Rain pattered down through the trees in an uneven rhythm, and the strings of solar-powered fairy lights swung in the breeze, making the tips of the wet grass below glitter like a lawn of diamonds for the taking. She pushed the door closed and locked out the night. For the first time in years, she felt a thrill of hope, and as she climbed into her old single bed in her old room with Artemis by her feet, she reveled in the luxury of having been kissed by a man who didn't take a thing.

25

SATURDAY'S DRIZZLE HAD been frozen out by Sunday morning, and the ice that'd formed over everything showed no sign of thawing yet. Every roof in the village was thickly white, and every pavement and car had swirls of frost painted over them.

Maggie sipped her double shot black Americano and tried not to be a coffee snob about Simone's half-fat, one shot latte with sugar-free hazelnut syrup or Star's decaf oat milk mocha, which were sat on the small table by the window waiting for their owners to arrive. Artemis sat on the chair next to her, taunting the cockapoo at the next table. She had left Verity watching Disney Christmas cartoons on the sofa with a massively hungover Patrick, who looked like a cadaver in a tartan dressing gown. This was her second Americano of the day, and she didn't imagine it would be her last.

So far, she and her sisters had done a lot of talking about the winter solstice celebration, but they hadn't actually set anything in motion. It was, she imagined, rather like being part of one of those government think tanks, where they spend endless hours talking about how to solve a problem without ever putting a solution into practice. Time was ticking on. The solstice was on the twenty-first, which gave them just eleven days to organize an entire festival. They had a list of things as long as their combined arms that needed doing and none had a tick beside them. If they didn't get a move on soon, they would fail without ever having tried.

"It's nice to have the three of you back in the village again," said Betty as she spritzed antibacterial spray onto a table just left by a group of gym mummies.

"Yeah," Maggie agreed. "I like having them around." She was surprised to find she actually meant it.

"I can't put my finger on it, but it feels right somehow. Balances the energy of the place. Used to feel the same when your father was back from his travels. But then I have always been very in tune with elemental energies."

She could well believe it. Betty had a sideline in herbal remedies and made her own essential oil blend candles to sell in the café.

"Betty, what do you know about winter solstice celebrations?"

Betty snickered. "What don't I know, more's to the point."

"You must have been too young to remember the ones held here, though."

Betty patted her short gray hair, flattered. "Nice of you to say. I was six when the last solstice celebration was held in Rowan Thorp, but oh, how well I remember them. Good memories stick. Old Bob Taylor had a veritable orchard at the end of his garden, and he would make the cider that would be used for the wassail. I kid you not, by early evening on the solstice you could have gotten pissed on the air alone with all that mulled cider brewing in cauldrons. Of course, everything feels like magic when you're knee high to a grasshopper, but what with all the candles and the smell of the bonfire, and oh my goodness the roast boar turning on the spit, makes my mouth water just thinking about it. I don't mind telling you: I am excited that you North girls are going to bring it back."

Maggie puffed her cheeks out. "If we can get our act together in time."

"It's the talk of the village." Betty was not making her feel better. "The Women's Institute have been champing at the bit waiting for you to ask for their cakes-pertise . . . See what I did there!"

"You think they'd help, then?"

"Course they would. At our last meeting, your winter solstice festival was at the top of our agenda. Just say the word, my girl. Everyone wants to help, but nobody wants to tread on your toes, so we're giving you space. Ask and you'll be inundated with offers."

"Really?"

Betty tutted. "That's the trouble with you young'uns. You think you're so connected, with your snappy-chats and your clock-toks. You're more likely to ask a virtual friend in Guatemala for advice than the people on your own doorstep."

Maggie could barely navigate Instagram, but she didn't bother to correct her, because she made a good point. She'd learned more about the winter solstice celebration through two minutes of idle chitchat with Betty than she had in the two hours spent trawling through Google in bed last night.

The bell above the door tinkled, and Simone and Star weaved their way through the café to the table.

"Took your time!" said Betty. "Your coffees are half-cold."

"Sorry, Betty," they mumbled together as they took off their coats and hung them on the coat stand next to the radiator.

Betty bustled off toward the kitchen with a tray laden with empty coffee mugs and plates. Simone sat down, smoothed first her hair, then her skirt, then opened her notebook and smoothed the pages on that too.

"So," she began, as though calling a meeting to order. "Where are we on how to actually start this thing? I was looking at the photographs again last night, and it looks like the bonfire used to be set up in the middle of the street, but I'm not sure the council would allow that now. Health and safety and all that."

"What about if we have it in Dad's garden? It's got access from the street, and we could have the celebration down near the woods," Star suggested.

"Not too near," said Maggie. "We don't want to start a forest fire."

"Halfway down, then. The council can't complain if it's on private land, can they? And we own the land now, so we only need our own permission."

Simone tapped her pen to her red lips and then nodded and made a note in her book. "We'll need to figure out a route for the procession as well," she mused.

"Maybe we could hold the banquet in the garden too, I mean it's probably long enough. Although I'm not sure it's a good idea to have a marquee near an open fire." Star was pondering.

"A marquee?" asked Maggie. "Do you think that's necessary?"

"I reckon most of the village is going to turn out for it," said Star. "We need to think big."

"Plus, it's the middle of December in England, so there's a good chance it'll be raining," Simone countered. "If we have a marquee, we can get some of those patio heaters in to keep people warm."

"Couldn't we just hold it in the village hall?" Maggie asked.

Star screwed her face up. "It's not very inspiring, is it?"

"We could spruce it up a bit."

Betty set down a plate with three sweet and salty chocolate tiffin bars between them.

"Brain food," she offered. "The village hall is booked out on the twenty-first of December every year for the annual Wealden Darts Tournament."

"Oh, of course, dammit," Maggie agreed.

"So the village hall is not an option," said Star brightly. "Ooh, thanks for these, Betty."

"Marquee it is, then. This is starting to look expensive," said Maggie, chewing her pen. "I wish we knew how much money was in Dad's solstice fund. I don't want to be a party pooper, but I really haven't got the money to be renting marquees or patio heaters, and I'm pretty sure neither of you have either. We need to figure out a way to do this on a shoestring budget, just in case the fund doesn't cover it all."

"Is there anyone in the village who could loan us one?" asked Simone.

"I reckon we could ask Troy and Kev if we can borrow their patio heaters for the evening. I'm sure they won't mind, especially if we promise to make sure the procession ends up in the pubs," Star suggested.

"Now that *is* a good idea." Simone approved, and Maggie saw Star's shoulders straighten a little at the praise.

"Maybe we could ask the parish council if we could have the banquet on Holy Trinity Green. They do it for the summer fete every year. It's plenty big enough." Star was on a roll.

"Yeah, but the incentive is that all money goes toward church restoration fund," Maggie replied.

"Plus, the whole pagan aspect of it might be a step too far, even for Belinda."

Belinda had come from a parish in North London, and due to her inclusive views and her launching of the annual Rowan Thorp Pride March in conjunction with the Women's Institute, congregation numbers had grown exponentially.

"The way I see it," Star began, "if God is supposed to have created everything, she must also have had a hand in the seasons and the sun's position in the hemisphere and the pagans who celebrated it. So to not support the winter solstice is kind of rude to God."

Simone and Maggie studied their sister for a long moment.

"Okay," said Maggie. "I nominate you to go and ask Belinda. And now that I think about it, the church summer fete always has a marquee for the cake contest and largest vegetable competition. I wonder if it belongs to the church or if they rent it." She tapped her pen on her chin. "Ask about that too."

"Yes, ma'am." Star saluted.

"Next on the agenda is alcohol. Dad's scrapbook is insistent on it being wassail, and he also says that the apple trees of Rowan Thorp make the best cider, as does Betty . . ."

"If Bossy Betty is insistent, we'd *definitely* better make it happen." Star snickered.

"I heard that!" Betty called, mid–loading a cake stand.

"Ears like a bat," whispered Simone.

"I heard that too!"

Maggie was struck by inspiration. She turned to the front of the shop and called, "Do you think if we held a village meeting, people would come?"

Betty rolled her eyes and settled her hands on her hips. "Try and stop 'em."

"What about if we held a meeting tomorrow night? In the village hall? Is that too short notice?" Simone was thinking out loud. "I'm not sure how we'd get the word out."

"You leave that to me, dear," said Betty. "I'll spread the word. Half the town would come just to see the spectacle of the North girls working as a team."

"Rude!" said Star.

"Jebediah at the newsagent's has been keeping a book on how long it'll take the 'North nemeses' to throw in the towel."

Some of the locals at nearby tables became flushed and began to concentrate on newspapers and slices of cake. Maggie guessed from their guilty faces that Jebediah's under-the-counter bookmaking business was booming.

"The North nemeses! Is that what they call us?" Simone was offended, but Maggie only laughed.

"I don't know why *you're* so uptight about it—I *live* here! What are the odds that we don't pull it off, Betty?"

"Twenty to one against."

Maggie felt both her eyebrows rise.

"O ye of little faith!" Star retorted.

"Don't shoot the messenger." Betty held her hands up.

"Have you placed a bet?" Simone asked.

"I have indeed. I've got money on you *making* a go of it, so you'd better not let me down. I expect to be picking up a tidy sum on the longest night of the year."

Maggie grinned. "We'd better make sure we get it done, then."

The sounds of chairs scraping against the wooden floor and the sudden mass exodus suggested that the people of Rowan Thorp might just be hedging their bets. Jebediah was about to have an influx of customers.

"What time do you want to hold this meeting?" Betty asked.

"Seven o'clock?" Maggie suggested.

Betty nodded. "Consider it done. Make sure you come with a plan and a list of things you need. People don't like having their time wasted. They'll give help when it's asked, but they won't do it all for you." And with that warning ringing in the sisters' ears, Betty went back to dolloping clotted cream onto the biggest scones Maggie had ever seen.

26

LATER THAT AFTERNOON, Maggie found herself alone in the flat. Patrick had taken Verity to a pantomime in Tunbridge Wells. Her son having never shown any inclination toward panto before, Maggie surmised it must have something to do with a certain young woman called Louella, who was playing the part of Princess Jasmine.

She was taking advantage of this rare peace and quiet to make some notes for the speech they would have to give at the village meeting tomorrow. Simone and Star had both agreed to take their turn to speak, but as usual, the planning had fallen to her.

She'd written out note cards of the things they should include in their appeal. She hoped Betty was right and that people were simply waiting for them to ask. If not, she had no idea how they were going to pull this thing off. She felt sure that if Augustus had had the faintest idea that she was about to be evicted, he would never have tasked her with this. It seemed cruel that she was putting so much energy into a celebration for a community to which she might no longer belong in a few short weeks. She sighed, sipped her tea, and continued to scribble words to rouse the village of Rowan Thorp to action.

The kitchen door opened, and she felt Joe behind her chair.

"Hello. How was your run?"

"Invigorating," he replied with a smile in his voice. "What are you doing?"

"Writing speech notes."

"Speech notes! Do you think you'll need them?"

"I get tongue-tied when I'm nervous."

"Relax," he said, rubbing her shoulders. The cold of his fingers brushing the skin above her collar made her shiver in a good way. "Everyone wants to help you succeed. It isn't a test, nobody's judging you. Just be yourself."

"Easy for *you* to say. *Your* self is all easy charm."

"Okay, firstly, that's not true. And secondly, you have no idea how beguiling you are. Don't get me wrong, it's sexy as hell that you don't recognize it in yourself, but you really have nothing to worry about. From where I'm standing, the people in this community would do anything you asked. You want my advice?"

"Of course."

"Speak from the heart and don't overthink it."

She let out a long breath. "Speak from the heart," she parroted like a mantra.

"Are you finished with your note cards?" he asked.

"Pretty much."

"Good. Come with me."

"Where are we going?" she asked, secretly hoping he would lead her to her bedroom.

"You'll see," he said. He was smiling. "You'll need a coat."

Dammit!

The sky was sepia-tinged gray, and last night's ice looked set to be joined by more tonight. All along the high street, chimneys pushed out curls of smoke, and in one of the back gardens someone was burning leaves. It was only three o'clock but already lamplight spilled out from windows and Christmas trees twinkled behind net curtains.

They hadn't taken the van, so he wasn't whisking her off to a motel somewhere for an afternoon of passion, more the pity. They crossed the road, and Joe led her to the side gate that led into Augustus's garden. This was becoming less romantic by the minute. What was it that he had to show her? A new compost bin? When he took her hand and led her to the end of the garden and into the woods, her hopes rose again, although she would definitely be keeping her coat on if they were going to attempt sex in the wild.

Birds feasted on the tight clusters of ruby berries that clung to spindly branches. Voluminous ferns dotted the ground in clumps between the corpses of woody bluebell stems and tenacious frilly capped fungi. They wandered farther into the wood, until all the sounds of the street outside had been replaced by birdsong, the crunch of leaves, and the scurrying of busy woodland creatures in the thicket. Squirrels flashed past in a whirl of gray bottle-brush tails and disappeared up tree trunks.

They reached a clearing encircled by trees whose topmost branches arched over to form a vaulted ceiling and cast shade on the ground below. In the middle of the clearing a two-person tent had been erected. Maggie felt a stirring in her apple-catcher knickers and was pleased she'd shaved her bikini line this morning. *Not a motel room but an improvement on being bent over sacks of potatoes in the storeroom*, she mused, cheeks flushing at the remembrance.

"And what is this?" she asked, unable to hide her smile.

"This is the tent of intent."

"The what?"

"You avoid talking about us. And I get that it's hard with two kids in the house and the business and now your sisters and all this solstice stuff. So, this is the tent of intent, where we set aside time to talk about us."

"Talk?" She balked. Her hopes for an afternoon of torrid tent sex were deflating fast. Such a pity; she'd never had sex in a tent before.

"I'm not ruling out other activities," he said with a lazy smile and a raised eyebrow. "But in the tent of intent, talk comes first."

"Like dinner before pudding."

"Exactly like that."

"You didn't go for a run at all, did you?"

"No."

She had known her stalling would catch up with her eventually. If she'd discovered his cunning plan sooner, she would have feigned an excuse, but she'd been so eager to get laid, she hadn't bothered to ask. *That'll teach you to think with your lady parts!*

She tried a different tack: she sidled up to him and began to trail kisses down his neck.

"What if my intentions for the tent of intent are physical rather than verbal?" she whispered.

Joe cleared his throat and shook himself, and she was pleased to see she had him flustered. But he took her hands in his and used them to gently push her arm's length away from him.

"My tent, my rules," he said. "We are going to have a grown-up conversation about us."

"God!" she huffed. "So unfair!"

Joe smiled and lifted the flap to the tent. "After you," he said.

She sighed and climbed inside. The floor was lined with cushions and a double sleeping bag lay unzipped across them. She fixed him with a stare as he climbed in beside her.

"That's a little presumptuous," she said, gesturing to the sleeping bag.

Joe settled next to her and zipped up the tent flaps. "Oh, I think not." He grinned knowingly at her. "But first, we talk."

She rolled her eyes as though disinterested, but inside she felt leaden with dread.

"I am in love with you . . ." She opened her mouth to protest, but he held up his hand for her to be quiet. "Please, Mags, I need to tell you this. I have fallen in love with you, and I want to be with you. Properly with you, not sneaking around, not pretending we are only *friends with benefits*. I want people to know about us. I know that you're stressed with the flat and the shop and everything, but losing the building needn't be the end of something. We can make a new start together, find a place and put both our names on the lease. Start a business together. And if that feels like it's too fast or too much for you, then we'll go at any pace you like, so long as we go public."

"Public?"

"I don't want to hide in the shadows like your dirty little secret anymore. I want us to be a couple, and I want the people that matter to us to know it. I want us to sit down with Patrick and Verity and tell them we're going to be a family."

"I haven't even told the kids we're being evicted yet. I think one bombshell is enough to be going along with, don't you?"

"Why would your kids finding out we're together be a bombshell? What we've got going is a good thing, a positive, life-affirming thing. Don't put our relationship in the same category as your eviction."

She pulled her knees up and hid her face in them. She so desperately wanted all the things Joe wanted, but it wasn't realistic. Sooner or later he would see it too and it would be messy, and she would be heartbroken, and Patrick would say "I told you so" and he'd be right. She pulled her head away from her knees and took a deep breath.

"I am not a good bet. You could have anyone you wanted . . ."

"I want you!"

"Joe, I let you talk, now you have to listen to me. I'm forty-four years old. I am not going to have another baby at my age—I don't want one, I've done the baby stuff. Plus, I'm pretty sure I'm perimenopausal, so the clock is ticking on that one anyway, even if I did want another baby, which I absolutely don't. And by the way, do you really want to be with a perimenopausal woman when you could be with some perky little thirtysome-thing? You've seen me have a hot flash, right? It's not pretty and it's probably going to get worse. I can't deny you the chance to have a child of your own. You would make a wonderful father, I won't stand in the way of that. And that's before all the compli-cations that come with me, my kids, and my precarious financial and living status, not to mention a myriad of hang-ups about allowing myself to depend on somebody. If I was on the outside looking in, I would see a whole lotta baggage and very few ben-efits to recommend me."

"Do you love me?" he asked.

"Did you hear all the things I just said? Think seriously about what you would have to lose by being with me."

"I am not afraid of menopause, Maggie."

"That's what they'll start calling me, you know? *Menopause Maggie!* Do you want to be associated with that?"

"Don't do that."

"What?"

"Make a joke to avoid talking about this."

She began to play with a tassel on one of the cushion trims. Boy did he have her number. "Sorry."

"As for your other worries. I'm not fussed about procreating. I mean, kids are great, and I'd be happy to be someone's dad, but I've never felt that push to have children of my own, it's just not a big deal for me. But I know I could be a good father to Verity and, with time, a good friend to Patrick."

Maggie sighed. "I can't commit to someone who might change their mind in a year or two years or five years, I just can't. And that's why I can't tell the kids. Not yet. You have to understand, I loved someone and he died, and everyone else I've loved has left in some way or other. I don't think I could stand that kind of rejection again, I just can't risk it."

Joe had been staring at his feet but now he looked her dead in the eyes.

"So your only objection to being with me is your belief that I am somehow in denial of my need to father my own children, and your worry that I will break your heart because of it, or that I'll die?"

"Well, I mean, obviously that's the oversimplified version, but essentially yes."

"Firstly, I can't promise you I won't die; I'm afraid that's out of my control, but I will do my level best not to, at least not until I'm in my nineties."

She let out an amused huff of a laugh.

"Now let me put something to you. Say I was fifty, never had kids, and told you I never wanted to?"

"Well, that would be different, wouldn't it? You'd be older . . ."

"So, what, at thirty-three years of age I'm too young to know my own mind? Immature for my age?"

"Joe!"

"Answer the question."

"No, obviously not. But . . ."

"I am in love with you, Maggie North. I am in it for the long haul. You are the only woman I see in my future. I promise you that is not going to change. I just. Want. You. Now, I'll ask you again: Do you love me?"

"Joe."

"Do you?"

"Yes! Okay? Yes, I love you! I love you! I love you! But . . ."

She didn't get to finish her very sensible next sentence, because he leaned in and kissed away her protests. He didn't stop kissing her as he pressed her down onto the sleeping bag. Nor did he stop as he undid the clips on her dungarees and expertly divested them both of their underwear. It was a cold afternoon. But inside the tent of intent, Joe and Maggie found a way to keep themselves warm. Twice.

27

BELINDA WAS SEATED in the front row of chairs in the village hall on Monday evening, her purple glitter Dr. Martens just visible below the hem of her black cassock. She gave the sisters an enthusiastic thumbs-up and whisper-shouted "Loud and proud!" as they took their seats on the stage.

Star picked nervously at her nails as the last few stragglers found chairs and got settled. Despite only having put the word out yesterday, they had a full house. Betty was sitting in the middle row surrounded by a few of the WI—Women's Institute—members; others she recognized were sitting with their husbands and significant others. The Cussing Crocheters huddled together in a row near the back, and when Star gave them a tentative wave they stood, each holding aloft a piece of crocheted granny-square bunting that read *GIVE 'EM HELL AND GIVE NO FUCKS* in red and green wool. She'd say this for Rowan Thorp: there was no shortage of strong women in residence. She liked to think that maybe her ancestor Patience North had started the trend. Since returning to Rowan Thorp, Star was finding it easy to fill her daily magic quota.

The crowd began to quiet down.

"Right, remember what we're going to say," whispered Maggie. Star instantly needed the toilet. "I can't do it," she said.

"Neither can I," Simone agreed.

"You have to!" hissed Maggie. "I'm not doing it by myself."

"We'll stand next to you."

"Oh, for goodness' sake!"

Her oldest sister pushed her shoulders back and gathered herself up and Star wished she owned that kind of can-do attitude. In fairness they were all out of their depth: a greengrocer, a physiotherapist, and a wandering hippie, none of them used to public speaking or asking for help.

Only her sisters would notice the slight tremor in Maggie's fingers or the telltale quickening of her breath that belied her nerves as she looked out into the sea of faces smiling back at her. Most of these people had known them since they were kids—some had grown up with them.

"Ahem." Maggie cleared her throat, and the microphone that Sonja had insisted she use reverberated with a deep *boff!* sound, followed by a high-pitched whistling. She jumped and looked helplessly over to Brian Moorhen, who was sitting in the wings and had adjusted the dials on the amp. He motioned for her to continue. "You probably all know by now that as per our dad's final wishes, we are reinstating the winter solstice festival in Rowan Thorp." The audience clapped in encouragement. "You probably *also* know that the three of us are *way* out of our depth on this. We stand before you today to ask for your help. I don't know why the solstice celebrations stopped. Perhaps it simply fell out of favor, as old-fashioned things do . . ."

"Same thing happened with vinyl," piped up Ron Docherty. "And now it's all the rage again! My grandkids are asking for vinyl records for Christmas!"

This was met with murmurs of agreement from the audience.

"And Polaroid cameras!" came another voice, to further agreement.

"And double denim!" called someone else.

"Doesn't make it right, though, Peter!" heckled one of the Cussing Crocheters, giving him a knowing look. Peter unapologetically flicked up the collar of his denim jacket and straightened the denim shirt, which was tucked into stonewashed denim jeans with stiff creases ironed down the middle.

Maggie cleared her throat again. "Yes, well, like those things, our dad obviously felt it was time for us to bring back the winter solstice festival." She looked down at her speech notes with shaking hands. Star slipped her arm around her waist and squeezed, earning her a grateful smile.

"Augustus had a deep love of this village and the people in it. I have asked myself why he tasked my sisters and me with reinstating the winter solstice festival, and aside from because he wanted to be a pain in the bum, I think it is because he didn't want us to drift as he did. I think he wanted us to be ensconced in this community. What better way to ensure Rowan Thorp continues to be a supportive, tight-knit neighborhood for years to come than to install a festival into our village calendar, one that makes us come together every year and join in celebration, like our ancestors did before us? If you can help us make this happen for our community and for our dad, then us North girls will be forever grateful." She let out a shaky breath and stuffed the note cards into her dungarees pocket.

Simone and Star each linked an arm through hers. Star rested her head on Maggie's shoulder, and Simone, who was taller, mirrored the image by resting hers on top of Maggie's head.

"You were amazing," Star whispered.

"I'm so proud of you," echoed Simone.

The response in the hall was overwhelming. The clapping began and seemed like it would never stop. People got up out of their chairs in a standing ovation. Whoops and whistles—the loudest coming from Belinda—and a stamping of feet vibrated through the wooden floorboards all the way up onto the stage. When the applause began to abate, Belinda climbed the steps, cassock swinging, and took over the microphone. The sisters gratefully sank back into their plastic chairs.

"Right, then, you motley lot!" the vicar boomed into the mic. "You've heard the North girls' plea, now let's hear what you've got and see if we can make this thing happen." Star watched as Artemis weaved in and out of the chairs in the hall, as though joining Belinda in chivying the crowd along. "To my mind, God and Mother Nature are one and the same—and both female, obviously." Belinda gave a wink that earned a few disgruntled noises from some of the octogenarian men in the hall. "So let's honor them both by celebrating the winter solstice!" She punched the air like a dog-collared rockstar, and Star marveled at her ability to work the crowd. If this was the kind of energy Belinda brought to the pulpit every Sunday, it was no wonder St. Swithun's had seen an uptick in attendance. "I'll start proceedings by saying I've got a mate who rents out marquees for festivals. I'll tap him up and see if I can wrangle us one. Who's next?"

The Myerses were the first to raise their hands. Gerry had retired with a golden handshake after being something big in the city and these days haunted the local golf club. Parminder Myers was manager of the Rowan Thorp library and what she didn't know about Rowan Thorp wasn't worth knowing. "As soon as we heard about your father's will . . ." Parminder began.

Someone in the audience—possibly Troy—quipped, "Approximately fifteen seconds after it was read."

Parminder gave a little side nod and a wry smile in acceptance of the probable truth of the statement.

She continued: "As soon as we heard that you would be reinstating the winter solstice festival, we changed our habit of making our famous apple jams and chutneys from our little orchard and began the cider-making process."

"It's good stuff," added Gerry, whose ruddy complexion would appear to verify his statement. "It'll put hairs on your chest and blast away the winter chills. And if hairs on your chest isn't your thing, it works wonders on brass; it's brought my fireplace tools up like new."

Parminder, in a stylish kurta over trousers, her salt-and-pepper hair pulled into a loose chignon, flapped her hand good-naturedly at her husband for him to shut up, and continued.

"Historically, the apples from our land were always used for the traditional wassail drink at the winter solstice celebrations, back when it belonged to old Bob Taylor—and even before—and we would be honored if you would accept our homemade cider for the newly reinstated solstice festival."

"And don't worry," added Gerry. "We've got flippin' tons of the stuff, so no whistle will go unwetted!"

Parminder smiled graciously as uproarious clapping and whooping rang through the little wooden hall. Maggie was too stunned to speak, so Star gave an appropriate level of grateful thanks, while Simone crossed *cider for wassail* off their very long to-do list.

Next came the WI, who donated their cake-making services to include the traditional bûche de Noël—chocolate yule log cakes—along with ginger parkin, fruitcakes, and their own take on the Black Forest gâteau, aptly named Rowan Thorp gâteau.

"We've been perfecting the recipe for some time," said Betty. "Mostly made using ingredients that grow nearby, but don't panic, there will be lots of chocolate included."

An audible sigh of relief whisked around the hall. Belinda said they could borrow trestle tables, chairs, and tablecloths from the village hall. Simone was greedily ticking things off the list.

For cooking the feast, Kev and Ryan, owners of the Stag and Hound, offered the use of the pub kitchen, which also happened to be a cookery school. Kat, the Stag and Hound's chef, promised her help and expertise.

Troy donated himself and his bar staff to the cause, promising to be an extra pair of hands on the day for food running, table waiting, and general helping duties. The Stag and Hound and Rowan Tree Inn would close to the public during the feast, and open up again later in the evening, "For a proper good knees-up!"

"Both pubs have applied for a special late-opening license for that night," said Troy. "I dropped the paperwork off personally into a pair of very safe hands." He turned to grin at Anita, a willowy woman with flawless dark skin, round glasses, and a halting manner, who worked in the village council building next to the library.

Anita was a quiet-spoken powerhouse whom everybody knew they could rely on to get a job done, and any who underestimated her did so at their peril. She gave Troy a self-conscious thumbs-up and said, "I am pleased to inform you that your joint applications have been successful." She delicately punched the air and added, "Hurrah to late-night openings!"

The hall exploded again into whoops and cheers.

When the noise had quieted down again, Ellen, leader of the Cussing Crocheters, announced their intentions to dress the banquet table and decorate the marquee with wintry displays. Nobody doubted they would do an excellent job. These women were the Banksys of the crochet world. One never knew when you would wake to find crochet dioramas of village scenes attached to the tops of postboxes or garden gates festooned with crochet characters from popular children's literature.

There was a natural crossover between the various groups and clubs of Rowan Thorp. Some members of the Cussing Crocheters also belonged to the Women's Institute or the historical society or the library book club or the church flower association, and all of them were happy to join forces should the need arise. It seemed the winter solstice warranted just such a call to arms.

One of the farmers who supplied Maggie's shop with free-range eggs promised to donate ten chickens to the feast. This spurred more offers of homegrown garden produce and an abundance of stewed fruits from various households.

Belinda, no stranger to calling upon the parish for volunteers, had come equipped with a clipboard and a stack of paper. As proceedings drew to a close, she urged people to write down their names, contact details, and what they could contribute to the winter solstice event. To the North sisters' delight and relief, there was a queue for the sign-up sheets.

Antonia and Troy walked over to the stage to congratulate them on a successful meeting.

"I'm so excited!" Antonia smiled. "We used to celebrate it

back home. It's so nice to see you all together! You must all come into the pub for a meal." She put an arm around Star. "This one comes in for discounted dinners." She kissed Star's cheek. "But we don't mind. She brings out the Italian mama in me; she makes me want to feed her. Simone, we've hardly seen you since you arrived."

"Oh, I've been around. You know me, always busy." Simone smiled. "We will all definitely come in for dinner before we head our separate ways."

Slowly the community of Rowan Thorp trickled out into the evening and made their way home to warm houses and suppers in front of the TV. Not for the first time, Star felt the pull of the village like a physical force. If, as she was coming to understand, her heart had always truly belonged in Rowan Thorp, perhaps it was time to stop forcing herself to fit elsewhere and accept that this was the place she had been searching for all along.

28

SIMONE WAS ALMOST at the gate to Dalgleish cottage when Star came up beside her, keeping step. There was no one else around; the hubbub of moments before had dissipated and the street was quiet.

"Fancy a hot chocolate at mine?" Star asked.

"Yours?" Sometimes she surprised herself with how easily the snark came.

"You know what I mean."

"I'm pretty tired," said Simone. "I'll see you tomorrow." She was relieved when Star stopped walking beside her. She didn't want to be mean, but she was hanging on by a thread and needed to be alone. She pushed open the gate to the front garden.

"It's because Antonia's pregnant, isn't it?"

Simone stopped dead.

"That's why you haven't been in to see her. It breaks your heart."

She was angry with herself; she thought she'd hidden it so well. The last person she wanted to get into this with was her irresponsible sister. Without turning to face Star, she snapped, "I don't want to talk about it."

"Of course you don't. You're Simone—unflappable, unemotional, and unapproachable. At least, that's how you act. That way no one can see what's really going on in your head."

"Don't try to psychobabble me, Star, I'm married to the real deal."

"And where is your wife?"

Simone still hadn't turned around, but she could feel Star's eyes boring into the back of her head, picture her face set in challenge. "Go away, Star!"

"Sure, push me away like you have with Evette."

Simone spun on her heel. "How dare you! You know nothing about my marriage. Nothing! And you know even less about me."

"Well, that's where you're wrong. I know that you and Evette are the strongest couple I have ever seen. I know that you love each other fiercely. I know that the only reason your wife would have let you come down here to sort Augustus's shit out alone is if she was at her wit's end. And I know that every time you see a pregnant woman or a baby it cracks your heart into a million pieces."

The truth of her words hit Simone like a slap. The shock of it stole her breath and smashed a fist through the wall she'd been hiding behind. Suddenly it was all too much, the repressing and pretending.

She covered her face with her hands as she gasped for air. She wouldn't cry. She wouldn't. Her sadness was a hand around her throat, choking her. She couldn't breathe. She kept trying to pull in air, but it came in tiny gasps she couldn't seem to let back out. She thought her sorrow might actually kill her if she kept it in, but she didn't know what would happen if she let it out. She felt Star wrap her arms around her.

"Let it out," she said softly. "I've got you and I won't let go. Let it out."

"I—I can't," she stammered.

"Yes. You can. You must. You have nothing to lose with me."

She found herself gripping hold of the back of Star's coat, her open mouth pressed to her sister's shoulder as she tried to stifle her sobs. Star was so much smaller than she was and yet she was practically hanging off her and Star was holding her firm.

"What if I can't stop?" she managed to gasp.

"Then I'll wait with you until you can."

Simone sagged further. The weight of this interminable grief wanted to pull her under the earth and bury her alive.

"Come on," Star said. There was a garden bench tucked beneath the front bay window, hidden from the street by an arbor, draped in the forlorn limbs of a rambling rose. Simone allowed herself to be guided to it and almost collapsed onto the cold wood. Just inside the porchway behind the log store was a basket of thick blankets—Mrs. Dalgleish liked to drink her morning coffee sitting on the bench, whatever the weather—and Star hastily grabbed two, shaking them out and wrapping them around Simone before pulling her close.

Simone allowed herself to be swaddled by her baby sister, leaning in and resting her face against Star's chest. Star rocked her gently and she didn't fight it. The tenderness of Star's hands rubbing her back through the thick blankets finally untied the tourniquet around her chest.

For a few minutes she couldn't speak. There was no room for words as the grief spilled out of her in wracking sobs and a high-pitched keen. Her sadness was visceral, primal, every lament convulsive. Star didn't speak either; she simply held her tightly, still rocking her, letting Simone know that she wasn't alone, that she was safe.

It took a long time.

When Simone finally felt as though she could control her voice, she looked up at Star.

"I feel so sad all the time," she said in a voice still shaking with sorrow.

Star nodded, her eyes shining with tears. "I know." She sniffed. "I know."

"I don't know what to do."

"We'll work it out. Together."

She didn't know how long they'd been sitting on the bench beneath the window, but Simone suddenly realized that she was very cold and if she was cold wrapped in two blankets, Star must be freezing. She took a shaky breath.

"Fancy a hot chocolate?" she asked, her voice catching in little hiccupping spasms, the aftermath of crying for so long.

"I thought you'd never ask." Star smiled, the lift of her cheeks causing the tears balancing on her lashes to spill over. She sniffed, wiping her face with her coat sleeve. "Watery eyes. Must be the cold."

"Must be."

With frozen fingers, they managed to get the front door open. Without saying a word, Star helped to build a fire in the hearth and then followed Simone out to the kitchen to make hot chocolate. Simone knew that her sister was staying close while giving her space. She appreciated it. She felt rinsed out. Tonight had been cathartic but exhausting. She wasn't cured. She hadn't expected to be. But her chest felt looser somehow.

They took their drinks back into the sitting room, and Star pulled the two armchairs in front of the fire. They sat: frozen fingers curled around hot mugs, the firelight casting dancing shadows on the walls.

"I don't know where to begin." Simone stared into the flames.

"Start at your first round of IVF. Tell me everything. And I mean everything—don't leave anything out."

"That's going to take a while."

"I've got time." She blew on her hot chocolate and took a sip.

Simone sighed and closed her eyes. What she'd have liked to do was go to bed and sleep for three days, forget any of this happened, go back to stuffing it all down. But Star was right. She needed to say it all and she needed to say it now. To creep back into denial would be easier, but it wasn't going to help her mental health and it certainly wasn't going to save her marriage. Now was the right time.

She started right at the beginning, that first appointment in their local GP surgery. Back when she was convinced that it would be easy, despite all the warnings from friends and health professionals not to get her hopes up. How could she fail to get pregnant when every fiber of her being was telling her she needed to be a mother? It was inconceivable that someone with such a strenuous desire to become pregnant could fail.

The first few sentences stuck in her throat. She felt mortified, like she was making a fuss or being a bore—two things she couldn't abide in others and especially not in herself. But as she went on, her words no longer felt like they were laced with razor blades. The edges smoothed and the words flowed, and she found she couldn't stop.

"We signed up to a fertility clinic that had good feedback from other female couples and then we found a great sperm donor. He's Evette's complexion and hair color but with green eyes, tall, athletic build, and an academic."

"He sounds like a catch. Do you have his number?"

Simone spluttered out a snotty laugh. "You know, I kind of thought we'd done all the hard stuff. I'd had my eggs harvested and we had the donor and I had successful embryos . . . After all that, the actual getting pregnant part felt like a foregone conclusion. It isn't like they didn't warn me, they did, I just didn't imagine it wouldn't work. But they just wouldn't take." Her voice cracked again. "My womb is a fucking inhospitable environment. Why wouldn't they stick?"

Star reached over and took her hands. "I don't know." She said. "I don't know why. But I'm sorry."

Simone looked down at her sister's freckled skin, fingernails bitten down to the quick on child-sized hands. She sniffed and swallowed hard. "So, I've still got embryos frozen. I mean, technically, if we had the money, we could just go on and on trying."

"And would you? If money wasn't an object?"

She started sobbing again. It was like she had an endless supply of tears. "I don't think I can. I think to keep going will end me. It will definitely end my marriage. But at the same time, how can I give up when there's still a chance? When I've still got healthy embryos on ice?"

"Do you need someone to give you permission to stop?"

Simone looked up sharply. *How can she know that?* More tears, falling and falling, dripping off her nose and chin in a stream.

"Yes!" she managed to gasp out.

Star nodded and said quietly, looking into her sister's eyes, "I give you permission to stop. You've tried really hard. And now it's okay to stop."

There was more to be said. Things that she couldn't say to anyone else, even Evette, for shame and fear of judgment. Star listened, never taking her eyes off her, prompting Simone gently when the silences fell and asking questions about terms she was unfamiliar with. After an hour, Simone was tired of the sound of her own voice, and she felt sure her sister must be too, but Star remained attentive.

The hours ticked past. It was gone two o'clock when they climbed the stairs, and Star, dressed in a pair of Simone's pajamas with the legs and sleeves rolled up, climbed into bed with her sister.

"I love you, Twinkle-Star."

"I love you too, Simona-Mona."

They slept in a spoon shape, Star's arm draped over Simone's waist, Simone holding her sister's hand to her chest in both of hers, just like they used to when they were children. Evette had been right: Simone did need her sisters.

29

STAR HAD CALLED a family meeting. She had made up her mind last night, lying beside Simone, who had fallen into a heavy exhausted sleep. But to be sure, she had spent all day listening to her inner self, meditating and testing that her determination stood firm in the cold light of day. It did.

On this chilly Tuesday evening, they were now sitting in the cozy sitting room in Augustus's flat. Star had lit candles along the fireplace and an incense stick smoked lazily on the coffee table.

She had deftly navigated the conversation around to Simone, and after some gentle cajoling, Simone had opened up to Maggie in the way she had to her the night before. It was important that Maggie knew the full story before Star made her proposal.

"The thing is," she began when Simone had finished speaking. Suddenly she felt nervous. "The reason I called this family meeting is because, well, I've thought a lot about it, and I know this is the right thing for me and I think for you too . . ."

"Star, you're jabbering. Stop it," said Simone, blowing her nose after having sobbed unashamedly for the second time in as many days. Maggie was crying too. Their sister's sudden uninhibited displays had left the other two without an emotional rudder, and the result was blubbing havoc.

"Sorry." Star took a breath. "The thing is this. I could have it for you, your baby. I could have your baby for you if you'd like me to."

Maggie let out a breath in surprise, while Simone glared at Star, as though this was a joke that she didn't find funny. When no one spoke for a full minute, the vibe in the room began to feel uncomfortable, and Star wondered if she'd made a monumental faux pas. But she rode the discomfort because this felt like the right thing to do, something she knew she *could* do for her sister that maybe no one else could.

"You mean, like surrogacy?" Maggie ventured.

"Yes. Only, I wouldn't want paying. I might need help with expenses, but otherwise it would be a simple case of me growing your child for you and then handing it over."

"You're serious, aren't you?" said Simone.

"Of course."

More blank looks.

"When you think about it, it's actually very simple. You really want children, you haven't been able to get pregnant yet, and I know that I can get pregnant, so it makes sense."

Simone winced but recovered herself and said cautiously, "A somewhat generalized statement, but there is truth to it, unfortunately."

But Maggie had picked up on something else. "What do you mean 'you know you can get pregnant'?"

Star shifted in her seat. She looked at Simone, unsure how her next confession would go down with a woman who was desperate to have a baby. But if she was going to do this, it would doubtlessly come out in the course of doctors' appointments down the line. She took a deep breath and began. "I was fifteen. I knew I couldn't keep it, I could barely look after myself, I was in no way equipped to have a baby."

She gave her sisters a moment to let this sink in.

"Was it Troy's?" Simone was bristling.

"No, it wasn't Troy's." she snapped. "I existed outside of Rowan Thorp, you know."

"Of course, sorry," said Simone.

Star shook off her annoyance. She'd never really discussed this with anyone, and though she knew she'd done absolutely the right thing, she couldn't help feeling defensive.

"I made a silly mistake with a friend of a friend I'd met at a party. We'd both had too much to drink. I'd never really believed the teachers at school when they'd said it only took one slipup. I sort of thought they were just scaremongering. But there we are."

"Did you tell him? About the pregnancy?" asked Simone.

"No. I didn't see him again after the party. And anyway, what would be the point? He wouldn't have been any more ready to become a parent than I was. It would only have complicated things."

"But your mum helped you . . . sort everything out?" asked Maggie.

"God no! She was in one of her delicate spiritual states. But I told Troy. I'd found out just before I was due to come here for the summer, and although I knew I couldn't keep it, I didn't know how to go about getting an abortion. I couldn't tell my mum. I'd hoped you'd both be here, and I'd tell you and you'd help me. But you weren't. So I blurted it all out to Troy on my first night back, and together we told *his* mum. She was great.

She spoke to Dad, and between us all we managed to get it done. Simone, you always wondered why Troy and I are so close—that's why."

"How did we not know about this?" asked Maggie.

"You weren't around, either of you. You'd pretty much ditched Rowan Thorp by that time." *And me!* she didn't say, but the inference wasn't lost on her sisters. She didn't want to feel her old hurts, but it was impossible not to when reliving them like this.

"You could have called us," said Simone.

Her signature defensiveness acted like a flame to Star's touch paper. She'd made calls, but they were never returned.

"Really?" Her chin jutted out in defiance. "I literally didn't hear from you for like two years, longer for Maggie. You just stopped coming. I was all alone. Summer used to be my favorite time of the year because I got to see my big sisters, and then suddenly it was like I didn't even exist. I was all alone!" she repeated. She thought she had laid those ghosts to rest, but apparently not; the sting of abandonment was fresh.

Simone shook her head and muttered "Shit!" under her breath and then said, "I'm sorry. I didn't think. I was a teenager, wrapped up in my own dramas. I guess I never thought about it from your point of view. I just felt like I was too old for playing in tree houses . . ."

Star took a breath and centered herself. "Look, it's not your fault. I absolutely didn't mean for this to turn all recriminatory. You had your own lives; I totally get it. I just missed you both."

"Oh, Star." Maggie held one hand to her heart. "I'm sorry we weren't there for you. You shouldn't have had to go through that alone."

"I had Troy and his mum, and while Dad didn't exactly talk

about it, he made sure I was comfortable afterward and cooked me soup."

"That's not good enough. We're your sisters! We should have been there. We let you down." Maggie's lip wobbled as she spoke, and Star wondered if she was imagining Verity finding herself in the same predicament and having no one to turn to.

"I did wish you were here with me." Her voice was quiet. "That was probably the time I missed you the most. But I got over it and I'm fine. It was the right thing to do."

Simone nodded. "Of course it was."

"Absolutely," agreed Maggie, dabbing at her eyes. "No question about it."

"So that's how I know I can get pregnant. I know we haven't always seen eye to eye, Simone. And I might be the last person on earth you'd want to carry your child. But the offer is there. No strings attached."

"What if you decide you want to keep the baby?" asked Simone. "You'll have carried it for nine months, you'll have bonded with it."

"I won't," she assured her. "It will be *your* baby. I'm not going to change my mind. I'm healthy; I eat well, I don't smoke, I haven't done drugs for years, not class A's anyway, and I'm still young enough—just. And most importantly, I want to do this for you."

"I—I don't know what to say," Simone stammered. Her face was a flurry of conflicting emotions.

"Quick, put out a news bulletin: *Simone North is lost for words!*" Maggie joked.

"Can I think about it?"

Star laughed. "Of course! You don't have to decide right now.

I'm just telling you that the offer is there, and it's a serious one. Take your time, although you know, don't take so much time that I start the menopause like Maggie."

"Cheers, Star!" Maggie snorted and gave her the bird. "I'll have you know that I am in my prime. Hot flashes, sleepless nights, and yo-yoing emotions aside, perimenopause has gifted me with the libido of a horny teenager."

"No wonder Joe always looks so chipper!"

"I'll need to talk to Evette, is that okay?" Simone was oblivious to the sidetrack the conversation had taken.

"Well, obviously! It's Evette's baby too."

"Of course. I'm not really thinking straight. I have to go," she said. "I need to talk this over with Evette."

"Okay." Star smiled reassuringly.

"Are you all right?" Maggie asked, standing up and taking Simone's arm to steady her. Simone was swaying.

"I'm fine. Just . . . a bit overwhelmed."

"Let us walk you back to the cottage," said Maggie, a crease of concern between her eyebrows.

"No, honestly, I'll be fine. It's just—it's a lot."

"Oh, for fuck's sake, Simone!" Star chuffed. "Stop trying to be so bloody stoic all the time and let us in. You don't have to handle everything on your own!"

"Says the woman who went through an abortion all by herself at fifteen!" said Maggie pointedly.

Star smiled grimly. "Touché."

"Or the woman who didn't tell us she was being evicted because she didn't want to be a burden!" Simone added, regaining some of her composure under the protection of a sister on either side of her.

"Double touché." Maggie laughed.

The sisters linked arms as they walked out into the cold night.

"Let's make a pact," said Star. "Here and now. Let's promise to stop being islands and start being sisters again."

"That's a good pact," said Maggie. "I promise."

"Me too," said Simone, tilting her head to rest it against Star's.

It was a cloudless night and the stars looked as though they'd had their wattage ramped up. There was no wind now, and it was so quiet that the clock in the church tower could be heard ticking its way to midnight. Nothing had changed; each sister's future was still as uncertain as it had been the day before—maybe more so. But that night, with the stars above their heads and promises warming their hearts, their worries didn't seem quite as insurmountable.

HER SISTERS HAD gone, and Simone was alone with her thoughts in the cottage, phone in hand, ready to call Evette. A mental ravine of possibility had opened up before her and stopped her in her tracks. She was looking down into it, her feet right on the edge of a precipice, deciding if she was brave enough to jump. Could they do this? Could it be as simple as Star was making it out to be? They'd have to find the money for the embryo transfer, which wouldn't be easy. Okay, so she wouldn't be pregnant herself, but it would be her egg, her baby, and her own biological sister carrying her child for her.

Her mind flip-flopped between the positives and the dangers. Obviously, she would need to make sure that Star fully understood the implications of what she was proposing to undertake. She'd always been impulsive, often to her own detriment, and this wasn't something to be taken lightly; if they went down this road, sudden cold feet would have dire consequences. Simone's head began to swim. It was too much. All of it. The hope and the worry were piling in on her from a great height and she couldn't breathe—she was drowning in a cacophony of feelings that were too big.

Unlike Star, she was not *in tune* with the universe, she did not entrust things to fate. Simone was measured and methodical. Lying back on the sofa, she took a calming breath and began to compartmentalize her feelings. The worries went in one box, the excitement went in another, and so she continued, sorting her mind in this way until all that was left was the very essence of the issue: herself and Star. And then she knew. Star was many things, but above all she was her sister, and she knew within her very atoms that her sister would rather break her own heart a million times than risk Simone's. She allowed the calm acknowledgment to flow through her.

This was how she was going to have her baby.

She pressed the call button on her phone and waited for her wife to pick up.

AT FIRST STAR couldn't place the vibrating sound that had punctured her sleep. When she finally realized it was her phone ringing, she snatched it up clumsily as though she were wearing mittens and saw that the time was nearly 2 a.m. No good phone calls ever happened in the dead of night.

"Hello? What's wrong? Who is it?" she asked in disorientation and panic.

"It's Evette. Don't worry, nothing's wrong. I'm sorry to call you so late, again, but it couldn't wait. I need to talk to you."

Star flicked on the bedside lamp and pulled herself up to sitting, blinking in the light. "Okay. Good morning, Evette. What do you need?"

"Are you serious? About being a surrogate for us?"

"Yes."

"You don't think you're rushing into this? I mean, you only found out a few days ago that we were even trying for a baby. I'm not sure you've had enough time to properly think through the implications. It's a huge decision. Life-changing for you. Your world will be tipped on its head, your body will be irrevocably changed, your hormones will be all over the place. It could affect your future relationships. And that's before we get to how you will feel handing over a child that you've carried for nine months. Or the fact that you will have to watch it grow up from afar. Have you thought about any of these things? I don't want to make accusations, but are you sure you're not being irresponsible with your sister's feelings, and mine? Simone is desperate to be a mother and she feels like you've offered her a lifeline. I know it comes from a place of love, but you can't say things like that off the cuff. It isn't fair. Worse than that, it's unkind."

"Are you finished?" Star asked when the line had finally gone quiet. She guessed from the way Evette—usually a thoughtful, measured speaker—had blurted it all out that she had been stewing for a while.

"For the moment."

She could hear the annoyance in Evette's voice. She thought she was a flake, just like everyone else did. "I understand your concerns. And I know it *seems* quick and impulsive."

"It is without question both of those things, Star."

She had never heard Evette speak so sternly. "Let me give you some background. I didn't tell Simone this because, well, the shock of my offer seemed to knock the stuffing out of her. I was going to discuss it with her when she'd had some time to regroup."

"Okay." Evette was listening.

"I realized a long time ago that having children wasn't a priority for me. I also realized that I had all these perfectly good eggs that I might never need and that I could help someone who really *did* want children. So, I began donating them to a fertility clinic. Long story short, someone at the clinic introduced me to a couple who were thinking about surrogacy. She suffered from endometriosis and was unlikely to ever conceive. I'd not really considered it before, but once I started looking into it, I decided that surrogacy was something I could do, something I *wanted* to do, not as a career or anything, but just once to help someone who needed it. Anyway, there was lots of back-and-forth and eventually everything was in place, and we agreed on a date for insemination. Only, that week, she found out that against all the odds, she was pregnant. It was kind of a miracle. And naturally my services were surplus to requirement."

"Was everything okay? For the couple, with the pregnancy, I mean?"

"Everything was perfect. They have a little girl, Tansy, and I am her godmother."

Evette let out a long sigh.

"I get how, for you, this seems to have come out of nowhere," Star continued. "But I know what I'm getting into, what I'm offering. I was happy to do it for relative strangers. I am ecstatic to be able to do it for my sister. Do you believe in fate?"

"I don't know. I believe in the power of coincidence."

"Good enough. Once I'd learned about surrogacy, I knew without a doubt that I was meant to help someone else become a parent. I'd thought it was my calling to help Tansy's parents, but fate had someone else in mind. Don't you think it's crazy that all the while Simone's been trying to get pregnant, I've been waiting to become a surrogate? I had no idea until the other night that you guys were even trying for a baby. I mean, hey, why would my sister tell *me*? I'm like her least favorite person. And yet, some higher force seems to want us to work together."

"You're not her *least* favorite person. That honor is reserved for the barista who always gets her order wrong, even though she orders the same thing *every* morning."

Star laughed, mostly out of relief that the anger had gone out of Evette's tone. "Yes, I can see how that would annoy my sister."

"Thank you for talking to me. There's still so much to think about."

"There is no hurry and no pressure. All I'm doing is giving you another option."

"Thank you. I'm sorry for waking you."

"It's fine."

"Well, good night."

"Don't let the bedbugs bite."

Star snuggled back down under the duvet. She could hear the wall of clocks in the shop downstairs ticking along together. The old water pipes creaked and the naked branches on the tree outside her window tapped and swished against the glass. These were the sounds of home to her. To Simone and Maggie, this building was always a holiday house, temporary, a brief respite from the normalcy of their home lives. Life with Perdita wasn't routine or suburban. They lived in lots of places, sometimes caravans, sometimes yurts, periodically during winters they rented flats, ready furnished with someone else's castoffs. The one and only thing in her childhood that never changed was this house. And she loved it.

The idea of selling it was heart-wrenching. She couldn't tell Maggie or Simone. It wouldn't be fair; they needed the money. *She* needed the money. All the same, she couldn't imagine this house not belonging to her in some way. To lose this house would be to lose the only dependable part of her life.

30

MAGGIE BURST INTO the curios shop on Wednesday morning and began speaking without preamble. She had woken up in the early hours worrying about her eviction and the festival and been unable to get back to sleep. She had also been drinking coffee since 5 a.m., and now she had to keep her caffeine levels topped up or risk a slump before lunchtime.

"Okay, I've just heard from Belinda, and her festival contact has come through with the marquee. It's an old one that he doesn't rent out anymore, so he'll let us borrow it for free, and since he's a big fan of Belinda, he'll loan us his team to build the thing as well. He'll deliver the marquee on Monday the seventeenth. It's going to need decorating, of course. We need to make it cozy and festive on a budget, and we'll need volunteers. Do we have posters? How are we on garlands? The flower association? Ideas? I've been googling edible decorations for animals and birds. I don't know how many takers we're going to get for helping to make them, but we are going to need ingredients. I've spoken to Vanessa this morning, and she's arranged to get us the funds we'll need. I've borrowed Kat's business loyalty card for the cash and carry, as I think we'll need to buy bulk. Simone, how are we doing on dates for things?"

"That was intense," said Star. "Good morning, Maggie."

"No time!" she trilled.

Simone was sitting in an armchair with her laptop open, Artemis stretched lazily in the gap between her stomach and the computer. Cat and sister eyed her with the same torpor.

"You are manic. Have a chamomile tea and calm the fuck down. I'm working on a spreadsheet and timetable of things that need doing. I'm also mocking up a poster to advertise the decoration making, which I've set for the eighteenth, as the schools will have gone on break, and which hopefully can happen in the marquee if it's getting delivered on the seventeenth. The flower association are already briefed and ready for garlands, as are the Cussing Crocheters; I met both Ellen and Anita in the queue for coffee at Betty's this morning. Then on the nineteenth we've got tree decorating in the woods from six p.m. In between times we've got to organize the food. And the rest happens on the evening of the twenty-first."

"We are going to be so busy." Maggie rubbed her forehead. "The twenty-first is going to be a nightmare day. Where are we on the running order for that?" She looked at Star, who put down the loupe she'd been using to date a gold mourning ring—complete with a lock of the deceased's hair visible beneath a cabochon crystal—and picked up her phone.

"Do you actually know what you're doing with that thing?" Maggie asked, motioning to the loupe, which Star had taken to wearing permanently around her neck.

"As a matter of fact, I do." She touched the loupe, smiling. "It's easy once you know how. Duncan is a very good teacher."

"It's not that easy at all," Duncan interjected. "She's being modest. I've never known anyone to pick it all up so quickly! I show her how to do something once and she's got it." His expression was one of a man well and truly smitten.

"Oh my god, these two." Simone gave Maggie a pained look. "It's like being in an episode of *The Brady Bunch*. They're *nice* to each other all day long."

"Maybe some of it will rub off on you." Star poked her tongue out at her sister, who poked hers right back.

"Star's a natural," Duncan continued, clearly not finished gushing. "She has a great eye for antiques. I'm serious, Sotheby's would snap her up."

"Patience North would be proud," said Simone. "Genuinely," she added for clarification.

"Forget Patience—*I'm* proud," added Maggie.

Star flushed a deep pink and concentrated on her phone. "Okay." She cleared her throat and read from the screen. "Everyone to assemble in the garden at four p.m. for bonfire lighting. I think we need professionals for this; you know, safety and whatnot. Then over to the marquee at four thirtyish. Allow two to three hours for the banquet. Then the procession with some wassailing around the trees and a bit of a singsong, which ends up in the pubs and we all get pissed and go to bed."

"Good call. Simone?"

"On it." Simone tapped something into her spreadsheet. "On my way to get the posters printed I'll drop in and ask Betty if she knows anyone who's good with fire; there must be at least one qualified pyromaniac in the village."

Maggie nodded. "If we're going to have a proper bonfire to dance around, we really ought to start collecting things we can burn; otherwise we'll be cavorting around a wastepaper bin."

"I'll add it to the spreadsheet." Simone began tapping away at her keyboard again.

"So, I was thinking, how great would it be if we booked a folk band for the evening? Someone who knows all the old songs?" said Star.

"Oh my gosh, that would be perfect!" Maggie was beginning to picture how all this would look. A folk band with fiddles and tambourines would definitely fit with what she had in mind. "But I'm not sure we can afford to hire a band."

"I used to date a guy in a traveling folk band," said Star.

"Of course you did," butted in Simone, but she was smiling.

Star didn't skip a beat. "They were really good. I was thinking, if I could track him down, maybe we could ask the band to play at the festival." At his desk, Duncan winced ever so slightly. "When I knew them, they pretty much played for food and drinks."

"Now that we *can* do." Maggie smiled. "We'll be feeding the five thousand anyway; a few more mouths won't make a dent."

"Great, I'll get right on it." Star smiled and scribbled on a notepad.

"I don't want to jinx it, but it's starting to sound like we have a plan!" said Simone.

Maggie rubbed her head again and let out a puff of breath. "There's still a hell of a lot to organize until the get-pissed-and-go-to-bed part."

"It'll be fine." Star waved a flippant hand.

"Can I ask, what exactly is wassailing?" asked Duncan, looking up from the ledger. "It sounds like we'll be doing a lot of it; I just what want to be clear on what I'm getting into. If wassail is like mulled cider, is wassailing just the act of glugging it back?"

"I'll hand you over to our resident hippie," Simone said, without making it sound at all like an insult.

Star picked up the mantle and began explaining.

"So, traditionally people wassailed—sang and danced— around orchards to frighten off the bad spirits who caused bad harvests and to entice the good ones, who bring protection and plentiful crops. Kind of like a blessing ceremony with hot alcohol. For some communities, wassailing was more like caroling, going from door to door and singing and toasting the neighbors. But I think because Rowan Thorp was always a rural community, our ancestors probably did the former, to ensure a plentiful harvest."

Simone lifted one eyebrow as though marginally impressed.

"I can see how that would make sense," said Duncan. "It's like hedging your bets."

"Exactly," agreed Star. "And you can get drunk while you're doing it, so it's a win-win. And also, why wouldn't you? I mean, in the days before electricity when the winter nights must have seemed interminable, it would have been lovely to have a big party with singing and dancing and booze."

"As a historian of sorts, I am very much looking forward to being immersed in my first pagan ritual." Duncan looked genuinely excited.

"I'd be looking forward to it a lot more if we weren't organizing it," said Maggie glibly.

"Give us a list, and Star and I will go to the cash and carry and get a head start on provisions," Simone said. It was evident that Maggie was beginning to spiral. "You go back to work and leave this with us."

"Are you sure?"

"Maggie, there's no point in us being here if you're just going to keep doing everything by yourself."

"Simone's right. We're not juggling jobs and kids and *sexy grocers*." Star gave a wink. "Let us help you."

TWO HOURS LATER, having tapped Vanessa up for a chunk of cash from the solstice kitty, Star and Simone emerged from the sliding doors of the cash and carry pushing a flatbed trolley loaded with enough birdseed to feed all the robins in southeast England and enough mixed nuts to satisfy all the vegetarians in the same catchment.

When the boot was fully loaded, they started back toward Rowan Thorp.

"Evette called me to ask if I was serious about being a surrogate," Star said.

"Did she? When?"

"Last night. She was worried that I was being flippant with your feelings."

"Sorry. She can be overprotective."

"Don't be sorry. I'm glad she is. It means she's looking out for you and that makes me happy."

"Who looks out for you?"

"Oh, I look out for myself. I am quite self-sufficient."

They were tootling along behind a tractor they'd encountered almost as soon as they'd left the main roads. Simone was keeping her distance after a stone had flicked up out of one of its huge wheels and chipped the corner of her windscreen.

"Do you ever think about doing more with your life? You're an intelligent woman. You could be anything you want to be."

Star threw her arms up in exasperation. "I'm so sick of people saying that to me. It's such a cliché, 'you could be anything you want to be.' How? I barely went to school. The knowledge I have doesn't translate to a recognized education and doesn't mean shit in an interview. In fact, it doesn't even get you through the door. But all of that is beside the point because I don't want that life. I want to live small and happy, I want to leave only the tiniest footprint on the world. Why isn't that something to aspire to? My life goal is to feel contentment; to me that's the only thing worth striving for."

For once Simone didn't argue with her. "You're right. I am judging you through the same lens that I view myself. That's the way I'm programmed. In my family, achievements were measured by certificates and qualifications that could be framed and quantified. Sometimes I think my mum studied art less for the love of it and more to conquer the enigma of it. 'Contentment' could only be achieved through accomplishment; anything less would simply be laziness."

"But surely that's relative, or at least dependent on your definition of 'contentment.' Dad was at his most content when he lived out of his van."

"Our father was the reason my mum pushed me so hard. She was terrified I'd inherit his lackadaisical nature."

"No chance of that."

Simone laughed grimly.

"Whatever could have made Rene fall for Dad? I mean, I can totally see it with my mum—two stoned wanderers, makes sense. And even Lilibeth I can sort of see; she was older and lonely, and Dad was friendly. But your mum? What was that all about?"

"God only knows. I can only imagine that he must have talked her into bed."

"He was a very smart man," Star agreed.

"Knowledge is like catnip for my mother."

"And here we both are. Unlikely sisters."

Simone smiled at her baby sister. "I'm sorry I wasn't there that summer."

Star was quiet for a moment. "Thank you."

"I was trying to figure out what I was doing that year that kept me from coming to Rowan Thorp. And the answer is not very satisfactory. I wasn't doing anything much, hanging out with friends and going to parties, nothing that was worth leaving you to go through that on your own." She bit her lip as though considering whether to go on. "I know that you tried to reach out to me. I remember my mum saying you'd called the house and I didn't call you back. I was feeling guilty about not coming down and I didn't want to have to talk to you because I knew I'd feel worse. And now I feel *really* bad. If only I'd not been so selfish."

This was an unexpected admission from her sister. She hadn't meant to make her feel bad; she'd only wanted her to understand that she was serious about her offer.

"It's in the past. Looking back, I can see why you wouldn't want to come down."

"It must have been frightening."

"Yeah. I was terrified." Star gave a little half laugh, to lessen the awfulness. "I'd so hoped you'd be there; I knew you and Maggie would help me. And when you weren't . . ." She'd felt so lost. That whole summer had a nightmarish quality to it. "Well, it all turned out in the end. Luckily I was only six or seven weeks gone, so it was very straightforward. It could have been a lot worse."

Simone pursed her lips. "And Perdita never knew?"

"No. She wasn't neglectful, exactly; she is a very loving person, she just wasn't very present. She never would have coped."

"*She* wouldn't have coped? You were just a kid! You deserved better."

Star shrugged. Laying blame never solved anything.

They sat for a while in companiable silence as they crawled along behind the tractor. This was new. Simone and Star were only usually silent with each other because they'd had a falling out or simply had nothing to say to each other, nice or otherwise. Star couldn't remember a time since childhood when they had been simply happy to sit quietly and enjoy being together. It was nice. Peaceful. She sent a little prayer of thanks to the universe.

31

IT WAS THE thirteenth of December—unlucky for some, which was rather how Patrick felt when he was woken by Maggie that morning. She had entered his bedroom, proffering hot tea and using the voice she reserved for when she was going to ask him to do something he didn't want to do.

"You want me to do what?" His hair was mussed, and his eyes puffed with sleep. Maggie suspected he'd had another heavy night with his old school friends.

"Dig a pit in Granddad's garden."

"Have you killed someone?"

"Not yet."

"What day is it?"

"Thursday. Why does this matter? Are you unable to dig pits on Thursdays? Or do you have a pressing engagement?"

"Ugh! I hate it when you're so chirpy in the mornings."

"I'll try to be meaner. We need a pit dug before we start laying the bonfire wood in it. I am reliably informed by Milton and Harini, our resident fire-safety experts, that this is an important measure. They're going to supervise you. I've been over there this morning, and they've already measured it all out for you."

Rowan Thorp possessed one retired firefighter, Milton—Doreen's husband—and one Harini, who worked full-time as manager of the post office and also part-time as a firefighter for the surrounding rural areas.

"Arrrghh," Patrick groaned dramatically. "Why me?"

"Because you're young and haven't yet slipped any discs in your spine or recently had a gallstone removed. Please, love. I really can't have Milton and Harini digging holes with their various ailments."

He rolled over in bed and pulled his head under the duvet.

"Make Joe do it, and I'll help you out in the shop," he mumbled.

"Okay fine, I'll do that. Sorry to have woken you at the crack of *nine a.m.*," she said sarcastically. She moved to the bedroom door, then added, "Harini said her granddaughter is coming to help. You might know her. Her name's Louella?" she said archly. "I'll just call and tell them to expect Joe instead of you because you don't like getting up."

Patrick's head popped out from under the duvet just as she was stroking her imaginary evil-genius beard.

"No fair," he said, laughing. "I'm complaining to the ombudsman for devious mothers."

She shrugged, all innocence. "*I* didn't invite her. But wouldn't it be a shame for Louella to miss out on all those muscles you've been building up in the uni gym?"

Patrick scowled and then grinned. "Give me half an hour," he said.

Maggie left the room rubbing her hands together. "One job down, eight hundred and sixty-two left to go," she said to herself.

KAT ALMOST FELL into the greengrocer's, the bell jangling furiously above her. "I've run out of onions!" she panted. "I'm in the middle of making a savory tart."

"Didn't I drop, like, ten kilos of onions into you this morning?" Maggie laughed.

"Yeah," agreed Kat, maniacally stuffing her arms full with bunches of coriander and parsley. "But most of those went into the French onion soup special, and then I made tomato sauce for meatballs, and now I haven't enough to caramelize for the tarts."

"Blimey." Maggie began to tip onions into the burlap bag Kat had thrust at her.

By now Kat had added several vines of cherry tomatoes and had a large daikon radish tucked in her armpit. Maggie held out a cardboard box, and Kat gratefully dropped her spoils in.

"How's it all going with the solstice arrangements and the curios shop?"

"Oh, you know, getting there slowly but surely."

"Must be nice having your sisters back."

"Do you know, I never thought I'd say this, but it actually is."

Saskia Brannigan—Vanessa's mum—came in for a kilo of clementines and some brussels sprouts, followed by Ellen of Cussing Crocheters infamy.

"Here," said Ellen, thrusting a paper bag at Maggie. "I've made you something."

Maggie opened the bag and pulled out a crochet hat with crochet mistletoe in the place of the more traditional bobble on the top and the words *kiss me, you twat* embroidered around the band.

"Wow. Thank you, it's . . ."

"It's a double whammy. Keep you warm in the shop and keep that Joe thinking about your lips." Ellen waggled her eyebrows.

"Oh!" Maggie was taken aback. Despite their afternoon in the tent of intent, she hadn't yet told anyone that she and Joe were official.

"He's terribly handsome," agreed Saskia. "You'd make a lovely couple."

"Um, thank you," she said awkwardly.

"I've seen people giving him the eye," said Ellen. "There's some lonely ladies who make a special effort when they know young Joe will be delivering their veg box."

Really? Should she start doing all the deliveries herself? Ellen broke her train of thought by asking, "Now does Simone do private consultations? Apparently, she's got 'healing hands' and I've got this hip, you see . . ."

THREE HOURS AFTER he'd left, Patrick strolled back into the shop, looking mightily pleased with himself. He plucked a green apple from a basket, spun it around in his palm, and took a bite, wiping the juice off his chin with the back of his hand.

"How did you get on? All done?" Maggie asked.

"Yep. I dug it all out and then we built up the outside edges with big stones and old bricks we found around the place."

"And was Louella there?"

Patrick grinned and his windburned cheeks turned pinker.

"You'd better go easy on that girl's heart. I've seen Harini throw a grown man over her shoulder after one too many G and T's."

"Ahh, don't worry, Harini loves me," he said with due smugness. He finished devouring the apple and bowled the spindly core across the room, where it landed in the bin. "And anyway, you've been lecturing me about being careful with people's hearts since I was like seven. But I can't be held responsible for all the lovesick ladies I leave in my wake just by being me." He puffed out his chest and struck a caricature muscleman pose.

"It's strange." She rubbed her chin musingly. "I don't remember raising you to be such a cocky little shit, but there we are."

Patrick laughed and grabbed a banana.

"Stop eating all my profits!"

He held his arms wide, all innocence. "I'm just trying to get my five-a-day, Ma."

"Can't you eat the bruised ones?"

He pulled a disgusted face and then said, "Hand them over and I'll make chocolate banana bread if you like?"

"You know how to make banana bread?"

"Don't look so surprised. I cook a lot at uni. How else will I impress women?"

She grabbed a bowl of dark brown bananas she'd set aside as freebies for customers who like to bake and handed it to Patrick. "Here you go, smarty pants. Knock yourself out." She remembered Ellen and Saskia's comments earlier. "Patrick?"

"Yeah?"

"Joe and I." *Oh god, how I am supposed to do this?* "We're, well, we're a bit more than just friends." This was excruciating. Why did she suddenly feel like a teenager?

Patrick took a measured breath. He managed to look mature and awkward at the same time. "I guessed as much," he said finally. "Is it serious?"

"I don't know," she lied, and hated herself for it.

Patrick brightened. "If it makes you happy, then I'm good

with that." There was a pause. "I just worry because you've put your faith in men before who didn't deserve it."

That was an understatement.

"I understand your concerns, my darling. We're just enjoying each other's company for now." It was better to make it seem casual, just in case. Despite her reasoning, she couldn't help feeling as though she was betraying Joe by downplaying things between them. She added guiltily, "But I'd like you to keep an open mind."

He nodded. "Okay. I'll try."

"Thank you."

He smiled self-consciously and left the shop clutching his bowl of brown bananas. He'd grown into a good man.

She'd not been much older than Patrick when she'd met Josh. She couldn't remember feeling that young; Josh's death had rendered her careworn before her time. On her young shoulders, the label "widow" had weighed heavy and she'd reacted by hurling herself into the path of reckless men in the hopes that she could shake off her own morbid title.

Now in her forties, she felt more comfortable in her own skin than ever before. She didn't need to try to be anything other than her herself, and Joe seemed to love her just as she was. So why couldn't she throw herself in completely? Though it had felt like a big step telling Patrick, she knew she was holding back by giving him a pared-down version of her feelings for Joe. Neither of them deserved that. She might be older and wiser than her twentysomething self, but she'd carried some of her fears down the decades with her, and those ghosts were proving hard to shake.

32

OVER THE LAST couple of days, donations for the bonfire had grown exponentially, and Maggie's fear that they would be dancing around a wastepaper basket was put to rest. Star left the gate open at the side of the shop for people to drop off their unwanted wood in the garden and then she and Duncan would leave the shop at intervals to pile the wood as Milton had shown them.

They'd been growing closer ever since he kissed her cheek. But as of yet there had been no actual snogging. This was very confusing for Star, whom men usually wanted to snog whether she liked them or not.

They spent all day every day together in the shop, and she learned everything he taught her as though by osmosis. She was thrilled by his knowledge and the history and provenance of the things in her father's curiosity shop. After a lifetime of happily bobbing around in her head untroubled, her brain was suddenly parched and the only thing that quenched it was dousing it with information.

She was acutely aware that while Duncan had unwittingly

ignited a passion within her, she brought little to the party. True, she had traveled a lot, she'd had no shortage of adventures, some which were best kept to herself, but all she could do with these was to tell them as stories and amusing anecdotes, like Augustus used to do with her. She had nothing tangible to offer, no skills to captivate a man like Duncan.

For his part, he didn't seem unhappy to be spending so much time with her, far from it; he arrived early each morning and often didn't leave until well into the evening. On more than one occasion, they had ended the day having dinner together. Yet at the end of the night, he would only kiss her cheek chastely. She was beginning to lose hope.

On Saturday afternoon, they were back out in the garden. It was freezing cold, and they were both muffled up in big coats. The sky was a strange camel color, which cast an eerie light over everything. The forecast promised a heavy frost with the possibility of snow.

The weekend had brought a flurry of wood donations, and they were busily arranging them on the growing pyre. Star had successfully wedged an old headboard into a gap when Duncan gave a yelp and jumped away from the stack as though he'd been burned.

"Are you okay?" she asked.

He was clutching his left hand with his right. His eyes were huge. "S-splinter," he stammered. "Big one."

"Here, let me see." She went to him and eased his hand away from his chest.

She didn't want to alarm him, but it was the biggest splinter she had ever seen in her life and it was embedded deep into the fleshy part at the base of his thumb.

"It's bad, isn't it?" he said, his head turned determinedly away. He had begun to take very deep breaths and seemed a little unsteady on his feet.

"*No*." She tried to inject some jolly nonchalance into her voice as she eyed the giant splinter. "It's no big deal. We will have to get it out, though."

At this, Duncan began to sway, and she noticed a sheen of sweat on his forehead. He was a tall man and had a long way to fall if he passed out. She didn't fancy her chances of getting him up to the flat, or at this point even back into the shop.

"I've gone hot," he said. "Really hot." He didn't sound like himself at all.

"I tell you what," she coaxed, "why don't we sit you down over here." She led him away from the pyre and over to a mossy bench by the garden wall. Duncan allowed himself to be guided and helped to sit. "Maybe pop your head between your knees for a couple of minutes while I go and get the first aid kit."

He did as he was told. "I feel sick," he groaned from between his legs. His splinter hand rested limply on the bench.

"I know you do, it's okay. You've had a nasty shock and it's made you feel a bit faint, that's all. You're going to be fine. I'm going to fix you right up."

"I feel stupid. I'm sorry," he managed between deep breaths.

"Don't apologize. This is a perfectly natural reaction to finding a foreign body in your body."

Duncan moaned in response. She rubbed his back.

"You're okay," she cooed. "Everything is going to be fine. Will you be all right if I nip up to the flat to get supplies?"

He gave a strangled "Yeah." Followed by, "I'm just going to keep breathing."

"Always best to," she said, and walked casually away until she was sure he couldn't see her, and then she broke into a sprint.

In the flat she grabbed a bowl of water, a pair of tweezers, some antiseptic, and the biggest plasters she could find. Then she changed her mind and ditched the plasters for some gauze and a bandage. That mother splinter was going to leave a hole.

She raced back downstairs to find Duncan exactly as she had left him.

"I'm back," she said quietly.

"My ears are whistling."

"Righty-ho. Now, do you want me to tell you what I'm doing, or shall I just do it?"

He made a retching sound but recovered himself. "Probably better to just do it," he whimpered.

"Hold very still, okay?"

"Very still," he echoed, his head wedged firmly between his legs.

Star took his hand and he groaned.

"Very still."

"Still," he whispered.

She picked up the tweezers and gently secured them over the end of the splinter. She didn't want to leave any wood behind, which could cause infection later, so she had to do this slowly.

Very gently she began to ease the splinter out. He whimpered and she made soothing noises and continued to tease the wood shard out of his hand. It took a while, but at last the end of the splinter relinquished its hold and came free. She looked carefully into the wound and at the splinter itself, but there was nothing left behind. She let out a sigh of relief.

"All done," she said soothingly.

"Really?"

He raised his head. He looked first at the splinter she held proudly between the tweezers and then at his palm. A glob of thick red blood pushed out of the hole, and he immediately fainted.

"Whoa!" She had just enough time to drop the tweezers as he flopped in a lazy forward roll off the bench onto the grass. Luckily his puffer jacket softened his fall. She managed to stop him from hitting his head and deftly rolled him into the recovery position. She pulled off her coat and laid it over him. This wasn't her first roller coaster with a fainter; when you'd been to as many festivals as Star had, you saw a lot of minor medical incidents.

She set about washing and dressing the wound. By the time Duncan began to come around, she was securing the clean white bandage and all traces of blood had been removed.

He groaned and rubbed his head. "What happened?" he asked, his voice muffled with confusion.

"You fainted. But you're all right now."

"Oh no, how embarrassing," he moaned.

"Don't be silly. It could happen to anyone."

He went to get up.

"Easy does it," she said gently, helping him up to sitting. "Sit for a while. I'll make you a nice cup of sweet tea to get your blood sugar back up."

He sat with his back against the wall, and Star sat down next to him, their knees touching.

"I'm wearing your coat," he said.

"I didn't want you to catch cold."

He looked down at his bandaged hand. "You fixed me."

"It's no big deal." She smiled. "It'll smart for a few days, but the splinter came out clean. I can come to the pub and change your dressing for you in the morning before you go to your sister's for Sunday lunch."

"You're the most amazing woman I've ever met."

"You might be delirious; I only got a splinter out." She laughed. But before she could say another word, Duncan leaned over and kissed her, long and sweet. His lips were as soft as she'd imagined, and when he deepened the kiss, Star wondered if *she* might faint. When they parted, she was indeed light-headed.

"I've wanted to do that since the day I met you," he said quietly.

"Why didn't you?"

"Because I wasn't sure that someone like you would be interested in someone like me."

"What? Why?" She laughed. "I'm nobody . . ."

Duncan put his finger to her lips. "Don't do that," he said. "You always put yourself down. You are fascinating. You only ever have to be told a thing once and you understand it and remember it like you've known it for years. You're kind and you're *always* thinking about other people, putting yourself in their place and seeing things from their perspective. Nothing fazes you. Not even giant fainting men. You laugh *all* the time, and it sounds like sunshine, and when you smile the freckles at the edge of your right eye line up to form a leaf shape."

No one had ever said anything like that to her before. She tried to speak around the finger pressed to her mouth but found she had no words.

"You have become somebody very special to me, Star North," he said. And he kissed her again.

They left the pyre to manage itself, and after a cup of strong sweet tea each, Star and Duncan took each other on their first official date, to the Stag and Hound.

33

VERITY WAS HOLDING court in the greengrocer's. Last night she had performed as a singing pomegranate in the school play, and the praise had gone to her head. It had also marked the last day of school, which only added to her high spirits. She was more than happy to recite her lines this Saturday afternoon for any customers who confessed they hadn't been fortunate enough to see her play.

"Aunty Simone, what did you like best about the play?"

Maggie had asked her not to indulge her daughter's ego, but Simone couldn't resist. Why shouldn't Verity be proud of herself?

"Definitely your pomegranate scenes. I have never heard such an eloquent fruit."

Maggie rolled her eyes. Verity smiled, satisfied, and continued making multicolored pom-poms from the basket of wool donated to the cause by the Cussing Crocheters. As she finished each one, she dropped them into a box at Simone's feet. She was grateful that her niece was so open to embracing her presence.

Simone was perched on a crate, tying pine cones, pom-poms, and crochet poinsettia flowers into long garlands of twisted spruce and ivy. The church flower association had kindly made the garlands yesterday, and Anita and Sonja had dropped them into Maggie's shop this morning for embellishments, ready for the marquee to go up on Monday. They took up a third of the shop's floor space, coiled like giant green anacondas, so Maggie had to keep stepping over them to reach her produce.

"How many of these are there?" Simone looked at the snaking pile, wondering if she was going to give herself a repetitive strain injury from tying knots.

"About seventy," Maggie said, sitting on a crate next to her and picking up a garland. "They've got to stretch widthwise along the length of the marquee."

"Shit the bed!" she exclaimed. "We'll be at this till kingdom come."

"Uh! That's a swear! Mama, Aunty Simone said 'shit'!"

"Thank you, Verity."

"Sorry, Verity," said Simone humbly. "I meant *poop* the bed."

The bell jangled, and Doreen blustered in carrying a large cardboard box, which she dropped next to the garlands.

"There's a load more pom-poms for you," she said. "I see young Verity is doing a cracking job of making them as well."

Verity looked pleased. "Did you see my school play?"

"I did. Never was there a more holy pomegranate in all of Rowan Thorp."

Verity beamed.

"Thanks for those, Doreen. The garlands are going to look great." Simone was surprising herself with her amiability.

"Ellen's going to drop in another batch of poinsettia in a bit. We're working at full capacity to get the rest of the decorations ready for Monday."

"Thank you so much!" Maggie gushed.

"Well, we all benefit from the festival. The decorations will last, the crochet ones at least, and we can add to what we've got year on year. This year is only the start. Just saw your boy with Harini's granddaughter, by the way. What's going on there, then?"

"Oh, they're just—" But Maggie was interrupted by her daughter's loud tutting.

"Patrick is *well* stupid around her, and his cheeks go all red when she laughs." Verity rolled her eyes as she continued to wrap wool around her plastic pom-pom disks.

"Is that so?" Doreen had the look of a woman who had just banked some excellent gossip. "Might as well get a few bits for tomorrow's roast while I'm here."

Maggie left the decorations to serve her just as Kev from the Stag and Hound walked in with his signature broad smile.

"Baked orange slices for the garlands," he said, putting the box carefully down beside Simone. "Having twelve ovens in the cookery school has come in very handy this morning; the whole pub smells like Christmas. Your sister's in there with Duncan, enjoying a cozy candlelit lunch for two," he said. Doreen squeaked out a yip of delight, which she tried to smother with her hands—more first-rate gossip. "Afternoon, Doreen." Kev smiled knowingly.

"Kevin, lovely to see you. How's that handsome husband of yours?" she asked.

"Would you believe he's making salt dough angels to hang from ribbons in the marquee?"

"I would. I've always thought he was the crafty sort," said Doreen.

Kev smiled fondly. "I'll be sure to let Ryan know."

"These are brilliant. Thanks, Kev," said Maggie, picking up an orange slice and sniffing it.

"No worries. I'll take some more portobello mushrooms while I'm here. Kat's doing stuffed mushrooms for the veggie roast tomorrow."

"Ooh, that sounds good. I might pop in," said Simone.

"Maybe we all should," Maggie suggested. "I can't remember the last time I ate out."

"We'd love to see you. Now while I've got you, Simone, I've got this shoulder, just needs a tweak . . ."

Oh, for goodness' sake! "Honestly, I'd like to help you, but there are certain protocols . . ."

"Tell you what, let's not even mention your professional credentials and just call this one friend lending another her expertise. Five minutes of your time. Miss Radley described you as having sorcerer's fingers."

"Good god. I'd forgotten what it was like living here," Simone grumbled. The audacity levels in Rowan Thorp were far higher than in Greenwich.

Maggie laughed. Kev was already taking his jacket off.

"You can use the storeroom," she called.

"Lovely jubbly!" said Kev.

Seven minutes later they emerged from the storeroom. Kev was windmilling his left arm delightedly.

"Old Miss Radley wasn't wrong. You've got a gift. All your dinners are on me tomorrow. I'll book you in for three p.m.," he called over his shoulder as he left the shop, swiftly followed by Doreen, who waved energetic goodbyes.

"I am going to start pimping out your 'sorcerer's fingers,'" Maggie chortled. "I wonder what else I could get for free?"

"If Evette leaves me, maybe I'll move down here and start my own practice," she said dryly.

Verity looked up, mid—pom-pom, her expression quizzical. "Mama, what's pimping?"

34

STAR HAD GONE to bed on Saturday night floating on a cloud of romance and possibilities but had woken early Sunday morning knowing that before she let this go any further, she had to be straight with Duncan. She liked him. A lot. But her commitment to Simone came first, and she knew it wasn't a straightforward thing for a potential boyfriend to have to accept that his would-be girlfriend might be about to become pregnant with her sister's baby. She wouldn't blame him if he couldn't hack it, but equally, she couldn't be with someone who couldn't respect her decisions with regards to her own body.

She had called him early and asked him to meet her in the tree house because there was something she needed to tell him. And now she waited, sitting among the piles of cushions and warm throws she'd hauled up into her old hideaway in the trees.

The weather was bright and cold and her old china tea set, now Verity's, was covered in a sheen of condensation. The woodland had frosted to a crisp that crunched underfoot and sparkled in the dappled shards of winter sun. In this frozen otherworld, sugar-dusted thorns lost their menace and the diamond-clustered rowan berries made fitting jewels for a snow queen.

"Dear Universe," she prayed, her entreaties carried in a cloud of her breath, "I don't often ask to have my cake and eat it, but please, if there is a way I could have Simone's baby *and* keep Duncan, that would be great!"

She pulled a blanket around her like a cape and leaned her back against the solid tree house wall while she waited for Duncan. This place had always been her escape; she felt safe within the organic structure, ensconced in nature, which was why she had suggested meeting here.

She smiled when his head appeared at the bottom of the doorway and waited as he scaled the last few rungs and clambered into the tree house.

"Thanks for meeting me," she said, tugging the sherpa blanket tighter. "Pull up a cushion and help yourself to a blanket."

Duncan did as he was told.

They took up position on cushions opposite each other. Star produced a fresh dressing and bandage from the first aid kit she'd brought with her. "Here," she said, motioning to his hand. "Let me change the dressing while we talk."

He gulped but held out his hand. "All right, hit me with it. What do you need to tell me?" His eyes scrunched tightly closed as she unwrapped the bandage.

Suddenly this was much harder than she'd expected. Her stomach wound into knots as she tried to find her words.

"I have offered to be a surrogate for Simone and Evette's baby."

She watched Duncan's face for his reaction, but his eyes stayed tightly shut. A moment later, the words having finally registered, he opened his eyes and looked at her.

"I'm sorry, what did you say?"

"I have offered them my services as a surrogate mother so that they can have a baby. Simone has been trying for a baby and it hasn't worked, and she's sad and desperate, so I said I would help her." She blurted it all out, watching the micro changes in Duncan's expression as he absorbed each nugget of quick-fired information.

"Surrogacy."

"Yes."

"How would that . . . ?"

She knew what he was getting at. "Simone has embryos already frozen, and they would be placed in my uterus. No sex involved."

"But you would be pregnant with somebody else's baby."

"Yes."

"I thought you said you were ambivalent when it came to having children."

"I am, for myself."

"But you'll have one for your sister."

"It won't be mine."

Duncan was quiet, thoughtful. As the minutes ticked by, Star began to feel an unpleasant sinking feeling. She finished dressing his hand and he held it to his chest.

"It's a lot to take in," he said finally.

"I know. That's why I'm telling you now. I really like you, Duncan. I want nothing more than to see where our attraction takes us. But if Simone asks me, I have to do this."

"I get that. I do. And I commend you for it. I just don't know if this is the way I want to start a relationship. I know it sounds selfish, but we've barely begun to know one another, and this will impact *how* we get to know one another. Instead of sexy weekends away, I'll be rubbing your swollen ankles. The baby inside you will become the priority over everything else, and rightly so."

"We can still have sexy weekends away," she said lamely.

He looked pained. "But you'll be pregnant, and it won't even be my baby. Oh god, I'm sorry, I know I sound like a dick. You've thrown me a curveball with this one. I've watched my four sisters go through twelve pregnancies between them. I am fully aware how impactful carrying a child can be." He looked down at his hands. "You are clearly committed to this, and it only makes me admire you even more. But I don't know if *I* can commit to it."

Even though she had known that this might be the outcome, it didn't stop her from feeling like she'd dropped through the floor and hit every branch on the way down.

"I understand," she said. There was no sunshine in her voice today.

"I think I need a little time to wrap my head around it all, if that's all right." Duncan looked at her pleadingly.

"That's fair."

"For the record, I really like you too." He rubbed his hand over his head and sighed. "I need to go; my sister will kill me if I'm not there to help with the gravy. Gravy's a big deal in my family." His words were light-hearted, but they sounded flat.

"It's an important component." She forced a smile.

Duncan folded the blanket neatly and laid it on top of the cushion he'd been sitting on. Then he bent and kissed Star softly on the lips, lingering just long enough to make her ache with longing. It felt so much like a goodbye that it took all of her willpower not to reach for him and beg him not to leave.

"I'll see you at the shop tomorrow," he said as he began to climb back down the ladder.

"See you tomorrow," she echoed.

Duncan would remain her friend, there was no doubt about that—he was too nice a guy not to—but she may have lost the promise of something lovely with him. The disappointment made her want to press her face into the cushions and howl. She had been so tantalizingly close, like warming your face on sunbeams pouring through a window only for someone to come along and pull the curtains shut.

But even as she watched him stride away and felt the tears prickle at her eyes, she couldn't regret the choice she had made. This was her chosen path, an integral part of her life's journey and all the roads she'd trodden up to now had been leading her to it, guiding her toward the time when she would help her sister to become a mother.

35

ON MONDAY AFTERNOON, Belinda's festival friend came through and the marquee took its place on Holy Trinity Green. There were a fair number of rips in the PVC that had been fixed with duct tape—many times over, by the looks of it—but it was free and they were in no position to be picky.

The sun was hiding, and the frost had settled in for the duration of the day, though with so much to be done to decorate the marquee, coats and scarves were soon being discarded as folks worked up a sweat. Merriment was distinct in the air, even more so when the church choir, chivied on by Belinda, began singing Christmas carols. The festivity was infectious and soon everyone was joining in while they worked. "Deck the halls with boughs of holly" had never felt more apt.

Simone's fingers ached from tying decorations onto garlands over the last three days, but it was all worth it to see them strung across the ceiling, punctuated by twelve holly wreath chandeliers running down the center length. They lent a medieval opulence to the tatty marquee; the lush green foliage with splashes of vibrant color from their embellishments made the space feel warm and inviting.

"It's actually happening." Vanessa had taken the afternoon off from the solicitors' to help with the decorations while her rowdy children—she had three boys aged between four and seven—ran up and down the length of the marquee screeching, "bum, willy, pants, poo face, boobies . . ." and a myriad of other words favored by small boys.

"Against all the odds, it is," Simone agreed.

"I never doubted you."

"Liar."

Vanessa chuckled. "For the record, I found it in poor taste to place a bet. No, I always knew you'd be *capable* of doing it; my concern was that you'd fail simply because you couldn't work together."

"To be honest, I thought the same."

"But things seem to be rather quiet on the home front."

"That's as much of a surprise to me as it is to you." Simone smiled.

"I'm glad of it. We used to be firm friends, you and I. Perhaps we could be again?"

"I'd like that."

Two of Vanessa's boys had begun to sing "Jingle Bells, Batman Smells," and she hurried off to bribe them to stop.

Simone looked around, feeling a rare calm while all about her was frenetic energy. Star stood on tiptoe on a garden chair, carefully looping the red ribbons of Ryan's salt dough angels onto hooks, her tongue poking out as she concentrated. Then she turned to look at Maggie, painstakingly fastening crochet Christmas tree bunting around the sides of the marquee. That acerbic twist of animosity that had flooded her system whenever she'd thought of her sisters was gone.

Through years of practice, she had convinced herself that her sisters were deadweight, but being here now, she realized that it was being *without* them that weighed her down. Watching them, she felt an effusion of warmth and, beneath it, a quiet lament that their dad wasn't here to see his girls working together. This was a different grief from the one she battled daily. It didn't bite but rather settled itself in gently for the duration.

Joe set a voluptuous fir tree in a pot at the far end of the marquee, and Vanessa's children, along with all the other children they had invited to decorate—including Verity—swarmed toward the boxes of donated decorations and began to festoon the tree with glittery baubles. With the small humans thus occupied, chairs and tables were ferried across from the village hall and set up in two long rows ready for bird feeder making tomorrow and the banquet beyond.

Maggie sidled up beside Simone. "What do you think?"

"It's beautiful." To her horror, her voice gave a wobble. She cleared her throat. "Very Christmassy."

"Now it's all here, I'm actually quite excited."

Star skipped over to them, which would look bizarre on any other grown woman, but on her seemed a completely reasonable way to travel.

"Isn't it wonderful!" she gushed. "It's making me so happy! Look at it—did you ever see anything more festive in your life? Imagine how it will look when all the tables are dressed." And then quite unexpectedly, she threw her arms around Simone's neck and kissed her. "I'm so happy we're friends again."

At once Simone was overcome and overwhelmed. Her joy was a Catherine-wheel firework spinning out love hearts.

"Me too," she croaked.

"Are you crying?" Maggie asked incredulously.

"No!" she sobbed.

"Oh, come here, Simona-Mona." Maggie laughed, muscling in on Star's hug so that they were a messy tangle of sisters, and kissed them both.

"You're not going to believe this!" Gerry Myers called in through the tent flaps. "It's only bloody snowing!"

As everyone rushed outside to watch the snow, Artemis hopped from a table onto Doreen's shoulder and mewed in her ear. "Well, quite," said Doreen. "When the North sisters come together, there's bound to be magic."

36

IT WAS TUESDAY morning. With the schools out, sign-ups for making edible decorations for the local wildlife were high. The North sisters were grabbing a quick coffee at Betty's before the hordes began to arrive at the marquee. Artemis was sitting under the table on top of Maggie's feet. Two ordinarily yappy Jack Russells belonging to the local counselor sat beneath the next table, chins on the floor, eyes doleful as they watched her.

A stiff breeze was picking up, and the fairy lights outside Betty's café were clinking against the windowpanes. Yesterday's flurry of snow had been short-lived, but the temperature had dropped further still, painting the village chalky white with its bitter breath.

Maggie peered out toward her shop through a hole in the condensation. The green matting that covered the display shelves outside was flapping in the wind, but she figured the wooden crates of fruit and veg were sufficiently heavy to hold it.

Verity was sitting in the reading corner of the café, her head bowed over a copy of *The Nutcracker and the Mouse King*. She'd woken up early and so had accompanied Maggie on her morning deliveries before they met the bleary-eyed aunts for coffee.

It never ceased to amaze Maggie how she would have to practically drag her daughter out of bed each morning at half past seven on a school day, but she would be up with the birds on holidays.

"Verity asked me this morning if Joe could be her dad." Maggie's lips flattened into a thin line. Her daughter's request had crushed her heart like a beer can. Verity had never made the slightest intimation that she wanted a dad. How long had she been secretly wishing for one?

"Whoa," said Simone. "That's heavy."

"I think it's lovely," Star gushed.

"She's putting it on her Christmas list."

"At least you know you've got her blessing on your relationship," Simone reasoned.

"It's so much more complicated with kids. If it was only my heart I had to take into consideration it wouldn't be so bad."

"It sounds to me like Verity's already given her heart away if she wants Joe to be her dad. It's sweet. Did you tell Joe?"

"He was there." Maggie covered her face with her hands. She'd watched him swallow down his emotions, knew he had wanted to swing Verity up into the air and then take them both in his arms and call them his family. He'd looked at her for permission but she'd stood frozen, the cruel gatekeeper to their joint happiness. It was one thing to tell Patrick there was *something* going on but another to raise the hopes of a child.

"Oh my god!" Star squealed. "What did he say?"

"He said any man would be proud to call Verity his daughter."

"That was diplomatic," said Simone.

"Oh my god, could he be any lovelier?" Star threw her arms in the air. "For heaven's sake, Mags, stop being so bloody cautious."

She had a point. Was her incessant caution protecting them? Or was it ruining *all* their futures?

"I know this sounds stupid, but it's like, if I don't make it too real, nothing can jinx it. While it's casual, we're safe."

"What are you saying? You need to fly under the radar because fate is out to get you?" asked Simone.

"Something like that," she admitted.

"Oh, Maggie!" Star took her hand. "You had some really shit luck, but that doesn't mean you're fated to always be disappointed. You need to have a little faith in the power of love."

"She's a goddamned hippie," Simone said, nodding, "but she's right."

Maggie shook herself. "Okay. Enough of that. Back to business. You know what would be really nice?" she mused, spooning the froth off her cappuccino.

"A lie-in?" yawned Simone.

She ignored her. "If we open Dad's garden for the duration of the winter solstice celebration."

"What, like a public park?" Star asked.

"Kind of, yeah. I mean, it's on the procession route anyway and we'll be decorating the trees in the woods. It feels like a nice way to honor Dad's memory. I thought we could leave the gate open and maybe put a sign outside so that people could just go in and have a wander around the woods when they fancy."

Simone looked thoughtful. "I think Dad would like that. I've spent years carrying around this sort of low-level anger because I wanted more from him than he could give. I was so hooked up on his absenteeism that I'd blocked out all the wonderful things about him. Being back here—I don't know, maybe it's being with you two—it's like I can suddenly remember them all." She gave a small laugh. "And now I miss the old bugger more than ever."

"I've felt closer to him in these last two weeks than I have for a long time." Star picked at the skin on her fingers.

Maggie took her hand to still her nervous fingers. "I miss him too. He had his faults. He was *terrible* at keeping in touch." Her sisters smiled knowingly. "But in his own way, he loved us fiercely. I believe that more now than I ever did before. He was fascinating and infuriating, and we are lucky that he was ours. It's easy to feel like we were short-changed, but I truly believe we got more of his consideration than anyone else *ever* did."

Simone raised her coffee.

"To Dad. You really were one in a million."

Maggie and Star raised their own and clinked them with Simone's.

"To Dad!" they said in unison.

Maggie added, "May you be loving your new adventure in your camper van in the sky."

37

DUNCAN WAS ALREADY in the marquee. He was in charge of edible garlands. Bowls of all kinds of dried fruits sat beside a mountain of popcorn. He was studiously threading long lengths of garden twine through large bodkin needles and knotting the ends, ready for makers to push the treats onto them. There was something going on between Duncan and Star that Simone couldn't quite put her finger on. They didn't appear to have fallen out, but there was a caution between them that hadn't been there before. It would be a shame if things didn't work out for them; she had felt that their personalities complemented each other rather nicely.

Simone had set up a Winter Solstice WhatsApp group chat, with all the names of people who had signed up to help at the village meeting. It was extremely handy. A shoutout on the group chat yesterday afternoon had seen them inundated with cookie cutters by teatime—stars, hearts, gingerbread men, snowmen, Christmas trees, snowflakes, candy canes, menorahs, and dreidels aplenty. Beside these, trays lined with baking paper ran along the center of the tables for the suet shapes to be plopped onto them and left to set. It was going to be messy.

Duncan glanced up and smiled as the sisters approached.

"I wonder what Sotheby's would say if they knew we'd dragged you into our pagan festivities?" Simone quipped.

"I won't tell if you don't," he replied. "Speaking of Sotheby's, remember that little wooden box of 'tat' I was going through? The one you found in the cupboard under the eaves?"

Simone nodded.

"Was that the one with the half-eaten packet of Parma Violets in it?" Star asked, pulling a face.

"Yes. Your father had a peculiar regard for antiques; on the one hand he had a truly excellent eye for collecting them, and on the other, he treated them like bric-a-brac."

"He had a similar stance when it came to women," said Maggie.

Duncan adjusted his glasses, which meant he was feeling mildly embarrassed. "Anyway, in among the jumble I found a miniature portrait of what I think might be a courtier, which I am almost sure is an early Hilliard."

Simone sucked in a gulp of air.

"Is that good?" asked Maggie.

"If it's a Hilliard, 'good' would be an understatement," she replied a little breathlessly.

"Who's Hilliard?" Star asked.

"Nicholas Hilliard was most famous for painting miniatures of Elizabeth the First and her court," Duncan explained. "With your permission, I'd like to have the painting couriered up to Sotheby's for further analysis. If it is indeed a Hilliard, then there will likely be a lot of collector interest."

"That sounds promising. What are we talking here, a couple of thousand?" asked Maggie. "That would split nicely three ways."

Duncan smiled broadly; he was enjoying himself. This was the closest anyone had seen him come to crowing.

"Try a couple of *hundred* thousand," Duncan said. "At least."

Maggie flopped down on a chair. Star barked a loud "HA!"

"How sure are you that it's a Hilliard?" asked Simone. A part of her wanted to rush off to call her mum; Rene would get a kick out of this.

"I'd hate to mislead you, but I'm ninety-five percent sure."

"He kept a two-hundred-grand piece of art in a broken box with some old sweets?" Maggie was stunned; this was a new level of insouciance, even for Augustus.

"Not just sweets," said Duncan. "There were also a couple of Matchbox cars, some shillings, a pack of nude lady playing cards—with the queen of hearts missing—and a plastic spider. It was wrapped in an old handkerchief," he added.

"Well, all right, then. For a moment there, I was concerned our father had behaved irresponsibly with a piece of fine art history," Maggie replied sardonically.

"When will you know if it's a genuine Hilliard?" asked Simone.

"I can get it couriered up to Sotheby's today. They'll have their expert look it over, and we can take it from there. A week, tops."

"You're an expert," said Star.

Duncan looked bashful. "I'm more of a general practitioner of antiques. I'm not an art specialist. But I would be very surprised if it wasn't a Hilliard."

"Is it too early for wine?" asked Simone. "I feel like I need a drink after that revelation."

"Me too," Maggie agreed.

"It's half past ten," Star replied.

"Yeah, but it's nearly Christmas," Maggie countered.

"Patrick says wine makes you stupid, Mama," said Verity, having finished her inspection of all the crafts on offer.

"Patrick needs a smacked bottom," Simone replied dryly.

"What did *I* do?" Patrick stepped in through the canvas door, grinning.

"You're supposed to be helping Joe out over at the shop—what am I paying you for?" asked Maggie.

"Technically I'm out on a delivery," he answered, holding aloft the bag he'd been swinging at his side. "Kat's making nut roasts, and she's run out of mushrooms."

"Ooh, we should definitely do nut roasts for the banquet," said Star. "That's very in keeping with the wholesome vibe."

"Agreed," said Maggie. "Can you ask Kat how far in advance we can make nut roasts, please, darling, and also if she'll help us make them?"

"You see, *this* is what you're paying me for," said Patrick. "I'm your nut roast dealer."

"I know how to make nut roasts," piped up Star. "I used to help in the kitchen tent when Mum took me to live in that commune in Dorset."

"I'm not sure we'll find a recipe more authentic than one from a genuine commune," said Maggie. "You are now our official nut roast guru, Star."

Star beamed.

Patrick grabbed a handful of popcorn and stuffed half of it in his mouth before screwing his face up in disgust. "Plain?" he complained.

"Birds and squirrels aren't as keen on sweet and salty popcorn as you are," said Star.

"Have you asked them?"

"Yes, of course," she replied without a hint of sarcasm.

"Oh, I also brought you this." He pulled a small Bluetooth speaker out of the mushroom bag. "Thought you might like some festive music while you work."

"Oh, thanks, darling, that's a great idea. How do I do it?" She turned the oblong speaker in her hands.

Patrick smiled, shaking his head. "Give it here," he said, taking her phone too, and after a couple of swipes, Bing Crosby began to croon *"I'm dreaming of a white Christmas"* out of the speaker.

As Patrick left, the crafters, young and old, began to trickle in and take their seats. Thoughts of Elizabethan heirlooms and day drinking were pushed to the side as the sisters walked up and down the tables assisting.

Doreen arrived with her husband and eldest grandson in tow. "Suet mix!" she hollered. Each of them carried a catering-sized stainless steel stockpot, which they dumped heavily down onto the tables.

"Brilliant!" said Maggie, looking over into the pans. "It actually looks quite tasty."

"Lard, nuts, birdseed, berries, oats, and peanut butter. Different variations in each pot. Some heavier on the seed, some on the berries. All heavy on the lard. This one's got mealworms in it, fancy a taste?" Doreen gave a wink.

"Umm, I think I'll pass. Would you like me to talk them through the process or . . ."

"I've got it," she said.

All eyes turned to Doreen as she showed the crafters how to take handfuls of the stiff mixture and smoosh it into their cookie cutter shapes. The shapes would then be pushed out onto the baking sheets, holes made in their tops for threading later, and left to set overnight.

Artemis padded up and down the center of the tables inspecting proceedings, but nobody paid her any mind. The wind had picked up further and it buffeted the walls of the marquee. But people seemed happy enough to work in their coats and scarves, and the Christmas music had a warming effect. There was something about being inside, even inside a tent, when the weather was blowing a hooley outside, that made people glow with gratitude. And when Belinda arrived with a catering urn of hot chocolate, and a pillow-sized bag of mini marshmallows, the cozy factor ramped up to ten.

Simone couldn't quite believe the response to their call to arms. Two weeks ago, she firmly believed reinstating the winter solstice festival would be an impossible task. She certainly hadn't expected that she would enjoy herself after decades spent looking down her nose at what she'd felt was a provincial little village. And now she was standing in a decorated marquee filled to bursting with that same community, who had welcomed her home with open arms. Perhaps she didn't need to choose between being the confident, accomplished woman in Greenwich and the girl she'd been in Rowan Thorp. Maybe there was room for both.

38

THE STORM'S NAME was Holly, and Holly had been busy. No one had expected the low-pressure weather front pushing over from France to exact a freak blizzard upon Kent. Holly had raged throughout the night while Simone had laid in bed listening as rubbish bins were toppled and twigs, ripped from their branches, scratched the windows.

She had got up twice in the night to peer out through the bay window, craning her neck to try to see the marquee. But it was almost impossible to make anything out between the thick dark and the swirling mass of snow.

At six o'clock in the morning, her phone buzzed with a text. It was Maggie.

> The storm took out the marquee. Come now.
> I'll bring coffee.

Simone's heart sank. Surely it couldn't be completely gone? She threw her coat over a pair of hastily chosen jogging bottoms and a hoodie. She hadn't brought any boots with her, but Mrs.

Dalgleish had a pair by the back door, which she wriggled her feet into and headed out into the dark morning. Artemis was waiting for her on the gatepost.

"How bad is it?" she asked.

Artemis gave a long slow blink, then threw her head back and meowed mournfully like a werewolf at the moon.

"That bad, huh? Come on, then, let's go." The cat jumped softly down into the snow and trotted beside her.

As she passed her car, she noticed a crack right along the center of the windscreen. "Great!" It had either been walloped by flying debris or the chip in the glass made by the tractor had fractured in the cold.

Holly's histrionics had burned themselves out, and the air was calm with a glacial sting. The village was transformed. Snow banked up against garden walls and postboxes and crunched under her boots. Fairy lights lit the predawn streets.

She saw it as soon as she turned the corner: the marquee skeleton was a buckled and bent carcass; torn strips of fabric hung limply from its brittle bones. The trestle tables had been overturned; some had been blown into the gardens of the Rowan Tree Inn and the Stag and Hound. The white tablecloths were scattered around the green, having been redistributed by the wind. Some of the garlands hung listlessly from the ceiling beams, but most had been ripped apart and lay scattered in the snow along with the trays of lovingly made bird feeders.

In the dim glow given off by the snow, Simone could see Maggie's eyes were red rimmed. At the same moment, a gasp from her left made her look around; Star was raking both hands through her bed-mussed tresses and shaking her head in disbelief. They'd worked so hard.

Maggie bent and handed them each a mug of coffee she'd set down on a torn piece of PVC. They said nothing. Simone didn't know how long they stood there quietly contemplating.

"I know this sounds stupid, but it feels like we lost him all over again," she said finally.

"It's not stupid," said Maggie.

"I know what you mean." Star sniffed. "We did it all for him and now it's gone. Just like he is."

Simone put an arm around her. "We really tried. I think he would know that."

Star nodded. A tear splashed into her coffee.

One by one, lights started to appear in windows as people began their day. Maggie continued to stare at the shreds of canvas that littered Holy Trinity Green. Her usual can-do attitude appeared to have been temporarily stymied.

Simone cast her gaze around the rest of the high street. The Christmas trees hadn't suffered too badly; a few baubles had loosened and the tinsel had bunched in places, but they were otherwise unharmed. If anything, they looked even better now that their fairy-lit branches were laden with fresh snow. It was as though Holly had focused all her attention on the marquee, like Dorothy's house in Kansas.

Duncan jogged up the high street and came to stand by them. He was wearing shorts and a sweatshirt, which looked faintly ridiculous in this frozen landscape. He bent, resting his hands on his knees while he caught his breath.

"Bloody hell," he said presently.

"And then some," Simone agreed.

"I went out through the back of the pub this morning; I didn't see any of this."

"Is there damage anywhere else?" Maggie asked.

"No. There're a few branches down but nothing serious. The snow's not even that deep, considering. Bloody hell," he said again, and then, noticing that Star was upset, he immediately went to her side to comfort her.

THE SKY WAS taking on the orangey glow of the sun trying to rise. People were coming to join Duncan and the North sisters on Holy Trinity Green, some on their way to work, some with dressing gowns pulled tightly around them, Wellington boots poking out of the bottoms.

The obligatory high-spirited commentary that attended any shocking event seemed to break the spell the sisters had been under. Maggie grabbed an overturned crate and began to pick bird feeders out of the snow. Star and Duncan joined her. Duncan's long muscular legs in tiny shorts seemed to be causing as much distraction as the storm damage.

"You never really think about what goes on beneath a man's trousers, do you?" mused Beth, Ryan's mum, who was wearing a Dalmatian onesie with Wellies. "I mean, everyone makes such a fuss over women's legs but hardly at all with men."

"Perhaps because they are less shapely as a rule?" suggested Parminder. "Gerry has legs like a Highland cow. I don't think anyone would be clamoring to see them in a pair of shorts."

"Nor my Ron; he has the knees of an arthritic flamingo. But some men's legs are very shapely."

"Made for shorts," Parminder agreed.

The popcorn garlands and peanut butter pine cones had been boxed up at the end of yesterday, and though the boxes had been tossed about, they didn't appear to have lost their contents. A large section of the fabric roof lay scrunched in a heap on the ground. Simone tramped through the snow to it and lifted a corner. Troy joined her, and together they rolled it slowly back. Underneath, the bulk of the birdseed pomanders had thankfully made it unscathed, protected from the worst of the storm by the fallen roof.

People began to join them with boxes and baskets, retrieving as many decorations as they could. Simone was heartened to see that what had looked like a total loss when she'd first arrived wasn't as bad as it had seemed. Though the marquee was undeniably totaled, much of their combined efforts were not entirely destroyed.

By eight o'clock the sun was fully up, and the villagers of Rowan Thorp were fully out. Troy offered the woodshed behind the pub as storage for the edible decorations, and people began to-ing and fro-ing with the boxes and bags.

Verity and the other children in the village were treating it as a treasure hunt, salvaging suet bird cakes and baubles from beneath the snow. Simone found herself unable to stop advising people on the correct way to bend without causing strain on their spines. Really, this was basic spine health stuff; no wonder people kept asking her for massages.

"All the duct tape in Kent won't put this thing back together," Betty noted grimly.

"I don't know where else we can hold the banquet," Maggie lamented. "Do you think we could squeeze everyone into the village hall? Maybe share with the darts tournament?"

"Unfortunately, the village hall is not an option for anybody," said Belinda. "The roof has sprung multiple leaks, the snow is melting in the sun, and I've got pots and pans all over the floor trying to save the parquet if possible. Water got into the fuse box and blew the lot, so we've got no power in there either. It's a no-go, I'm afraid."

Duncan had taken a step back and seemed to be lost in thought.

"What's going on in there?" asked Betty.

He squinted like he was loath to discuss his ideas yet, but Betty was not a woman to be denied.

"I think I might have an idea of how we could do something with these scraps and, if it works, maybe a venue for the banquet."

All eyes turned to Duncan, who looked uncomfortable under the glare.

"Come along, young man, spit it out!" said Betty.

He rubbed the back of his head. "It would take a few sewing machines, and maybe some extra canvas, and some guy ropes."

"The Women's Institute sewing machines will be at your disposal, and I'm sure we can rustle up some canvas. There must be tents languishing in sheds all over the village," said Betty.

"Count the Cussing Crocheters in with whatever plans you're hatching," said Ellen.

"Abso-bloody-lutely!" echoed Doreen.

"Knew I could count on you ladies." Betty smiled warmly.

"What exactly did you have in mind, Duncan?" Maggie asked.

"I was thinking, what if we make a kind of patchwork tarpaulin out of the bits of canvas left and tie it to the high branches of the trees in the rowan tree woods? The clearing near the tree house is plenty big enough to get everyone together. It'll mean a longer journey getting the food from the pub kitchen to the tables, but the space will be dry and sheltered."

Many heads nodded as the possibilities took root in their minds.

Simone found her spirits rising.

"You'll still have the patio heaters," said Troy, and Ryan agreed. "I'm just glad we didn't leave them in the marquee last night."

"Do you really think you could make something out of this lot?" Maggie asked, waving her arm at the mess.

"I do," said Duncan. "We'll need to clean it up a bit, but other than that, it's just like putting together an oddly shaped quilt—easier, in fact, since it doesn't need lining or to be particularly neat, it just needs to be fit for purpose."

"Piece of cake!" said Ellen.

"Right, we have a plan. Let's get cracking," shouted Betty.

"What about work?" asked Maggie. "I don't want you to get into trouble."

"I'll call Sotheby's myself if they're going to be dicks about it," piped up Doreen.

Similar offers of being rude to his employer ensued. Those Cussing Crocheters sure knew their cusses.

"That won't be necessary," Duncan assured the small army of women who appeared ready to do battle for him. "I've got some time owing from all the extra hours at North Novelties."

"That wouldn't have anything to do with a certain North sister that happens to be staying at the shop, would it?" asked Ellen.

Duncan studied his snowy trainers. Simone looked over to see Star looking anywhere but at him. Something was definitely off with those two; she'd noticed a distance between them yesterday at decoration making.

"Right! It's a plan!" called Betty. "I'll close the café at two o'clock today, and we can stitch and bitch in there. In the meantime, we'll need this canvas cleaned up a bit and a search of all sheds in the area for more. Bring your sewing machines and your can-do attitudes, and I'll provide the mince pies and mulled wine."

A cheer went up, and the village of Rowan Thorp sprang into action.

"I knew that Duncan was a good egg," said Betty as she passed by Simone. "Excellent knees."

Simone couldn't help feeling a strange rush of affection as she watched the scene before her. People bustled about helping to clear the mess, some in pajamas and boots, others dressed for blizzard conditions. Mugs of hot tea were handed over garden walls, and plates of toast were ferried back and forth while children made snow angels on the grass. Belinda flung open the church doors so that everyone could hear Ron's masterful organ playing, his fingers performing a kind of musical alchemy as haunting melodies of medieval Christmas carols suffused the cold morning air. This is what it was like to be a part of something bigger than herself. For too long she had been in a desert of her own sadness with nothing to see on the horizon but more of the same. There was no miraculous cure for her pain, but she felt ready to step into the little oasis that the village of Rowan Thorp was offering.

39

WHEN MAGGIE HAD put the word around that there would be tree decorating in the rowan tree woods on Wednesday evening, she hadn't expected almost the entire village to show up. Especially since many of them had not only helped with the cleanup that morning but also spent the best part of the day fashioning a patchwork tarpaulin that would be hung tomorrow, ready for the feast on Friday evening.

Joe had spent most of the afternoon replacing all the old strings of garden lights left by Augustus and adding twice as many more. Using the tree house as a kind of central flagpole—and performing some hijinks at the top of a ladder that were definitely against health and safety—he'd fixed strings of LED fairy lights to the base of the house and then stretched them across to the tops of the rowan trees around it. He wound lights around gnarly trunks, dropped them over bramble patches and up-lit mounds of ferns, and was rewarded with Maggie smothering him with kisses.

Now, well insulated against the determined chill in the air, the summer sisters stood by the open gate to Augustus's garden to welcome everyone onto their father's land.

At the far end of the garden by the entrance to the woods, Verity and Patrick guarded the wooden crates loaded with salvaged decorations from some rather bumptious squirrels. The pyre in the center of the long garden had steadily grown over the past few days and now looked set to rival any Guy Fawkes bonfire.

The trickle of familiar faces became a torrent, and soon a queue to get through the gate had formed, which trailed back along the high street.

Now that it was dark, the effect of Joe's lighting display and the snow was magical. Appreciative gasps ran through the crowd, with arms full of edible garlands and baubles, as they chose trees to decorate. Miss Radley began to sing Christmas carols and soon everyone joined in as they worked. The rowan tree woods were alive with the tinkle of laughter and voices raised in song.

Children hung bird feeders on the branches they could reach, while the adults draped the garlands over the higher limbs. The WI brought a supply of gingerbread stars hanging from garden twine and added them to the crates of decorations, along with strings of dried orange slices studded with star anise.

"We made extra," said Betty, eyeing a boy in a bobble hat who had just devoured a star, "to ensure that at least some of them make it onto the trees."

"Thank you, Betty. You've done so much to help." Maggie felt herself welling up at the scene before her, their little woods alive with activity.

"Oh, pish!" Betty batted away the thanks. "If I've said it once I've said it till I'm blue in the face: we're a community; help will always be offered if you'd only ask."

. . .

"AH, GOOD, THERE you are!" Gerry Myers said, intercepting Maggie on her way to see how Verity was getting on. "Now, I'm sure you know about the Rowan Thorp Twitchers."

Everybody knew about the Rowan Thorp Twitchers; the local birdwatching group had hides set up in fields and groves surrounding the village. As well as rigorously keeping score of the common birds they spotted and being deeply competitive about documenting the rarer varieties, the hides were well known to double as places the twitchers could explore their naturism tendencies.

"Yes." Maggie couldn't quite keep eye contact with Gerry.

"What we'd like to do is set up a couple of bird cams here in the woods, so that we can watch the birds and mammals enjoying the feeders in real time. We thought we could stream it live on our webcast so that the whole village could enjoy the *fruits* of their labors." He snorted at his own joke. "It'll be educational for the kiddies and great for us twitchers. We thought we'd call it *Bird Brother*!" He snorted again. "Do you get it? Like *Big Brother* but with birds! What do you say?"

Maggie recalled her afternoon of bliss with Joe in the tent of intent. There'd be no more of those shenanigans if the twitchers were live streaming the woods for all to see. And then she remembered that the tent of intent had been donated to the great tarpaulin sewing bee and smiled.

"It sounds like a brilliant idea," she said. Everyone had been so kind, and Parminder and Gerry had been especially generous by supplying them with their homemade cider for the wassail. The least they could do was let them pop a couple of cameras up. "I'll have to check with Star, since she's living here at the moment, but I don't think it'll be a problem."

She was fairly sure Star had grown out of her naked outdoor yoga phase, but it wouldn't hurt to check.

"No need," blustered Gerry, slapping her on the back with a meaty hand. "I'll do the honors." And he strode off in search of Star.

BY SEVEN O'CLOCK every last decoration had been hung, draped, and balanced, and everyone stood back to admire their handiwork. The effect of the bejeweled trees was one of majestic abundance. Every tree was festooned in a cornucopia of edible adornments, every branch dripped with fruit and nut embellishments, gingerbread pendants, and popcorn necklaces. It was a feast for the eyes as well as for the woodland critters, and Maggie wondered why they'd never thought to do it before. She couldn't remember a time when she'd felt as connected to her community as she had done these last few days. It made the idea of having to leave at the end of January even more of a wrench.

The little crowd began to thin. Parents shepherded tired children home for cocoa and bedtime stories, while others headed back for well-earned glasses of wine and perhaps some last-minute present wrapping. There was a feeling of bonhomie in the air as neighbors and friends called cheery goodbyes.

Joe appeared carrying Verity, her arms tight around his neck, her legs clamped about his waist. Patrick walked beside them.

"Verity," Maggie scolded lightly. "I've told you, you're too big to make Joe carry you."

"But I'm tired and my feet are cold. Joe doesn't mind, do you, Joe?"

"Far be it from me to make you walk on cold ground," he said good-naturedly.

Maggie rolled her eyes. "You'll give yourself a hernia," she warned. But he only laughed.

"I'll sling you over the other shoulder if you're not careful."

"You *are* a glutton for punishment," Patrick joked, and Joe laughed with him.

The thought was in her head before she could check it: *We sound like a family.*

"WHAT'S GOING ON with you and Duncan?" Simone asked in a low voice.

"Nothing," said Star.

"Don't give me that. A few days ago, you two were making gooey eyes at each other, which I might add was making me feel a bit sick, and now you're acting like polite strangers. Have you had a fight?"

"No, nothing like that."

She could see the tightness around Star's mouth. She was keeping something back. "Then what? I know I usually give you a hard time about your taste in men, but Duncan is one of the good guys."

"It's probably better if he stays away from me, then." Star's tone was playful but edgy.

"Why would you say that?"

"I find it easier to say it before you do; it stings less. I know what you think of me, Simone. I know you don't think I deserve someone like Duncan, and I agree with you. Maybe he's coming to realize it too."

Simone was crushed. Is that how she'd made her sister feel about herself? Evette had warned her often that what she considered straight talking could be taken as unkind. And yes, sometimes she snapped out a sarcastic comment before she had time to think better of it. She and Star had certainly had their differences, and maybe in the past she *had* wanted her words to hurt, but not anymore.

"Star, I think you misunderstand me. The reason I go on at you about the men you become involved with isn't to put *you* down—it's to try to make you see what *they* are! You deserve so much better than Stu and the like. It annoys me to no end that your bar is so low."

"So you don't think Duncan is too good for me?"

"No! I think Duncan would be lucky to be with you. What has always infuriated me about you is how little you think of yourself. Your shine is so effortless it's slightly sickening. You're like fucking Snow White with bluebirds flying around your head and you can't even see it. I would give my left nipple to have even half your natural vivacity. And yet you sell yourself short time and again, you give all that shine to people who are unworthy of you. I have *never* thought that you didn't deserve to be with good men, Star, quite the opposite; I didn't feel that the boyfriends you chose were deserving of *you*."

Star was quiet for a moment and then she asked, "Why the left nipple?"

A laugh burst out of her, and she shoved Star away hard, before yanking her back into her side and folding her arms tightly around her, kissing her head.

"It's my least favorite one, dickhead," she said, smiling. "I love you."

"I love you too."

Maggie doubled back from the garden gate and held her arms out for them to stop. Her expression was grim.

"I don't want to alarm you, but Stu's outside."

And just like that Simone's good mood deflated.

"Shit!" said Simone and Star in unison.

40

STU WAS SITTING on the front step of the curiosity shop, his knees pulled into his chest, his arms holding them in place, as though he were trying to curl himself into a ball like a hedgehog. Star's stomach dropped. She felt defeated, like she'd never be free of him. What hope did she have of starting something with Duncan, or anyone, while the ghost of Stu trailed after her?

When he saw her, he unfurled himself and stood, rubbing his hands down his jeans in a nervous gesture. Simone flew at him.

"I told you if I ever saw you again, I'd call the police! What is it? More money? I'm not going to keep paying you to leave my sister alone."

Stu ignored Simone and looked pleadingly at Star, his hands outstretched, motioning for calm. Across the street a car door opened, but Stu turned and shook his head at the occupant and the driver's door clicked shut again.

"I just want to talk," said Stu. "I don't want any trouble. I'll be leaving in a few minutes, and you won't ever have to see me again if you don't want to, but I really need to talk to you first. Please, Star."

She felt her resolve slip. He seemed so sincere, she couldn't turn him away. She went to Simone, who had been joined by Maggie, Joe, and Patrick in forming a human barrier between her and Stu, and laid a hand on her sister's arm.

"It's fine. I'm just going to talk to him." She tried to sound in control, but the looks she got in return suggested she hadn't done a good job of it.

"You don't have to talk to him." Simone was fierce, ready to pounce.

"I know. I want to."

"You don't owe him anything." Maggie echoed Simone.

"I know that. Please have a little faith in me."

"It isn't you that your sisters don't trust," Joe added amicably. Verity, still clinging to him, stayed quiet, unnerved by her mum's and aunts' reactions to the man outside her granddad's shop.

"I will be okay." She looked each of her sisters in the eye.

"Fine. Have your talk, and I'll wait here to make sure nothing gets out of hand," said Simone, going to stand on the pavement outside the shop and folding her arms defiantly.

"I don't need a bodyguard."

"You sure about that?" Maggie asked.

Duncan stepped forward and said calmly, "I'll stay. I'll wait over on the bench to give you some space." He turned to Simone. "I won't let anything happen to her. I promise."

Simone looked unconvinced. "I don't mean to be rude, Duncan, but you knit and get excited about old runcible spoons."

Duncan, who was half a foot taller than almost everyone gathered, raised his eyebrows. "I also box and run marathons. I can handle myself."

Star shot him a grateful smile. She was quite sure she didn't need protecting from Stu, but if she must have a bodyguard, better it be Duncan than her smart-mouth sister. Maggie and Joe took Verity home, and Patrick insisted on walking his aunty back to her cottage. As she left, Simone jabbed a finger at Stu and said, "One false move, pal, and I'll hunt you down!"

"You're not Bruce Willis!" Star snapped, exasperated.

"Yippee-ki-yay, motherfucker!" Patrick grinned and steered his aunt away across the street.

Star shook her head.

"I'll be just over there," said Duncan, pointing to the wooden bench outside the post office.

She couldn't deny she felt a thrill that Duncan wanted to watch over her. Finally, it was just her and Stu outside the shop.

"How have you been?" he asked. One of his knees bounced blurrily fast as though of its own accord, but she could tell from his eyes that he wasn't high. They both folded themselves down onto the stone doorstep to the shop. Within seconds she felt the cold seeping through her velvet trousers.

"Good. You?"

"Some and some," he said.

She noticed his hands were shaking. He clearly had something to say, but he was having trouble getting the words out.

"So what brings you here?" she asked.

"I'm going into rehab."

"Stu, that's great news. I'm so proud of you."

"Thanks. I think I finally hit the bottom, after a lot of looking for it. I OD'd in a park. A dog walker found me." He gave a nervous laugh, as though he was telling a funny story rather than talking about a near-death experience.

"Not with the money Simone gave you?" She felt suddenly sick.

"No! God no, I blew that before the next morning. This was five days ago."

She nodded. "I'm so sorry you went through that."

He smiled at her sadly. "It was only a matter of time. I'm surprised it hadn't happened before."

"And now you're going to rehab, a fresh start. When do you go?"

"Tonight. My brother's taking me." He motioned toward the car parked across the street. She squinted and waved. The driver wound down his window.

"Hey, Star," he said. "All right?"

"Yeah, Paul. You good?"

"I'll be better when I've got this wally into rehab." He smiled. "You look well. It's nice here, it suits you."

"Thanks."

Paul wound his window back up and went back to staring ahead. Across the way, Duncan was doing his own staring, each lookout giving his charge a bit of space.

"I wanted to see you before I went in. I need to apologize for so many things I don't even know where to begin." He ran his hand through his hair. "You put up with such a lot from me . . ."

"I could've done more to help you . . ."

"No, Star, please don't ever think that." He sounded desperately sincere but also like he was worried that if he didn't say his piece now, he would lose his nerve. "That's why I'm here. To take responsibility. To apologize for all the things I've done to you. You didn't deserve any of it. I'm sorry. I'm sorry for all of it. I needed to say it to your face, so that you know I mean it. I couldn't go into rehab without giving you that much."

She felt a rush of affection for her old friend and lover.

They'd been through a lot together over the last six years. Two lost souls careering through life in a haze of ecstasy and desolation.

"Thank you," she said. Her hands were cold, and her bottom was numb, but she felt a peace she hadn't known in a long time, as though Stu had taken a heavy burden from her.

"I know I have no right to ask this. And, full disclosure, the program at the center warns against starting relationships during rehab, but I wonder if you would wait for me? I want to be with you. I'll get my shit together and I'll be a better man. I need someone to be good for. I don't know if I can do it for myself."

A part of her would always love Stu, but not in the way he would want, and he would never understand if she tried to explain it to him. His was a personality that didn't deal in nuance, only obsession or indifference. She didn't want to be the reason he failed in rehab; she knew how delicate his emotional state was. For a fleeting moment, she considered agreeing to wait for him, just so that he would go into rehab with a sense of hope. She could break things off when he was clean. But that wouldn't be fair on either of them. Saying yes to Stu would mean closing the door on her and Duncan. She reasoned, judging by the past couple of days, that door may already have closed. But if there was even the slightest chance, she refused to sabotage it.

"I can't. I'm sorry," she whispered. She steeled herself for his reaction. She never knew which way he would go.

He bowed his head. Six years of "if only"s swam before her eyes.

Tears poured down his cheeks. They sat like that until his brother wound the window down and said kindly, "Stu, mate. It's time to go."

He nodded.

"I wish you all the best. I really do," she whispered. "You can do this. You know that, don't you? I believe in you."

Stu took her cold hand and kissed it before standing up. She stayed where she was.

"Goodbye, Heavenly-Stargazer Rosehip North."

And with that, he strode round to the passenger side of his brother's car and climbed in. The engine sounded loud in the quiet street. Paul gave Star a wave that was part salute and drove slowly out of the village.

She rested her chin in her hands, closed her eyes, and took a few deep steadying breaths. Nostalgia was an intoxicating perfume that could cloud judgment. She had loved him for a long time, but there were no roads that led back to him now. Maybe there were none that led to Duncan either. But she needed to be true to herself, and if that meant going it alone, well, that was good too; she'd never been afraid of her own company. When she opened her eyes again, she saw a pair of long, denim-clad legs in front of her. She looked up to find Duncan standing there. He held out his hands and she took them, allowing him to pull her up to standing. Her legs were stiff with cold, and her knees ached.

"He's gone." She didn't trust her own voice yet. "Into rehab. He just wanted to apologize, go in with a clean slate, I guess."

"I thought he might be asking you to get back with him."

She sighed. "That too. But I said no."

Neither of them spoke. She was suddenly very tired.

"Thank you for sitting out in the cold. It was very kind of you to watch over me."

"My pleasure," said Duncan.

"Well. Good night."

He nodded once, turned, and walked away.

SHE UNDRESSED AND climbed into bed. There was sadness, yes, but her decisions were sound, and they were the right ones for her. She had freed herself from Stu and she would give her sister a baby—there was much comfort in that.

41

"THIS IS VERY gentlemanly of you, Patrick, but you really don't need to walk me home. You can see the cottage from the high street," Simone said.

"It's no bother. You can never be too careful."

"All right, you got me."

"It's nice having you and Aunty Star here. Mum really loves it."

"I never thought I'd say it, but I like being here." She paused. "I feel like I haven't been the best aunty to you and Verity. I've not been very present for the last few years." She felt embarrassed, ashamed even, of the distance she'd kept.

Patrick shrugged. They were almost to the picket fence of the cottage.

"You're here now." He took a hesitant breath, and Simone sensed he was steeling himself to say something. "Aunty, is my mum serious about Joe?"

Ahh, there it is, she thought. She found herself caught between the truth and a promise. She didn't want to lie to Patrick, but there was no way she was going to break her sister's confidence.

"What do you mean?" she asked, stalling for time.

At that moment, a woman rose up from behind the arbor. Simone's heart gave a thud and she was suddenly weak, as though all her bones had rubberized.

"Evette? What are you doing here?" Just to see her wife's face was like walking into the light, dazzling and regenerating.

A flash lit the two.

"Got it!" said Patrick triumphantly, looking down at the photograph he'd just taken on his phone.

"What's going on?" she gasped. She was delighted and suspicious all at once, she couldn't take it in.

Evette smiled. "Star told me I should surprise you. I told her you hate surprises, but she was insistent. She said you'd all worked really hard on the winter solstice festival and that it would be a crime for me to miss it."

Simone laughed and threw herself at her wife, kissing her and then squeezing her in a bear hug before kissing her again.

"Well, I'll be off," Patrick said cheerily. "Hope you weren't waiting for too long on that cold bench, Evette. That's a recipe for hemorrhoids."

"Cheeky shit." Evette laughed.

"It's good to see you again, Aunt Evette." Patrick grinned.

"You too, sweetheart."

"And what was your role in this little deception, young man?" Simone asked, smiling, still clinging to her wife as though she might disappear if she let go.

Patrick waved his phone at her. "Paparazzi." He grinned. "Aunty Star wanted to see your face when you saw Evette."

She rolled her eyes. "Heavenly-Stargazer inherited the North mischief gene."

"Aren't you glad she did?" Evette asked, squeezing Simone's hand.

She looked at Evette. She couldn't believe she was here. It had been a long time since her heart had been full of anything other than melancholy, but right now it was singing a glad tune. "Yes," she replied. "Yes, I am."

Patrick wandered back out onto the high street. His whistling "Let It Snow" carried on the crisp night air and could still be heard even as Simone, smiling, pushed the door to the cottage closed and turned to face her wife.

"I've missed you," she said.

"Me too," Evette agreed. "We have a lot to talk about."

"Not yet." She was hungry for her wife, and she was gratified to see Evette's lips twitch into a wicked smile.

"You're right," Evette said, yanking her coat off and slinging it over the banister. "Talking can wait. Where's the bedroom in this joint?"

LATER, AFTER THEY had reacquainted themselves, they lay spooning, Simone's big spoon to Evette's little, the duvet pulled tight around their bodies to keep out the chill.

"I told you it was a big bed," she said sleepily. She felt Evette smile.

"We'd never fit a bed this size into our tiny flat. There wouldn't be room for anything else. Only bed."

"I think I could live with that." She pulled Evette closer.

Evette laughed softly. "Not with your clothes-buying habit. Wardrobes are essential."

"We could get a bed this size if we had a bigger place."

"I think that's above our pay grade."

"Not if we moved out of the city." She felt Evette shift away slightly and cold filled the gap.

"What are you suggesting?"

The words seemed to have come of their own accord, but now that they were out, she realized she meant them.

"Maybe we could move here. Star's going to stay at Dad's place for a while; Maggie too while she gets sorted."

"You're serious, aren't you?"

"Maybe. I don't know. What do you think?"

"I think that so long as you're not using Rowan Thorp as a place to hide from the problems we've been facing, it's worth considering. You know my home is wherever you are."

"I can't be hiding from things if you're with me, can I? It'll simply be a fresh environment for us. I feel more relaxed here. Believe me, that's as much of a surprise to me as it is to you. You were right, I need my sisters. You're always right."

"Oh, no, don't put that pressure on me." Evette laughed softly. "It's only that sometimes I can see what you're too close to notice. You do the same for me."

"Thank you." She nestled her head into the pillow, reveling in having Evette so close.

"For what?"

"For coming here."

"Thank Star for being a pushy mare. That woman is tenacious when she's got a bee in her bonnet."

"Remind you of anyone?"

"I don't think any of those apples fell as far from the tree as you North sisters like to think."

Simone smiled and snuggled in closer.

"You tired?" asked Evette.

"Why?"

"I was thinking we should take advantage of this awfully big bed again."

●　●　●

FOR THE FIRST time in a long while Simone slept through the night without wakefulness or nightmares. She had missed Evette since she'd been in Rowan Thorp, but now that they were back in each other's arms, she realized she had been missing her for a lot longer than that. Over the last year, they'd been living simultaneously together and miles apart. She wouldn't let that happen again. Their path toward becoming parents might be unclear, but she would make sure they never lost sight of each other again.

A PATTER WOKE Star. A dripping tap? A branch against a window? A shower of little skitters against the glass. This better not be Stu again. "For fuck's sake!" she shouted. She jumped out of bed, threw back the curtains, and wrenched open the window in one smooth movement, shouting, "What!" against the wall of cold air.

"I don't care!" blurted a man's voice.

Her world tilted. Not Stu. Duncan. She gulped in a lungful of frozen night.

"Duncan!" Hope oxygenated her blood and catapulted through her veins.

His face was so earnest it made her knees weak.

"What I mean to say is, I don't care if you don't want to have children in the future. And I don't care that you want to be a surrogate for Simone. I only care about being with you. I will stand by you and your decisions. I'll rub your feet when you're too pregnant to reach them, I'll hold your hand while you're in labor with your sister's baby, I'll do whatever it takes to be with you. I just want us to be together, to see where this takes us."

"Why?" She couldn't help wondering what had caused this sudden assertion.

He smiled shyly. "Because I love the way you see the world, your positivity and endless hopefulness that people can be better than they are. You make *me* look with better eyes. I feel awake when I'm with you in a way I've never been before. I love that you look for magic in the mundane and how you shine when you find it. I want to search for magic with you. You are kind and principled and strong-willed to the point of ridiculous and you'd move the moon and stars for the people you love. I'd like to know you, Heavenly-Stargazer." He looked up at her imploringly. "Is that enough? I can go on. I've got so much more!"

She was dumbfounded. She clapped her hands to her mouth to stifle a laugh of joy. Her heart was beating so fast, she could feel the pound of it through her skin.

"Am I too late?" Duncan asked. "Please tell me I'm not too late."

"You're—no—you're not too late," she managed to stammer.

He smiled. "Then come down here," he urged.

She flew down the stairs in a dream, running to the garden gate in bed-socked feet and yanking it open.

Duncan walked slowly toward her, and she waited. Excitement pulsed through her. When he was so close that the steam of their breath mingled, she said, "I've got bed breath."

His chuckle was low and deep as he looked into her eyes. "I *really* don't care."

He bent to kiss her lips. They kissed slowly at first, tenderly, his hands cupping her face while she snaked her arms around his waist. But they'd missed each other over the past couple of days, and quickly a hunger awakened between them that couldn't be satisfied with gentle kisses. Their breath came harder as they pulled and pawed at each other, frustrated by the clothes between them.

"Get a room!" someone shouted from an upstairs window above one of the shops.

She giggled, burying her face in Duncan's chest.

"You know, that's not a bad idea," he said.

She looked up at him and smiled.

"How do you feel about single beds?" she asked, taking his hand and leading him through the back gate to the flat.

That night, the creatures in the woods discovered the feast laid out for them by the people of Rowan Thorp. And upstairs in Star's old bedroom, she and Duncan discovered each other for the first time and found magic aplenty.

42

BIRD BROTHER WAS an instant hit. Gerry and his fellow twitchers had installed the bird cams on Thursday morning, and within an hour of going live, most of Rowan Thorp was tuning in to watch the comings and goings of the rowan tree woods creatures. Betty—ever the canny businesswoman—had propped her iPad on the countertop so that people could watch while having their morning caffeine fix. The whole café stopped to watch when Joe and Duncan appeared on-screen and fixed the patchwork tarpaulin over the clearing in the woods, which would now be the banqueting hall. When it was done, everyone burst into applause.

Maggie, Simone, and Star had use of Ryan and Kev's cookery school kitchen for the day and they planned to get as much prep done as possible, starting with the nut roasts.

There would be chicken as well, ten of them in fact, which they would cook tomorrow afternoon, so that the meat would be warm and rested for the feast. Kev and Troy had gone halves on a whole pig, which would be roasted slowly on the day. Apparently, they had been wanting to branch into offering a hog roast service, and the winter solstice banquet was the perfect excuse for them to try out their skills before they committed to buying all the equipment.

"It looks like the bird food Doreen made for the decorations," said Simone, staring into her bowl of nut roast ingredients with distaste. "I think I'll be sticking with the hog roast."

"Don't knock it till you've tried it." Star was unperturbed. "This is not only utterly delicious but is full of vitamins."

"It looks like a recipe for explosive farts. I'm keeping Evette well away from it."

Maggie snickered but pulled herself up short when Star glared at her. The mixture was rich, heavy with mushrooms and lentils, and fragrant with fresh sage, thyme, and rosemary. Liberal handfuls of fresh cranberries added a burst of color and there was no denying it smelled like Christmas Day as they plopped the mixture into the waiting loaf tins.

Next was the soup, which could be made today and reheated just before needed tomorrow evening. The old solstice menu notes they'd found in the strongbox revealed that English onion soup, made with cider from Rowan Thorp apples, was the tradition. With Parminder and Gerry Myers having made enough cider to test the livers of the entire village three times over, there seemed no reason to mess with history.

Maggie dragged a sack of white onions across the floor to rest against the legs of the long stainless steel work area.

"Are you serious?" asked Simone.

"What did you think we were going to make onion soup with?"

"That's like two hundred onions!" declared Star.

"Don't be so dramatic," Maggie admonished. "It's barely a hundred."

"And we have to peel and chop them all?"

"That's how it usually works, yes."

"We're going to be in agony!" wailed Star.

"I have sensitive eyes!" protested Simone.

Kat walked in in her chef's whites, swinging a carrier bag.

"Don't worry, whiners, I've come prepared," she declared, pulling three pairs of welding goggles from the bag. "Put these on and you can chop onions all day long without shedding a tear."

The women goggled up and set to work. Kat put some Christmas tunes on, and they only had to suffer minimal grumbling from Simone about the risk of chopping-induced repetitive strain injury.

"How are things with Evette?" Maggie asked.

Simone smiled. "I think we're going to be okay. I was so fixated on becoming pregnant, I'd reached the point where I was saturated with it. There'd been no space for anything else. But I'm learning how to make room."

"Oh, Simone." Star looked up from stirring the onions that were caramelizing in one of three huge pans, her eyes cartoonishly large in the goggles.

"It is what it is." Simone shrugged. "Being away from it, and I guess being with you two, it's helped me reset."

"I'm glad it's helped," said Maggie, sliding a chopping board full of sliced onions and fresh thyme into the melted butter in her pan. "We have to do better for each other. All of us. I want you both to know, here and now, that I am here for you."

"Me too," said Star. "I don't want us to be estranged. You're my family, I need you—even you, Simone."

Simone swiped at her with a wooden spoon. "It's hard for you to see, what with the welding goggles, but that's made me shed a tear." Simone's voice was tight.

The North sisters closed in for a hug, three sets of goggles clinking.

"Thank you for offering to be our surrogate," Simone whispered into Star's ear. "You'll never know how much it means to me."

"I would do anything for you, either of you."

"For the record, I have no need of your womb," said Maggie. "But I'd appreciate a babysitter once a week now that you've decided to stick around for a while. It would be kind of nice to go out on actual dates with Joe."

"Done." Star smiled.

The scent of onions caramelizing in butter filled the kitchen, and when crushed garlic was added to the mix, a new layer of savory filled the space.

"I want to run something by you both," said Simone.

Maggie narrowed her eyes. "Go on."

"I'm on sabbatical for a year, and Evette and I thought, since our lease is up in January, maybe we could try and find a place to rent here."

"In Rowan Thorp?" Maggie exclaimed. "I mean, that would be wonderful! I'd love it if you lived here, but isn't it a bit quiet here for you London gals?"

"We love London, but we've lived there for our entire married life. We're ready to start a new adventure."

"Oh my god! This is so amazing! We'll all be together again! I'm so excited!" Star was shrieking with delight.

"How would it work with Evette's counseling?" asked Maggie, ever practical.

"If her existing clients want to stay with her, she could offer video appointments and then she could set herself up in practice here for in-person consultations. And if after a year we've settled in properly, I guess I'll look at getting another physiotherapy placement. To be honest, I'm looking forward to helping at the shop and just being around, you know? Being in the present, instead of living on fast-forward. I've been so busy chasing the future that I stopped appreciating the here and now, and that included my wife. We need a bit of time to bask in the greatness of our marriage."

"Sounds like you've got it all worked out." Maggie smiled. "I think it's a brilliant idea. The only fly in the ointment is that *I* might not be able to afford to stay here. How ironic that after all these years of living here without you both, I might be leaving just as you move in."

"What!" Star exclaimed. "No!"

"Interest from city dwellers wanting to move to the country—no offense, Simone—has pushed rents around here through the roof. I was barely hanging on over at the shop, and that was with the advantage of being a long-term tenant." Maggie couldn't help the wobble in her voice.

"Live at Dad's with me permanently," Star implored.

"Sweetie, that's not a long-term solution for either of us, you know that. We need to sell the building; we all need the money, and I need a job. I'm losing my livelihood; I've got to move where the work is."

"Which leads me to my next proposal." Simone pulled her phone out of her pocket and said in her bossiest voice, "Hello. Yes. I need you to come here now, please."

She had barely shoved her phone back into her jeans when Duncan walked in, holding a glass of orange juice and a plate with a chef's club sandwich teetering on top.

"I'm here," he said, resting his lunch on the worktop. "I was just in the bar getting lunch. Why are you all wearing goggles?

Blimey! It's a bit oniony in here!" His eyes instantly began to stream.

Star handed him a square of kitchen paper.

"Tell them what you told me earlier." Simone nodded at him.

The paper towel was already soaking, but Duncan struggled bravely on.

"It's a Hilliard," he began, "the miniature we found the other day. I just found out this morning. Simone caught me as I was taking the call; she asked me to wait until you were all together."

"Holy Mary, Mother of God!" Maggie reached for the work-top to steady herself.

"All praise the goddess!" Star trilled.

Simone smiled, pleased. "In light of the fact that our ances-tors appear to have hoarded some pretty mint heirlooms over the years, my suggestion is this. We don't sell the shop. We keep it going. Star, you are homeless and jobless . . ."

"Thanks for reminding me."

"My point is, you can live at Dad's and run the shop. You've been learning this stuff with Duncan, so keep learning. Become a buyer of interesting things like Patience and Dad and all the Norths in between.

"We can auction off some of the bigger-ticket items like the Hilliard and split the cash to keep us going. Two hundred grand split three ways would be about sixty-six grand each. More than enough for you to find a new place to rent in Rowan Thorp, Maggie, and give you a bit of breathing space while you find another job. We'll get a contract made up, Maggie and I can be silent partners in the business. We'll take our cut, and, Star, you'll have somewhere to live rent-free."

Star was nodding like one of those bobble-head dashboard dolls, her mouth an *O* shape of delight.

"You could work in the curios shop with me, Maggie. It's a family business, after all," she gushed excitedly, hugging herself as though to stop herself from exploding. Simone couldn't help but grin at the effect her words were having on her sisters.

"I can't quite take it in." Maggie laughed. "Sixty-six grand. Shit! That's more money than I've ever had in my life!"

"That's a modest estimate, in my fine art counterpart's opinion," Duncan put in. "That would be the reserve price; I'd expect it to go for a lot more."

"I think I might throw up." Maggie was dabbing her forehead with her apron.

Star was doing a strange kind of floaty dance of joy about the kitchen, which looked all the more incongruous for the apron that read *Dirty Bitch!* and the welding goggles. She paused to kiss Duncan, who had taken to stirring the three pots of onions to make sure they didn't burn, since the North sisters had all but abandoned their workstations.

"Well?" asked Simone. "What do you think, Maggie? It won't save your home, but it means you can stay in the village. Verity wouldn't have to change schools, and you could help out at the shop until you find your feet, or forever if you'd like? You have to admit it's a genius idea, if I do say so myself."

"I agree with your genius," said Maggie slowly. "I think it could work. It would be lovely to have you all here. I mean, you are a giant high-maintenance pain in the arse, and Star is a space cadet, but I wouldn't have you any other way."

"Who's a space cadet?" asked Star as she pirouetted about the kitchen.

Simone smiled. At long last, things were starting to look up.

43

"I'M GOING TO tell them both tonight," Maggie said, a half-empty crate of broccoli in her arms. "Over dinner."

She and Joe were bringing in the fruit and veg displays from the front of the shop. The weather had turned ominously cold, and a freezing fog hung along the high street. She had filled Joe in on the events in the pub kitchen.

"We could tell them about us too. Make it official. Hit them with all the good news at once." Joe smiled.

Maggie squirmed. "Maybe not tonight. We don't want to blow their minds." She laughed awkwardly. His face fell and she felt horribly guilty. "But soon," she added brightly, always playing for time.

Joe recovered his good humor quickly. "I've got say, I'm relieved," he said, dropping a crate of parsnips down beside a tray of sprout trees. "I understand your reasons for keeping the eviction from them, but I've felt uncomfortable about Patrick; he's an adult, he ought to be kept in the loop."

"I know. I was hanging on for a miracle. But what with the money from the painting and not having to sell my dad's place, it feels like I've got the next best thing. Honestly, I feel like a weight's been lifted. I know I gave it the big 'I'll be fine' speech, but I was scared shitless about what I was going to do."

"I know. You're not as good an actor as you think you are." He was smiling warmly at her.

"And here I was thinking I had you fooled."

"Don't give up your day job." Joe laughed and then realized what he'd said. "Sorry."

"My day job's given *me* up. I know it isn't glamorous, but I've always loved running a greengrocer shop. It's hard work, but I get to be out and about, I get to meet people and carry on something my mum built up. It feels like I'm losing a part of her with the business."

"I'm sorry, Mags. You know if I could I'd buy Gilbert out and give you the building."

"You are so sweet, no wonder I love you."

His face broke into a smile. "I don't think I'll ever get tired of hearing you say that." He paused for a moment and then said, "There's something I need to tell you. It's about Gilbert and Marks . . ."

The door that led from the shop up to the flat flew open and hit the wall so hard there was a definite sound of wood splintering.

"Patrick! What are you doing? You practically took the door off its hinges." And then she saw his expression. Pure anger.

"Why didn't you tell me?"

Patrick's voice was sharp and accusatory, shaking with rage. She recognized the blue letterhead as he shook the letter back and forth in his clenched fist, and her heart, so light a second ago, sank like a stone. From the corner of her eye, she saw Joe straighten up from lifting a box of clementines and dust his jeans down.

"Why wouldn't you tell me? I had to find out like this. Cheers, Mum! Happy fucking Christmas."

"Darling, listen, I . . ."

"I can't believe you! What were you going to do? Box everything up and hope we wouldn't notice? Or maybe move out on the sly when I've gone back to uni, send me a forwarding address in a text?"

"Don't be ridiculous . . ."

"Did he know, this whole time?" He jabbed a finger in Joe's direction. He must have seen the look that passed between them, because he raised his hands in the air in exasperation or resignation, Maggie couldn't tell which. "Of course! Of course you would confide in him before your own son. I'm sorry to be the one to tell you this, Ma, but you put your faith in the wrong person."

She could almost hear Joe's thoughts as his eyes tried to seek hers; *I told you you should have told him.* She kept her eyes on Patrick.

"I was going to tell you." She kept her voice level.

He barked out a laugh. "When?"

"I didn't want to ruin Christmas for Verity. I didn't want you to worry. But there have been some recent developments, literally today, and I was going to tell you tonight. I was *just* talking with Joe about it . . ."

But Patrick wasn't listening; he was too angry to be reasoned with. "What were you thinking? Spring it on us on New Year's Day maybe? Happy bloody New Year! We're going to be homeless!"

"I was hoping I could change the landlord's mind."

"This is our home. I had a right to know."

"You're right, but I'm your mother, and sometimes I have to make hard decisions for us."

"You know, you treat me like a kid when *you're* the one who's being childish."

"Come on, mate, that's not fair," said Joe.

Maggie felt him come to stand next to her, but it didn't bring her any comfort; if anything, her stomach squirmed with unease. Siding with her was only going to make Patrick angrier. He turned his attention to Joe. She couldn't read the expression on his face, but his eyes narrowed infinitesimally, and his mouth twisted into a sneer that didn't suit his kind face.

"I went on the Gilbert and Marks website," he said, voice low with rage. "Thought maybe there'd be a way to contest the eviction or make a complaint. I didn't find anything useful, but the About Us page had some interesting photographs of the happy landlord family picnic two summers ago."

She frowned, wondering where he was going with this. Patrick's eyes were still locked on Joe. His voice had taken on an oily menace that she didn't recognize. Beside her, she felt Joe stiffen.

"We can talk about this, Patrick," said Joe calmly. He held out his hands, palms facedown, making a tamping-down motion, as though he could physically smooth out whatever was brewing between them.

"Talk about what?" she asked, looking from her son to her lover and finding only animosity in both faces. "What's going on?"

"You're not the only one keeping secrets," said Patrick, eyes still locked on Joe, daring him to break the stare-off first.

"Let's not do it this way, Patrick. I promise you, you have this all wrong."

Patrick shook his head. "I don't think I do."

"Will somebody please tell me what's going on?" She felt sick; it was the kind of nausea when your body knows before your brain that something is about to mess up your world.

Joe took a deep breath but Patrick cut him off.

"Gareth Gilbert is Joe's uncle. I did a little digging. Your boyfriend is on the payroll. I guess this was an undercover job, huh? How much did you get for screwing us over?"

The room spun.

"What?" She looked from one to the other, confounded. Joe hung his head.

Patrick let the eviction notice drop to the floor. "Over to you," he said to Joe, and left the shop.

The shop was suddenly oppressively quiet. Joe put his hands into his pockets and smiled nervously at her.

"Well, that was quite a spectacular mike-drop moment," he said, trying to joke away the storm.

"You're my landlord's nephew?" She was having trouble making things fit in her head. *What did this mean? Why wouldn't he have mentioned this?* "Did you know I was a tenant when you took the job?"

"Not right away."

"But you work for Gilbert and Marks?"

"No. I did some freelance marketing for them occasionally; I haven't done any for over a year." He sighed, resigned. "Gilbert is the uncle who stole my mum's shares. I couldn't stay working for him after that."

"Why didn't you tell me?"

"Because I knew what it would look like."

"And what does it look like?"

He rubbed the back of his neck. "Like I was in cahoots with my uncle."

"And were you?"

"No!" His voice was desperate, pleading. "You have to believe me. I was looking for a job, and I saw yours on a website. I recognized the town name because I'd seen it when I was working for Gilbert and Marks. I knew my uncle had properties here, but I swear I didn't know yours was one of them until I got here."

"And when you did realize?" She felt sickeningly alert, like she'd just woken up in a strange place.

"I should have told you. I know that. But the longer I left it, the worse I knew it would look. I don't expect you to believe me, but I have been trying to help."

"Help me or help yourself? Get me into bed and out of my home? Was there a nice promotion in it for you? Were you all laughing behind my back? The desperate widow gagging for a shag, totally oblivious?"

Her voice was rising, but it quavered unsteadily, catching in her throat. Her hands were shaking, and she clenched her fists to make them be still. She was a tornado of hurt and humiliation. She knew it. She just knew it. *This is what happens when you give your heart away.*

"No! God, Mags, no, it was never like that. I told you—I didn't work for him when I came here. I'll admit I was curious when I first arrived, I remembered my uncle had plans for the building . . ."

"This is my life, my livelihood, my *home.* I grew up here, my mother died here, I raised my kids here!"

"Please just take a breath, let me explain."

She shook her head as though trying to stop his words from touching her. "Don't!" She put her hand up to stop him. "Just don't. You used me. I let you into my life—into *my bed*—and you used me. God! I feel disgusting. How could I have been so stupid?"

Joe reached out for her, touched her arm lightly as he looked searchingly into her eyes for a gap through her defenses. She shrugged him off, clutching at the place he'd touched as though he'd slapped her.

"You have to believe me; it wasn't how Patrick made it sound . . ." he pleaded with her.

"Just go."

The hurt in his face was too raw, she couldn't look at him, she didn't have enough left in her to feel sorry for him after what he'd done.

"Please give me a chance to explain."

"No. You don't get chances. Thank god I didn't let you talk me into making things official between us. Imagine if I'd told Verity!"

He shook his head sadly as he stepped away from her. "How did I not see it before? This is perfect for you, isn't it?" he said.

"What?"

"I've just handed you your Get Out of Jail Free card. Now you don't need to make room for me in your life. You never had any intention of telling Patrick or anyone else that we were serious, did you? There was never going to be an 'us' or 'ours' in this scenario. I was always going to be your dirty little secret because you are too afraid to let yourself be happy."

"You are in absolutely no position to accuse me of anything." The truth of his words sickened her further.

"Exactly!" He laughed bitterly. "I've relieved you of all responsibility. Stupid me, I walked right into it. Now you can throw me out of your life and still maintain the moral high ground.

"All I want is to be with you, but you make someone wanting to get close to you feel like an incursion. You push everyone away."

"You lied to me!"

"I omitted the truth—it's different!"

"That's semantics. How could I ever trust you again?"

"If that's the case, what about you? What about your lies? You want to talk about trust? I trusted you when you said you just needed a bit of time and then we'd tell the kids we were together, get a place together, start a life! I trusted that you felt the same about me as I do you, but the truth is, you were never going to let me in."

He was right. But so was she.

"You're turning this around. Don't gaslight me."

"I'm not. I know what I did. I take full responsibility for my mistakes. I fucked up. I should have told you straightaway and I will always be sorry that I didn't." He rubbed his hands through his hair, shaking his head. "I would shout my love for you from every rooftop in this village. For god's sake, Maggie, I would give you everything, all you had to do was say the word. Please. Please don't give up on us. Let me explain it properly."

This was too much. And the worst part was that even as her heart was breaking, a part of her knew that he was right about her, that she was too afraid to let him in, that this *was* the perfect excuse to end it all before she got in too deep. Joe was looking at her, his expression haunted, desperate, pleading. She couldn't let him see her tears fall. She couldn't let him know that he had broken her.

"Maggie."

"Leave me alone!"

"Please—"

"Leave! I want you out of my home. Go!"

He nodded once and left. She grabbed her phone and pulled up the Gilbert & Marks website. She clicked on About Us and scrolled through the pictures of staff until she found it: a picnic cloth laid out on the grass, loaded with food, a cooler to one side stuffed full of bottles of beer. And behind the feast, with his arms draped around the people on either side of him, grinning up at the camera with the gleeful expression of the freshly drunk, was Joe. Joe, who had joked on more than one occasion that he was an open book. Joe, who had made love to her and told her that he was in love with her. Joe, who had promised that her heart was safe with him. Joe, who was a liar.

44

WHEN SHE'D MANAGED to calm her breathing, Maggie called Star and asked if she would mind having Verity for an impromptu sleepover. She was not fit for good parenting right now. She was hanging on by her fingernails and she didn't know how long she had before she'd fall.

"Are you sure everything's okay? You sound weird."

"Everything's fine. I've got a ton of paperwork to do, and I just really need to get on. She's been badgering me for a sleepover with you ever since you got here."

"Bless her heart. Of course, I'm excited to have her over. And you're sure you're . . . okay? I thought we were meeting tonight to go over the final plans."

"I'm fine! Honestly, I'm just really behind on my paperwork, what with the time taken up with the solstice festival . . ."

"Is Joe there?"

"Um, no. No. Not tonight."

"Okay, I'll be over in ten."

"Thanks. You're a star, Star."

"Uh-huh."

Verity was beyond excited at the idea of a sleepover with

Aunty Star. She kept watch at the front window and when she saw Star crossing the street, she grabbed her rucksack and rushed down the stairs to meet her. Maggie followed her down and stood in the doorway, keeping the porch light off so that Star couldn't get a good look at her face as she waved Verity off. Verity bounded out onto the street to greet her aunty and was so insistent to get over to the curios shop that Star didn't have a chance to get within six feet of her sister.

"So, you're all good? Yeah?" Star called over. "Nothing you want to tell me?"

"Nope. All good." She forced a smile. Her cheeks felt like setting concrete as they lifted in response to her mouth's movement. "Sameera's dad is coming to pick Verity up in the morning at eight thirty for a playdate so that we can crack on with the festival. I'll text him and tell him to pick her up from yours."

"Okay, no worries."

Finally, having her sleeve tugged by a very excited niece, Star turned with a hesitant wave and left.

Maggie kept the rictus grin on her face until she closed the door and then she let the smile melt down her face like candlewax.

She spent the next hour vigorously cleaning the shop in an attempt to get her thoughts straight. Her sadness was a physical pain, throbbing with its own heartbeat. At the same time, humiliation burned her, searing her cheeks and making her stomach twist so that in one breath she wanted to curl up in a ball of her own mortification, and in the next, she wanted to set the world on fire and watch it burn to ash. Her feelings were too big. There wasn't room for them in her chest. She needed to scream them out, but there was nowhere in this goddamned village where a person could lose their shit without being seen. In the end, love would find a way to kick you in the fanny one way or the other. She set about mopping the floor with a violence that left no stain safe, and as the disinfectant fumes rose out of the steaming bucket, so too did the rage that was unfurling within her, and it wasn't only Joe who had incited it.

When there was nothing left to scrub in the shop and she felt she had her anger under control, she climbed the stairs to the flat and knocked on Patrick's bedroom door. He was sitting on his bed, reading. The bottoms of his white socks were a dirty gray and the room was littered with discarded underwear and hoodies. He sat up straighter when she walked in, locking eyes with her for moments but unable to hold her gaze.

"You could have come to me, quietly, taken me to one side."

Patrick didn't meet her eyes at all now. "*You* should have told me we were losing the house," he countered.

"Yes. With hindsight, I should have told you, and I'm sorry that you had to find out in the way that you did. I was trying to protect you, but I went about it the wrong way."

"You don't need to protect me."

"I will always try to protect you because I'm your mother and I'm hardwired that way. But your behavior today was unacceptable."

He looked up quickly and away again but not quick enough to hide the guilt in his face. He knew what he'd done.

It was a fight to keep her voice level, but she wouldn't raise it and give him an excuse to fight back. He wanted to rail against the unfairness of their eviction, he wanted someone to shout at because the situation made him feel helpless, but she wasn't going to give him the chance.

"You made me look a fool, and the worst part is, you did it on purpose because you were angry that I'd kept something from you, and you wanted to hurt me. Well, mission accomplished."

She shook her head. "How dare you try to pull that macho, man-of-the-house, misogynistic bullshit on me. I thought I'd taught you better than that."

He had the grace to look ashamed. "I was so angry, Mum." Tears stood in his eyes. He was still her little boy even though he was grown now.

"That's not going to cut it. You don't get to behave like an arsehole just because you're angry, that's not how respect works. You made me feel small and stupid. I do not deserve that."

He looked up at her then. "I know. I'm sorry."

She drew her hand across her forehead. She felt wretched. She and Patrick didn't fight, never had, even when he was in the middle of his sullen teenage years.

"Okay." She nodded. "I'm going to bed."

"Do you really think I'm a misogynist?"

She looked at her boy. She so wanted to make him feel better, but at the moment she was barely holding it together. The anger had acted as an Elastoplast over her heart, but now the rage had gone, the plaster was unsticking, and she was about to come apart at the seams.

"I don't know what I think at this moment; my brain is mush. I know that I love you and I'm tired and heartbroken and I need to go to bed."

"Heartbroken because of me? Because of my behavior?"

"No, my darling. You won't want to hear this, but since it's over I suppose it's a moot issue anyway. I love Joe. And I thought he loved me too. I guess that makes me just another desperate middle-aged woman. So, that's it. The whole story. We're being evicted and I'm a fool."

When he looked at her, his eyes were full of compassion and worry. "I didn't know that you actually loved him. I thought it was a fling or something. If I'd known, I never would have . . . We'll work it out, like we always do, it'll be okay . . ."

She forced a smile into her trembling lips and tried to make herself sound like a mother and not someone whose life was falling down around her ears.

"Don't you worry about me. Nothing that a good night's sleep can't fix," she lied.

She left before Patrick had the time to scooch off his bed and give her a hug because a hug in that moment would break her.

Pulling his bedroom door closed behind her, she ran to her room as the tears began to fall. Her head pounded from the pressure of holding in her sorrow. She waited until her face was firmly pressed into her pillow before she gave way and let the torrent roll over her. It was all too much. It wasn't simply about Joe, though his betrayal had been the final straw. Nor was it only the eviction, or losing her father, or arranging the whole funeral, or losing her business, or organizing a goddamned winter solstice festival, or trying to plan and pay for the Christmas her children deserved, or having to be so fucking upbeat all the time because if she wasn't, the people around her became nervous, because so long as Maggie was all right, then everything must surely be okay in the end. It wasn't only the thought of having to pack up her entire life. Or the thought of having to rebuild her business in an unknown location, or having to change careers entirely and start again, be the new girl at forty-four years old.

It was *all* of those things piling on and turning the screws like she was a flower in a press. And she had lost Joe. Just as she had known she would. All men leave in the end.

Amid it all, she wondered where Joe was now. What was he

doing? Was he drowning his sorrows in the pub or had he gone for one of his runs? Was he feeling like she was? God, she hoped so. She didn't know what to think. Could there have been an explanation like he had intimated? Should she have given him a chance, heard him out?

She turned over onto her back and stared at the ceiling. What did it matter? In the end, everything had played out just as she'd known it would. She'd made her heart vulnerable, and he'd stamped on it.

45

JUST AFTER HALF PAST eight on Friday morning, the door to North Novelties & Curios crashed open, slamming against the wall and causing multiple wind chimes to jangle.

"Blimey, Patrick!" Star exclaimed. "What did that door ever do to you?"

Betty was bent over Simone's massive to-do list for the evening's events, making appreciative noises at the spreadsheet. She'd left Doreen in charge of the café while she came over to check the running order for the day. The folk band had arrived in the early hours in two camper vans, had taken up residence in Betty's café as soon as it opened, and looked set to stay for the foreseeable future. There was a general feeling of excitement and expectation in the village, despite the early hour.

"Is your mum okay? Something was off with her last night and she's not returning our calls. Is she coming over?"

"I was just about to go over and check on her," added Simone.

"I've messed up," said Patrick. His eyes were wide. "I've really messed up. I don't know what to do. You've got to help me."

Simone and Evette immediately took control of the situation.

"Okay, first things first. Is anybody hurt?" asked Evette.

"Define 'hurt.'"

"Do we need the emergency services?" Simone snapped. "Is your mum in mortal danger?"

"No."

"That's a start, then. Come and sit down," Star soothed, taking his arm and leading him to the chair that Evette had pulled out for him. Patrick allowed himself to be pushed down into it. "Now, what's the problem?"

"It's Joe. Well, it's Mum but it's Joe. I got it all wrong and I've messed it up royally and now Ma's heartbroken. She's trying to pretend she's okay, but I know she isn't and it's all my fault."

Evette had her head cocked to one side and was nodding calmly, a look of concern and non-judgment on her face; Star surmised this was her professional expression and she was grateful for it.

"Okay, Patrick." Evette's voice was smooth like the sea on a calm day. "There's a lot to unpack here, so let's take one thing at a time and then we can see how best to help you. Why don't you start by telling us what happened with Joe?"

Patrick nodded, clearly soothed by Evette's calm demeanor. He took a deep breath and began.

"You know we're going to lose the house, right?"

"Did your mum tell you that?" asked Star.

"No." Patrick looked down at his hands. He was picking at his nails, which were already bitten down to the quick. "I found the eviction letters. I was angry and confronted Mum about it."

Star whistled out a breath at the ceiling. "Your mum was trying to protect you and Verity; you do understand that, don't you?" She had a horrible feeling that Patrick would not have taken Maggie's deception in the way it was intended.

He squirmed on the chair. "I do. Now. I didn't at first. I don't need to be treated like a kid."

"Perhaps you should stop behaving like one, then," said Simone.

Patrick looked up at his aunts, and for a moment Star wondered if he might take offense, but he only nodded and went back to his stubby fingernails.

"That's pretty much what Ma said too," he said.

"What happened when you confronted your mum about the letters?" Evette asked, her voice soft.

Patrick avoided eye contact. "I didn't handle it as well as I could," he replied.

"That would explain why Maggie was a no-show last night," said Simone, looking at Star.

"We argued and I blurted out what I'd found out about Joe."

"Wait, what you'd found out about Joe?" Simone asked, puzzled.

Patrick sighed. "Our landlord is Joe's uncle. Joe works for him. Or he did until a few months ago."

"What does that mean?" asked Star.

"I thought he was being paid to infiltrate the household, like an undercover operative or something."

"Have you been watching James Bond?" asked Star. She was having trouble picturing Joe as a spy. "And you found all this out how?"

"There's a photo of him on the landlord's website. 'Our family helping your family to find your perfect home,' or some such bollocks."

"Shit!" said Simone.

"My intuition knew something was wrong," Star said.

"So Joe was a spy?" asked Duncan.

"No, but I didn't know that then."

"What then?" asked Simone.

"I told her Joe was using her to get her out of the building. We had a row. A big one. Joe was there. Then he and Mum had a row."

"Patrick!" Star exclaimed. His head snapped up, his eyes pleading. Evette held up her hand for quiet.

Betty stepped forward. "What did you say? What's that about an eviction notice?"

Simone turned with what was clearly going to be a "Not now, Betty" sentence, but Star stopped her, with a gentle hand on her arm.

"Maggie's being evicted. She's got until January thirty-first to vacate the building and then it's being turned into a boutique hotel," she said.

Betty's eyes took on a squinty look as she absorbed this news. All eyes focused back on Patrick, who was wringing his hands nervously.

"And what's the situation with your mum now, Patrick?" Evette asked.

He took a shaky breath. "Mum threw Joe out. Now she won't stop crying. I couldn't get her to come out of her room this morning."

"You did the right thing coming here," soothed Evette.

"After the horse had already bolted," muttered Simone. "I'll go over there and check on her." She shot a daggered look at Patrick, which made him shrink into his chair. In that moment he looked much younger than his twenty years, despite the beard and bravado. He looked like his mum around the eyes, and Star found herself torn between wanting to coddle him and wanting to throttle him.

"It's worse than that," said Patrick quietly.

"How can it be worse?" Star asked exasperatedly.

"Joe was on our side. I mean, he was kind of a double agent but in our favor."

"How?" asked Simone.

"I went over to the Rowan Tree Inn, just now. I wanted to talk to Troy."

"Troy?" asked Star, surprised.

"I wanted to talk to a bloke, okay? Sometimes I just need to talk man-to-man with someone. I spotted Gilbert in there having a full English breakfast with some big blokes in suits. I couldn't believe he was here, in Rowan Thorp. He was moaning about his 'good-for-nothing nephew' who was making life hard for him. Trying to block his plans for the hotel and get him to let us stay. He's come down to have it out with Joe, face-to-face."

"Christ on a bike!" exclaimed Simone.

"I don't think there's much love lost between them," Patrick went on.

"If I might be allowed to interpose," Betty began, in a tone that implied she was going to whether she was allowed or not, "I think you'll find this Gilbert fella doesn't have the right to turn the building into a boutique hotel."

"That's not really our main concern at the moment, Betty," Simone said a little snappishly.

"I beg to differ," Betty challenged.

Simone huffed out a breath. "Whether he turns the place into a hotel or a bloody casino doesn't change the fact that he owns the property and is evicting our sister. I've a good mind to go over there myself and give him a rollicking."

"He owns the leasehold," Betty replied simply.

"What difference does that make?" Simone's voice was rising, but Evette motioned at her to be quiet.

"Go on, Betty," Evette urged.

"Gilbert owns the lease but not the freehold. The freehold is owned by the North estate."

There was a stunned silence, which felt as though it might stretch on indefinitely. Finally, Star asked, "How do you know this, Betty?"

Betty sniffed and jutted out her chin. "I am a member of the Rowan Thorp chapter of the Women's Institute, it's my business to know. And if you North girls hadn't been so flippin' secretive about the eviction, I could have stepped in before any of this nonsense." She cast a reproachful look at Star and Simone, who quelled beneath her gaze. "For heaven's sake! I've known you all since you were babes in arms. Why in god's name didn't any of you come to me?"

"Sorry, Betty," said Star, rubbing the toe of her boot along the flagstone floor.

"Yes, sorry, Betty," added Simone in a tone so meek that Evette did a double take.

"Well then." Betty smoothed down her apron. "I'll call an emergency meeting of the WI and let's see if we can sort this out. Gilbert and his cronies are still in the pub, you say?" Patrick nodded. "We need to keep them there. You, young man, Duncan. Get yourself over there and tell Troy what's going on. Tell him it's imperative that Gilbert doesn't leave."

Duncan started to sputter, but Betty's answering glare brooked no argument.

"I'll be off myself," Betty said. "Leave you to sort your sister out. Tell Maggie I need her to meet me outside the pub in two hours. You got that?" She tapped her watch. "Two hours!"

They all nodded, and Betty marched out of the shop and across the street like a woman on a mission.

AFTER A FEW moments of stunned silence, Simone gathered herself.

"Right," she said, returning her mind to the immediate business. "Okay. We can work with this. So, all we have to do is find Joe, tell him we know what he's been trying to do for Mags, and get the two of them in a room together to sort this shit out. And as for you, dearest nephew, your mother's relationship with Joe is none of your beeswax. What's the time?"

"Eight fifty," said Star, looking from the clock to the itinerary. "Plenty of time to get everything done for the festival and reunite the star-crossed lovers before the ceremonies begin."

"Let's do this!" Simone grinned and held her palm up to Star, who high-fived it.

"Joe's gone," said Patrick in a voice so small it was as though he hadn't wanted to be heard.

"What do you mean *gone*?" asked Evette.

"Troy told me. He left a note and the cash for this month's rent."

"Well, where did he go? Did he say anything in the note?" Simone demanded.

Patrick shrugged. "I don't think so."

"Have you tried calling him?" asked Star.

"It goes straight to voicemail. He's either switched his phone off or he's blocked me." Patrick gave an awkward grimace.

"I'll give him a try." Star pulled up his number and held her phone to her ear. A moment later she shook her head. "Straight to voicemail."

"Does anyone have any idea where Joe might have gone?" asked Evette. She was answered by shaken heads. "Maybe Maggie might have an idea?"

"Ahem." Duncan, who had shrugged into his jacket and was almost to the door, stopped in his tracks. "I, um, saw Joe this morning when I was out for my run. He said he was going to France, catching the ferry."

"France? Why France?" asked Simone.

Star rounded on him. "And you didn't think to tell me?"

"He told me in confidence. He was in pretty bad shape, it seemed like the least I could do. I didn't know the full story, only that he and Maggie had had a bust-up. He said it was his fault and he needed to get away from Rowan Thorp. His family live somewhere near Lille, I think he said. I got the impression he needed to lick his wounds. If I'd have known . . ." he trailed off.

"Did he tell you what time his ferry was?" asked Simone.

"Eleven o'clock—it was the only time he could get at such short notice."

Simone and Star stared at each other as if communicating via thoughts alone.

"My windscreen's cracked to hell; I can't drive my car," said Simone.

"I came by train," Evette added.

"Maggie's veg van, then?" said Star, and Simone nodded.

"You need to come too." Simone pointed at Patrick, who shrugged his shoulders and stood.

"What about the festival?" Star said. "With Maggie out of action, we're already one woman down and I can't do it all by myself. You're the organizer, not me. You've said it yourself enough times—I'm a shower of shite!"

"You'll be fine," said Simone with schoolmarm assuredness.

"We've got the plan all laid out. You know what needs to happen. Duncan can help you when he's finished helping Troy at the pub. Speaking of which, why are you still here?" She pointed a finger at Duncan, who jumped to attention and left without protest.

"I'm not sure I'm up to it, Simone, it's a huge responsibility."

"Look, one of us needs to get to the port at Dover and you can't drive. It's got to be me. I was wrong about you—you're not a shower of shite. You've got this. Just keep calm and follow the plan. With any luck, I'll be back with Joe way before the festival begins."

46

TEN MINUTES LATER, after some violent complaints from Maggie's old van as Simone got to grips with the gears, she and Patrick chugged out of the village, the engine roaring and the smell of diesel fumes in their wake.

Simone had driven vans before, but never one as old and clunky as Maggie's. There was a pervading scent of cabbage and earth hanging in the air, despite the efforts of a pine air freshener in the shape of a Christmas tree swinging from the mirror. There were no mats in the footwells, and the interior was skeletal. The heating had two settings, roast or freeze, and in between times they had to keep the windows down to stop the windshield from steaming up. She determined to use some of the proceeds from the curiosity shop to buy her sister a new van, and then remembered that Maggie would have no need for a work van if she had no business.

They had taken the country roads, because she was worried the van might shake itself to pieces trying to hit seventy on the motorway. The suspension was knackered, and every bump and pothole was a bruise in waiting. Thankfully, the snow was

mostly banked up at the sides of the roads and began to peter
as they reached sea level.

"Thanks for doing this," Patrick shouted over the clatter and
roar of the ancient vehicle; indoor voices were pointless.

"You've already thanked me."

"This seems like it deserves double thanks."

She smiled. "What is your problem anyway? Don't you want
your mum to find someone who will make her happy?"

"Of course I do! It's not that. It's just that she has really bad
taste in men. I don't want her to get hurt."

"You are not the gatekeeper of your mother's love life, Patrick. Does she have opinions on your girlfriends? Make them
feel unwelcome? Question their intentions?"

He balked. "No! Thank god."

"Then why do you feel the need to behave that way with Joe?"

"It's not the same."

"Then tell me how it is. No judgment. We've got time, and
this van—contrary to its physical attributes—is a safe space."

Patrick looked out the window. She could see him chewing
the inside of his cheek as he decided how much to tell her,
whether he could trust her with his feelings. She could wait. If
she'd learned anything from Evette, it was the art of allowing
space for dialogue, not pushing too hard but not allowing things
to settle either. She knew she was a bull in a china shop, impa-
tient with herself and those around her. But spending these last
couple of weeks with her nephew, watching as he climbed and
stumbled up the mountain of adulting, she understood the need
for a gentler approach.

Finally, he spoke. "You're going to think I'm a selfish cock."
She recognized a kindred spirit in her nephew.

"I'm going to think that you are a complex human being with complex emotions."

"What if she loves Joe more than she loved my dad? Joe is just so fucking *good*, and he's funny, he's brilliant with Verity, he makes Mum laugh all the time. He cooks! He's all the things that I always imagined *my* dad would have been, and that annoys me—I don't know why, it just does. It's like I missed out on my real dad and then the perfect 'stepdad' comes along too late, I'm already grown up, so I've missed out on that too. And it's gonna change everything. We've always been a three. What does being a four even look like? Where do I fit in? I'm away most of the time, so they'll be perfecting their new family dynamic, and I'll be an outsider. I want Mum to be happy. I'm just afraid of what will happen if Joe is the one to make her happy. Believe it or not, I actually like Joe a lot and I want him to like me. I feel like such a shit. He'd have every right to give me the finger and get on the ferry. I've fucked everything up. And I really upset Ma." His voice cracked and he put his head in his hands.

Simone swallowed hard to dislodge the lump in her throat. She pulled the van off the road and undid her seat belt so that she could bundle her nephew into a hug.

"Patrick Joshua North, you listen to me. You are a good person. There is nothing wrong with the feelings you are experiencing. Accepting a new person into your family is a big deal, and it is completely normal to have doubts and fears. Your mum loves you more than you can even imagine. You hurt her feelings, but she'll get over it, because love is bigger than everything else. And as for Joe, how could he not like you, you are fucking awesome! And if he doesn't accept your apology, then he's an idiot and he doesn't deserve your friendship or your mum's love, and *I'll* be the one giving *him* the finger, after I've kicked his arse!" Patrick snorted a laugh into her shoulder. She kissed the top of his head and released him. Pulling out her phone, she tried Joe's number again. Nothing. She wouldn't let Patrick see she was worried. "Right, let's crack on; we've a ferry to catch!"

Simone pulled back out onto the road and tried to channel her youngest sister's practice of pushing positive energy out into the universe. If she was going to make this right for Maggie, she would need to harness some of Star's eternal optimism.

47

THE FRONT COURTYARD of the Rowan Tree Inn was unusually busy. There hadn't been another snowfall since the storm, and with so much footfall on Holy Trinity Green the grass was making a reappearance. The glittering Christmas tree had been out-glitzed by an eclectic group of twenty or more women over-forty showcasing a style aesthetic that ranged from Fair Isle sweaters to leather trousers and everything in between. Some of the older women had gone gracefully with their gray hair, while others railed against it with fiery orange or Cleopatra black, and in one case a fetching flamingo pink. They looked as incongruous a group of comrades as you could hope to meet.

As Maggie looked on in a kind of trance, Evette gently steering her by the elbow, Betty emerged from the crowd looking resplendent in a cerise trouser suit with 1980s shoulder-pads-of-power and a white ruffled blouse exploding out the jacket. Her short sensible gray hair had been swept up at the front and gelled into a pompadour that would have made the most ardent New Romantic jealous. Maggie had only ever seen Betty in an apron over a floral tunic and slacks, and the sight of her now jolted her out of her daze.

"Good, you're here. We were starting to wonder how much longer we could keep Gilbert contained. Troy offered them free coffees, but they're making noises about leaving, so we need to move now," Betty half shouted.

Maggie shook herself, taking in the faces, which were now turned expectantly toward her.

"I'm sorry, who is Troy supplying with free coffee?"

Betty puffed out an exasperated breath toward Evette. "You didn't tell her?"

"I didn't know I was meant to. You just told me to get her here; that was hard enough."

"Not to worry, no harm done. She's here now. Let's get in there and bang this miscreant to rights."

"Who?" asked Maggie again, feeling increasingly like she had woken up in a parallel universe, or another decade.

"Your landlord, dear, the dishonorable Gareth Gilbert of Gilbert and Marks letting agents."

"Right. Why is my landlord in the pub at"—she looked at her watch—"ten forty-five in the morning and what are we going to do to him?"

"Scare the shit out of him if all goes to plan, eh, ladies!" A whoop went up behind her as the women fell in line behind Betty. "Ready?" she asked, looking expectantly at Maggie.

Maggie was lost and confused, so she nodded and stepped into the space left open by Harini.

Evette squeezed her arm. "Don't worry, I'm sure they've got this all under control," she said, though Maggie noticed she had begun to bite her lip.

"Oh, I'm not worried," she replied lazily. "At this point I really don't think much more can go wrong. Let the chips fall where they may."

Betty's voice drowned them out. "Ready, ladies?" The women of Rowan Thorp's wide and varied societies, institutes, and associations shouted and punched the air in a way that suggested they were *more* than ready. Maggie took a deep breath and followed Betty into the pub.

Gareth Gilbert was sitting in the far corner on one of the benches fitted against the wall, flanked by four archetypal *heavies*. He was so engrossed in his conversation that he didn't notice the wall of women headed toward him until they had clustered around him and blocked out not only the light but all available exits. He was momentarily taken aback but recovered himself quickly, no doubt bolstered by the human mountains on either side of him.

"Ladies!" he said, opening his arms wide in an expression of friendly greeting. "How can I help you? Are you collecting for the church roof fund? Or is it orphans today?" His voice had a nasal quality to it, oily and smooth so that every word came out as a sneer.

Troy came over and placed five pints of ale on the table in front of the men.

"On the house," he said and hurried back behind the bar to watch the show. The gift of free booze appeared to squash any thoughts the men may have had of imminent departure. Gilbert raised his glass to the women and took a swig.

"It's five o'clock somewhere." He gave a yellow-toothed grin.

Betty folded her arms and some of the women in the group shook their heads in disbelief and sympathy for his misguided ways.

"I knew your father," Betty began.

"Good for you," Gilbert countered. "Taught me everything I know about property; god rest his soul."

"Didn't teach you to read, though, did he?" piped up Harini. That got some titters.

Gilbert shifted in his seat, looking slightly discomforted for the first time but smiling through it. "Ladies, I don't mean to be rude, but I am a busy man, so if there is something I can help you with, let's get to it, shall we?"

"Your father knew how things stood in Rowan Thorp," said Betty. "He had respect."

Gilbert seemed to notice Maggie for the first time, and a kind of understanding dawned on his smug face.

"This is about Ms. North's eviction," he began, a smile fixed in place. "It isn't nice to lose a business in the village. I get it. I do. Small communities disappear when the hearts of the high street die. But I'm on your side. The hotel that will replace the greengrocer's is going to bring visitors and tourists to this charming corner of the weald, put you back on the map. Everyone benefits."

"We don't need to hear your sales pitch, Mr. Gilbert," Betty cut in. "We're just here to tell you, it's not going to happen."

Gilbert looked momentarily confounded but recovered himself quickly. "I'm afraid it's not up for negotiation."

"No, it isn't," agreed Betty. She turned and crooked her finger, and Maggie saw Saskia Brannigan push to the front of the little crowd, holding a large manila folder to her chest.

Saskia smoothed her hair down with one hand and then opened the folder at a page marked by a yellow sticky note. "You inherited the lease of the building currently rented by Maggie North," she began.

"Guilty as charged."

"The *lease*, Mr. Gilbert."

"Yes."

"Not the freehold."

Gilbert took a contemplative swig of his pint and set the glass down. "Get to the point, please, madam. I've got places to be and I'm sure you ladies have flower arranging or crochet granny squares to attend to."

Saskia straightened her back, and Maggie recognized the same steely glare as her daughter. A smile twitched at her lips. "As per the Rowan Thorp public records, Patience North purchased the historic land upon which Rowan Thorp is built in 1750. Over the next thirty years, she also purchased the freehold of several buildings on the estate, which have remained in the North name ever since."

"This is all very interesting, madam, but it doesn't affect *me*. I own the lease on the building, and I can sell it, with planning permission, to whosoever I choose."

"I'm terribly sorry to burst your bubble, Mr. Gilbert, but that's simply not true."

Saskia looked back and smiled as Parminder Myers, librarian, came to stand beside her.

"Patience North was a savvy businesswoman," Parminder began. "Women weren't entitled to own land in their own right in those days, but her tenacity garnered support from a team of London solicitors sympathetic to her plight, and certain loopholes were exploited to her advantage. Upon purchasing the estate and the property freeholds, she had covenants written into the deeds, so tightly knotted that they could not be undone by even the most cunning legal mind. This was her way of securing the future for North women down the centuries."

Sonja Moorhen had come to stand by Parminder and took up the story. "Though she remained unwed, she had three daughters. Her influence and high regard in the village as a good and fair landlord offered her protection against those who would have destroyed her for being an unmarried business-woman."

Gilbert put his hands up to stop Sonja. "I'm sorry, ladies, I realize you're on some sort of 'women's lib' trip here, but can you get to the point?"

Sonja looked about ready to poke Gilbert's eyes out with the laminated corner of the folder, but Parminder rested a steadying hand on her shoulder.

"Mr. Gilbert," Parminder said with a smile, "by law, as per the covenants placed on this land by Patience North, no North woman may be evicted from any property which bears the name North in the freehold."

Maggie's mouth dropped open, though not as wide as Gilbert's.

"Nah!" He grinned, shaking his head. "You're having me on. There's no such thing."

"Oh, but there is," said Saskia, stepping forward to wave a copy of the original freehold agreement and the leasehold agreement signed by Reginald Gilbert—Gareth's father—in 1955. Gilbert reached forward and snatched them out of Saskia's hand. She merely smiled serenely and watched with an amused smirk on her lips as he scanned the two documents.

He ran one hand through his thinning hair, greasy at the roots and beginning to clump. "I take it this isn't the only copy," he said with a kind of faint hope in his voice, as though he could rip these papers up and make it all go away.

"Really, Mr. Gilbert, what do you take us for?" asked Saskia sweetly. "There are copies held with the North family's solicitors, also in the library archives, the public village records, the historical society, and just as an extra precaution, in the Rowan

Thorp Women's Institute's own files. We like to stay informed. You will also find the covenants clearly marked out in the land registry and title deeds."

Gilbert's expression morphed from annoyed to perplexed as he scanned the documents. "Why would my dad agree to something like that?" he asked his associates, who simply shrugged their shoulders at him in response.

"There were no North women living in the property at the time he purchased it," said Parminder. "Presumably he didn't envisage that changing over the years. People often ignore the small print if it doesn't directly affect them at the time of signing."

"The bottom line, Mr. Gilbert, is that Maggie North is going nowhere." Betty had moved to the front of the crowd, arms crossed so that her ample bosoms rested on her forearms like two sandbags wrapped in polyester.

"I've shelved out serious money on this project!" Gilbert's face was turning dangerously red; a vein protruded above his left ear. "I've got planning permission. I've got a team of builders ready to come in and gut the place. I've got *planning permission!*"

Anita raised her hand. "If I may interject?" she asked.

"By all means, Anita," said Betty.

Anita smiled hesitantly and adjusted her glasses. "Thank you, Betty," she said. She spoke slowly and softly as though addressing a small child. "The planning permission—so-called—of which you speak, Mr. Gilbert, would seem to have bypassed the regular channels. That is to say, it didn't come past *me*. And *all* planning requests pass through *me*. Further inspection of this oversight has led to my discovering that you used a proxy company name when submitting your paperwork and that you submitted your paperwork via a third party, through the village council of nearby Warehorne. Somewhere between being redirected and arriving here, it was signed off, presumably by persons unknown, and filed without ever passing through my hands. In short, Mr. Gilbert, your planning permission has more holes in it than a builder's vest!"

The women grinned with a knowing smugness; Anita might look unassuming, but she was a firecracker when it came to procedure.

With a violent flick of his wrist, Gilbert threw the papers at them. The women quietly picked them up and handed them back to Saskia, who shuffled them into order and placed them back in the folder.

"You're making a mistake," Gilbert growled. "I'll sell the lease." He pointed at Maggie. "I'll sell it to one of the big building firms. See how your small-town politics stands up against a multimillion-pound company. They'll squash you like a bug."

"My family name will still be on the freehold," said Maggie. She glanced back toward Sonja, who nodded reassuringly. "The law is the law, no matter how big the bully."

At that moment, Vanessa rushed in, cheeks flushed and bobble hat bobbing.

"Sorry, ladies!" she chimed as she weaved to the front. "The football club had an away game and it ran over. I had to put this all together on my phone in between cheering and then dash into the office to print it off. Talk about short notice, Maggie. It would have been a lot easier if you'd told me about the eviction when you first got it."

Maggie gave a half shrug and muttered a bewildered, "Sorry?" She was feeling decidedly discombobulated. If last night's revelations had been devasting, then today's were confounding.

"No matter," trilled Vanessa. "Phew! It's hot in here. Where are we up to? Am I too late?"

"You are just in time." Her mum, Saskia, smiled. "We've challenged the legitimacy of the planning permission and provided evidence of Maggie's claim to remain on the property. Which team won?"

"We did. The boys have gone home with Tim to make celebration pizza for lunch," Vanessa replied, unwinding her scarf and pulling a William Morris binder out of her tote bag. "Good. Okay then, Mr. Gilbert. I have a proposal for you. Something that I think would be in all of our interests."

"Do you seriously think, after the attack of the menopause brigade here, that you could present me with *anything* I'd be interested in?" Gilbert was incredulous, but Vanessa ignored him, blowing her fringe out of her eyes and opening the binder.

"Now, there's room for a bit of back-and-forth, but the gist of it is this: taking into account Patience North's covenants and the fact that we have a North descendant in residence, the village of Rowan Thorp is willing to subsidize a mortgage in the form of a long-term loan in Marguerite North's name to purchase the leasehold from your good self, Mr. Gilbert." She turned to Maggie. "Should you want it, of course, Maggie."

Maggie had no words. She seemed only able to communicate by blinking, which she was sure she was doing more than the recommended daily allowance. Satisfied that Maggie's blinks were positive, Vanessa continued.

"Our coffers are not bottomless, you will understand, but I have compiled what I believe to be a fair offer for the leasehold." With a flourish, she pulled a printed sheet from her folder and handed it to Gilbert.

He looked it over and laughed unpleasantly, leaning back in his bench seat.

"I'm afraid you'll have to do better than that. You seem to have missed off a couple of zeros."

Vanessa was unperturbed. She pulled another piece of paper from the folder and smiled sweetly as she laid it in front of Gilbert and bent over so that her hands were flat on the table. Gilbert's stooges moved their pint glasses out of her way. Vanessa pointed to various lines on the page as she spoke.

"Ah, well, you see, I've actually done you a favor, sort of *cut out the middleman*, if you will. Let me explain. I calculated how much you will have to pay in court charges, fines, legal fees, compensations, and reparations when my clients—that is to say Ms. North and the village of Rowan Thorp—sue you for wrongful eviction, emotional distress, misconduct, and unlawfully gaining planning permission via willful deception and/or bribery." She took a deep breath; it was a long sentence. "As you can see, that is going to cost you a lot of money, and that is before we apply for a compulsory purchase order to buy the leasehold from you at a reduction of the market price in view of your misdemeanors. This figure represents the value were we *not* to press charges."

The stooge to the left whistled through his teeth. "I hate to say it, gov, but I think you've been snookered."

Gilbert's lip twisted up into a snarl. "When I want your opinion, I'll ask for it."

"Ooh! Somebody's tired!" came the singsong voice of Mrs. Philomena Russell—famous for her gooseberry jam—who had turned ninety just last week and given away all her shits twenty years before that.

Gilbert threw his arms up into the air. He looked every ounce a man who had been beaten. "Fine! Do you know what? You win. Let's do it. This project ain't worth the hassle. I hope you'll be very happy," he spat in Maggie's direction. "You lot deserve each other, bunch of fucking village witches. I hope you burn!"

"Oh, our foremothers in the seventeenth century did that already, dear, under James the First's reign," piped up Miss Eliza Radley—mistress of the WI Christmas quiz. "Nowadays *we* do the burning. Metaphorically speaking, of course. And metaphorically, I would say we burned you good and proper."

Gilbert shoved hard at the henchmen to his right, and the men began to shuffle along the bench seat to get out. It was hard to make a dramatic gesture of storming out when you first had to shimmy your bottom along a velour banquette. Finally, he stood, shrugged on his longline houndstooth coat, and flicked his collar up aggressively as though poison darts might shoot out of his lapel. None did. Then, with chest puffed and chin jutted, he pulled a wad of banknotes from his pocket, slammed it on the bar, and left the pub, his hired muscle lolloping along behind him.

At the sound of engines roaring outside, the women began to laugh and high-five one another.

"Drinks, Troy!" shouted Betty. "Fast as you can, please. We've got a winter solstice festival to conquer next."

"Coming right up," came Troy's answering call. "Orders, please, ladies. These are on the house!"

A cheer went up, followed by a stampede toward the bar. Maggie was dumbfounded. Vanessa gave her a smile. "You look thunderstruck."

"I am. Did what I think just happened, actually happen?"

Vanessa laughed. "Yes, it did."

"But how did you . . . ?"

"Well, I won't lie, it was a bit of a rush. Betty activated the phone tree as soon as she left Simone and Star in the shop."

"The phone tree?"

"Yeah, you know; we each have a list with everyone's phone numbers on it. In case of emergencies, the person at the top of the list calls the next person and they call the next and so on, until everyone on the list has been informed."

"I feel like I need to join the Women's Institute."

"You really do. So anyway, Miss Radley set up an emergency Zoom, and we all jumped on and, well, you know the rest."

"I had no idea about the covenant."

"I'd assumed Augustus would have told you all, otherwise I would have mentioned it. It didn't help that I wasn't aware of your eviction notice."

"In fairness to me, it's not the sort of thing you want publicized. I have my pride."

"Lot of good it did you. And anyway, it's not public, it's us, your friends, the people you and your kids have grown up with."

"I had no idea the Rowan Thorp women were so well connected."

"They're like gangsters, but with cake and fundraisers instead of organized crime."

Evette came over holding three sherry glasses. "To congratulate you and warm your cockles ahead of the solstice. It's freezing out there."

"Drinking before lunch?" Maggie raised an eyebrow.

"It's a special day." Evette shrugged.

"Were you in on this?" Maggie asked her sister-in-law.

"No, I simply did as I was told and got you here."

"Where *are* my sisters? They've missed all the fun."

"They're getting everything ready for tonight. I think they wanted to take some of the pressure off you."

Maggie felt a twinge of guilt. "I need to get over there. I've wallowed enough for one day."

She swallowed her sadness about Joe and stored it in the way that all good women trying to balance a million things had done for centuries: repress now, take antacids later. There was much to be thankful for. She could keep her home, she could keep her business going, more than that, she was on her way to *owning* her home, something she would never have imagined possible. Of the many emotions vying for her attention in that moment, it was gratitude for the women of Rowan Thorp that bolstered and empowered her to forge ahead with the day.

48

MAGGIE WAS HALFWAY to the shop when she was intercepted by Gerry.

"Ah, good, glad I caught you. Don't suppose you've tuned in to *Bird Brother* today, have you?"

"To be honest, Gerry, I really haven't had the time."

"No, quite right, that's what I thought. Thing is, I was just going back over last night's footage—there's a lot of activity at night—and I came across something that I think you ought to see."

Gerry pulled out his iPad and angled it toward her. Intrigued, she leaned in. The clock at the bottom of the screen read 5:52 a.m. The picture was grainy, but she could make out the outlines of the trees and the decorations gently swinging in the breeze. A mouse scurried along a branch and out of sight. There was a rustling somewhere out of the camera's range and then a face came into view. It was Joe. He was looking straight at the camera; the night vision made his eyes look strangely bright. Maggie's heart gave a jolt.

Joe cleared his throat. "Um, I don't really know where to begin. Since you've blocked my number, bird cam seemed like the best option." His voice was a scratchy whisper. "Maggie, I'm sorry. I messed up. And then instead of just asking for your forgiveness, I got defensive like a complete douchebag and turned things around onto you. You've done nothing wrong.

"I need you to understand how this all happened. It is true that I had been doing some freelance marketing for Gilbert and Marks. I had nothing to do with the lettings side of things; my role was to make the agency look appealing to landlords looking for a managing agent and to potential renters. I stopped working for my uncle when he conned my mum into handing over her shares of the business. I swear to god, when I applied for the job with you, I had no idea that he was your landlord." Joe paused to adjust his collar against the wind.

"By the time I discovered the link it was too late—how could I have told you without you thinking I had targeted you on purpose? Then when he started eviction proceedings, I knew I had to act. I even tried suing him for wrongful eviction. I was always on your side, Maggie.

"You are the kindest, most patient, most unselfish person I have ever met. You take everything onto your own shoulders so that the people you love have less to carry. I guess a part of me wanted to be your hero, wanted to prove to you that I was worth keeping around. I thought I could make things right, and instead I made a right hash of everything. Whatever you may think of me, I need you to know that I was never, ever in cahoots with my uncle. No matter what, I will always be on your side, fighting in your corner. Even if you never want to see me again. I love you, Marguerite North, and that won't change, however far apart we are."

Joe stared out of the screen for a few seconds and then he was gone. Maggie continued to stare at the dark outlines of the trees as though waiting for Joe to return. He didn't. Gerry stopped the video and tucked the iPad back under his arm.

"Shit!" she murmured under her breath. She was in daze; her heart was doing all kinds of wild things.

"Quite," Gerry agreed.

"As apologies go, that was pretty up there." She bit her lip. This morning had been a lot.

"Don't know what young Joe has done, but he seems like a good sort to me."

"He is a good sort," she agreed, feeling distant and muddle-headed.

"Probably shouldn't have let him go."

"Probably not, no." Her mind was stuck on Joe's final words: *however far apart we are.* Where was he? If only she hadn't been so hasty to block his number.

"When you think about it, there's not much you can't come back from if you really love someone. Apart from finding out that your dearly beloved is a murderer, or a bigamist, but beside those few exceptions, it's all just a storm in a teacup if you are truly in love," Gerry offered. "And I think you are truly in love, aren't you?"

"Yes," she said weakly. "I am."

FINDING SOMEWHERE TO park at the port had been impossible. Simone had trundled the noisy old van around the area so many times that the Port of Dover Police had begun to eye her suspiciously. When they began to talk into their walkie-talkies, she pulled off to one side.

"You need to go and find Joe. I'll park up along the seafront and catch you up."

Patrick paled. "Don't make me go by myself!"

"There isn't another option. In less than half an hour, that ferry is going to set sail with Joe on it unless you stop him."

"But. What am I going to say to him? What if he won't listen to me?"

"Make him listen to you!"

She took a breath and brought her voice down from snappish to merely forceful.

"This is going to be uncomfortable as hell, and you are going to have to eat some serious humble pie. But you will do it because it is the right thing to do and because it will make your mum happy. Trust me, when you find him, the words will be there."

He looked down at his lap as though steeling himself and then flung the van door, which creaked like an old farm gate, open.

"Okay. Let's do this." He jumped down. "Wish me luck!"

"Good luck! Go get that grocer!"

Patrick set off at a jog, and Simone looped back around and found a car park at the edge of the town, then began speed-walking in the direction she had last seen her nephew.

The wind came off the English Channel in salty gusts that knocked her sideways and whipped her hair over her face like damp seaweed. The only clues that storm Holly had been here were the gray piles of dirty snow clumped together in gutters and at the base of walls. The waves were whitecapped far into the distance; the sea swelled ominously, as if a behemoth was breathing below the surface. She was glad *she* wasn't traveling on a ferry today.

When she reached the port, she followed signs for the foot passengers' lounge and came upon a modern, glass-fronted building. Patrick stood outside, leaning against the windows.

"What happened?" she asked. "Where's Joe?"

Patrick shrugged. "All ferries have been canceled due to bad weather."

"Great! That ought to make it easier to find him. Come on."

Patrick pushed himself away from the glass. "He's not in there. I spoke to one of the concierges. Most of the passengers have gone into town, some have gone to find hotels. The ones who can afford it are heading back to Folkestone to catch the Channel Tunnel instead. He could be anywhere."

Simone tried not to let the disappointment show on her face even though it dragged through her from her head to her feet. She had so wanted to make things right for her sister. She cast her eyes around the port. Where would he go? It was a huge area to search, with no guarantee that he hadn't simply checked into a hotel in Dover to wait out the storm. In one last desperate attempt, she tried his phone again. It went straight to voicemail as before. Joe didn't want to be found.

Patrick was looking at her for answers, and she was all out.

"We tried, sweetheart, we really did. I guess we're just not going to win this one."

"But we can't give up! I have to make this right."

"You are not to blame for this. Your delivery was a bit shit, but Joe made his own mess. The best thing we can do now is head back and help your mum and Star with the festival."

Patrick's shoulders sagged, but he agreed.

"Let's get back to the van before we blow away. I'm not sure I'll be able to get a brush through my hair after this wind."

"Want me to shave your head?"

"You may have to."

With heads bowed, they made their way back toward the van. Waves smashed against the sea wall, sending explosions of spindrift into the air like a shaken champagne bottle.

They were almost to the van when a prolonged beep broke through the din of the storm, making them both jump. Simone put her hand to her eyes to shield them and squinted at the articulated lorry that was pulling up next to them. The passenger-side door opened, and a man with a hood pulled low over his face jumped down and approached them, pulling his hood back as he did so. Joe had dark half-moons beneath his eyes.

"Simone? Patrick? What are you doing here?"

"We've come to get you!" she called over the noise of the storm. "Why don't you answer your phone?"

"I forgot my charger, my phone died. Did Maggie send you?" For a moment his bloodshot eyes brightened.

"No," she said, and Patrick shook his head.

The light in his face blinked back out and was replaced with grim resignation. "Does she know you're here?"

"Well, no."

"Listen, I appreciate you coming all the way over here, but I think you've had a wasted journey. Maggie made it clear that she wanted me gone, and I don't blame her. I'm not going to force my presence on your mum if it's unwelcome, Patrick. You get that, don't you?"

"I'll explain it all to her," Patrick said with feeling. "I know what you tried to do for us; I overheard Gilbert in the pub this morning."

Joe raised his eyebrows. "Why was my uncle in Rowan Thorp?"

"He said he wanted to talk to you."

Joe shrugged. He had the look of a man for whom life holds no more surprises.

"Come back with us," Simone implored. "It's ridiculous for

you and Maggie to be apart—anyone with eyes in their head can see how much you love each other." She cast a sideways glance at Patrick.

The driver of the lorry leaned over and shouted, "If you wanna lift to the Channel Tunnel, we're gonna need to make a move, mate. You coming or staying with them?"

Indecision fleeted across Joe's face. Suddenly Patrick was climbing the steps to the cab. He grabbed Joe's duffel bag from the footwell and heaved it out.

"He's staying with us," Patrick told the driver.

The driver leaned over again. "Joe?" he asked. "You good? I don't wanna be witnessing a kidnap and have to tell the old Bill that I did nothing to help you."

Joe laughed uncertainly. "Ah, no, it's all good, thanks, mate. Not quite sure what this is, but pretty sure it's not a kidnap."

Simone stepped forward, pulling her hair out of her face. "It's really more of an ambush than a kidnap," she tried to reassure the driver.

He raised his eyebrows. "Well, if you're sure, Joe. I've got to get off. Hopefully I'll get to Belgium before midnight."

"I'm sure. Thanks for letting me hitch a ride, Nat, it was good to meet you. All the best. Merry Christmas!"

"Merry Christmas."

The driver gave a salute, and Joe slammed the passenger door shut. The lorry pulled back out onto the road and left them windswept and shivering on the pavement.

"Want to tell me what this is all about?" Joe asked, taking his duffel bag from Patrick.

"Mind if we discuss it in the van? My nipples are in danger of snapping off." Simone was trying to hold her hair down with one hand and keep her coat closed with the other. Joe made an "after you" motion, and Simone set off to the van with Patrick and Joe following behind.

There were a few moments of relief and exclamation as they closed the doors on the weather and settled themselves into the three seats in the front of the van, Joe in the middle.

She started the engine and put the heater on high to clear the windscreen. No one had said anything yet, and it was beginning to feel awkward. She wished Patrick would say his piece and get it over with. Eventually Joe broke the stalemate.

"Okay, you've stopped me leaving for France. Now what?"

She heard Patrick gulp. "I'm sorry about the way I dropped you in it," he began. "It was a dick move."

Joe took a moment to absorb Patrick's words. "Apology accepted. And I'm sorry that I didn't tell anyone about my involvement with Gilbert and Marks. I don't think we did ourselves any favors by keeping secrets. I'm sorry you had to find out about the eviction like that. Your mum never wanted that. She only ever wanted to protect you and Verity."

"I know. And thanks. So, are we good?"

Joe let out a long sigh. "This doesn't change anything. Your mum asked me to leave. She blocked my number. I don't think she wants to see me."

"I know that she *does* want to see you."

"Did she tell you that?"

"No. I just know."

Joe took another deep breath. "Let's say I come back with you and your mum accepts my apology. Where does that leave us? You block me at every turn, Patrick. I don't want to be your enemy. I would never, *could* never try to fill your father's shoes. I only ever wanted us to be mates."

"I know. I realize it doesn't seem like it, but I want that too."

"If push comes to shove, your mum will *always* choose you. I fell in love with her knowing that I would always come second best to you and Verity. I can handle that. The question is, can *you* handle having me around?"

"Yeah. I can. I want you to come back."

"Are we done?" asked Simone. "I don't want to hurry anyone's emotional journey, but I left Star in charge of the catering, and I am fearful of what that means for all of us."

Joe looked at Patrick. "This is your last chance to get rid of me," he said.

Patrick screwed his face up but then cracked it into a smile. "Nah, we're good. Let's go."

"Unless your mum kicks me to the curb as soon as we arrive."

"Let's cross that bridge when we come to it, shall we? For now, we need to get back to Rowan Thorp before Star decides it's a good idea to put cannabis in the trifle," Simone said.

The van roared to life. The weather outside was frightful, but inside, spirits were high despite the uncertainty waiting for them back in Rowan Thorp.

49

THE EARLY MORNING deliveries were still stacked up by the back door where they'd been left, and Maggie decided to take them in and stash them in the cold store, giving herself a minute to get her head in the game before she went to find her sisters.

She had just pulled the door shut when Duncan appeared behind her.

"Bloody hell, Duncan, I almost peed my pants!"

A closer look at his expression showed that he was distinctly shaken.

"Thank god I've found you!" he said, letting out a puff of held breath. "You need to come quickly, Star is freaking out."

"Star?" Maggie was incredulous. "Star doesn't freak out, she meditates."

"She's not meditating now." Duncan looked grim.

"Right, lead the way." There was nothing like another person's crisis to help you shelve your own.

When she entered the cookery school kitchen behind the Stag and Hound, the preparations for the feast were well under way. Saucepans full of parsnips and potatoes waiting to be parboiled before roasting covered half the hobs. A vat of red cabbage simmered gently, pushing out steam perfumed with red wine and cinnamon. Mounds of peeled brussels sprouts and carrots sat beside a pile of cauliflower florets ready for the leek and cauliflower cheese.

Across the kitchen ten large raw chickens in roasting tins were lined up along one long stainless steel worktop. A bucket-sized bowl of stuffing sat nearby, amid the detritus left by peeled garlic cloves and branches of herbs.

Standing beside chicken number eight, wearing rubber gloves that reached up to her elbows and a maniacal expression on her face, was Star. Her gloves were shiny with raw chicken and butter and smeared all over with stuffing. She was brandishing a lemon like a weapon.

"Hello, Twinkle-Star, everything all right?" Maggie asked in her most soothing voice.

Star's eyes seemed to focus, as though just realizing Maggie was there. "Nigella says I have to put lemons up chickens' bottoms!"

"Does she now? Pervert."

"She's made me massage butter into their crevices."

"Nigella is a very sensual woman."

"I don't eat meat. I've never handled dead birds. I've never handled dead anything. Do you know what massaging a dead chicken feels like?"

"As a matter of fact, I do. But I can see that this has been something of a baptism of fire for you."

Star shook the fist that clenched the lemon. "This is what love looks like. I've forced lemons into dead chickens' bottoms because you are sad. True love is lemons in chickens' bottoms!"

Maggie noticed that Duncan was backing toward the door. She didn't want to laugh at her sister's obvious distress, but it had been a hell of a weird day and this absurdity was just too much. Once the giggles started, she couldn't stop them.

"Star, I'm sorry you were left with all this," she said through her snickering. "I'm going to take over from you now, okay?" She was moving slowly around the worktop, one hand out like she'd seen Chris Pratt do with the velociraptors in *Jurassic World*.

"They're all dead!" Star squeaked, but she was starting to laugh too.

"Given the circumstances, that's probably for the best."

"I was supposed to be in charge of the nut roasts."

"I know, sweetie, and I'm sorry. I'm here now." Star still held the lemon, but her stance was beginning to relax a little and she burst out sporadically in paroxysms of laughter. "Star, I need you to step away from the chickens and put the lemon down."

Star looked at her hand as though only just seeing the lemon and placed it down on the worktop.

"Good girl. Let's get you over to the sink and rinse those gloves off, shall we?" She took her sister by the shoulders and carefully maneuvered her toward one of the sinks. The pair of them were practically squealing with laughter.

"That was intense," breathed Star once she was clean and divested of chicken gloves. Their giggles had subsided, and Maggie felt a sense of relief at having burned off some of the fire raging inside her.

"Of all the things, I never expected it to be raw chicken that would break your spirit." She smiled. "Where on earth is Si-mone? I don't understand why she isn't helping you." Maggie looked at her watch. It was just after one o'clock. "Shouldn't Verity be back by now? It was only a morning playdate. And where's Patrick?" It was like she was just coming back to her senses after a long dream.

"Verity's over with Antonia watching *The Muppet Christmas Carol*. She was here, but she got bored of breaking the cauliflowers into florets and grating cheese. She said both her arms were broken."

"That sounds about right. What about Patrick?"

"I'm here, Ma."

Maggie swiveled round to see Patrick standing in the doorway, looking contrite, and her heart instantly felt as though it would explode.

"Hello, love, where have you been galivanting off to? Have you seen your Aunty Simone?"

"She's been with me."

"Doing what? I've spent the last ten minutes talking Aunty Star down from a carcass crisis."

"I needed to make something right. I'm sorry I gave you such a hard time."

"Oh, my darling, none of that matters. We aren't losing the house—or the business—isn't that amazing!"

"What? I mean, yeah, but how?"

"It's a complicated story, but the long and short is Gilbert legally can't turn us out, because we're Norths. We don't have to leave. I'm sorry I didn't tell you about the eviction. And I should have told you how I felt about Joe." She swallowed the lump in her throat.

"I'm sorry I made you sad."

"We both made mistakes, my sweet boy, so let's promise to communicate better in the future, deal?"

"Deal." Patrick smiled.

Maggie pulled him into a tight hug. "Now," she said with a sniff. She released him and wiped her eyes. "Tell me what you and Aunty Simone have been up to, because I *know* it wasn't helping with the chickens." She cast a glance back at Star, who looked over at the chickens and shuddered.

"We were on a mission," said Simone, stepping in beside Patrick.

"Good god, what happened to your hair? You look like a cave woman."

"Salt spray," Simone replied, touching her hand to the matted beehive her usually straight hair had become.

"Salt spray? Have you been at the beach? I take a morning off, and you've all gone loco."

Joe walked in then, stepping around Patrick and Simone to stand in front of them.

"They came to stop me from leaving for France," he said.

Maggie stumbled backward. Her brain ceased to form coherent words or instructions to her limbs, and she wasn't sure her legs would hold her. Joe was here. Joe was here! Was this real? A hope that she'd dared not consider flooded her body. She loved this man, so wrong on paper yet so utterly perfectly right for her.

Joe approached her, slowly. Unsure. He couldn't know that every atom of her being sang at the sight of him.

"I'm so sorry I didn't tell you who I really was. Can you forgive me? I love you, Maggie. I don't care about the age gap, I don't care if we have to live in a tent, I don't care what the future brings. I simply love you, truly, madly, deeply, and that's never going to change."

Before she knew quite what she was doing, she ran at Joe, jumped into his arms, and wrapped her legs around his waist. He laughed, catching her with ease.

"Does this mean I'm forgiven?" he asked as she fervently kissed his head, cheeks, nose, any piece of his face she could get her lips on.

"This means I love you," she said, looking into his eyes. "And I don't care who knows it."

"Ahem!" came Kat's voice. "This is very unprofessional kitchen behavior, North sisters."

Maggie slid her legs down from Joe's waist and turned sheepishly to face Kat.

"Sorry, Kat," she mumbled, her cheeks burning.

Kat shook her head in mock disapproval. "I'm happy you two have finally made things official. Your relationship is the worst-kept secret in Rowan Thorp. Now, the feast begins at four thirty p.m., and we have a lot to get done, so it's all-hands-on-deck, aside from Verity, who came to tell me that she had two broken arms and needed to rest. Are we ready, team Winter Solstice?"

"Ready!" erupted the cheer from the kitchen.

50

THE ROASTING OF the hog began at midday. Troy and Kev had rented a portable hog roasting oven, which they set up in Augustus's garden and took shifts to monitor throughout the day. Within a couple of hours, the smell was already permeating the village.

Fable Folk—the folk band Star had invited to play at the festival—had a vibe reminiscent of the Mamas and the Papas. Three men and one woman, Helena. They came with only the instruments they could carry, no amps or electrical equipment. True to Star's predictions, they really did play for food and drink. Having filled themselves up at Betty's for breakfast, they played impromptu sets outside the café and then each of the pubs. They sang "Scarborough Fair," and "A Case of You," and a good smattering of Christmas carols. All day long they were inundated with hot drinks, wedges of Christmas cake, and mince pies from villagers with requests for certain songs or simply as thanks for filling the village with their music.

"So, um, which of the band were you 'friends' with?" asked Duncan as they set off up the high street to collect tablecloths.

Star laughed. "You're not jealous, are you?"

"No," he said, unbuttoning the top button on his shirt. "I'm only wondering who my competition is."

She reached up and kissed him. "You have no competition. Trust me."

"I can't sing or build a campfire. I've never worn a flatcap. I'm not . . ." He stumbled over his words. "I'm not cool or hip." He motioned toward the band, who were playing outside Maggie's shop now. "I'm a history nerd."

Star stopped walking and reached her arms up around his neck. He smelled of her patchouli shampoo from when they'd showered together after Verity had been picked up this morning.

"Firstly, history is hot. Every time I see you reading from a tatty old book, I have to fan myself. I'm not even joking. Secondly, you knit," she said, looking into his dark brown eyes. "Knitting is very sexy. And you designed the tarpaulin that saved our banquet—that was a truly maverick move." She gently turned his face away from the band and back to her. "Stop worrying. I only want you. Now kiss me like an antiques expert."

WITH THE PATCHWORK ceiling hanging above and the branches on the trees laden with bird feeders and fairy lights, the clearing in the rowan tree woods felt intimate and at the same time otherworldly, as though existing inside a fairy tale. The woodland surrounding the clearing was still a Narnian dream. Branches creaked beneath the weight of their snowy blanket and scurrying creatures left tiny footprints in the crisp white drifts.

Any garlands and bunting that could be salvaged from the marquee had been used to decorate the space. Duncan, Joe, and Patrick had arranged the tables and chairs not in a line as they would have been in the marquee but higgledy-piggledy to fit the unusual banqueting hall.

"It's wonderful!" Star gushed when she came bearing a tray of hot wassail for them. "The woods were always special in the summer, but in winter they have a magic all their own, can you feel it?"

"Almost as magical as this wassail," said Patrick appreciatively, sipping the warming brew. "It's like drinking Christmas."

"That'll be all the cinnamon and spices infused slowly into it," she said proudly.

"How have I never had this before?" Duncan asked, taking a sip and then leaning toward her for a kiss. "You even smell like wassail," he added, sniffing her hair.

"So would you if you'd just made fifty gallons of the stuff. The fumes in the Stag and Hound kitchen are enough to make Godzilla drunk."

"And how much wassail have you North sisters consumed during the brewing process?" Joe asked, one eyebrow quirked knowingly.

"Any chef worth her salt always taste-tests her creations before she serves them. That's just good practice." Star flicked her hair, stumbled slightly, and sashayed out of the clearing, zigzagging her way back to the kitchen to continue preparing the feast.

AT THREE O'CLOCK the Cussing Crocheters and the church flower association joined forces to dress the tables, which only added to the charm. Crochet foxes, squirrels, and other woodland creatures peeped out from garlands of dark green ivy which lay along the middle of each table.

The cutlery was mismatched, as were the mugs and plates,

thanks to the emptying of many a kitchen cupboard for the occasion. If the March Hare and the Cheshire Cat were discovered taking tea in the clearing it would have surprised absolutely no one.

Overlooking it all was the tree house, which was where Verity had insisted that she, Sameera, and a couple of other friends from the village should dine this evening.

At four o'clock, the revelers, muffled in hats and coats, gathered in Augustus North's garden to watch the bonfire being lit. Fable Folk sang "God Rest Ye Merry, Gentlemen" and "It May Be Winter Outside" by the glow of the fire as dancing flames of gold and magenta warmed the spectators. Spirits were high and the anticipation was palpable.

The hog roast was well and truly cooked, and even Star's stomach growled at the fragrant smoke that mixed with the bonfire. It was the epitome of wintry smells carried on the crisp cold air, at once both warm and sharp in the nostrils.

Betty led the walk down to the bottom of the garden and into the woods. Star and her sisters gathered near the entrance to the clearing.

"Listen!" she whispered, unable to stifle her delight. With breath held and hands clasped in childlike excitement they waited for people's reactions. Appreciative murmurs drifted back to them through the trees as friends and neighbors entered the enchanted dining hall. The whisper of many breaths sucked in in delighted surprise and exhaled in awe floated on the wintry air. The clearing looked even more stunning in the dark, lit only by the twinkle lights in the trees and the LED candles dotted along the tables. And when the guests took their seats, the woods themselves seemed to sigh contentedly, as though a long wait was finally over.

• • •

IT FELT TO the sisters like a never-ending trail of back-and-forth between the cookery school and the clearing, as they delivered the fruits of their labors to their hungry guests. But the revelers were kept well-oiled by two large cauldrons of steaming wassail, which was ladled into mugs by Betty and Harini, and spirits were too high to complain about the wait. Joe had fashioned a basic dumbwaiter out of some rope and a picnic basket and lidded mugs of warm spiced apple juice were sent up to Verity and her friends in the tree house.

Transporting each giant saucepan of onion and cider soup to the clearing was a two-person job. The waiting trestle table groaned as it received the weight of the pans, but the fragrant pottage was quickly spooned into bowls and passed eagerly along the tables to be scooped up with roughly torn chunks of crusty bread slathered in cold butter. The band took a brief break from serenading the diners to tuck into the warming soup, and when they took up their instruments again and began to sing "Good King Wenceslas" it was with a renewed vigor.

"I feel like I've traveled back to medieval times," said Simone, slurping a translucent tendril of onion off her spoon.

The first course had been served and the sisters were perched at the end of one table, hurriedly enjoying mugs of soup before the next round of fetching and carrying. The sweet choral voices of Fable Folk drifted around the woods and below that was the gentle hum of contented conversation, like midsummer honeybees in the hedgerows.

"I wouldn't be surprised if we evoked the spirit of King Wenceslas himself," Star joined in.

"I'd rather not have our woods haunted, even by a member

of ancient bohemian royalty," Maggie added, tearing off a piece of bread and plunging it into the thick soup.

A CHEER WENT up when platters piled high with roast pork and chicken landed on the tables. These were followed by the nut roasts and the vegetable dishes. Artemis, weaving between the legs of the guests, gratefully received the morsels they dropped in her direction.

The tables were groaning with food, and the patio heaters and wassail were doing their job to keep the banquet and the guests warm. When every mug was refilled, the North sisters raised their own for a toast.

51

MAGGIE TOOK A deep breath and felt the comforting presence of Simone and Star on either side of her.

"When Vanessa first read out Dad's wishes, I think my sisters and I unanimously thought, 'This is going to be an absolute ball ache!'" This got cackles of laughter from around the tables. "And in fairness, it has been." More snickering. "It has been challenging. At times, both my sisters have wanted to throttle me, and I them. But it has also been the most amazing experience. I have lived in Rowan Thorp on and off for much of my life, and yet I had somehow forgotten what a remarkable joy a close community can be, the bone-deep comfort of belonging somewhere. Thank you all for reminding me. Dad's caveats have made me appreciate where I live and the people around me, and I am deeply grateful to some *very* powerful women who have made it possible for me to continue living here. Tonight is a joint effort, and we thank you all for everything you have done to help make this winter solstice event happen. This experience has taught us a lot, and though I don't think any of us would profess to be suddenly overflowing with wisdom, we are wiser people than we were a month ago for sure. Our dad was one of a kind . . ."

Quips of "That's an understatement," "Hear! Hear!," "You're not wrong there!," and lively guffaws ran around the tables.

"He was by no means perfect. But by forcing us to work together, he made sure that me and my sisters found each other again; without this, I'm not sure we ever would have. So"—Maggie and her sisters raised their mugs, and everyone else stood to join them and raised their own—"cheers to all of you! Cheers to my sisters! And cheers to Augustus Balthazar North! You were a strange old bugger, but it turns out you knew us better than we knew ourselves!"

A unanimous "Cheers!" went up.

"Happy winter solstice!"

This too was parroted by the guests. The sisters sat down, and Vanessa stood and cleared her throat.

"Now that we're all gathered here, I have one final letter from Augustus, which, as he left in his instructions, was to be read out at the solstice feast."

"How unlike our father to have the last word," Simone quipped, and the guests around the tables tittered.

Vanessa opened a stiff envelope, just like the ones that had landed on the sisters' doormats three short weeks back, and pulled out a sheet of pale cream paper. Artemis jumped up onto a table and sat beside Vanessa like a sentry.

"Somehow I thought you'd make an appearance for this," she said to the cat. Vanessa cleared her throat and began to read.

My darling babes of the woods, if you are listening to these words, it means you have succeeded in reinstating the winter solstice festival. But, my girls, you have done so much more than that. You have found your way back not only to the community of Rowan Thorp but also to one another. Well done! Keep this sense of togetherness in your hearts as you move forward.

The winter solstice marks the longest night of the year and the promise that soon the sun will be back again. But winter is not merely a trial to be got through while we wait for warmer times. You must embrace the cold days and long dark nights and learn to find the joy in them, for there is much joy to be found. Hunker down and revel in the warmth of soft blankets when the weather is howling outside. Make the time to take time, not just for others but for yourselves. Read books, light candles, take long baths, watch the flames flickering in the fireplace or the rain dribbling down the windowpanes. Open your eyes to the beauty in the winter landscape and count your blessings every single day. Slow down. There will be time enough for buzzing around with the bees when the sun comes back. For now, let the moments stretch long and lazy. Recuperate, rejuvenate, reflect, and let winter soothe you. Let this winter solstice be the first of many times this winter that you come together to give thanks and appreciate the people in your life. Gratitude is everything. It is infinite, and even in death I know that the warmth of my gratitude for all of you lives on in the spirit of this season. My heartfelt thanks to the people of Rowan Thorp, whom I know will have helped my girls so much.

Marguerite, Simone, Heavenly-Stargazer Rosehip, I was not always with you in person, but my love for you was always and forever will be transcendental. I am

watching you from the stars and I am shining with pride.
Always yours, Dad.

A moment of peaceful reflection drifted over the little gathering in the rowan tree woods, as all around the tables thoughts turned to loved ones who were no longer here with them, and those who were gathered counted their blessings for the ones who remained. For Maggie, Simone, and Star, they had finally got the acknowledgment that they had hankered after from their father and each had the sense that they could lay at least some of their old ghosts to rest. They had found one another despite the obstacles between them and they vowed silently never to lose sight of one another again.

Through this quiet contemplation, the woods made themselves heard. Boughs creaked. Snow, dislodged from laden branches by the feet of small creatures, swished and pitter-pattered down onto the woodland floor. The bonfire outside crackled and hissed while the songbirds in the clearing sang their last melody of the day. And on a table, surrounded by the detritus of a very merry banquet, a large black cat with two white circles around her eyes purred contentedly.

52

DESPITE EVERYONE PROCLAIMING they couldn't eat another bite of dinner, they somehow found room for the Women's Institute's chocolate yule log and the much-whispered-about Rowan Thorp gâteau, which turned out to be a spiced chocolate and damson cake, layered with whipped cream and rowan berry jam and topped with a thick layer of dark chocolate ganache.

When they finally got up to move, Maggie considered that it might have made more sense to do the wassailing before dinner. People groaned and stretched and pulled at waistbands. Verity and her friends were summoned down from the tree house to join in the procession.

Outside the protection of the woods, the weather had turned very cold, and even the bonfire did little to warm the air. Mugs were filled once again, and with the band in tow, the villagers of Rowan Thorp began the wassailing.

Fable Folk played ye olde Christmas songs and carols that everybody knew, or thought they knew, and everyone sang along regardless. They began by standing around the bonfire; some even danced a little. The cider probably helped with that. It also helped to keep the chill at bay as everyone wended their way back along the garden and out onto the high street, where the lights glowing in the windows and on the Christmas trees warmed the frosty scene with their happy colors.

Joe held Maggie's hand for all to see. He beamed as though holding her hand was his every dream come true. Maggie felt as though her love for him was radiating from her. She didn't have all the answers, she didn't know what the future would bring—who did? But she had realized that it would be a waste of happiness not to welcome love when it came.

They wassailed along the high street calling out impromptu blessings on the businesses that they might prosper in the year to come. And they wassailed around Parminder and Gerry's orchard, giving thanks for the cider—really heartfelt thanks for the cider—and welcoming in the good spirits so that next year's wassail supply might be just as plentiful. They blessed the church and the pubs and the Rowan Thorp Twitchers and the Women's Institute and the Cussing Crocheters and the Rowan Thorp Historical Society and the library and anything else they could think of.

The more the little crowd acknowledged the things that they were thankful for, the better they felt. Their gratitude filled them up even more than the banquet had done as they counted their blessings and found them to be bounteous: beloved friends, pets, gardens, stars, flowers, views, trees, food, warmth . . . Once they began, there seemed to be no end to the things that they were thankful for.

Eventually the procession led them back to the pubs, and the villagers parted like the red sea to enter either the Rowan Tree Inn or the Stag and Hound.

The North sisters and their significant others, along with Patrick and Verity, wandered into the Rowan Tree Inn. Joe and Patrick went to the bar and the others took a seat in one of the large curved banquettes. Verity was desperately tired, though she pretended not to be, and objected to all of Maggie's suggestions that it might be time for them to go home.

"Please, Mama, can I stay up till the end?"

"This is the end, sweetheart, there's nothing else after this."

"Just let me have one blackcurrant squash."

"One drink and then bed."

"She's going to be a party animal when she's older." Star smiled, pulling a fleece blanket off the back of the chair and draping it over her niece.

"No, she is not," said Maggie. "She is going to work hard and then become prime minister."

"No pressure, Verity," Simone said, fondly stroking her hair.

"So, how do you feel about spending your first-ever Christmas together?" Evette asked the sisters.

Their smiles were enough of an answer.

"I *never* thought it would happen," said Simone.

"I always hoped it would," added Star. "But I don't think I believed it ever could."

"Our Christmases have always just been the three of us, just me and the kids. They've been lovely, but you know, sort of quiet, or as quiet as Verity ever is. She's going to love having a big family Christmas. You'll all come to ours, won't you?"

Star and Simone nodded emphatically.

"I've been thinking that we all ought to chip in. I've no doubt you'd make a delicious Christmas dinner, Maggie, but why don't we each make part of the dinner and bring it over to you, so that you're not doing everything?" suggested Star.

"I agree. How about this: Maggie makes the starters and me,

you, and Evette do all the rest?" Simone said. "Star and I will work it all out between us, that way you get to kick back a bit and enjoy Christmas Day too."

"Are you sure?" Maggie asked hesitantly. She was torn between loving this idea and feeling guilty about not being the sole provider of Christmas for her family.

"Yes!" said Star exaggeratedly. "We're all adults, let us help you."

"Let us share the load," said Evette kindly.

"In that case, oh my god yes please!" Maggie gushed. Christmas immediately ceased to be another monster she needed to slay and became something to look forward to. "But I'm still the big sister, right?"

"Always." Simone leaned over and kissed her cheek.

PATRICK CAME BACK to the table empty-handed.

"Joe's still waiting to be served," he said. "It's like a rugby scrum at the bar."

Maggie looked down at Verity, who—despite her protestations and the cacophony in the pub—had fallen asleep across her lap.

"Tell Joe not to worry about getting drinks for Verity and me. I think I'm going to get this little one home to bed."

"Why don't I take Verity home and you stay here and enjoy the rest of the night?" Patrick suggested. "You've worked so hard to make this evening happen; you deserve to have some fun."

"That's kind of you, love, but to be honest, I'm knackered myself. I'm probably not long from bed either. You stay and enjoy yourself."

"If you're sure," he said.

She nodded, and Patrick disappeared back into the throng at the bar. A few moments later, just as Maggie was wiggling herself and a snoring Verity along the banquette, Joe appeared.

"Your packhorse awaits, my lady." He grinned.

"You don't have to leave just because I am," she said, though she couldn't deny she was pleased.

"As if." He smiled warmly at her. "You know I'd rather be anywhere with you than here without. Hand Sleeping Beauty over and let's go home."

Joe picked up Verity, who flopped her arms around him and buried her head into the crook of his neck.

The music suddenly grew even louder, and a cheer went up around the pub.

Maggie called her good-byes and left them to their merriments. Simone had one arm slung around Evette's shoulder as they rocked side to side singing "I Wish It Could Be Christmas Every Day!" Star and Duncan were face-to-face, laughing as they sang loudly at each other. She noticed Louella slip between the punters at the bar and sidle up next to Patrick. She wouldn't be expecting her eldest offspring home for a while yet.

Outside the pubs was just as busy, as patrons of each establishment mixed and mingled. The snow on Holy Trinity Green had almost gone, but as Maggie and Joe walked slowly along the high street, thick snowflakes began to flurry down around them. By the time they reached the flat, the snow had become a shower of feather-white lint, falling thick and silent, bright against the inky sky.

She shivered as she pushed the key into the lock and opened the front door. *My wassail warmth is waning*, she thought. Joe climbed the stairs to the flat, slow and steady with Verity in his arms. Maggie followed.

Her home was warm and welcoming, lit only by the fairy lights on the tree. Together they got Verity into her pajamas and tucked into bed. She woke briefly but quickly dozed back off.

Back in the kitchen, Maggie put the kettle on. "Tea?" she called out quietly. She turned to find Joe standing in front of her and instinctively she wrapped her arms around him.

"You pulled it off, Mags, it was an amazing winter solstice celebration."

"*We* pulled it off," she corrected. "That was a hell of a joint effort. It went okay in the end, though, didn't it?"

"Okay? It was amazing. You're amazing."

"Oh, you're just saying that to get me into bed." Maggie winked at him.

"Is it working?"

"Hell yeah."

Joe kissed her, gently at first and then more deeply, and she felt herself unfurl like one of the fern fronds in the rowan tree woods. She let herself melt into him as his hands moved to hold her waist. They kissed their way out of the kitchen, but when Joe angled them toward the sofa, she stopped and broke away. He looked at her quizzically, and she took his hand and led him toward her bedroom.

"No more sneaking around," she said. "No more scurrying back to your single bed at the pub. Tonight, all night, and every night hereafter, we sleep together."

"Are you sure?" he asked, searching her eyes.

"Positive."

He smiled, pulling her roughly to him and kissing her, his

hands splayed across her back, keeping her close. "I can't guarantee that all we'll do is sleep," he whispered in her ear, his voice a low growl.

Maggie was breathless. "Oh, thank heavens for that." They stumbled into her bedroom, where she paused only to kick the door closed.

In the kitchen, the kettle came to a boil and clicked itself off, but nobody came to make tea.

EPILOGUE

FIVE YEARS LATER

THE WINTER SOLSTICE celebration at Rowan Thorp was a tradition now firmly set in the hearts of the villagers. Each year, more and more people gathered to dance about the bonfire and sing songs of old and join the procession around the village, bestowing blessings on one another and the land and welcoming the spirit of thankfulness into their hearts.

The blessings certainly seemed to have worked on Gerry and Parminder's orchard. Their crops had been so plentiful in the last few years that as well as donating cider to the winter solstice celebration, they had taken to bottling their own wassail and selling it in the local shops. It was very popular with tourists.

While the general merriment was open to all, the winter solstice banquet remained a village affair only. Though the village hall roof had long since been made watertight and the option of a marquee on the green was still in the cards, it was unanimously decided that the banquet should always be held in the clearing of the rowan tree woods. The patchwork tarp had been mended and reinforced, and the crockery was still a colorful mishmash pulled from many cupboards.

Star had acted as a surrogate for Simone and Evette and

delivered to them little Ava North, who was now three. A few months after Ava was born, she fell unexpectedly pregnant again—this time with Duncan's baby—and nine months later Primrose North was welcomed into the world. All her previous ambivalence at the idea of having children of her own had evaporated the moment she'd held Primrose in her arms. Star was obsessed; she hadn't imagined a love so all-encompassing was possible until that moment. There was a time when she'd had to search for her daily dose of magic, but now her daughter supplied her with all the magic moments she could ever need.

That said, Star was not a woman who glowed during pregnancy. It had tested every ounce of her natural spark. Duncan had been consummately patient as the love of his life grumbled and grimaced her way through heartburn, swollen ankles, mood swings, backaches, insomnia, all-day sickness, and constipation during her pregnancy with Ava. Simone had once described Star's pregnancy temperament as a cross between the Wicked Witch of the West and the Hulk, and Star, ever self-aware, had agreed with her.

When she fell pregnant again so soon after, it was decided that if she and Duncan could get through another nine months like the last, they could get through anything else life threw at them in the future. Star's midwife was less than pleased to see her again so soon, given the risks of tightly spaced pregnancies. But despite being a self-confessed miserable cow and grumpy mule, Star was also as healthy as a horse. When their beloved Primrose finally arrived, Star immediately got a contraceptive implant and Duncan underwent a vasectomy to be doubly sure. She and Duncan were united in their decision to pour all their love into their daughter and that Star should *never* become pregnant again.

After a happy trial run, Simone and Evette moved permanently to Rowan Thorp. They opened a joint practice on the high street, called Mind & Body, where Simone eased the villagers' physical aches and Evette took care of their mental health. Simone's days of freebie physiotherapy consultations in storerooms around the village were thankfully a thing of the past and she now received proper remuneration for her professional services. A year after Ava was born, the couple welcomed a daughter into their family via adoption, a four-year-old named Natalia, who epitomized all the mischief of the North sisters combined, and their family was complete.

The three little cousins were the apples of everyone's eyes and had their aunty Maggie and uncle Joe wrapped around their little fingers. It was an endless source of joy to Simone and Star that their children would grow up so close together, both in age and proximity.

Star and Duncan reopened North Novelties & Curios, and it was by far the most popular shop on the high street, bringing in tourists from far and wide. Duncan kept his links with Sotheby's and still did some freelance appraisal work for them. Star surprised everyone by completing an Open University degree in art history, and her natural eye for spotting a hidden gem at flea markets was even keener than Augustus's.

When Patrick finished his degree, he got a job in Dorset, and Louella joined him soon after. Joe had become Patrick's go-to for all matters of electric, career, and man-to-man advice. Patrick and Louella saved enough holiday each year so that they could spend three weeks in Rowan Thorp at Christmas. Maggie always cried happy tears when Patrick finally arrived and she had all her ducks in a row.

Verity was now fifteen with a stroppy age exactly appropriate for a fifteen-year-old. She was rebellious and forthright, and

Maggie secretly loved that her daughter was such a force of nature, even as she grounded her and slapped her with curfews on school nights. She didn't even really mind the tattoo that Verity had had done illegally, though she'd made a good show of parental outrage at the time. Despite her often prickly demeanor, Verity was a gooey blob of softness with her little cousins. Natalia had already decided she was going to have tattoos like Verity when she was a big girl.

With the proceeds from sales of the Hilliard and several other choice items, Maggie and Joe had saved enough money to take over the mortgage from the village of Rowan Thorp and now owned the grocer's and the large flat above it outright. Between them, they had completely refurbished the flat and made it truly their own. They had also taken on two part-time employees in the grocer's, which meant Saturday mornings were now for staying snuggled up in bed till 8 a.m. followed by a leisurely breakfast for two at Betty's.

That first flush of love and passion had never waned for Maggie and Joe, and it continued to grow year on year as they settled into a life of togetherness. Maggie would never tire of stealing kisses with Joe and Joe would never stop feeling proud to have Maggie by his side; after having to hide their love for so long, Joe still reveled in the feeling of Maggie's hand clasped in his as they walked down the street.

IT WAS THE morning of December 21, the day of the winter solstice celebration, and the North family were sat together in Star and Duncan's garden—formerly Augustus's—on four large garden sofas. They wore thick coats and hats and hugged steaming paper cups of coffee—hot chocolate for the children—

which Maggie and Joe had brought from Betty's café. Artemis was curled up asleep on a folded blanket. It was the quiet before the storm . . . well, relatively speaking; the children were definitely making themselves heard.

"This coffee doesn't taste very strong. Is this a single shot?" Verity asked.

"Yes," said Joe.

"I have a double shot now," she replied, in that way teenagers have of making statements lilt up at the end like a question.

"Not on my watch." Joe smiled.

"Da-ad," she complained. "I'm not a child anymore."

"You've got years ahead of you to become a caffeine head like your mother . . ."

"Cheers." Maggie grinned and raised her triple-shot Americano in a toast.

"I just want you to embrace the natural energy that comes with your youth; you'll need coffee to get going soon enough," Joe finished.

"You sound like Aunty Star."

"She's a wise woman," said Duncan fondly.

Primrose and Ava were sitting between Duncan and Evette, working on their Christmas coloring books.

"Is Sameera coming tonight?" Patrick asked his sister.

"Yeah, if she can bear to be apart from her *boyfriend* for two minutes!" Sameera was not abiding by the "sisters before misters" rule. "I was thinking, I know we usually sit at the tables with you guys these days, but I feel like it's time Natalia got her first taste of the solstice banquet in the tree house. Can we eat up there together?"

Natalia's eyes lit up and she looked hopefully at Simone, who smiled and said, "It's fine with me."

Evette nodded and said, "I think that sounds like a wonder-ful idea."

"But not Ava and Primrose," Natalia clarified. "They're still practically babies."

"Don't worry," said Star. "Ava and Prim will be on the ground with us for a couple more years. It'll just be you big girls."

Natalia looked like she might float with happiness.

"We saw Fable Folk arrive on our way over here," said Patrick.

"Betty said she and both the pubs have brought in extra stock just to keep them fed. I couldn't tell if she was serious or not," added Louella, and they all laughed knowingly.

"Right," said Maggie. "Let's finish these and get cracking."

By now Maggie, Simone, and Star had the winter solstice preparations down to a fine art.

"I vote myself not to stuff the chickens," said Star.

Simone laughed. "You haven't stuffed a chicken since the first solstice!"

"And I want to make sure I never have to do it again." She shuddered.

In an hour, Troy and Kev would roll the giant hog roaster into the garden. Their joint side venture had become a very suc-cessful business; demand was high for the Rowan Thorp Roast-ers. But they always kept their calendar free for the solstice celebration.

Duncan and Evette were in charge of childcare, which left the North sisters free to focus on the preparations. As usual it was a whole village affair, which meant there was no shortage of volunteers.

Maggie stood, and her sisters followed her back along the garden, leaving the others to continue catching up with Patrick and Louella.

"Shall we grab more coffees before we head to the kitchen?" Maggie asked.

"Of course," Simone replied.

"God, I love the winter solstice," said Star.

"Me too," agreed Simone.

"I think I love it even more than Christmas," Maggie added, and her sisters nodded.

"What do you think Dad would say if he could see us now?" asked Star.

"Probably something annoying like 'I always knew you had it in you, my little babes of the woods.'" Simone tried to mimic his gravel-with-a-smile-in-it voice.

"I'll bet he's chuckling his arse off." Maggie smiled.

The forecast was for snow, and the pale lilac clouds didn't look like they would disappoint. The three giant Christmas trees on Holy Trinity Green glowed resplendent in the gray morning light, and every shop window glittered with snow globe perfection. The North sisters' breath clouded out in front of them and the cold bit at their cheeks as they linked arms and walked with heads bent together, the bobbles on their hats shaking as they laughed at some joke known only to them. No more were they sisters bonded by summers alone. That first winter solstice had marked the beginning of a new journey, one they would take together, always.

ACKNOWLEDGMENTS

I always find acknowledgements hard to write because I am so deeply thankful to so many people and I worry that my words won't properly convey my gratitude. So please know that everyone mentioned here is appreciated more than my meagre words can ever express. And if I've missed anyone, then I am truly sorry; it is only a result of my scattered brain and no reflection on you.

To Hayley Steed, my agent at Madeleine Milburn, thank you for your faith in me when I have none in myself, and for being so fiercely supportive; you are like a feisty mother hen in agent form. Thank you, Elinor Davies, for being a ray of sunshine and a helpful star. And to the rest of the MM team—which is the very best team to be a part of—thank you for all the work you do to push my books out into the big wide world: Hannah Ladds, Liane-Louise Smith, Georgia Simmonds, Valentina Paulmichl, and everyone working so hard behind the scenes, I am grateful for you all.

I have a whole bunch of love and gratitude to give to my Putnam family. My US editor, Kate Dresser, is marvelously funny, kind, and supportive. Kate, thank you for making my stories better and keeping me from disappearing down the many rabbit holes I find myself teetering over, like the time I panicked because I don't write spicy books and I felt like I ought to, so I tried to write a spicy scene and it was so incredibly bad and you said "What was *that*? Don't do *that* again!" Thank you for telling me it's okay to be me and not to worry about trying to be somebody else.

Thank you, Tarini Sipahimalani—editorial assistant and lovely human—for guiding me through the editorial process with patience and kindness and for writing the most brilliant discussion guide questions for *A December to Remember*. The glorious book jacket was designed once again by Sanny Chiu, whose talent blows my mind and makes me feel lucky indeed; thank you, Sanny. Production editor Claire Sullivan and copy-editor Kathleen Go, thank you for your editing wisdom. I always look forward to your comment boxes; you make editing fun and keep me on my toes. I especially love the bafflement that my Britishisms create! And to proofreaders Ryan Richardson and Leah Marsh, your eagle-eyed observance is deeply appreciated. Thank you, Elora Weil, publicist, for setting up events, talking me through my nerves, and making sure everyone knows about my books; you go above and beyond, and it doesn't go unnoticed. My heartfelt thanks go to the rest of the Putnam publishing team, without whom there would be no book at all: Shina Patel, marketer; Maija Baldauf, managing editor; Emily Mileham, senior managing editor; Alison Cnockaert, interior designer; Ashley McClay, marketing director; Alexis Welby, publicity director; and last but definitely not least, Sally Kim, publisher.

Jayne Osborne—formerly my editor at Pan Macmillan—

you may have left Pan Mac for new and exciting adventures, but you will never leave my heart. Thank you for championing my books from the very first. And thanks to Kinza Azira—my new editor—for stepping in and hitting the ground running to get this book published. Already you are tackling my panicky emails with good grace, and I thank you for it!

To you, dear reader, I will be eternally grateful that out of the millions of brilliant books on offer you chose to read mine. I still can't believe I get to fulfill my dream of writing books, and that is all down to you. Thank you! To the wonderful, creative people on Instagram, Twitter, and BookTok, thank you from the bottom of my heart for your support, your kind reviews, and for sharing my books on the interweb. It means the world to me. I have found my booky family on Bookstagram, and you are awesome! Bianca-bemused-tree-frog, Kate-of-sock-knitting-genius, and Jean Meltzer, sublime human and writer, I'm so glad we met. Thank you to Lauren Bethancourt and the amazing Bayou Book Babes for letting me be a part of your book club; I love our meetings and I am so thankful for you all. And to Lauren Garcia, fearless leader of the Read Rovers Book Club, thank you for your friendship and support. Book people are the best people. To my friends in the flesh, a million thank-yous for tolerating my long absences while I write and for welcoming me back when I re-emerge bewildered and desperate for cake.

Thankfulness plays a big part in the end of this book, and I am blessed to have so many people in my own life to be thankful for. I feel lucky every day that my greatest friends happen to be my siblings; Linzi and Simon, you are the best. Thanks, Mum and Dad, for being the loudest, proudest cheerleaders for all your children and grandchildren; you give us power. Thank you to my boys, Jack and Will, for being an endless source of joy. And for Dom—husband, best friend, soother of perimenopausal wife, and fellow plant nerd—thank you for letting me be extremely dramatic when writing is hard and for telling me that it will all be okay in the end.

Kindness is everything. My heart is full.

DISCUSSION GUIDE

1. North Novelties & Curios was passed down to Augustus through generations. What does the shop—its name, history, and unique trinkets—tell us about Augustus's commitment to family and legacy? To what extent is Augustus's approach to life admirable?

2. Evidenced by the late Augustus's warm reception, the people of Rowan Thorp held a shared, beloved impression of Augustus. Still, he remained a mystery. What quality of his described at the beginning explains this discrepancy?

3. In their youth, the three half-sisters eagerly awaited their summer reunions, when they were free to eat ice cream for breakfast, climb trees, and sleep under the stars. But overtime, the sisters became estranged. Discuss the transition from childhood to adulthood. What did the sisters lose and gain during this period? In what ways did Augustus defy this process for them?

4. Early in the novel, we witness Joe's undying support for Maggie. What attracts them to each other? To what extent is circumstance a culprit of their romantic tug-of-war? Discuss whether true love is possible in the absence of circumstance.

5. Simone and Star have a unique relationship. How would you describe their dynamic? To what extent do Simone's reactions toward Star reflect her feelings around motherhood?

6. Nomadic and unconventional, Star (full name Heavenly-Stargazer Rosehip) is described as a free spirit. Identify and explain a moment in which Star lives up to her name. If you were Star's sister, how would you have dealt with that moment? Who in your life shares Star's spirit?

7. Displacement is a major theme in this novel. Discuss how this manifests in each sister's life. For each sister, what does it mean to return home?

8. Later in the novel, the sisters reinstate the old Rowan Thorp winter solstice celebration. Discuss, in relation to the spirit of the holidays, the impact this has on the sisters' relationships. Compare and contrast this celebration with the essence of their summertime reunions.

9. To unlock their inheritance, the sisters must complete tasks. How did you react to each task? How can we apply this approach to our own life?

10. Whether it's climbing or lighting up a tree for Christmas, trees play a big part in driving the story's aspirational ideas. Referencing the phrase "to see the forest for the trees," discuss the sisters' relationship to the woods. In what ways do trees evoke nostalgia?

11. Rowan Thorp is a tight-knit community where people know one another's business but still have one another's backs. Using a character as an example, discuss how proximity to community impacts the formation of one's sense of self.

12. In the end, Augustus's caveats proved fruitful. Discuss the bizarre or unconventional ways you've received love. How did you react to these displays of affection in the moment?

ABOUT THE AUTHOR

A former professional cake baker, **JENNY BAYLISS** lives in a small seaside town in the UK with her husband, their children having left home for big adventures. She is also the author of *The Twelve Dates of Christmas*, *A Season for Second Chances*, and *Meet Me Under the Mistletoe*.

JenniBayliss
BaylissJenni